In the very long ago men encased in steel and riding huge four legged creatures fought in what, for them, was a new world. Being men, they did what men are apt to do. They mated and mixed their blood with the native girls who were sometimes willing and sometimes not. Through the centuries the blood line continued, as did memories of ancient ways. Later, far to the north a red-headed Irishman met the daughter of a shaman. The Cheyenne were a tall, well-built people. The daughter was knowledgeable about the ways of the spirits, of healing, of keeping a clean, well-fed camp, and of pleasing her man. When the Irishman quit his roaming, he took her with him. Their daughter, married a man from Mexico whose ancestors went as far back as did hers. She died when influenza swept through the world. Her daughter, Margarita Maria Namid Gomez, married a cowboy named Stanley and produced three boys for the Diamond MiK or the McKaid ranch if you prefer.

As the world celebrated the end of a long war, Deedee let her widowed granddaughter and her father-in-law celebrate with their own prayers. She sat on the porch of her little cabin smoking the long pipe that came from her tribe, thanking her own gods. When the Purple Martins came swooping in, gathering for their long flight south, and Brother Eagle came to sit on the porch railing, Deedee smiled at the five deer who came to say hello.

"Your princess is close, David," she murmured. "Now find her and make her yours, and bring her home." All was right with her world. She had waited long for this day.

Other books by Barbra

Angel's Choice

I offer my thanks to Teri Valentine who was so helpful throughout the development of this story. Sandy Richards, Caroline Davis, Rita Meagher, and I thank you for your patience with my terrible typing talent.

Always, I thank my sons for their help and support. Without them I would be lost. I particularly dedicate this book to my youngest, Gilbert, who spent the last year and a half of his life watching me at my computer.

A Lick of Sense is a work of fiction. The characters have never existed, but I hope they give my readers a sense of how the world was in 1945.

A Lick *of* Sense

a novel by

Barbra Heavner

Order this book online at www.trafford.com
or email orders@trafford.com

Most Trafford titles are also available at major online book retailers.

Printed in the United States of America.

ISBN: 978-1-4269-5312-5 (sc)
ISBN: 978-1-4269-5313-2 (hc)
ISBN: 978-1-4269-5314-9 (e)

Library of Congress Control Number: 2010919281

Trafford rev. 01/25/2011

North America & International
toll-free: 1 888 232 4444 (USA & Canada)
phone: 250 383 6864 • fax: 812 355 4082

Chapter 1

Texas-July 8, 1915

Once upon a time in the not so long ago, in an enchanted land called Texas, near the fabled town of Austin, lived two families, side by side. Now they were neighbors, but they weren't necessarily friends. They were close to the little village of Kaidville. Everybody knew the McKaids. Buck McKaid, his given name was David, was a fair man, and he made the best of all the acres his people had put together. The Diamond MK, they called it. Lots of acres, lots of cows, not much ready cash.

His son, Stanley, loved that ranch. he did, and enjoyed riding the across it after those pesky and sometimes dangerous critters. At an early age, he'd learned to handle a rope and branding iron and had been given a sharp knife for turning those little ones into steers.

However, on his eighteenth birthday, Stanley McKaid wasn't riding the range. Neither was he relaxing. He was tense and worried, his long legs stretched out underneath the big ranch table, one hand curled around a glass of old Elmer Simpson's white lightning. He looked at his father and spread out the cards.

"Full house. Aces over eights."

Both men had that lean, hard look of the outdoors, blond hair, sun-bleached in spite of the hat always worn, the years telling on Buck's face. Strong hands held the cards, hands used to handling a rope and a horse, but hands capable of a soft touch as well.

Young Stanley had heeded his father's words.

"A wife works hard as any man," he had told him. "She cooks for all the hands, does the washing, keeps a clean house, and tends to the little ones. She deserves respect from her man. Any man strikes a woman ain't worth wiping your feet on."

Actually young Stanley couldn't imagine anyone being rough with Margarita. That first day, when old Deedee had brought her six-year-old granddaughter to the one room schoolhouse, he had been ready to slug any boy who teased her or, when you came right down to it, any girl who shunned her.

He hadn't needed to though. Everyone respected old Deedee. They might look down on some who had mixed blood, but they knew who to call whenever there was sickness or a baby to be born. They were not ready to risk insulting her. Who knew what kind of a spell the woman could weave? Deedee was Cheyenne, and her husband was Patrick Ryan, an Irishman straight from the old country, a man who had ridden with Kit Carson and his ilk. Margarita's own father and mother had been killed in some kind of a ruckus over land.

"Would you like to tell the children your name?" the teacher asked.

A couple of the girls giggled. Everyone knew she was called Maggie.

"I am Margarita Maria Namid Ryan Gomez," the little black haired. blue-eyed girl announced. "I am named for both my mother, my grandmother, and my grandfather."

Stanley never again thought of her as anything but Margarita. Later he learned that Deedee's Cheyenne name, Namid, meant She Who Dances with the Stars. Sometimes, when they were in bed, Stanley felt that they were both dancing with the stars. Margarita and her grandmother could lull the roughest cowboy with a few quiet words. Stanley looked forward to hearing his young wife sing lullabies to their babies.

"Beats a pair of kings," Buck announced. They weren't playing for money. It was just something to do while trying to take their minds off what was going on upstairs.

"Relax, boy," Buck told him. "Women have been having babies forever. Deedee knows what to do."

"She's just a girl, Pa. Didn't figure on getting babies this soon."

"What you think was going to happen. You been keepin' that bed busy for most a year now. Margarita's a fine girl. Your ma was glad to have her in the family. Too bad she didn't live to see her grandbaby."

"You still miss her, don't you?"

"Damn tootin' I do. She kept me on the straight and narrow when we were young."

"It's taking too long." Stanley pushed the glass aside and started rolling another cigarette.

"She'll be fine."

"Can't stop worrying. Not after what happened at the Simpson's."

"White trash," Buck snorted. "Not got the sense of a jackrabbit. Been inbreeding for generations." Buck started dealing out the cards. "Thinking she could have her baby all alone. If anyone could have saved her, it would have been Deedee. "

"E2 says no matter what Elmer Number One says, he's calling in Deedee if this new wife has one."

"Saw her and the boy in town t'other day. Looks pretty bright for a two-year-old Simpson. Too bad he'll grow up being nothing but Number 3 and learning nothn' but makin' moonshine. He'll probably be like every other Simpson and keep holding on to that measly forty acres."

"Would think they'd stop naming them all Elmer," Stanley remarked.

Upstairs sixteen-year-old Margarita McKaid was chomping on a rope tied to the brass rail of the double bed, trying to bite back the scream that wanted to tear her in two. Old Deedee stopped the singsong tune she'd been chanting. "Push, daughter. Your baby's about to say hello to you."

With good reason, most of the young men in the county had courted the beauteous Margarita. Her hair was a lustrous black. A pert little nose, but she had the high cheekbones of her Comanche ancestors. Favored the Mexican part of her heritage with her skin.

She could run like a deer, but she had never run away from Stanley, not even when they were children. She had an infectious laugh. Hearing that laugh one would think she was a cheerful but empty-headed girl. Not so. She was smart as any boy in the county. She had helped Stanley's mother though her last illness and taken on the responsibilities of the household right well.

A baby's cry had Stanley on his feet, crushing his cigarette in the ashtray.

"Guess I'm a grandpa." Buck smiled.

Stanley rushed up the stairs, looking over Deedee's shoulder even before she had the baby cleaned up.

"It's a boy." The baby's lusty cry was music to his ears. He found himself grinning at the child, black hair fine as down, skin that looked like it might be a little like its mother's or Mamaw Deedee's, arms waving, and legs that would grow long enough to reach the stirrups on any horse. A boy. He had a boy. It felt pretty good to know he was man enough to have sired a son. He could pass out cigars at the Kaidville bank and the feed store with pride. He had a son.

He went to his pretty wife, her glorious black hair wet with sweat. "What do we call him, honey?"

"Davy, just like we talked about. David Stanley McKaid, for you and your father." She smiled an exhausted smile.

"Buck's gonna like that."

"This one will grow up to be a fine man," old Deedee said, putting the squalling bundle into his arms. "Men's gonna look up to him, and there's a little princess waiting to be born who will adore him forever."

"Got lungs loud enough to out-cry a coyote." Stanly held his newborn son a few short moments before placing him in his wife's arms. He watched as the babe turned his head, arms waving, and tiny mouth seeking a nipple. "Lord a'mighty," he breathed, "ain't he a sight. He already knows enough to go after what he wants."

"Just like his daddy," Margarita said.

"He's going to get a good education, honey." Stanley told her. "I'll make that happen. He'll be first McKaid to go to college. He'll make the Diamond MiK proud."

It was a big promise. The McKaids, like a lot of ranchers, were land poor. Their ancestors had amassed thousands of acres with cows roaming all over the place, but ready cash was scarce as green grass in August.

August 3, 1917

There were cousins a few years older than two-year-old David, and a baby girl cousin only a few months old. Sometimes they played together, but on this particular day Deedee had brought four year old Elmer Number 3 to the house for Margarita to watch.

"This one not going to come out easy," she told her daughter. "We should give this little boy a taste of a good home once in awhile. He deserves better than he's getting."

She went back to Elmer Simpson's miserable little shack on the forty acres next to the Diamond MiK. She spent part of her time tending the woman in labor, but starting by cleaning the bedroom a bit. Old Elmer Number 1 made himself scarce, but when Number 2 started to follow him she put her hands on her hips and stared at the man.

"That's your wife in there, and you're going to stay right here. You go wash your hands and get yourself in that pig sty of a kitchen and cleanup those dishes, and boil me some water."

"Yes'um, Miss Deedee. Whatever you say. She aint been feelin' up to doing much lately,"

"And whose fault is that. You put that baby in there, you can help her when she needs help. Your sister. Adelaide could be doing her share."

"Yes,um she could, Miss Deedee, but them two women don't cotton to one another. Adelaide calls her a slut jist cause of where I found her."

She went back into the bedroom knowing that as long as she was there he would follow orders. The fool was scared to death of her. She wondered if he even knew his wife's name.

Hours later, her heart ached as she cradled five pounds of trouble. Elmer Number Three was turning out to be a fairly normal little boy, but this girl baby made her skin crawl. Her mama didn't want to anything to do with her, and Deedee was pretty sure she knew why. She had seen the way old Elmer Number One looked at his daughter-in-law and the way she tried to avoid him. No one was going to mourn that man when he was gone.

The woman had screamed curses at every man she'd ever slept with, the vilest of which went to her husband who had sweet-talked her about life on a ranch. When she wasn't cussing, she was declaring that life in the Austin cathouse had been better than the hellhole she was in.

Deedee was inclined to believe her. However, the troublesome babe was going to live and be part of this miserable excuse for a family. The child would have to be fed. She put the babe into her mother's protesting arms.

"Feed her," she ordered. "She's half yours. What are you calling her?"

"Betty Lou's as good as any." The red head in the bed scowled at her. "I'll feed her, but just as soon as she's weaned I'm outa here. Ain't spending my days being no brood mare for neither of the Elmers."

Deedee nodded, feeling the truth of it. Nothing good came out of this house. She returned to her little cabin, and not even looking around, she stripped herself of her garments, leaving them beside the door. That night, while all the world was fast asleep, she stepped out to burn them, all the while chanting a prayer to all the gods she knew, begging forgiveness, not because she had felt the urge to snuff out the life of that baby girl, but because she hadn't done it.

* * * * *

Life went on at the ranch. Everyone remarked that David was going to grow up to be a tall man. Margarita was giving his hand-me-downs to the Simpsons because David was soon taller than little Elmer Number 3. Adelaide Simpson did a little better at keeping the place clean and the boy and his sister half decent because Deedee had a habit of dropping by to check on the children.

Betty Lou's mother was true to her word. She took off one day when the baby was three months old, and no one knew where she went.

In 1919 Stanley McKaid came home from his days of duty in France. He'd put in his time in the trenches across the pond and was glad to be back in Texas. Never could figure out why the army hadn't put him in the Cavalry, but he was glad he'd come through the war to end all wars in one piece. Leastwise he'd done his part in assuring that young David would never have to be a soldier. It sure was good to get horse between his legs again, even better to have his wife there.

Buck had kept the place going. Four-year-old Davy was already pretty good at twirling a rope. The little stinker followed Buck around like a puppy dog. He was tall for his age, had a way of talking to the dogs and horses as if they could understand him. He had the makings of growing into a good-looking, hard riding man. Buck already had him sitting on one of the gentler horses.

Nine months later Stanley was feeling even better. Took a real man to have two sons at one time. Named them Taylor Lee and Timothy Walker, names they could be proud of. David might have his mother's black hair, high cheekbones, and a skin that looked as though he'd been in the sun forever, but Taylor and Timothy were McKaid freckled and red headed. Two peas in a pod, they were. Life might be hard, but it was good.

Chicago, Illinoise-1919

Mark Rollins wasn't a big man, and he hadn't been sent to the trenches, but he wasn't going to apologize for his part in the war. The army had needed number crunchers as well as fighters. He would have fought if he'd been sent over to France, but he'd been satisfied to stay behind with a desk in front of him. Washington wasn't all that far away, but he hadn't been home in all the time he's been in the army.

Still in his uniform, he stopped by the Smith home before going out to the farm to see his folks. He just had to see Gracie Ann Smith. He had spent many a day thinking about his best friend's sister. He had been smitten with the pretty little blonde as soon as he had met her. His parents had warned him that such a delicate girl was not suited to farm life, but that was all right with him. Before the war, he had already finished his training and passed the test for being a Certified Public Accountant. Let his brothers have the farm. He had spent much time rereading Gracie's letters, and dreaming about the way her hair sparkled like gold and the way those brown eyes of hers made him want to kiss her. If it hadn't been for the war maybe they would have already been married.

He'd written her faithfully, often expressing hope that she wasn't charming some other man with those golden locks and brown eyes. She had written back, telling him that she was saving all his letters.

Her father met him at the door. Mark had always been in awe of the man, but the army had matured him. Had the man always been a good three inches shorter that he was, or had he shrunk? He seemed so much older that he remembered.

"Is Gracie home?"

"We need to talk about that." There was an uncomfortable silence as the two took their places on the porch swing. "Are you planning on staying in the army?" her father asked.

"No, sir, I've been promised a job at a movie house. It's doing the books and whatever else needs doing."

"That's a bit of luck. Jobs won't be easy to come by." He was silent again. "Mrs. Smith read your letters," he finally stated. "Seems you mentioned marriage without consulting me."

Mark frowned. He couldn't help it. His letters had been meant for Gracie, not her family. Though he had been very proper in writing them, he didn't much like the thought of her parents reading them.

"Only natural she'd do that, son. Gracie is not one of these young women who thinks she has to go out in the world and make her own way. We've always protected her from that sort of thing."

"Pardon me, sir, I don't mean to be rude, but I couldn't see talking to you before how I knew how Gracie feels about it. If she's agreeable, I'll take good care of her, and never hurt her. She's all I've thought about all these months."

"Brad tells me you're a good Catholic. Go on in, and ask her proper like." The old man almost smiled at him. "She threatened to run off to a convent if we didn't approve. Mrs. Smith and I already talked about turning the upstairs into an apartment. Might as well pay us rent as give it to a stranger."

Six month later, the apartment completed, Mark married Gracie at St. Mary's church, and after a small reception, walked through the parlor to the fully furnished second floor apartment. Mark's boss gave them a soup tureen and said Gracie could come watch the movie anytime she wanted. Her mother saw to it that Gracie didn't overdo it and made sure she took a nap every afternoon. On his Sundays off Mark sometimes thought it would be nice if he had more say in his wife's life. By the time they attended High Mass with the old folks, had the usual chicken dinner with them, and he sat with them while Gracie took her nap, well, by the time all that happened they didn't have much time alone.

Chapter 2

Kaidville, Texas-1924

The little church was filled. It was the kind of wedding people would talk about for a long time. It was also hot. Dressed in his first long pants, David was sweating and trying to remember not to tug on the unfamiliar necktie. The plain gold ring was fastened to the little pillow with a straight pin taken from his mother's red pincushion.

His Uncle Bob was marrying Adelaide Simpson, Elmer Number Two's sister, and David knew why. Elmer Number Three had told him. Adelaide had a bun in the oven, and he might be nine, but he knew what that meant. That's what Bobby got for fooling around with white trash, but did they have to let Betty Lou hold a basket of Dogwood petals to throw down the aisle? He hated that girl. She was clean for a change. Somebody had combed her red hair, but she was still a pain in the you know what, always following him around. He didn't like that. Usually she smelled like she hadn't had a bath in a month, and she had a mean streak. More than once he'd seen her kick a dog when she thought no one was around.

The piano player started playing the Wedding March.

"Go on," the bride whispered to the seven-year-old. "Walk, just like we showed you yesterday."

Instead the little girl turned to him.

"Ask me to marry you, Davy."

"Go on down the aisle."

"No. I want to marry Davy."

"I wouldn't marry you if somebody paid me to."

Children on a ranch found out about the facts of life a lot earlier than their counterparts in the city did, and probably a lot more accurately. His Sally was going to have a colt, and Pop and Gramps sure hadn't chosen any old nag for the sire. He might be young, but he had ears and knew breeding was important, and Betty Lou was a Simpson.

The piano player paused and started over.

"Be a good girl," her father urged. "Show everyone how pretty you look today."

"I am pretty," she chirped. "Davy will marry me when we grow up?"

"No, I won't." He glared at her.

Little Betty Lou stamped her foot, bouncing some of the petals out of the basket. "Will too."

Heads were turning. The piano player stopped playing and looked toward the back of the church. When the minister said something to her, she started a third time.

"Davy, you tell that little girl what she wants to hear," old Elmer Number One said. "This here church is an oven, and we have to get this here wedding on its way. It's the onliest big wedding this family ever had."

"I'm not gonna marry her."

"You're only nine years old, boy. You're not a gonna marry anyone for a long time. Just say it, or I'm going to shoot Sally"

"You wouldn't shoot my horse." On looking at the man, he was afraid he just might do it. After all he was a Simpson. "Willyoumarryme," he mumbled.

"Oh, yes, Davy." The waif thin seven-year-old skipped down the aisle, and it was a good thing Dogwood blossoms weren't stones because most of them landed on the guests instead the floor. As for

Davy, when he took his place next to the best man who was also an uncle, the man whispered to him.

"Thanks, fellow. Maybe she'll die in childbirth."

David decided he was going to be very careful around girls. He wasn't going to be like his uncle and marry a girl just because her Pa had a shotgun handy. Girls meant trouble, and he especially hated Betty Lou.

* * * * *

The little redhead was thrilled to be in the wedding, but she didn't particularly like her aunt. She hadn't let her wear the pretty pink dress to school. Aunt Adelaide was always telling her what to do. She didn't even care that it hurt when she combed the tangles out of her hair. She was the only one who paid much attention to her, but that didn't mean she had to like her. The only babies she has been around cried all the time. She heard what Davy's uncle said, and wondered what would happen if Adelaide fell down the attic steps. She could always get her way with Pa and Papaw. Her brother, E3, pretty much ignored her except for seeing she got to the schoolhouse on time.

Chicago- January 18,1925

Mark Rollins watched the storm clouds gather. At an early age he had promised himself that he wasn't going to spend his life behind a plow. He'd made good on that promise. He was quick with figures and enjoyed his job as bookkeeper for a local radio station. It paid better than the old movie house had. One thing though. Even when he went into the confessional, he had never mentioned just how much better it paid. If he had, his greedy father-in-law would have upped the amount they paid for rent and utilities. The old skinflint counted every penny.

It wasn't easy living in that upstairs apartment. The Smiths felt entitled to walk in any time they wished. He had hated that from the start. He hated not telling his wife about his private bank account, but there was no way he was going to let the Smiths find out about it.

Sitting in the apartment that was part of his in-laws big house, he was contentedly watching his wife finger her rosary. Gracie was so little and delicate. Even with her belly swollen in the last stage of pregnancy, she was pretty. How he enjoyed brushing that long. blonde hair each night before they retired. Once she had mentioned bobbing it, but he had talked her out of that in a hurry. Her hair was her crowning glory.

He might not be a big man, but he still knew that he was the man of the house. Taking care of his woman was a man's job. They were the weaker sex and needed a strong man to tell them what to do and how to vote. One of these days he would have enough in that secret account to buy their own little house.

He was almost sorry they hadn't decided to go to California with Gracie's brother and sister-in-law. They had been tempted, but at a time like this he knew Gracie really did need to be near her mother. Mother Smith knew how much Gracie needed her rest. He insisted it really didn't matter if it was a boy or a girl, but in his heart he wanted a boy. He just hoped there wasn't going to be a heavy snow. The doctor had said, "Any day now."

"Oh." Gracie dropped her rosary. "Maybe you better go downstairs and get Mama."

Hours later, Mark and his father-in-law sat at the table with the doctor playing dominos. The snow had arrived, and the doctor didn't want to take any chances of not getting back when Gracie really needed him. Every so often he went upstairs to check on her. Gracie's mother came down once to fix sandwiches for the them. She came back down a little later to clean up after the men, and make sure they had coffee. Five and a half hours later, Mark looked down at the tiny bundle in his arms and fell in love all over again.

"My little princess. Lucinda Jane will be the most beautiful girl in the world. She's ours, Gracie. All ours. I'll make sure our little princess is always safe." Keeping the boys away would be the biggest problem because he just knew she was going to be the prettiest girl on the block.

Far, far away old Deedee looked at the moon and listened to the sounds of the night. Every coyote in the area was yip-yip-yipping, and the stock was mooing and neighing. A little princess had been born somewhere. It would be a long time, but someday David would bring her home. She'd have to spin some powerful spells though. That little Simpson girl was a problem, worse than any ugly stepmother could have been. Bad blood there. She was a sly one.

That wedding had been a disaster. After only five and a half months Bobby had been turned into a widower. No one quite knew why Adelaide had been up in the attic. Eight months along, she must have fallen from the very top step to cave in her head that badly. Not a thing anyone could do to save her or the baby. By the time she was found, it was too late.

Betty Lou had cried, telling everyone how good Adelaide had been to her. Crocodile tears, Deedee thought. Her eyes betrayed her. The girl was still insisting that she and David were engaged. No matter how he tried to avoid the girl, she always managed to be near.

June 4, 1926

Seventeen–month-old Lucinda looked up from the doll she was covering with the little quilt Grammy Smith had made. Her brown eyes were red from crying..

"Putting her to bed?" Dr. Watkins asked.

"She's sick like mama." She shook her head, her golden hair swinging loose. It was much too long for a little girl, but her father wouldn't let anyone cut it. "She's got a sore throat like Mommy. Hurts. Mommy's yelling." She picked up the doll, hugging it. "Won't let me see Mommy."

"Well, we'll just see if I can't make your mommy well." He patted her on the head.

"Nap time, Princess," her father said. "You use Grandma Smith's bed this time,"

When she woke from her nap Grammy Smith and her father finally took her up into the bedroom to see her mother. Her eyes opened wide. She didn't know mama had a doll to sleep with. She reached up to touch it, and pulled her hand back in surprise.

"Baby?" It was a question.

"You have a little sister. Her name is Letitia Fay." Mark lifted her so she could see her.

"We have to be very careful with her," her mother told her. "She's real little, and we don't want to hurt her."

"Soft." Lucy reached out to touch the baby's cheek. "Can I play with her?"

"When she gets bigger."

"Buy me one, too."

"The doctor brought her in his bag," her grandmother told her. "He doesn't have another one right now. We'll let your mother rest now. She's tired."

For a long time little Lucy peered at the doctor's black bag every time she saw him, wondering if he had another baby in it. Finally one day she asked him if it did.

"Goodness, no," he had replied. "The stork brings the babies."

She tried to imagine a bird big enough to carry a baby. She was a precocious little thing, already asking why and what about everything. When Mommy or Grammy changed the baby's diaper, she was there to pick it up with two dainty fingertips and carry it to the diaper pail on the back porch. In her little mind she had decided that the more she helped the sooner her little sister would be big enough to play with. She would have to get her own doll though. Baby doll was hers, not Tish's. Lucy had trouble saying Letitia. By the time her sister was a month old everyone except Grandpa Smith was calling the baby Tish.

Kaidville, Texas-June 1928

Margarita felt lost standing under the canopy. She had loved Stanley all her life. The thought of going on without him hurt deep inside. Her mother's black dress was pinned in several places because she hadn't been able to go into Austin to buy her own. The little black, veiled hat was from one of the women in Kaidville who had lost her mother last year. She just had been too busy nursing her husband over the past weeks, praying that Mama was wrong, that he would recover after the old bull had turned on him.

The three boys were waiting by the fence surrounding the little country church's cemetery. David shouldn't have come, but he had insisted. That boy really was something, The way he had rushed out, trying to help rescue his father. . .

Five men had seen the whole thing, and they had five ways of telling it. The only three things they all agreed about was the fact that Stanley had known the old bull was dangerous, David had screamed as he rushed to his father's side, and Buck's one shot had killed the bull before he had stomped Davy, too. Thank the good Lord above, Davy had only gotten a broken leg out of it.

The cast on his leg, grimy with Texas dust and dozens of autographs, was due to come off in two more weeks. As usual, Betty Lou was hanging around, still pouting because she was the only one Davy hadn't let scribble her name on the thing. The twins bravely stood on either side of him so the girl couldn't get close.

"Church ladies will be waiting at the house," her father-in-law finally said.

"I don't know what I'll do, Buck. I never thought I'd be a widow so young. I don't know where I'll go."

"Margarita, you ain't going nowhere. You and the boys and your mama are staying put."

"You've been good putting up with Mamaw Deedee and me. Not many men would have welcomed us into the family the way you did."

"Stanley loved you. That's just how it is. People might think she's strange, but we've got a mighty fine healer in that grandma of yours. Taylor and Tim missed it, but you can see a touch of Cheyenne and Mexico in Davy if you know what to look for it. He's going to wow the girls when he grows up. Lord a'mighty, he's already taller than any thirteen-year-old oughta be."

"I don't want the boys growing up knowing nothing but roping cows and trying to make ends meet."

"Ain't gonna do that without a good education. Had a talk with that wildcatter Stanley chased off while back. He's mighty sure there's oil under us."

"Stanley didn't want to dirty up the land."

"Better than starvin', girl. Times are tough. Them boys have good minds. Tim's already got your mama's healing touch. Gonna talk to an Austin lawyer next week. Don't want to have oil all over the place and still be poor. Might take Davy with me." He looked over to the fence and raised his voice. "Come on, boys. Get yourself in the back of the truck. Betty Lou, you better go find your folks."

"They already left. I told Pa you'd bring me. He says girls should be with their boyfriends time like this."

"You're not my girl friend." David snapped. "You're not getting in the back of the truck with me."

"I'm a gonna marry you, Davy." The little redhead appealed to the grown-ups. "Can I sit up front with you, Miss Margarita?"

Buck helped his grandson and his cast onto the tailgate.

"Bad enough I was sitting on the fence when the old bull broke loose," the boy told him. "Lost Pop, and now I still have to put up with her. You really going to take me to Austin with you?"

"Almost fourteen. I recon you're old enough to know what's going on. You're sure enough old enough to find out there's a life outside of cows. Want you to know about things. Can't do it all myself. Need your help."

1930

Fifteen-year-old David and his twin brothers watched in awe. School was out for the day, and all three were on their horses, as close to the drilling site as Buck would allow. They could see it spewing forth. The black crude was raining down on all the men around the drilling rig. Boys and horses stood still..

"It's a gusher." David's voice fought between awe and excitement.. "It's a God damned gusher."

"Don't let Mom hear you swear."

"Don't care. Not this time. You know what this means. I can go to the university. I can be a lawyer, and you two can go to any college you want. Hot damn, boys, we're rich. It's a damn gusher, and Patrick's already has a second spot primed to drill."

There was both rejoicing and sorrow on the Diamond MK that night. Oil meant an end to scrimping and saving, but a portion of the land was black and would it ever heal?

* * * * *

Betty Lou smiled when her brother told her the McKaids had struck oil. She'd be rich when she married her Davy.

When word spread, old Elmer Number 1 frowned at his son and two grandchildren.

"The McKaid's have all the luck. Buck's gonna lord it over all of us."

"He's a nice man," Elmer Number Three told his grandfather. "He said I can help out at round-up. Pay me a wage."

"Won't need a wage when I marry Davy," she told him. "We'll be rich, too."

"No kin of mine's gonna have any truck with that bunch. You just remember what happened when Adelaide married one of 'em."

Thirteen-year-old Betty Lou said nothing as she looked at her grandfather and older brother. She just smiled. The baseball bat she had stolen from school was still in the attic. She had practiced with it a lot before she had persuaded her aunt to come to the top of the attic steps. Then she turned to see what her father was thinking. Pa had waited a long time to be number one. The flowers called Foxgloves she had been growing in her little garden were coming along right well. She wondered how they had gotten that name. Pa knew everything about the still he had to know. Maybe Papaw's heart wasn't too strong. After all, he was a really old man. Maybe with one less mouth to feed she could buy a dress. Davy would be impressed to see her in a pretty dress when they were in church.

Chapter 3

Chicago, Illinois-1930

In the upstairs window, Gracie watched as Mark parked the car. Lucy was sitting on the second step, her little face big with tears.

"What's the matter with my princess?" he asked..

"Grandpa pulled down my panties and spanked me."

"He did what?" Mark stooped down to his daughter's level. His little girl violated? He took out his handkerchief to wipe away her tears.

"He said I lied. He spanked me."

"Lied about what?"

"Grammy's good dishes. He said I broke them. I didn't, Daddy. I really didn't. It hurt."

"Run upstairs, Princess. Wash your face, and tell your mommy to get baby Lily ready. We'll all go out for ice cream after I talk to your grandfather."

At the upstairs window, Gracie watched him storm over to the front porch and heard him fling open the door without bothering with the knock her father insisted upon. She could imagine him ripping her father's afternoon paper from his hands. She could hear the angry words her husband was shouting.

"If you ever touch one of my girls again, I'll kill you."

"If you can't teach them the difference between right and wrong the nuns at St. Mary's will," the old man said.

"I am their father. I told you they will go to public school, and that's where they will go. You had no right to spank her. She's only six."

"She broke Gracie's mother's dishes. For the last three days one a day has been broken. She lied about it. A child who lies is an abomination in the eyes of our Lord."

"She said you pulled down her panties. What does that make you?" He stared at the man he had come to resent. "Don't you ever touch one of my girls again. If you so much as kiss them goodnight, I will kill you."

Gracie busied herself with coats for the girls. Mark walked up the steps slowly, giving himself a chance to cool down. Lucy and Letitia met him with sweaters in their hands. Gracie was wrapping a blanket around baby Lily.

"Lucy said ice cream."

"We have to talk."

"About the letter we got from my brother?" He nodded. She almost smiled. "I miss Brad and Jane."

Neither spoke while in the old Ford. Mark by-passed the local drug store, driving instead to the usual one close to the radio station. He helped the two older girls into their wrought iron chairs before he took baby Lily.

"Can I have a strawberry milk shake?" Lucy asked as a boy came over to take their order.

"Princess, you can have anything you want. How about you, Tish?"

The five year old looked at her sister.

"She likes chocolate," Lucy told him.

For a time, all silently sipped their milks shakes. It was almost a tradition to come here when the wanted to talk. It seemed to be the only time they had real privacy. Gracie's father had always insisted that Mark knock before entering the downstairs apartment, though both he and his wife felt free to walk upstairs at any time.

"We have to get out of that house?" he finally said. "Would you be happy in California?"

"We've been married twelve years," Gracie said. "Don't you think it's about time we have our own home?" She reached over to wipe chocolate ice cream from Tish's chin. "We'd need a down payment and some furniture. You have enough in your secret bank account." She smiled at his shocked look. "The bank book you keep in the inside pocket of your good suit," she added.

"You go through my pockets?" He had never thought his quiet wife would do anything like that.

"Mama says it's the only way a woman can know what's going on."

"Your mother?" That did shock him beyond belief.

"She doesn't think we should let Papa know until the day we leave. That way he won't have a chance to blow up. You might never have a chance like this again. Brad's letter said the old man is retiring next month." She put her hand on his arm. "Mark, I want a home of our own. It's not right for him to be able to walk in any time he pleases and try to tell us how to raise the girls. Besides," she almost laughed a little, "if we have to spend our life eating ice cream every time we want to talk alone, I'll get as fat as a pig."

"We can't let that happen."

* * * * *

Later that evening Mark visited Doctor Watkins.

"Usually don't see you in here. You have always been one of the healthiest men I know."

"It's not me," Mark told him. "It's Gracie and Lily I'm here about."

"Want me to come out to the house."

"No, they're both feeling okay. I just want to know if they are strong enough for a trip to California."

"A visit to her brother would do Gracie a world of good."

"I'd appreciate it if you keep this confidential, not say anything about it to her folks."

"Won't say a word, boy. You having trouble with them?"

"I've put up with a lot, knowing how delicate Gracie's health is, but with the girls growing up. . ." He pounded his right fist into his left hand. "Doc, I'm just not going to send my little princess to a school where the nuns will slap her hands with a ruler every time they feel like it. I just won't do it. That old man has run my life long enough. I've been talking to Gracie's brother. Been using a phone booth away from the house. Brad says there's an opening for a bookkeeper at the radio station he works for. I can have it if I want. Gracie's willing to go, but I just don't know if she's up to the trip, and Lily's only six months old." He kept his eyes on the old doctor's face. "I just never intended to spend our whole lives living in the same house as her folks. Doc, he spanked my Lucy because he claims she broke some dishes and lied about it. I don't think she did. If Mother Smith dropped them I'm not sure she would tell him. He's got no right."

"Just between you and me," the doctor took his stethoscope from around his neck, "the only thing reason Gracie is delicate and can't do a lot is because her mother and father would never let her do anything. She's been told all her life she's delicate. She's given you three healthy little girls with no trouble at all. You go ahead and do what you want, but you know the old man's going to squawk."

"We're not going to tell them until the last minute." Mark relaxed for the first time in days. "I have to get a bigger car. I've got my eyes on a 29 Studebaker. It's in good condition and low mileage. It's got a nice big trunk on the back. Have to give two weeks notice where I am."

"I don't mean to pry, but I brought Gracie into this world. She was only the second baby I delivered. Do you have enough for the trip?"

"I'm fine, Doc. I sorta fudged on what I made when I moved to the radio station. If I hadn't that old skinflint would have upped our rent." He walked out of Doc's office knowing that tomorrow he was going to buy that Studebaker and give notice. He was going to be a bookkeeper in Hollywood.

Chapter 4

Along Route 66-1930

She wasn't any old scaredy cat. She wasn't afraid of dogs or spiders or the weird things that might live under the bed, but six-year-old Lucinda Jane Rollins didn't like these curvy roads with the sides so steep they went down to nowhere. She wanted to cover her head with the blanket just like Letitia was doing, but she was big sister and had to be brave. Mama had brushed her long blond hair before they left the tiny little cabin, but she didn't feel very clean wearing the same dress she'd had on when they left Chicago.

The 1929 Studebaker was nicer than the old Ford had been, but the trunk on back didn't hold a lot, and Lily's things and mama's dishes had to come first. Babies sure needed a lot of things. She and Tish both had their favorite dolls here in the back seat A bag of clean diapers was on the floorboard along with a couple of pillows.

A cry came from the basket between her and Tish. Lucy wrinkled her nose.

"Mama, Lily needs a clean diaper."

"You know how to do it." Gracie Rollins turned to look at her oldest daughter.

"We're going to have to stop. She smells."

"It won't be long, Princess," her father said. "We'll be stopping as soon as we see a motor court."

"We might have to find a store where we can buy a few more diapers," Gracie told her husband. "It's so wasteful throwing so many away"

"We budgeted for it. We sure can't stop long enough to wash things. You didn't help much when you gave some to that Oakie woman yesterday.

"She needed them, Mark."

"I know, honey. I guess I didn't know how lucky we are until I talked to some of these men. At least I have a job to go to, and we have the money I've saved. Most of these people don't have a thing."

"How long is this old Route 66?" Letitia asked for the umpteenth time. "I'm tired of riding."

Lucy shook her head. She was tired, too, but Daddy had already said they would reach the place called Hollywood the next day. Uncle Brad and Aunt Jane had already found a house for them, and Daddy wouldn't even have to drive to the radio station where he'd be working. He could walk, and that would save money.

Even at six, Lucy knew money was important. She heard Daddy talking about it a lot. She'd heard him tell mama that the car had been worth every penny just knowing that they wouldn't have car trouble. He'd wanted a new one, but that cost too much. This one wasn't quite two years old. They'd only had one tire blow out.

She wound down the window. One thing about baby sisters. They could just plain stink when their diapers were dirty.

Austin, Texas

The Senator's little get together was the usual mob scene. David had a lot of respect for his godfather. At the Senator's suggestion, he had brought along his roommate and his date. The senator was a frequent visitor at the Diamond MiK. He and his father had been friends. However, David suspected that he wasn't the only reason for the man's frequent visits. Mom was still a beautiful woman.

Just last week the Senator had introduced David to TJ Jefferson. He would spend his summer as an intern at TJ's firm. Life couldn't get much better. Jefferson, Colby, and Smith was just about the best law firm in Austin, and he had the luscious Trudy on his arm. He was going to ask her home for the Memorial Day barbeque, maybe even look into a ring. She might be the way to put a stop to Betty Lou.

He picked his girlfriends carefully, and he did have his pick. He would never be called handsome, but there just seemed to be something about him. Six one, wavy black hair, and with the look of a perpetual tan, girls just seemed to be attracted to him. Of course, the fact that he had his own Studebaker and was heir apparent to the Diamond MiK didn't hurt his popularity.

Actually he didn't date a lot, and when he did it was always with another couple. Betty Lou Simpson and her ridiculous claim that they were engaged was enough to make him wary.

In his dreams he often found himself making love to a fairly well endowed little blonde. He often wondered about that because he actually preferred the taller, dark haired girls.

Trudy Collins was the one he'd brought to the cocktail party. She was one of the prettiest co-eds at the university. She and her mother had gone to New York to find the gown she was wearing. In her high heels, they were only a couple of inches away from being eye to eye. They made a striking couple, her hair as black and wavy as his own.

His mind was wandering a bit. The college years had been good to him. He had worked hard on his speech and manners. If he was going to be a lawyer, he was going to be the best. His aim of getting that diploma in three instead of four years had been a grind, but it had been worth it. In September he would be on his way to that law degree. Still, he was looking forward to getting back to the ranch on weekends. There wasn't anything better than mounting Tiger and feeling the wind on his face as he and the palomino raced across the fields. If Trudy visited, she could ride Pretty Girl. She was getting more comfortable on a horse, and Pretty Girl was gentle. Mom wouldn't mind.

He hadn't been paying much attention to the conversation between Trudy and Jim's date until Trudy's remark made a sudden impression.

"Really," she was saying, "I didn't know her kind would be here. Look at her. Talking to the Senator as though she belongs here. Those pearls have to be costume jewelry."

"Why don't they stay where they belong?" the other girl asked.

"Well, they do know how to cook and clean, and Daddy says they'll work for next to nothing. She is pretty enough. Do you suppose she and the senator are— you know?"

Instantly, David forgot about looking at rings. He decided that, after all, he didn't like this girl he had been dating. His roommate looked as though he was about to say something, but David shook his head and took Trudy's arm. "Come on, Tom, I'll introduce you all to Senator Clayton."

He walked them over to the imposing man in the white suit. Senator James Clayton of the Texas legislature held out a welcoming hand.

"How you doing, boy? You got that palomino calmed down?"

"Yes, Sir."

"You named him yet?"

"Tiger. He's man's horse. If we breed him to Pretty Girl, we ought to get a mighty fine colt." He turned to the pretty Mexican woman beside the Senator. "Mother, you know Jim, of course, but I don't think you've met Trudy and Pamela. I believe they noticed you." He almost enjoyed the mortified look he saw on the girls' faces. "In fact, I do believe I heard them say we ought to go back to where we came from. I can't help wondering if they meant the Spanish Conquistadors. Of course, perhaps they meant Ireland. Your grandfather did come from there before he rode with Kit Carson. Or maybe Mamaw's Cheyennes? If I remember my history, they were here first."

"David," she chided, "you are embarrassing your friends."

"Trudy," he turned to the girl he had brought to the cocktail party, his voice cold, "I would like you to meet my mother, Margarita Maria Namid Ryan Gomez McKaid. Everyone at the Diamond MiK is quite proud of her. She and Gramps do pay all our Mexican workers a living wage, and the pearls didn't come from Woolworths."

"Oh, David, I didn't mean. . ."

"Don't.," he interrupted.. "It's good that we discovered that I'm not suitable before we made a mistake. I'll take you back to the dorm. I should be studying anyway." He looked at his roommate. "Jim, are you coming? You can talk to the senator at the Memorial Day barbecue."

Maybe he'd try to find time to read the book Mamacita had given him. She'd said to read it and remember that it could have been his life. Steinbeck had written it, and he was one powerful writer. Grapes of Wrath, he called this one.

1941

Nothing could stop the battles raging on. Stanley McKaid, along with thousands of others, had believed in the war they had fought. They had had believed that their sons would never have to march away from the shores of this beloved country called America.

They were wrong. Across that protecting body of water called the Atlantic Ocean, in a place called Germany, a maniacal ogre reigned. He had great ideas, and he believed in his evil plans. To him, his were the chosen people. His people, he believed, had bloodlines purer than all others. It was not enough to have the ones he called Storm Troopers eradicate from his own country the ones he feared and hated. He sent them to all his neighbors to pillage, destroy, and kill.

The leaders of David and Lucy's country had tried to help their friends with what they dubbed a Lend Lease Program. Help, maybe, but bodies were needed— young, strong, idealistic bodies of America's finest.

There were those who believed that America should and would join the fight.. There were those who would keep to their own shores, secure in the knowledge that the great Atlantic protected them. Somehow, few gave thought to the greater waters, the one called the Pacific Ocean. That is, until one Sunday morning. The calendar said December. The year was 1941.

David McKaid had walked out of Jefferson, Colby, and Smith Friday afternoon quite pleased with himself. T.J. had congratulated him. The case hadn't been a big one, but the verdict had gone his way. He slid his boots into his new Buick convertible, anxious to get to the ranch and into something more comfortable than the navy suit he was wearing. Always, in court, he wore navy and the white boots with the Diamond MiK's brand embroidered in plain view. Pure vanity, and he knew it, but he loved that M and K within the diamond shape. Wherever he might go it would be a bit of home, of riding horses, and of seeing that first gusher spew its Texas Tea into the clear blue air.

He also knew that Patsy had been hoping to be invited for the weekend. He'd always been up front with her. No way was he ready for marriage. She was fun to be with, but that spark just wasn't there. He wanted a girl with the flair to match his, one who could wear boots and maybe flout conventions a bit.

Once he was clear of the Austin streets, he pushed down a little harder on the accelerator. He'd bought the Buick in April. His mother had given him the sheepskin seat covers for his birthday. The twins would soon be home for the holidays. Tim was going on to Vet school after he finished at Texas U. Old Doc Kelso was waiting for him to take over the care of the county's animals. Taylor already was giving Gramps some pretty good ideas. When he finished at Texas A & M he'd be ready to take over. Those two new bulls he'd picked out should produce some fine calves. Gramps was talking about building a new house. In a way, he would hate to see the old homestead go. Added on to over the years, it was part of the McKaid legacy. Yes, life was okay.

Sunday morning he was out riding fence with one of the hands when the three quick rifle shots rang out. Recognizing the universal call for help, both turned their horses and urged them into a gallop. By the time they got to the house every hand on the place was gathered around the back porch. His mother held the rifle. Mamaw Deedee was beating on the dinner triangle, and Elena, the cook and housekeeper was clutching a cup towel and crying. All the men were quiet, waiting, wondering what was wrong.

"President Roosevelt just came on the radio." His mother's voice was grim. "The Japanese bombed Pearl Harbor."

"Where's that?" one asked.

"Hawaii. They weren't prepared. Took them by surprise. Almost the whole Pacific fleet was there."

"We're in it now," Buck declared. He looked at the men, "You married men better go see your wives. The rest of you come on in and we'll listen for news."

David led his horse away. Tiger had been ridden hard. He needed to rub him down before he could go into the big kitchen, and he needed a few minutes alone to think. Which of them would be wearing a uniform, and how many would be coming home.

Chapter 5

Hollywood, California
August 14,1945

"Tell him I've gone to bed."

Because no one closed the windows in August, the window was already open. Lucy didn't hesitate. Without a second thought, she unhooked the screen, slid one red clad foot out, then the other. She was well past her twentieth birthday and tired of being treated like a child. Both feet on the ground, she pushed the screen closed, straightened her skirt, checked to see that she hadn't damaged any buttons, and straightened the red hat covering her blonde, pageboy hairdo.

At least she didn't have to worry about getting a run in her stockings. Now that the war was over maybe she would soon be able to get the new nylon hose instead of painting her legs with colored goo. Her mother had made the beige suit two years before, and she had never told anyone that, though the fabric had been on sale, the gold buttons that looked like knots hadn't been They had cost a dollar ten cents apiece. It had been extravagance but each time she wore the suit she was glad she has spent the money. They were just plain pretty.

It was VJ Day. The Japs had surrendered, and no way was she going to miss the celebration. She pulled on her red gloves and met Sophie as she coming out of her house across the street. They began walking down toward Hollywood Boulevard.

"I'm broke," Sophie said, but I have my bus pass. Let's go downtown."

"Sounds like a good idea. I have seven dollars. Hill street ought to be exciting tonight." The way she felt, she didn't even want to stay close to home. The Hollywood Palladium would probably be too crowded for dancing anyway.

"Not still carrying that torch, are you?" Sophie asked.

"I'm over him." She snapped out the words through gritted teeth. "I'll find someone who appreciates me. Might even find one who doesn't gamble. I've had enough of guys whose idea of a date is a burlesque show and a hot dog, and while I'm at it. I'm walking out the door next time. Climbing out windows is for school kids."

"We're in luck. The streetcar is coming."

All the seats were taken, but two sailors offered them theirs. Sophie scooted into the window seat. Lucy looked up at the sailor left standing by her side.

"Thank you."

"Anything for you, beautiful." He bent down, his head close to hers. "Know why a sailor has thirteen buttons on his uniform?" he asked.

That one again. How many times had she heard it? But usually not as an opening line. She didn't want to have anything to do with him. With that breath, he'd probably already had too many beers.

"Yeah," she told him. "It's to give a girl thirteen chances to say no. A smart sailor knows enough to believe it on the first button."

She was silent for the rest of the ride downtown, her mind replaying the scene with her father.

"Lucinda Jane Robbins," he had said, "you are not taking one step out of this house tonight."

"It's a special night. Sophie and I are going out."

"Not tonight, you aren't."

All three of her eight-year-old brothers had been making faces at her, happy to witness another confrontation between her and her father. She loved the triplets, but they could be exasperating.

"Great." The word boiled out in anger. "I can give you half of my paychecks. I help Mom with the ironing and cooking and the boys, but I can't go out when I want. Isn't it about time you admitted that I've grown up?"

"I remember how it was when we licked the Huns back in WWI," he told her. "It was chaos on the streets. No daughter of mine is going out tonight. Our Little Ladies are staying home where they are safe."

Our Little Ladies. The words grated on her nerves. She hated them almost as much as she hated the way he had always called HER his little princess. That wasn't fair to Tish and Lil. She hated the house not being big enough for a family with six children. She hated the daybed she slept in. When it came right down to it, maybe she hated the whole wide world. I deserve better. Damn it, I deserve a lot better.

The telephone had rung, and she had grabbed it before Dad or one of the boys could. Maybe she could find someone who wouldn't put a ring on her finger and then disappear from her life. She wanted to get away, away from the hurt, away from teasing triplets, away from her father. "It's me." Me, of course, had been Sophie, calling from the house across the street. "Mom and Dad are being unreasonable," she said. "I'm going out anyway."

"Same here." Her father could give out all the ultimatums he liked. There was no way she was going to miss the celebration.

"I'll be in my room reading," she had snapped as she flounced out of the living room and into the tiny room she shared with her two sisters.

It seemed that she and her father argued more than they talked. They disagreed about finances, about the news, about Father O'Toole's sermons. Maybe it was just the stress of the last few months. Maybe it just hurt so much that no one other than her sister Tish seemed to care that night after night she had cried herself to sleep until there were no more tears left in her, and now she had to worry about Tish as well. That sailor she was dating was bad news. She just knew he was. It was more than just his lack of good manners and the tattoos he was so proud of. She just didn't trust him, but Tish seemed to excuse all his faults. Her sister was changing. Couldn't Mom and Dad see that?

Earlier in the day she had felt so wonderful. The long war was over. Rationing would probably stop, and she would be able to buy a new pair of shoes. The three growing brothers had been using all the family's shoe stamps. She had bought the red wedgies she wore with her first paycheck when she was still in high school. They weren't leather and hadn't needed the ration stamps, but they were getting pretty well worn.

She'd told her father she wanted to celebrate, but now she had lost that feeling. Now she really wasn't feel very festive. While her parents said little about Tish's Eddie who was a real jerk, they had been very vocal about Jerry, especially about him being so much older and not in uniform. They didn't seem to care about how much she missed him, how it hurt to have him gone. Hurt? That was too mild a word for what she had been feeling. Devastated? Worthless? Abandoned? How could she put a word to the way she felt?

What hurt most was that even as he had put the ring on her finger he hadn't been honest with her. If she had known that he was an undercover cop, she would have understood the times he hadn't shown up or been late. Worst of all, when she had finally been told, she had been sworn to secrecy and couldn't tell anyone the truth.

Having him just disappear after they had planned the wedding for Christmas Eve was bad enough, but almost by accident finding out about the truth was hard. Both her parents had quit asking when she was going to stop wearing the ring. Maybe it was because they didn't take the opal seriously. It wasn't a diamond, but he had put it on her finger, and engagement rings didn't have to be diamonds. That night was the last time she had seen or heard from him. Could anything hurt more?

Maybe she had no more tears to give him, but the pain was still with her. She didn't think it would ever go away. It had been twisting in her heart for eight months. This was probably the most important night of the century and her father, standing by the door, telling her she couldn't go out, was almost too much to bear. She was tired of being treated as a child and wanted to be anywhere but in her parents' house. Maybe it was time to take the ring off and put it away. Jerry would never be coming back.

* * * * *

Probably Sergeant David Stanley McKaid was the only person in all the whole U.S. of A who wasn't deliriously happy. Hell's bells, probably the only one on all five continents. He should have been sitting on top of the world. Someone in the firm, probably his god-father, T.J., or maybe the senator, had pulled some strings, and he'd been discharged three weeks earlier, and here he was, still in his custom tailored uniform, on a crowded street in downtown L.A., putting off going home.

Damn Betty Lou Simpson. Gramps' last letter had said he'd seen a ring she was wearing around her neck. It sure wasn't any ring he'd bought. The only redeeming feature any Simpson had was the White Lightning their still had been putting out for generations. It had been a mistake for Uncle Bob to get involved with the finest example of white trash the county had. David Stanley McKaid sure wasn't going to be the second in the family to make that mistake.

Yeah, he remembered the whole disaster all right. The only thing was, now he was certain old Elmer Number 1 would have shot his horse. He wanted to get home to the ranch, to get Tiger, Jr. between his legs, and ride with a rope in his hand and a gun in his holster. Problem was, he dreaded it. His mother and Gramps needed him. With Taylor and Timothy both gone— yeah, the ranch needed him, but at the same time he owed the firm for still wanting him after almost three years in the army, making sure he hadn't been sent to the Pacific so Mom wouldn't lose her oldest son as well as the twins.

Half of L.A. must be out on the streets. He had to admit that it was good to see all the lights. The blackout was over. There were couples clinging to each other, girls by themselves getting kissed by every servicemen who passed. He was beyond that stage in his life. The girls he had kissed when he was younger had only one thing in mind, and it wasn't him. The McKaid name and money were all they wanted.

Maybe it was time to forget it all, go back to the hotel, check out, and head for home. Maybe he could turn into a real bastard and foreclose on the Simpsons. T.J. had bought the mortgage for him, and they were so far behind in the payments that anyone else would have done it a long time ago. Of course, that would have every cowboy for miles around griping. Nobody knew how they did it or where they had the still hidden, but they sure depended on the Elmers' bootlegging. He knew where the still was hidden, but it was a thing he had kept to himself ever since the twins had found it. Trouble was, the older he became, the more it worried him. The consequences of the government guys finally finding it on McKaid land would be catastrophic.

He looked up the street. That was when his eyes paused on golden hair streaming out of wide brimmed red hat. Now if he had something like that to go home to. A neat little suit almost the color of Pretty Girl. Wouldn't she be something at the Christmas parade on one of the high stepping palominos

She wasn't very tall, but even at a distance she did look good. Her hands were covered with red gloves. That alone set her apart. Most of the girls were dressed a little more casually. He'd been around enough to wonder if her shoes matched the hat and gloves. Wasn't there a saying about girls who wore red shoes? Definitely not his type, but there was something about her. Maybe it was because she looked as lost as he felt. For the first time in days, a smile came to his lips as he started working his way through the crowd.

* * * * *

Betty Lou was kneeling in front of the rickety table. The place was little more than a shack. It didn't show any sign of ever having been painted. It had two bedrooms and a kitchen, but she slept here in the upstairs attic. One hand was on the old lunch box, her most treasured possession. The other clutched the belt buckle. The snakeskin Davy had thrown at her was there as well, but she wasn't seeing it. All her mind saw was the big house over on the

Diamond MK. Soon. Soon she would be there in reality. Her Davy was coming home.

The stairs going from kitchen to attic were steep and rickety, but once when she had been seven and had held a baseball bat she found that to be an advantage. Age had dimmed the bloody stain on the kitchen floor, but she knew it was there, satisfied that her aunt would never again boss her or pull the tangles from her hair. The girl didn't like to be hurt, and combing those tangles had hurt.

The wind blew through house in the winter, and everything that flew or crawled managed to get in when hot weather came. There was a pump over the kitchen sink, but that's as modern as the place had ever gotten. The McKaids had indoor plumbing and everything. Old Elena was still doing the cooking. Betty Lou looked forward to that. She hated to cook . When you came down to it, the little building with the half moon in the door and the two holes inside was tended better than the house. She shivered at the thought. Cold in the winter and smelly in the summer.

In the attic the moonlight struggled through the grimy window. She had unrolled the blanket from the Diamond MK stable. The bloody baseball bat, the tattered bandanna, and Elsie Mae's hair ribbon brought back all the memories of her triumphs. This night she didn't have a candle to put on the rickety table, but she placed her hands on Davy's things anyway and said her little prayer.

"Davy McKaid is handsome and dark.

Davy McKaid always tells the truth.

Davy asked me and I said yes."

After that she thought of the earlier scene in the kitchen.

The August sweat had poured off her as she finished putting away the supper dishes. She had on her a gingham shirt and tattered blue jeans. She had wished she could take off her shoes, but she had learned young that it wasn't much fun to step on an odd scorpion or two. Pa and E2 were complaining about the stew again. "Too bad," she had told them, suddenly feeling brave by the thought of her Davy coming home. "That's all you're gettin' till I git that new stove. I'm tired of hauling wood in and having the place hot as hell all summer."

"Keeps the chill off in the winter," Pa had said. "Propane's expensive. Wood don't cost nothin.'

"Propane's plenty cheap enough to buy for the still. I been askin' for a new stove for years. I'm sick and tired of haulin' wood. You're gettin' nothin' but stew til I git the stove."

"Don't sass me, girl." Pa's open hand slapping against her cheek had reinforced his words. Pa was gonna be sorry for that one of these days.

"Leave her be, Pa," E 2 had told him. "I'll go see that new foreman Davy brought home. I ought to be able to hire on for the round-up."

"Got a son that don't even know how to keep a woman in line," old Elmer Number 1 muttered.

"I'll tell him to hire you," she had told her brother. "Davy'll be coming home, and it's time we got hitched."

"Told you before, Betty Lou, no McKaid is going to marry a Simpson."

"Aunt Adelaide did."

"Lot a good that did her," her father had said. "Fall'n down the stairs thata way. Got herself and her baby killed trying to be somebody she wasn't."

Maybe she'd tell him about that someday "He'll marry me. He proposed, and I said yes."

"You were children." That had been her brother again with the words she'd heard so often.

"A proposal's a proposal."

She had tossed the cup towel on the cabinet and come up here in the attic.

Davy would marry her all right. She already had the ring around her neck. Pa was just lucky it took two to manage the still. She didn't like it when he slapped her like that. Leastwise he'd believed her when she told him he better not come in her bedroom the way his daddy had. When she was twelve she took care of that. She'd known how to take care of vermin no matter how many legs they walked on. Her grandfather had hurt her bad and kept on hurting her. Nobody did that, just like nobody got close to her Davy and got away with it. She had all mementos in the blanket she'd snitched from the Diamond MiK's stables. Davy's things were different. They were carefully arranged on the rickety old table. When she had a few pennies to spend, she always bought a candle and lit it while she said her prayer. This night she repeated it a second time.

"Davy McKaid is handsome and dark.
Davy McKaid always tells the truth.
Davy asked me and I said yes."

This time she added, " Someday soon, Mrs. David McKaid I will be.

She had been chanting it for twenty years

Chapter 6

Hill Street was alive. Los Angeles was out in force. Up and down the street soldiers, sailors, and Marines were kissing girls. It was New Years Eve all over again. Both Lucy and Sophie had been kissed a dozen times, but Lucy started watching a soldier elbow his way through the crowd. Tall and rugged looking, if he'd been in the movies he would have been the villain, not the hero. The stripes said sergeant, but he had the look of an officer. She had noticed him, standing still, as though he was lost, almost a look of despair on his face.

Oops. Must be six feet, maybe taller. Way too tall, but in his dress uniform he looked as neat as a general. How did he get that uniform to fit so well? A sailor grabbed her, kissed her, and went on to Sophie. The sergeant was coming her way.

Lucy was still burning about her father and the fact that he had forbidden her to leave the house. She was twenty for heaven's sakes. What was she going to do? What kind of a job could she get? Tish worked at Woolworth's and Lil was babysitting when she had a chance. She'd been making good money running the spot welder until the Germans had surrendered. She could have had her own apartment, but now she was probably stuck at home forever, sharing that dinky little room with her two sisters.

The sergeant carried himself well. When he stopped in front of her she wondered if he realized she had been watching him come closer. She started to turn away, but her eyes kept going to the double row of ribbons on his chest, including ones she couldn't identify. The gray rifle on a blue background that he wore on his right side was a one she had never before seen. The smile appearing on his face was to die for.

"What's a pretty little filly like you doing out on a night like this?"

Even with all those battle ribbons he was wearing, not only were his lips smiling, his eyes were as well, deep, dark eyes that almost had a hint of silver in them. He was talking to her, not grabbing her. The war hadn't turned his eyes bitter. The soft hint of a nasal twang told her that the movie would have to be a Western. A man like this would probably be on the side of the Indians, not the cowboys, maybe the Indian Chief on a horse, aiming his bow and arrow at the soldiers.

"Pretty little thing like you shouldn't be out all alone."

"I'm old enough to do as I please."

He looked her up and down. His face broke out in a broad grin.

"Dang, it all, girl, I'm old enough to know better. You're not the type I usually go for, but you're the prettiest thing I've seen in a long time. Saw you half a block away, and had to see for myself if you're a girl worth meeting."

"Let me guess." She cocked her head back a bit to look up. "You like your ladies to be long, lean, and willing. That lets me out on all three counts."

"We can find a box for you to stand on." He was grinning at her. "That would take care of the long part."

"No one's ever mistaken me for lean. I like to eat too well."

"Curves just could be a mite more comfortable at that, and if I'm paying for dinner, I expect a girl to eat every bite on her plate."

"I was taught to do that." She was enjoying herself. "It's that last part that's the stickler. You won't find anyone who will tell you I'm willing."

"We'll have to work on that a bit."

He didn't grab her. His arms were gentle as they enveloped her. The kiss started out soft, but rushed into something else. Suddenly it wasn't brief, and it wasn't shallow. She felt it was as though she had never really been kissed before. His breath was nice. No cigarette or beer taste. She liked that, and let him explore her mouth all he wanted, and did a bit exploring herself, all the while feeling that something special was happening. Jerry's kisses had been nice, but they hadn't overwhelmed her with the desire to sink into him and be part of him. It was as though the tall stranger was twisting her into a knot and setting her on fire. She could feel that kiss run through every nerve in her body. Her arms reached out to cling to him. He looked down, meeting her eyes.

"You'd better be footloose and fancy free, little girl." He looked as shocked as she felt. "You pack quite a wallop for someone who isn't going it take up much room in a bed."

"Do that again," she whispered.

"You feel it, too, little girl?"

"Just don't let go of me or I'll fall." *Don't walk away from me.* The thought pounded its way through her head.

"Couldn't if I wanted to, and I don't want to. We're going to try that again and see if it's real. Never had a woman do this to me in one little kiss. Tell the truth, makes me wish we weren't in the middle of a crowded street."

Their lips met again, and Lucy wondered if she could even walk. Her whole being was exploding. *Please. Please, Mother Mary, don't let him walk away.* It was the first time she had prayed in a long time.

"Seems I've heard something about girls who wear red shoes and their lack of underwear." His words were quiet, for her ears only. "A little too public for me to find out if it's true."

"Not true, Sergeant," she murmured. "I wear them, and I keep them on."

"You'll take them off for me, little girl, because I'm going to marry you. Where do you live? I'll see you home. You're through being kissed by every soldier and sailor who comes along."

"Hollywood." He had a surprised look, and she shook her head. "Not the expensive part."

"What do I call you?"

"Lucy."

"Short for Lucille?"

"Lucinda. Lucinda Robbins."

"Lucy doesn't sound right. Lucy wouldn't wear red shoes. Lucy's prim, and proper and shy, and that's sure not you." He hooked his arm into hers, claiming her, letting the street know that she was his. "Anyone ever call you Cindy?" The crowd swirled around them.

"No. Are you ready to call it a night?" she asked Sophie. A Marine was holding her friend's arm.

"Bone structure's not right," the sergeant said, looking at Sophie.

"What's wrong with my bones?" Sophie asked.

"You're not sisters."

What did that mean? The tall sergeant was holding her pretty close, but not close enough to quell the longing she felt. Life wouldn't be worth living if he didn't kiss her again.

"Sophie lives across the street from us." She had to look up to see his face. It didn't seem to matter that he was so much taller than she was. "We go out together, and we stay together. You do have a name, I presume."

"At your service, ma'am. David Stanley McKaid, rescuing sad looking little girls a specialty of mine." He swept off his hat and gave a slight bow. "Oldest of the Texas McKaid boys. Only one left thanks to this war." That hint of a twang disappeared. He could have been swashbuckling Errol Flynn, sweeping off his plumed hat. There was a tinge of pain in the last part. Evidently the war had hit home. That would hurt to have a brother killed.

"Looks like you came close." She touched the purple ribbon on his chest.

"Purple Hearts are a dime a dozen in combat, Cindy girl. Got my car around the block. I'll take you home."

Cindy not Lucy. She liked the sound of that. Next she touched the blue rifle. "What's this one?"

"Combat Infantry Man Badge."

"Must mean you didn't spend your time behind the lines." She touched the winged pin on his lapel, the one the army was giving discharged soldiers. " Ruptured Duck. You're already out of the army."

"Got out three weeks ago. Where in Hollywood do you live?"

"Nothing fancy. Just off Vine before the hills start." She liked the way he was looking at her. There was a question in it, maybe even respect. He wasn't stripping her with his eyes. "Crowded. I have two sisters, three brothers, a mother, and a father who has a hard time paying all the bills. Gives lie to the picture of a glamorous Hollywood."

"Thought you looked like good breeding stock. Nice hips."

"Gee, thanks." What was that all about?

"Sorry. Habit I guess. The McKaids run a few mama cows."

It was her turn to check him out. Not drop dead gorgeous, but not bad. The most beautiful eyes she had ever seen. Hair as black as midnight. She wondered if it might be wavy when that GI haircut grew out. If his nose had been as high as his cheek bones he really could be cast as that Indian chief she had thought about. Nicely tanned. Taller than she liked, but he didn't smell of cheap booze or peppermint. Nice and neat.

"Do I pass inspection?" he asked. "Do I get to take you home? My car is parked on Seventh Street."

"How about a get acquainted drink first." A car? Texas was a long ways from Hollywood and her father. Who knew? They just both might get lucky. *Jerry's ring? Why hadn't she stopped wearing it? Maybe she could slip into the ladies room at the bar and ditch it before he saw her hands without the gloves.* "There's a little bar around the corner. It will be crowded tonight, but it's a nice place." Who cared if he came from a farm with a couple of cows? He didn't look the type who would stay on it

* * * * *

David looked around. As the girl had said, the small bar was indeed crowded. It was little more than a hole in the wall, sandwiched between two other businesses. There was a bar along one wall and three booths along the other. The juke box against the back wall was playing a Glen Miller tune. Empty, there might be room for one or two couples to dance. This night that was out of the question. He saw a couple of privates hunkered down in one of the mahogany colored booths, alone, no girls with them.

"Wait here, Cindy girl." He gave the girl's hand a slight squeeze. "I'll get us a booth." As he walked over, his hand going for his wallet, a devastating thought hit him. He was sure he had felt a ring under that glove. That was a disappointment. Still, he pulled out a twenty and handed it to one of the privates. There was a chance there wasn't a wedding ring with it. Maybe he was wrong. It was worth finding out because that little girl had him wound up tighter than a fiddle string.

"You'll know her when you see her," Mamaw Deedee had said as he had left her little cabin. Those two kisses had eaten him alive. He didn't drink much because his grandmother's people had too much trouble with alcohol, but right now he needed something to calm him. He'd been telling the truth in what he had told her. It had been a long time, but one kiss shouldn't have made his trousers too tight.

"Twenty for the table, boys."

"There are two of us, Sarge."

With no hesitation, David pulled out another twenty and beckoned to the two girls and the Marine. When he asked the girls what they wanted to drink, almost in unison they said rum and Coke. At the bar the Marine started to pull out his wallet, but David shook his head.

"My treat."

"Didn't know you soldiers liked us gyrenes."

"Lost a brother on Guadalcanal. Heard tell it was pretty bad."

"Our own little bit of hell right here on earth."

"You've got that right." *Guadalcanal and D-Day. Two dates his family would never forget*. "Lost us a lot of good ones all over." *But why had he had to lose both twins? Why had fate left him as the only McKaid male to take over from Gramps?* The bartender placed the drinks on the counter. One of the rum and Cokes had a maraschino cherry floating in it.

"That red hat deserves something special," he remarked.

"Keep the change." David slid a bill across the bar. Back at the table he put the glass in front of her and put his own bourbon on the table, all the while noticing her left hand was without a ring. Had he imagined it, or had she taken it off? "Bartender said the red hat deserves something special."

She popped the cherry in her mouth, drank part of the drink, and, with a nod, handed it back.

"Take it back to him and tell him to put in the rum you paid for. Then tell him to mind his own business."

"Relative or business partner?" He questioned, quietly meeting her eyes. No B-girl he'd ever heard of dressed like her. Those girls dressed to show off what they had. Surely a stint in the army hadn't blunted his knack for reading people.

"Your wallet's safe. I don't roll soldiers or anybody else, Sergeant McKaid. He's just a friend. Name's Tony. He knows I don't drink much."

"Hot damn, girl, I'm liking you better by the minute. You're straight up with a fellow." He took the glass from her hand and went back to the bar. He watched as Tony added the Bacardi.

"Don't hurt that little girl," the bartender told him. "She's a nice one. She's had enough of that. She's not the kind for a one night stand. Tell her for me I'm glad she finally came to her senses."

After that David relaxed a bit. He was smiling when he handed her the drink. "I'm supposed to tell you he's glad you finally came to your senses. Want to know what else he said?

"No."

"It's something nice." In one easy move he planted a kiss on her forehead and sat down. A girl who didn't drink much suited him just fine. "I'm to respect you because you aren't the kind of a girl for a one night stand. Told him not to worry. I'm roping you in, and taking you back to Texas with me, letting the whole state know I've brought home the prettiest gal in California." He put his arm around her, drawing her closer. "Love the way you kiss," he whispered in her ear.

Chapter 7

Did this sergeant mean it? Take her home with him? Intrigued, Lucy watched him closely as the four sat in the little booth for a couple of hours and just talked. She had listened to a number of servicemen talk about ships which had been sunk and battles that had been fought, but that had been at the Palladium or bowling alley when it was one on one. With David and the Marine it was talk of the weather, how they liked California, and the speculating of when rationing would be lifted. She and Sophie told the guys how they had climbed out the windows. David and the marine thought that was pretty funny.

"What are you going to do when you get home?" Lucy asked David.

"Hug my mother and grandmother, and give Tiger, Jr. an apple."

"Is that what you call your son?" Her heart dropped a couple of inches.

"Tiger Jr. is the prettiest Palomino you ever want to see. He's out of Tiger and Pretty Girl."

"And you," she asked the Marine, her heart back where it belonged, "what will you do?"

"I am thinking of making a career out of the Corps. I could retire after I've put in thirty years and have a pretty good pension. We probably won't have another war."

"That's what my father thought," David commented.

"We have something in common," she told him. "My father thought the same thing."

"It never stops," David said. "We humans are a stupid lot. Anyone ready for another round?"

No one was. Cindy was glad. She and Sophie had their a rule, never more than two drinks. One was just fine with her. Eventually they left the bar. She noticed that David's glass was only partly emptied. Two hours and only one drink apiece? Tony probably could have killed them, but the tip David handed him as they left probably made it all right, but she did wince at the hundred dollar bill and hoped it was legal.

Sophie and the Marine exchanged addresses, and she gave him her telephone number. He had to get back to his base by morning but Sophie stayed with them for the drive home. David's car was a surprise. It was a shiny Buick convertible, black with a red leather interior. The top was down. It was as new as the war would allow. Clean and neat, it didn't look as though it went with a farm and a couple of cows.

"Had a leave after I got out of the hospital," he explained. "I drove back with it, but I haven't used it much. One of the mechanics at the fort checked it out before I left."

"Ration stamps don't go far" was all Cindy could think of to say. Of course he had been in the hospital. He did have the Purple Heart

"The old man and some of the boys manage to send me a few. Got enough to get me home. Mind sitting in the back?" he asked Sophie as he pulled open the door.

Lucy slid across the red leather, and once he had the car going, his right arm pulled her close.

"It feels new."

"Hasn't been used much. Been in the garage most of the war. Leather gets pretty hot in Texas. I put the seat covers in the trunk. Didn't want anyone taking a shine to them. They were a birthday present from Mom."

The sergeant was looking better all the time. *Likes his mother. Bet he wouldn't give a girl a ring and leave her wondering where he was.* At that thought a familiar wisp crossed her mind. *Had Jerry really been an undercover cop killed in the line of duty?* She had only a stranger's brief word for that.

David drove all the way to Hollywood with one arm around her, and when they dropped Sophie off at the end of the block they waited until she had disappeared down the drive.

"Back door?" David asked.

"The window. I'll do the same. Tish won't have closed it." Somehow neither of them were using full sentences. It was sort of a cozy feeling, almost as though they were reading each other's mind. With one hand, David started massaging the back of her neck. Heaven. That's what it felt like to her. His hand felt strong and comfortable.

"How old are you really?" he asked.

"Like I said before, twenty."

"I'd have said a couple years older. At a guess, you must be the oldest sister who was given a lot of responsibility."

"I grew up fast when the boys arrived. Mom needed a lot of help."

"Still even at twenty it seems your father's the boss."

"It just wasn't worth arguing about." She was feeling very relaxed as his hands stroked her neck. "That feels so good." She was waiting for him to kiss her. "I'll wait until I'm twenty-one to get my own place. I have to find a job first. Dad's people came from the old country. He's terribly old fashioned about his daughters. Tish and Lil don't seem to mind. I do. I've been giving him half of my salary ever since I graduated. He wanted me to give him the whole thing and put me on an allowance, but I fought that."

"I can't quite picture you crawling out a window."

"It's easy," she told him. "The screen's on a hinge at the top, and there are no bushes underneath. My daybed's in front of the window. All I have to do is crawl up on it and slip out. I'm pretty good at hoisting myself up a bit to get back in." She nestled a little closer.

"Daybed?" he asked.

" Tish and Lil have the bed. The room's not big enough for a double bed and a single one. It's pretty crowded. I had my own room before the boys came along. Dad and Uncle Brad added it on just for me. He promised it would be only temporary, that we'd soon be moving to a bigger house. That never happened. I've always refused to call it my bed. Foolish maybe, but it's my own little touch of rebellion. I know I shouldn't, but I've never forgiven my father. It wasn't his fault. I know he regretted it, but I have to blame someone."

"It's getting late. You sure you don't have a job to go to in the morning?"

"No, I'm collecting unemployment. We really were laid after the Germans surrendered. Besides, it's morning already. Somewhere around two I think." She wondered what he was thinking as he looked at her. That had been a petty remark about her father. She shouldn't have made it. It wasn't the daybed she was angry about as much as it was the way he had forbidden her to go out. She was an adult, not a child. Had she spoiled it all, or did this man want to kiss her as badly as she wanted him to?

"A lady of many talents. How about seeing the sunrise from those hills up there?"

"The house with the light?" She sat up straight, looking down the street. "If Dad made a bed check, I'm already in trouble. Another hour or so won't make any difference."

Maybe she was feeling a little reckless, but she was so tired of the endless arguments with her father, so very tired of it all. There was also the fact that David's two kisses really had been something special. She wanted to feel his lips again. She wanted to have his arms around her. Never before had a kiss caused her to feel this need, this feeling of an emptiness that only this man could fill, almost a feeling of wanting to crawl inside his skin.

Both were quiet as he made his way up Mulholland Drive. David found one of the scenic pullovers and turned off the engine. It was dark, quiet, and peaceful. A light had never before been turned on when she had come home late. That probably meant her father was waiting. She wasn't looking forward to walking into the house and confronting him. When David turned, he lifted her hat, tossing it into the back seat.

"Anyone ever tell you you're a beautiful girl?"

"Must be a rule somewhere you have to say that. They probably teach it at boot camp."

"If they do, I missed the class. You stood out down there in the street. You're something special, Cindy. Once I laid eyes on you, I couldn't see anyone else." He ran his fingers along her cheek, his other hand going though her hair. His touch moved something deep inside her. He lifted her left hand. "What about that ring you managed to lose?" he asked. "I like kissing you. I want you, but I need to know where we're going."

"You're quite observant."

"Learned young. Broken leg at thirteen taught me that. Being observant sometimes keeps a man alive. It came off with your gloves while we were getting the drinks, didn't it?"

"A mistake." she said. "A big mistake. It's an opal, not a diamond. They're supposed to be bad luck, and maybe they are. I haven't seen him since the night he put it on my finger eight months ago. He never told me he was an undercover cop and might get killed." Her hand went to her mouth. "I had to swear I'd never tell anyone that. Forget I said it. There just hasn't been a reason for taking it off until tonight."

"That's all right." His hand drifted through her hair. "We need to know each other. All I heard was the reason part. Mind sharing that reason?"

"Simple. I want you kiss me again. I want you to hold me. He never made me feel what I'm feeling with you."

"Thought it was mutual. I've been looking for you all my life. No woman has ever stirred me up the way you did with one little kiss."

His lips were on hers, and this time his hand was wandering a bit. "God, how I want you, but I'd better tell you something," he said eventually.

"You're married." She pulled away. "Take me home."

"No, but there's a girl named Betty Lou who claims we're engaged because I proposed to her when I was nine and she was seven."

"When you were nine?"

"At my uncle's wedding. I was the ring bearer and she was the flower girl. Last thing the old man told me before I left was to find me a girl I could live with. I can see myself kissing you fifty years from now. I know just the spot for a house of our own. I don't even care if you can't cook."

If that was a proposal, it sure was an odd one. If she could cook? She'd been doing that for years. They were sitting under the stars in a convertible, and this sergeant, whom she had just met, was talking about fifty years and a house of their own. Certain that he was about ready to kiss her, she watched his hand go to his right wrist.

"Would you be willing to exchange that ring for this?"

His hand came away with an ID bracelet. Many servicemen wore them - heavy links on either side of a flat surface carrying their name and service number.

"You're a strange man. You do have a way of talking. Sometimes it's country and sometimes not. Your folks have cows, but you sure don't strike me as a farmer. I don't even know how old you are. Just because your father wants you married isn't a good reason to latch on to me."

"Thirty. I graduated from Texas U. He's my grandfather. Pop got stomped by a bull when I was thirteen. That's the first time I broke my leg. My number came up in the draft, so I've been in the army for three years, and Gramps doesn't have anything to do with it. It's purely and simply that we belong together. My great-grandmother told me I would know the girl for me when I met her. She was right." He was ticking off the items on his fingers. "That's almost more than I know about you."

"You forgot to mention that you're from Texas. What do you know about me?"

"You climb through windows, so you don't take kindly to being told what to do. You come from a big family with not a lot of money. In spite of that, you look like a million dollars. I don't care how many idiots you've been engaged to. You kiss real nice. I've kissed a lot of girls, but you the only one who ever made me feel like I've been lassoed, rolled over and stomped on. I've got a feeling life with you wouldn't be dull. You're the prettiest thing I've ever seen, and I want to carry you right back to Texas with me."

"The ring's in my purse." It was almost a whisper as she let him fasten the bracelet around her wrist.

"We'll have a couple of links taken out." Instead of kissing her, he started stroking the back of her neck again. "God, but you kiss nice, and this car is damned inconvenient for what I want from you."

"Sergeant McKaid," she told him, "I'm a very good cook, and I think kissing you is a little more than nice." Who knew? Maybe that was as good a reason as any. Texas was certainly a long way from Mom and Dad. New name, new start. Maybe it was worth a try. She didn't even have the feeling that she wanted to say no to this man. There was enough moonlight to see how serious he was, and if he didn't soon kiss her again she would have to kiss him.

"I've got a room at that big hotel on Wilshire Boulevard. Might be more comfortable."

"Probably." Now what kind of an answer was that? Sure, she put up a good front, but knowing that Jerry hadn't been honest had done something to her ego. She had been holding onto a dream for months. Enough was enough. She'd been flirting with David all evening. It was nice having someone approve of her for a change. He wanted her, and she didn't want to go home and face the anger of a father she was tired of arguing with. She was aching for him to take her in his arms again. Never before had she ever felt this need to be closer to a man. Even with Jerry she hadn't felt this urge to ignore the edicts of religion - to be part of him.

"Father a violent man?"

"No, he's a good father. Just over protective."

"That's good. They say in Nevada there's no waiting period." He turned the key and pulled back onto the road. "You ever been to Las Vegas?"

"No."

"Stopped there when I brought the car back with me, but we'd better wait till morning when filling stations will be open. I don't think there's enough gas in this thing to get us there, and to tell the truth, I don't think I can wait that long."

She took a good look at him. As far as she knew there was only one hotel along Wilshire Boulevard. If he had been staying there, he'd be broke before he got halfway home. Was he registered there or just trying impress her?

Chapter 8

Lucy had butterflies fluttering through her as they took the elevator up to the fifth floor. David hadn't lied. He really was registered. He had just held out his hand for the night man to hand him his key. The man had smiled and nodded as he exchanged the key for the folded bill David had in his hand.

Watching David put the key into the lock on the door, she wondered what was she doing in a hotel with a man she had just met. Was she really that desperate? That feeling vanished when he scooped her up in his arms. David McKaid was one strong man, and his arms felt mighty good.

"What are you doing?"

"Well, maybe it's not official yet, but don't all brides get carried over the threshold? We'd take off for Las Vegas tonight but we need a few hours sleep first, and I really don't want to run out of gas in the middle of the desert."

She doubted if sleep was what he was thinking of any more than she was. Her arm just automatically moved around his neck. He didn't put her down until he reached the bed. The room was larger than the one she shared with her two sisters. It had a big dresser with a mirror, and the space for hanging clothes was roomier than the closet at home. There was a little table with two armchairs beside it. David's duffle bag was propped up against the wall. Her memories of the time she was six were dim, but they hadn't been anything like this room. She had only vague recollections of the tiny cabins they had stopped at when Lily was a baby. She didn't think she had even been old enough to be in school when they had come to California. She did remember that she and Tish had slept on the floor while her parents and baby Lil took the bed. It wasn't so much the size of the room as the pure luxury of it. It was the sort of thing she had only seen in the movies.

"I would have booked the bridal suite if I had known I was going to meet you," he told her.

That statement, as much as the ID bracelet on her arm, convinced her that he really meant it about eloping to Las Vegas. Still, she was feeling a little edgy. She could see a private bath. That was a welcome sight. She nodded toward it. "Do you mind?"

When she came back from a bathroom that was bigger than the tiny one at home, David had his jacket and tie off, and the bed was turned down. While he took his turn in the bathroom, she took off her suit jacket and reached for a coat hanger. Her hand paused in mid air. She hadn't said take me home.

She was in a hotel room with a thirty-year-old sergeant who thought she had nice hips. His family had a couple of cows. He owned a convertible, and had gone to a school called Texas U, which she presumed was a college. The ribbons on his jacket told her he'd seen s lot of action in the war. He had mentioned getting out of a hospital, and he did have a Purple Heart. He must like his mother because he took care of the seat covers she'd given him for his birthday. What kind of a recommendation was all of that? Did she really want to get away from home that badly?

That wasn't the real problem though. His kisses had awakened something inside her. No one had ever before had reached into her soul. From behind her back, his hand reached for her jacket.

"Second thoughts?"

"Kiss me," she whispered, shaking her head. "I do like kissing you. It doesn't make sense, but it feels like I've never really been kissed before."

* * * * *

David was more than glad to oblige her, and his body was quick to react. The kiss he meant to be gentle turned into a feral thing that was demanding all of her, and she was responding with her own demands. When it ended, he slowly undid the buttons of her blouse. He wanted to prolong the agony he was feeling. He wanted to enjoy every inch of this girl he had found. The blouse and slip were coming off her shoulders and his hands were working at the hooks at her back. He cupped her breasts in his hands. It was a gentle touch. His fingers were gentle as he rolled them around a nipple. "Perky little puppies," he whispered, and he unbuttoned and unzipped her skirt. When the skirt and slip fell to the floor a touch of a smile touched his mind. The old saying was wrong. This girl might flaunt her red shoes, but she wore all her underwear. The smile was because in place of elastic the pink panties had a red ribbon tied into a bow. Almost making a ceremony of it, he untied the it. "God, girl, but you are lovely." He lifted her and carried her to the bed.

* * * * *

As he unbuckled the red shoes and tossed them aside, Lucy knew, after all, that the deciding factor hadn't been about getting away from home. She had been heading here after than first unbelievable kiss. Her days of saying no were over.

"Your heart's going a mile a minute. You that nervous, Cindy girl? Maybe we better take it a little slow, and give you a chance to calm down."

She tried to catch her breath at the unexpected sensations that ran through her when he lifted left hand and took a finger in his mouth, sucking on it.

To think that she had once had the idea that a man wouldn't want to see her naked. The magazine articles she and Tish had read, the ones telling how to undress modestly if there wasn't a closet to use? They must have been written by a dried up, prune faced old maid. She just wanted to feel his arms around her, but when he dropped his army issue boxers and wore only his dog tags and a small brown bag around his neck, she had a few doubts. With the triplets she knew what a man looked like, but she had never imagined anything like that. She knew the rudiments of what was going to happen, but did wonder if it was really possible.

David was gentle though, and he didn't rush.

"Kiss me again," she whispered. "Hold me close, David. I want to be in your arms."

He did. Then his hands stroked and teased until she was whimpering with pleasure and exploding with a feeling she had never dreamed of having. He brought every inch of her body to a flaming desire. By the time he got through with his mouth and hands, she wasn't thinking. She was feeling. She was needy, emotional, and she didn't know it was possible to feel so glorious. His mouth on her nipples was making her whole body come alive. All she could think about was the need to be closer to him.

"You're ready, girl. God, but you're tight. You're. . ." He looked down at her. "Oh, God, Cindy girl, you're never done this before."

"I've been waiting for you," she managed to whisper.

"You just wrap your legs around me, and hang on. After I break through we'll see if we can go over the top together."

She did and they did, and afterwards he brushed her hair away from her face. "No wonder you were nervous. You surprised me. I didn't think it would be your first time."

"Are you disappointed?"

"Disappointed? Good God, girl, how could I be?" He smiled, and lifted her hand to his lips. "How could I be, but why? Why, when we've just met?"

"I couldn't say no." It was the truth. "I watched you come to me, and when you kissed me I wanted to crawl inside your skin. We belong together."

"Cindy honey, I'm going to put a diamond as big as all outdoors on your finger tomorrow before you change your mind. Maybe I should ask if you want a regular wedding with your family."

"Las Vegas will be fine." She pulled his head down so their lips met. Her folks couldn't afford a "big wedding even if she had wanted one. "Do they have a minister there?"

"We'll find one."

"I knew the sermons were wrong," she whispered. "This is why God created men and women. I'm glad I didn't stay home."

* * * * *

No wonder all the tall, money hungry brunettes he had dated hadn't satisfied him. This little blonde was the girl who had haunted his dreams. She was the one his grandmother had promised him, the one he would build the house for. There, close to the main road and the trees where the old Live Oak was, the house he had dreamed about building would be their home. He would build it large enough to last a lifetime.

"You'll know her when you see her, boy. She's waiting for you," Mamaw Deedee had said. "You just go off and fight this war. Sadness will come to the Diamond MiK, but it won't come through you. Your little girl won't have dollar signs in her eyes. You'll know her when you hold her. She's waiting for you." A chill had descended on the little cabin, and he had wondered which one of them would not be coming home.

The biggest wonder, though, as he felt the softness of Cindy's skin against his, was the fact that for the first time in his life he hadn't given a thought to protection. Perhaps it was nature taking its own course. He smiled. Just for a little while he wouldn't tell her about what awaited them in Texas. He ran his hand over her back. The night had been long, but he wasn't ready for sleep.

* * * * *

Along about nine a.m. Lucy opened her eyes and realized she was curled up against David, his arm holding her close. This was what she had been longing for, what made her complete. Love at first sight wasn't a myth after all. She never wanted to be away from this man. She had spent the whole night with him - well what had been left of the night. David had filled her with a contentment she had never known. Never for a moment did it occur to her that she might have made a mistake.

David was awake and watching her. She felt so comfortable and safe feeling the warmth of his bare skin against hers.

"I've never spent the whole night with any woman before," he told her.

"Neither have I."

"I know." He had a satisfied smile on his face. "Do you want that diamond? Are you going to marry me?"

"How long does it take to get to Las Vegas?"

"Not long." He moved his arm away from her. "I would like to stay in this bed, but right now, if we want to get to Las Vegas, we better force ourselves to be sensible and get dressed. Go freshen up while I order breakfast. Phone's on your side of the bed. How about handing it to me? How do you like your eggs?"

"Over easy." She rolled over and complied.

"Dial zero for the front desk, then go fill up that tub and soak a few minutes while I call room service."

"Isn't that expensive?"

"You're sounding like a wife already." He grinned, then turned his attention to the phone in his hand. "Mornin', honey." That Texas drawl was back. " Would you tell room service that room 510 wants breakfast? Coffee, orange juice, eggs over easy and bacon for two. Then get Las Vegas on the line, *Hotel El Rancho Vegas*. Ring me when you have them."

Lucy slid out of bed and started running water into the tub. She looked at the counter by the washbasin. David's shaving cup, comb, and straight razor were placed very neatly beside his toothbrush. She wondered if her brothers would ever be that precise. She also wondered if the comb in her purse would get the tangles from her hair, and wished she had a hair brush and her own toothbrush. When David entered and picked up the shaving cup, she was looking at the bracelet he had fastened around her arm the night before. There was only an M and a K inside a diamond shape. The initials and diamond were a gold color.

"It only has your initials." She reached to turn off the running water.

"Name and serial number are on the underside." He looked at her, and shook his head. "I didn't realize they ration water around here." The water barely covered her knees.

"Habit. Water costs money, and with eight in the family, things like that matter. I've often thought the ultimate luxury would be a leisurely bubble bath."

"Tonight," he promised, "you can fill the tub with bubbles and soak as long as you like. I might even join you, but right now, honey, please get dressed or we will never get out of this room. I can only take so much of looking at you before doing something about it." Even so he watched her every move as she dried herself and picked up her panties with a look of distaste.

"You'll need some fresh things. Don't those things usually have elastic instead of drawstrings?"

"Drawstrings are safer than wartime elastic. I should go home and get some clean clothes." She slipped them on, fastened her brassiere, pulled the slip over her head, and reached for the white blouse, all the while glancing at him. "Are the scars on your hip and leg the reason for the purple heart?"

"I was lucky. They didn't have to take it off. I can still ride a horse." Somehow, when he was speaking to her the accent disappeared. "Might have healed faster if it hadn't been the third time that leg's been broken We'll do some shopping. Somehow, I don't think your folks are used to having you stay out all night."

She didn't even want to think about that. Though she wasn't feeling guilty, she sure wasn't looking forward to confronting her father. Both were dressed by the time the breakfast cart arrived. Eating in the room had her feeling slightly unreal. The boy wheeling in the cart with its covered dishes was something that only happened in the movies. She felt like pinching herself but settled for taking her place in the chair David held out for her. He, however, seemed at ease with it all. As if he was used to doing it, he slipped a bill into the boy's hand. The bacon and eggs were a real treat. At home she had the choice of corn flakes or Rice Krispies. Ration stamps didn't allow meat at breakfast, but even before the war breakfast had only meant cereal. They were just finishing when the phone rang. She could only hear David's side of the conversation.

"I'm David McKaid. I stayed with you about three months ago." He paused. "That's right. The Texas McKaids. We'll be arriving late tonight. We're in L.A. right now. Can you have a minister waiting for us?" Another pause. "I understand. It is short notice. One of the bungalows will do. Just have that parson and the necessary paperwork waiting. It might be a mite late before we get there so don't cancel us." David hung up and winked at her. "The honeymoon suite is already booked, but they'll have a place for us. You have until we get there to change your mind. Got a couple of things to do first. Can't go gallivanting around the country in just what you're wearing now. You have anything at home you can't do without?" She shook her head. "Just as soon not meet your father and brothers until we get that ring on your finger. I saw a couple of shops in the lobby."

"I can't afford anything they'd be selling here." That was true enough. "I'm sure they don't even have a blouse I can afford. Mom made this suit. I have seven dollars in my wallet. That won't buy much."

"Don't fret your little head about that. I've got a few bucks in mine." David walked over to where the jackets were hanging. As he held the beige jacket for her to slip her arms into, she couldn't help feeling that for a farmer, he had impeccable manners.

"You sure you want to go to Las Vegas," he asked.

"If you still want me to."

"Nothing I want more. You surprised me." He put his arms around her, almost lifting her off her feet as he bent to kiss her. "I think I owe you an apology. A beautiful little thing like you with all the right answers and having a ring on your finger. I figured you'd had some experience. Are you sure you don't have any regrets?"

"For your information, David McKaid, I'm a world champion at saying no. I didn't stomp on your toes with my high heels; I didn't jam my knee into your groin; and I sure didn't reach for the old fashioned hat pin in my hat. That must say something about the way I feel about you. I have one War Bond, two hundred and forty-four dollars in the bank. I'd say let's find a pawn shop, but there's a fifty-fifty chance that stupid ring is hot. I'm going to toss it out while we're in that convertible of yours."

"Sounds like you've been keeping the wrong kind of company." He laughed and started putting on his jacket. "Cindy gal, you're going to fit in just like you were a born Texan. We're known for being rebels. Every man in the county is going to envy me. Put on your hat and hat pin. Money is my department from now on."

Just as he reached for his duffle bag there was a loud knocking at the door. She started toward it, but he put out a hand to stop her.

"Let me, little girl."

Chapter 9

Lucy stood back as David opened the door. The man standing there was heavy-set, wrinkled, and not smiling. "I hear you got a woman in your room, Sergeant," he rasped.

"I sure do. What's it to you?"

"I realize last night things got a little hectic, but this is a respectable hotel. We don't allow. . ."

"Guess you must be the hotel dick, David drawled. He reached for her, his arm going around her. "Didn't know the little woman was going to get her mother to take care of the twins so she could meet me." The Texas twang became more pronounced. He wasn't sounding like a college graduate.

The detective looked around. "I don't see any luggage for her."

"Would you believe it was stolen? After I kissed her hello I looked down, and there wasn't a suitcase in sight. We're going to have to go shopping before we head back to Texas. Anyway, the two of us are checking out and heading for Texas. Like you said, things were pretty hectic last night. Lucky thing she left her jewelry at home."

The man didn't look as though he believed him, but he left.

"Shall we go get that ring?" David picked up his duffle bag

"You lie pretty convincingly."

"No, I don't." That engaging grin was back, the country boy sound gone. "I didn't know I was going to meet you, and for all I know, two of those brothers of yours might be twins, and after I kissed you I sure didn't see a suitcase. I just asked if he believed me."

She couldn't help it. The co-incidence was so unlikely. Her laughter startled him. He put his bag on the floor.

"Why are you laughing? Even if we never see him again, I couldn't let him think you were a lady of the evening."

"They aren't twins," she said. "Jimmy, Jack, and Jason are triplets."

"Triplets?" He lost the grin. "What is fate trying to do to us?"

Her laughter stopped.

"My grandmother. . ." he hesitated. "I guess I should have told you right off. She's very old, and some people think she's a bit strange. She's really my great-grandmother. Mom's mother died in the great influenza epidemic. To be honest, Mamaw Deedee's Cheyenne. My great-grandfather was a wonderful old Irishman who told us tales of riding with Kit Carson and some of the other old-timers. Her father was a medicine man. She's delivered most of the babies in the county, and she's a fine healer. She has a way of knowing things.

"When I was on leave before I left for the army she gave me a blessing, saying I would come home and to remember that two and three don't always make five. Sometimes, she said, they make a beautiful pair. It didn't make much sense then." He grasped her hand. "Taylor and Timothy were twins." He took a deep breath. "Cindy girl, I want to marry you more than anything I've ever wanted, but if you don't feel the same, now is the time to tell me."

She didn't hesitate. "If you don't marry me, I'll die a little." She took his free hand and looked up to meet those eyes so dark they were almost black. "When I first saw you, I pictured you in a western. I almost had you playing the part of an Indian Chief. How's that for women's intuition? Going to bed with you wasn't a sin. God had me wait for you. We belong together. It's as simple as that. If that means we won't have quintuplets, that's more than fine with me. I don't think I could handle that many babies. If you have a mixed background, I don't care. It's not all about getting from way from Dad. I can't imagines life without you."

"It's mixed all right. My other grandfather was Mexican. We might make a go of it if we try. I'll be honest with you. Part of it's that I don't want to be coerced into a marriage with a senseless idiot. The old man's right, but that's not all there is to it. The minute I kissed you I knew you were the one for me. I want to spend the rest of my life making love to you. Might be you want to get away from here, but maybe one of these days you'll learn to love me."

"I don't have to learn. I never believed in love at first sight until you kissed me." Nothing less could account for the way she had felt. She never wanted to be away from this man. "I don't think it has anything to do with Dad. I couldn't keep living if you walked away from me."

"No danger of that." His smile returned as he hoisted the bag over his shoulder. "Let's get moving, girl. We have a busy day ahead of us."

* * * * *

The hushed reverence of an empty church permeated the air as Lucinda, on David's arm, stepped into a jewelry shop located along Hollywood Boulevard. Alone, she never would have been in so expensive a place. Fine glassware and silver items were displayed on open shelves, but every last bit of jewelry was in a glass display case. In front of one filled with rings were two comfortable looking chairs. David guided her to the one to the left, seating himself in the other. She was suddenly all too aware of the fact that the green stones on her ears had cost twenty-five cents at Woolworth's.

The shop was empty except for the two well-dressed men conversing behind the counter. One came their way.

"What can I do for you, Sergeant?" The salesman's hushed tone emphasized the expensive surroundings. At the same time she had the feeling that he wasn't too thrilled to see them.

"Little lady needs a set of rings for her left hand." The man looked at David's stripes and her ears. He reached for a tray of rings.

"She needs diamonds big enough to see," David told him. "Try the ones in the front."

"Don't be foolish, David," she said. "Those are going to cost too much."

"You're going to wear them the rest of your life. Can't be ashamed of them."

Just what kind of a spendthrift had she agreed to marry? Hot dogs and bowls of chili were one thing, but this was going way too far in the other direction. Reluctantly the clerk pulled out the tray David had indicated. Stunned, Lucy just couldn't bring herself to select anything that looked that expensive. She watched David pick up a set that took her breath away.

"See if this fits."

Never had she envisioned anything like the diamond he slid onto her finger. In its gold setting it gleamed.

"It's. . ." Words failed her. She tried to say she didn't like it, but that would have been a lie and Lucy didn't lie. The words just wouldn't come. She just held out her hand looking at the sparking stone, and the look on her face would have denied anything she might have said. David smiled.

"Looks mighty fine. Just a gold band for me," he told the waiting clerk.

"David, these are for movie stars and Oscar nights, not for people like us."

"Looks fine to me. Just what your finger needs."

"Sergeant," the clerk began, "that is a blue white, emerald cut, two carat diamond. It has. . ."

"I said we'll take them." His voice firm, David didn't let the man finish. He just produced a checkbook from inside his jacket. "The bracelet the lady is wearing is a bit large. If you can do it in less than ten minutes take out some links." The clerk beckoned to the other man standing by. He seemed a little edgy about taking a check. She didn't blame him.

"Mr. Kohn, the sergeant here has just selected the ring set the young lady is wearing, and he wants her bracelet shortened. He'd like to write a check."

"Show the man your arm, honey." David looked at the second man. "The links come back to me." He took his wallet from his back pocket and extracted a folded paper and a card. He handed them to the man. "My banker figured you Yankees might not cotton to out of town checks. It's notarized. I would tell you to call the bank, but we need to get to Las Vegas before dark and one never knows how long it going to take to place a long distance call. Besides," he shrugged, "chances are pretty good that Cal is still at home sleeping off last night's celebration." There wasn't a trace of the good-old-boy tone he had used on the telephone at the hotel. He was firm. cultured, and sure of himself. For a brief moment she wondered just who he was.

The man called Mr. Kohn glanced at the paper, looked at her arm, and slipped the ID bracelet over her hand.

"A lovely piece, Sergeant McKaid. Step this way, and I will make out the bill." He handed the bracelet to the clerk. "Tell Morrie to take care of this immediately. Two links should do it."

Lucy didn't know what the paper said, but the hesitation was gone. David wrote the check and she kept the engagement ring on her finger while he put the velvet box holding both weddings rings in his pocket. *Don't ever lose it,* she told herself. David's ID bracelet no longer had a tendency to slide off her hand. The two links were in her purse

"Saving them in case you want it back?" she teased.

"Not a chance, honey. Just not going to leave a couple of chunks of sterling behind."

He really didn't mean that the ID bracelet was solid silver, did he?

Out on the street he stopped in front of a window showcasing a soft brown dress with tiny pearls at the neckline and cuffs.

"That looks like you," he told her.

"Where on earth would I wear anything that fancy?"

"Church maybe. Cocktail party. Who knows? It would look good on you."

Cocktail party? Did Texas farmers attend such things? She doubted it, but she did let herself be led into the shop. David was right. It did look good on her, and she did like it. She had never had anything so lovely. An ivory crepe with short sleeves and a lace collar looked just as good, as did a vibrant pink with long sleeves and a pale green, with puff sleeves and a perky peplum. David touched the ivory crepe.

"Would you rather shop for a wedding gown?"

'I think this would be fine, and I can wear it later." As she looked at herself in the three way mirror, she also studied the man standing behind her. What had she gotten herself into? *Please, dear God, she prayed, please don't let this be a mistake.*

A few minutes later as she was standing in the little dressing room the clerk opened the door, handed her a navy blue pants suit with a western look, and grinned.

"He said you'll look sexy as all get-out in this."

* * * * *

David enjoyed himself watching her try on the clothes. He had almost forgotten how it was to worry about how much something cost. He would have to tell her that he was no farmer, but for now it was actually nice to hear her worry about money. If it hadn't been for that mean old bull he might not have been able to carry a hefty check book. His father had sent Patrick away, but Gramps had taken a chance on the wildcatter. Even after all these years, Mom still took flowers to church every Sunday, putting them at the headstone before the service.

It's a wonder he hadn't been killed himself, the way he had tumbled off the fence in an effort to get to Pop. Luckily, all he'd gotten out of it was a broken leg. Gramps had put a shot through the bull's head before he could do any more damage. It was the only time he had ever seen his mother cry.

Cindy walked out of the dressing room wearing the western outfit. How had he ever thought women should be tall, slim, and sophisticated? God, they couldn't get to Las Vegas fast enough. Was he going to spend his life wanting a bed every time he looked at her? His body was recalling how it had felt to slip into her. A few minutes away from her might help. He'd seen a leather shop a few doors away. They couldn't be carrying her things around in a paper sack. She was going to have to have some luggage.

"Pretty as a new-born calf," he told her.. "Just the thing for the rodeo. All you need are boots and a hat. Take care of whatever unmentionables you need, while I skip out to a place I noticed two doors down. I'll be back to settle up real quick like."

Chapter 10

Shopping with David was an adventure she'd never dreamed of having, but it worried Lucy. She didn't know how much mustering out pay he had. She couldn't believe how much those dresses cost. Each and every one of them cost a good deal more than she had made in a week of overtime. He seemed a bit careless with money. The way he had tipped Tony at the bar, and the boy who had brought breakfast. , .on the other hand the man at the jewelry store had taken his check for the diamond she was wearing. Still, she wasn't sure how long it would take to drive to Texas, and she sure didn't want to spend the next few days wearing the same pair of panties she'd worn since yesterday morning. Without looking at the price tags she picked out what she needed.

The clerk looked at the pile of clothes and turned her head to see if anyone was listening. "For special customers we have a couple pair of nylon hose." She almost whispered the words.

Why not? "Wonderful." She added a garter belt to the pile.

It was more like twenty minutes before David walked in carrying an expensive looking suitcase.

"Took me longer than I thought. Had him put your initials on it."

Sure enough, there they were. Two shiny gold letters. CM. Not Lucinda Robbins. Cindy McKaid. The clerk packed all her new purchases into the suitcase and started to close it.

"I sure won't object, Cindy girl, but you plan on sleeping in the buff?" David asked

"Pajamas," she exclaimed.

"Not in my bed." He wandered over to the lingerie department, coming back with a negligee set, sheer, lacy, and fire engine red.

"I thought men didn't like shopping for things like that."

"Real men know what they like on their women. Besides, there's no one here I know. Even if there was, all they would be doing is envying me. We'd better get started if we want to get to Las Vegas before it gets dark."

When he put the suitcase in the trunk, she saw the rest of a full set of matching luggage. Goodness, she would never need that many suitcases.

Their next stop was a filling station, where the gas tank was topped off, the attendant checked the tires and the oil, cleaned the windshield, and they used the facilities. David had one of the attendants put on his sheepskin seat covers and handed the boy a five for doing it. She was sure the boy would have done it for a dollar. She admired the comfort of the soft wool.

"About the only thing a sheep's good for," David told her as he pulled four Coke bottles from the red icebox sitting next to the door.

"If they have any Dr. Pepper, I would rather have that," she told him.

David replaced two of the bottles, wrapped the four in a blanket from the trunk, raised the top, and they were on their way to Las Vegas. Neither said a single word about getting in touch with her parents. As soon as they left the city traffic, he pushed harder on the accelerator and pulled her close.

"Not a scenic route," he said. "Nothing but a straight road. We'll see more on the way home. We want to see the Grand Canyon. They say it's really something. I'd like to see Hoover Dam, but they've got that locked up tight. It will take time for them to change that."

"It sounds like a wonderful trip."

"We can take our time. It will give us a chance to know one another a little better. What do you like to read, for instance?"

"Anything I can get my hands on."

"Is UCLA your school?"

"I went to work. There was no way I could afford to go to college."

"I thought UCLA was free for residents."

"Books, supplies, and clothes aren't. I went through high school with a dollar a week allowance. Considering that it was Hollywood High, that was next to nothing. I got a part time job in my senior year."

"Any hobbies?"

"I sketch a little, and do a bit with pastels when I can find time."

"Do you do anything with oils?"

"Can't afford that, and I don't think the family would appreciate the smell."

"What does your father do?" He reached over to turn off the radio. They had lost the station.

"He's a bookkeeper at CBS. He could have gone to work in one of the aircraft factories and made more money, but he said if he stayed where he was he would still have a job when the war was over. Maybe he was right."

"Those brothers of yours? What do they do?"

"They just see how much trouble they can get into." She smiled as she thought of the boys. "They're only eight. You said your grandmother was part Cheyenne. Does she live with your folks?"

"Full-blooded Cheyenne. She has her own little log cabin on the place. It's older than the house, but it's been worked over a couple of times. Mamaw Deedee knows things most of the world's forgotten. You'll like her, and I know she will like you. She's the reason I don't drink much. Too many of our American Indians have trouble with alcohol. It just doesn't seem smart to test how far down the line that applies. Nothing can ruin a man quicker than drink."

"Is that thing around your neck with your dog tags an Indian thing?"

"Mamaw Deedee made it when I was a boy. I've worn it all my life." He was quiet for a few minutes. "Taylor and Tim didn't like wearing theirs when it would be seen. They said it looked odd with the red hair they inherited from our Irish great-grandfather. Sometimes I wish they hadn't felt that way."

It was her turn to be silent. Finally she said, "Think she'll make one for our children?"

"I know she will." He reached for her hand. "Thank you. You really are something special. We'll have a good life together."

She leaned against David, closed her eyes, and slept until he brought the car to a stop in front of a low building with a giant windmill atop it.

* * * * *

A big sign proclaimed that they were at the *Hotel El Rancho Vegas*. Someone hurrying to take the suitcases and David's duffle bag made Lucy think it might be about expensive as the hotel on Wilshire Boulevard had been. In the middle of the desert, the grass was as green as a tropical forest. Inside the first things that caught her eyes were all the slot machines placed in convenient locations. It might all have a western look, but it was sure upscale western. The way David just breezed into the lobby and announced himself surprised her.

"McKaid," he told the desk clerk. "I called this morning. The little lady might want to freshen up before we see the parson."

She watched as he signed the register book. Mr. and Mrs. David McKaid. Oh, what a feeling that was.

"The boy will take you to your bungalow."

Her first glimpse of the bungalow almost overwhelmed her. A box of chocolates on the table and an ice bucket with a bottle of champagne next to it.. An orchid corsage was there as well. The big bed in the bedroom had a spread that matched the draperies, and a chocolate mint on each pillow.. She felt as though she had fallen into a movie set.

She also wondered who in the heck David McKaid was. One minute he sounded like a poor cowboy in a western, the next time he was Cary Grant. The rings and dresses? The car, the story about a Cherokee grandmother? If he was a con man he was a slick one.

Whoever or whatever he was, she didn't care. He was the most fascinating man she had ever met. She could no longer imagine a future without him. She was anticipating the look he would have when she put on the red lace thing he had picked out. That's what life was really all about.

"Big enough for two," David told her as she looked at the fluffy towels and the big tub in the bathroom. "All the water and all the bubbles you want."

"You don't have to spend this much money on me."

"We only get one honeymoon, honey. I told you to let me worry about finances. Why don't you slip into that thing the girl called ivory so I can pin that orchid on you?"

"I don't even have a comb or brush, not even a toothbrush."

"You just get yourself into that dress. There's a minister waiting. After dinner we're coming back here, and I'm going to spend the night making love to you."

"Got something to do first." All doubts disappeared. He really did mean marriage, and the jeweler certainly hadn't hesitated in taking his check. Opening her purse, she took out Jerry's ring, led David to the bathroom, lifted the lid, dropped the ring and flushed. "Just so you know."

"Really afraid it was stolen?"

"A chance, even if he bought it from someone."

"It's good that you did it this way," he said. "If he was stupid enough to walk away from you, I know it hurt you. This way the water will wash away the past. If you had tossed it out, the evil would still be looking for you."

"I like the way you think."

They stood there in the bathroom kissing. Lucy closed her eyes. She had burned her bridges. She didn't know what lay ahead but hoped it would be good.

While she opened the suitcase, he picked up the phone and dialed.

"Think that gift shop might have a nice lady's comb and brush set? Maybe one with a mirror as well?" he asked. "Need a little old toothbrush as well."

Twelve minutes later Lucy was running a Lucite comb through her hair, wondering if the backs of the mirror and brush really were silver. They sure looked like it.

When they went back to the main building a colonel and his wife were registering. There wasn't anything shy about David. He walked right up to the officer and gave him a snappy salute.

"Excuse me, sir. Could I have a word with you?"

"What can I do for you, son?" The officer glanced at David's ribbons. "Looks like you did your part in this war."

"Did my best, sir. I have a favor to ask." His Texas twang came out loud, clear, and appealing. As she listened to him, she realized that he turned it on or off as he pleased. The college education was there only when he wanted it. "My girl and I are getting married in a few minutes. Her family's all back in California, and mine are outside of Austin. I was wondering if you and your lovely wife would be our witnesses."

"Oh, do say yes, Henry," his wife pleaded. She was as tall as the colonel. Lucy could well imagine she was a take-charge woman.

"See what you're getting yourself into," the colonel told David. "Whether it's stripes, birds, or stars, these women think they're the boss. We'll be glad to."

"Thank you, sir." He laughed a little. "She's already after me about my spending habits."

"Sensible girl."

The two were beside them as she and David stood before a minister who had introduced himself only moments before. In a spontaneous gesture she reached for the hand David held out to her. She was wearing cheap red shoes she had bought years before, an off white dress which that afternoon had cost over a hundred dollars, a two carat engagement ring, and twenty-five cent ear rings. At home she slept in a second hand daybed, squeezed into a small bedroom with her two sisters. A whole luxurious cottage was theirs for tonight.

Last night had been so real. She hadn't been the least bit embarrassed to be naked with David. Making love for the first time had been a glorious experience. David, indeed, had been what she had been waiting for. Ever so gently she felt the pressure as David tightened his hand around hers. She suddenly realized the minister was saying something about till death do you part.

"Oh, yes," she said, "I do."

The minister smiled as he asked the same question of David, whose eyes twinkled at her as he echoed her words, "Yes, I do." Then he was slipping that incredible wedding band on her finger, and she knew that she was glad she had been on Hill Street the night before.

It didn't matter in the least that it was a minister and not a priest who said, "I now pronounce you man and wife." Her father hadn't walked her down the aisle; her mother wasn't wiping away the tears during a High Mass, but it didn't matter. She had decided long ago that a minister was probably as much a man of God as a priest. They all worshiped the same God. They were married, and she loved the idea that whoever he was, she would be with David Stanley McKaid for the rest of her life. He called her Cindy, but she felt more like Cinderella.

* * * * *

David made sure that when the photographer, who would be roaming later that evening, took pictures of the wedding, the colonel and his wife were included. The four of them had dinner together in the *Round Up Room*, where the atmosphere was western, the food good, and the entertainment nice. Not one word was spoken about the war that had just ended. It seemed the colonel had spent some of his army time in Texas and hadn't thought much of the state.

"There's no place like Texas," David told him. "The army was just looking for the toughest conditions they could find. We have anything you want, mountains, deserts, piney woods, and seashore. We've even got the right to secede from the union if we want. No other state can say that."

"McKaid," the colonel's wife said. "Seems as though I heard something about the name. Are you near the King Ranch?"

"No, ma'am. They're south. Our little place is a little east of Austin."

"Little?"

"Everyone's little compared to the King Ranch, ma'am."

"You're going to have to watch this one?" she told Lucy. "If those rings are any indication, he likes to spend money." The diamond engagement ring rested next a row of five diamonds definitely large enough to be seen.

Lucy had to agree with that, but she already loved her rings. Mrs. David McKaid. The name sounded nice. She liked it. Last evening she was arguing with her father. Tonight she was sitting in Las Vegas wearing a dress she couldn't have afforded, along with two very expensive rings, and calling herself Mrs. David McKaid. Cindy McKaid was a far cry from Lucy Rollins. She even had an orchid on her shoulder. No one had ever given her flowers before.

"I've told him he doesn't need to impress me by spending money," she replied. "At least we'll have a wonderful memory of today."

"To wonderful memories." David lifted his glass of champagne. "I'm looking forward to life with my beautiful wife and her thrifty ways."

Chapter 11

As he sipped the very nice wine he had ordered, David contemplated the pleasure he would have when he introduced Cindy to his family. His thoughts drifted back to the time he had taken a girl named Trudy to the senator's reception. He was doubly glad that he had had escaped the clutches of her and others like her. The girl beside him had such a beguiling smile, yet she was strong enough to defy her father and priest, caring enough to try to protect her sister, and caring enough to help her mother raise three little boys. Quite by chance he had found the perfect mate.

He stared into the bubbling wine. Last night he had made love to the girl in his dreams, but it hadn't been a dream. She was real; she was beautiful; she was full of life; and she was just what he needed. Cindy was so refreshing. She didn't have four years of college behind her, and she undoubtedly had never ridden a horse, but she had a natural grace and beauty.

For just a little while longer he wouldn't mention the ranch and the wells. All his life he would value the knowledge that he didn't have a money grubbing wife who had wanted the Diamond MiK more than she had wanted him. She didn't even scorn his great-grandmother's ways. That was an unexpected bonus. He loved Mamaw Deedee and was proud of his Cheyenne blood.

* * * * *

They said goodnight to the colonel and his wife. Lucy took her new husband's arm as they walked through the lobby. They hadn't quite reached the main exit when David spied the ladies dress shop and almost dragged her through the doors. He picked up a tan colored suede skirt decorated with fringe.

"You're going to look cute as a button in this." He gave her one heck of a sexy smile.

Half an hour later Lucy inspected herself in the mirror. Was a sergeant's mustering out pay really as big as this? Shouldn't he be saving some of it to live on? The girl in the mirror didn't even look like her. That girl was not only wearing the skirt, she had on a white silk blouse, a beaded vest of the same suede as the skirt, a white Lady Stetson hat with a leather cord under her chin, and a pair of white boots. How David had finagled those without ration stamps, she didn't know. Somehow when she looked down at her feet and looked at those boots with their fancy stitching, she knew. She knew she was Cindy McKaid, not Lucy Rollins. The trouble was, all she knew about Cindy McKaid was that she loved being in bed with David McKaid.

"You can wear them tomorrow," he said, "if we ever decide to get out of bed."

"David." She blushed as the young sales clerk giggled.

"Just married me the prettiest gal in California." He winked at her.

This was a teasing side of him she hadn't seen. She took his arm as they walked out. No, it wasn't all about leaving home. She had never known, but it really was possible to fall in love just like that? She was happy.

The next afternoon they ventured into the casino.

"You know how to play poker?" he asked.

"I don't play." That wasn't lying, just evading the question. A terrible sense of deja-vu struck her as she recalled the back room of the drug store with Lance, and the bowling alleys and poker games with Jerry. A book and Jerry had taught her all about the game, and he had been elated when she had bluffed her way to a good pot with nothing more than a pair of sixes. "I'll watch."

She never wanted to see a pair of aces or a straight flush again. Were all men gamblers, or did she just attract them? She tried to smile, but didn't succeed because after two hands David looked at her.

"Something wrong, honey?"

"No." She was twisting the rings around her finger.

He picked up his chips, slid off the stool, slipped his arm into hers, and guided her out the door.

"Let me guess. He was a gambler, and you're afraid I am."

"I hope you're not."

"You lend him money?"

"No, he wasn't like that."

"Don't you cry, Cindy girl. An occasional card game doesn't make me a gambler." He turned her face up to his. "And don't you worry. You'll never have to wonder where your next meal's coming from as long as I'm around. Does your father work on Saturday?"

"No."

"We'll leave for Hollywood. Saturday morning."

"Hollywood?"

"Why, sure thing, honey. Sort of figure I ought to meet your folks, and you'll want to pick up your things. How old are those brothers of yours?"

"Eight." Would she ever know what was coming next with this tall sergeant of hers? She had thought they would be going straight to Texas. Only one thing bothered her. What on earth would her father have to say about such a quick marriage, and without a priest?

"Boys that age ought to get a kick out of souvenirs from here."

They spent the rest of their second night together in the bungalow doing what newlyweds do best.

* * * * *

Friday morning when Cindy woke , David was standing across the room in his khaki undershirt and boxers, talking on the telephone. She watched him and listened.

"I'll be heading home soon, but I'd like to have some ready cash. I don't want to be traveling with just a checkbook." A pause. "I'm calling from Las Vegas. The Hotel El Rancho Las Vegas." Another pause. "No, it's not that kind of hotel. How much? Name a figure." He listened. "Double it." A pause. "Now triple it, and no, I did not pick up some bimbo in a bar. You know me better than that." This time there was a real frown with the pause. "I'll tell you when I get there. Just send it to the Western Union office here, and you don't need to mention it to Mom."

He nodded to her as he replaced the receiver. "Just having Gramps wire some cash. I put his name on my checking account when I left for the army. Gas stations don't take checks."

"David," she murmured, "you don't have to keep spending money on me. It doesn't take money to be happy."

He walked over and sat on the bed next to her. "Did it ever occur to you that I might like spending money on you? If we push it, we could be in Texas in three or four days."

"I imagine you'll be glad to be home."

"I will," he admitted, "but what I been thinking - well, things will be a mite hectic for awhile once we get there. We could maybe take our time, do a little sightseeing, and learn to know each other a little better. We didn't give you a crack at a big wedding, but that doesn't mean we can't have a real honeymoon."

"Just the two of us. It sounds wonderful, but. . ."

" I - maybe I'd better get used to saying we," he corrected. "We can afford it." He kissed her, pushed the sheet aside and started drawing circles around her left breast. "God, girl, I can't keep my hands off you. I like loving you. I've been waiting for you all my life." He kissed her again. "How many children do we want?"

"Does four sound about right?"

"Two girls and two boys? Sounds fine to me." He was running his fingers through her hair, brushing it away from her face. "I think we ought to take back something for your folks as well as the boys. We'll do some shopping this afternoon."

They bought caps with Las Vegas stamped across the brims for the boys. He would have bought cap guns, but she assured him that they already had them, so he settled for belts and holsters for them. There were turquoise earrings for the girls, a silver broach for her mother, and a bolo tie for her father. Cindy acquired new earrings as well. Under the glass counter there was a turquoise necklace that ended up being dangled before her eyes.

"Would you like this?' he asked.

"It looks too heavy." Maybe that sounded better than too expensive.

When they stopped at the Western Union office and picked up the money that David's grandfather had wired, David peeled off five twenties and handed them to her.

"Better put them in your purse. You'll probably be needing a few things."

She certainly hadn't expected that, but took it, all the while wondering just how much his grandfather had sent, but not sure enough of herself to ask. One twenty went into her wallet beside her seven ones. The other four she folded and tucked between her senior picture and Leticia's. She just couldn't imagine spending that much money.

"Would you consider giving me that picture for my wallet?" he asked.

"I have a couple more at home." She removed the picture and found another spot for the bills.

They did leave early Saturday morning. Her new wardrobe filled one suitcase and spilled over into the second, almost filling it. The silver comb, brush, and mirror set, a toothbrush, and an expensive perfume resided in the matching cosmetic case. A shopping bag held the gifts for her family.

* * * * *

Cindy stayed awake on the way back. Deserts had always evoked the images of the empty sand dunes of the Sahara, but that wasn't true of Nevada. As the Buick purred along, she saw several species of cacti, sagebrush, and once a jack rabbit darting across the sand. She wondered how it managed to stay alive. It had its own kind of beauty, but it wasn't a place she would want to have as her home. Driving faster than the speed limit and having the windows open made the morning heat bearable.

"Do you drive?" he asked her.

"I know how, but I don't have a license. I learned on a stick shift." She wasn't going to mention that Jerry had taught her to drive his old Ford.

"We'll get you a car when we get home. You can get in some practice along the way."

"My father's not going to be happy about us."

"I will talk to him."

She doubted anything David could say would placate her father, but she didn't put that doubt into words.

They were about half an hour inside the California border when a State Patrol car passed and made a sharp u-turn, his siren suddenly wailing in the desert air. David stopped the car immediately. The siren died as the patrol car stopped behind them.

It was as though the bottom dropped out of Cindy's whole world. There in the August heat she was chilled to the bone, feeling everything draining out of her. An icy fear swept through her when both uniformed men approached the car with drawn guns. The older, heavier trooper was beside David, barking out an order to get out of the car. Had she made the biggest mistake of her life? David couldn't be a wanted man, could he? The younger officer standing beside her was quieter. His gun was pointed at David, but he spoke to her in a steady, even voice.

"Get out of the car, Miss. It's all right. We've got him covered. He can't hurt you now."

Chapter 12

Can't hurt me? What did that mean? For the first time since she has learned to talk Lucy didn't know what to do. Her first instinct was to edge closer to David, but there was a state trooper with a gun telling her to get out of the car. She hesitated.

"Don't move, Cindy." David's voice was soft but steady.

"Leave her alone." It was a sharp order from the trooper at his side. "Just do as I say. Out, real easy like, and keep your hands in sight."

"I'd like to see some identification first and your badge number?" David's voice suggested a practiced authority. "If you don't mind," he added politely, "my wife stays in this car until I know she is safe."

"Wife? You got a driver's license and registration for this vehicle?"

"Cindy honey, there's an envelope under the maps in the glove compartment. Will you get it out? Open it slowly so he can see there's no weapon in there."

She was a little shaky as her hands moved to the glove compartment. After landing the maps half on her lap and half on the floor of the car, she handed the envelope to David, who in turn gave it to the trooper, who stepped back while he looked over the papers.

"My business card should be in there as well," David told him. "I own this car, and I would like to know why you are holding guns on me and my wife. You're frightening her. My driver's license is in my wallet. I'm going to have to reach my back pocket to get it. I'm not going for a gun or anything other than my wallet." Slowly, using only one hand, he withdrew his wallet and handed it to the officer.

"Should have known it took a lawyer to ask for a badge," the officer sighed after looking over the papers in the envelope. "Even with a gun on him he asks for it."

"Down my way we're used to guns. Need them sometimes. People aren't always who they say they are. Anyone can get hold of a uniform. At the risk of repeating myself. suppose you tell me what this is all about."

Now she was really confused. David sounded so firm and business like. Who had she married? A con man, a Texas lawyer, or a farmer with a few cows?

"What's your name, Miss?" The officer was looking at her.

"Lucinda."

"Rollins?"

"It was. It's McKaid now." She wriggled her left hand in front of the trooper beside her, and then past David to the older man. "Aren't they just the most beautiful rings you've ever seen?"

"We were married Thursday night in Las Vegas," David told the officer. "Do you have an explanation for this outrage?"

"There's an APB out on you. You know what that is?"

"It doesn't take a lawyer to know. It's an all points bulletin."

"Give the man a prize. Lucinda Robbins, five two, blonde, last seen with tall, black haired army sergeant driving a black Buick convertible with Texas plates. Maybe stolen. Possible kidnapping."

"Sophie," Cindy muttered. "My friend has a habit of over dramatizing things. David didn't kidnap me. We're on our way to tell my family about our marriage."

"Would you like to see our marriage license?" David asked. "It's in one of the suitcases in the trunk."

"Guess those rings are big enough. Put away your gun, Paul. Looks like we've got a couple of love birds here." They both holstered their weapons. He looked at David. "What's a Texas lawyer with money enough for those rings doing being just a sergeant?"

"Just managing to stay alive, sir. I was drafted and probably could have avoided it, but that would have been the coward's way out, but the last thing I wanted was to be an officer."

"There's no need for us to take them in." He was speaking to his partner. "I'll call it in as soon as we see a telephone booth." The man turned his attention back to them. " Just let her folks know she's okay."

They watched the two troopers drive away. Cindy stuffed the registration and maps back into the glove compartment.

"Thought you had a farm and cows. Are you really a lawyer? Trials and courtrooms and all that?"

" Taylor and Timothy were always more interested in working the stock than I am, but with them both gone, I probably won't go back to the firm." He leaned over to give her a quick kiss. "Is living with you always going to be this exciting?"

"I hope not. Guns make me nervous."

"I thought you kept pretty calm. I will admit that I don't like looking at the wrong end of one. Didn't want them searching the car though. My thirty-eight's under my seat and it's loaded. They might not have been understanding about that. Your father hunt?"

"No."

"We'll have to teach you to shoot." He grinned at her before turning the key to start the car. "Most Texas girls carry a little one in their purse. Thirty-eight's fine for rattlesnakes, but you better have a rifle for a wolf or big cat."

He turned on the radio before starting out again, leaving her with her thoughts. What kind of a place was she going to call home? Rattlesnakes and mountain lions? She wondered if the Westerns she had seen prepared her for a farm in Texas.

* * * * *

So now she knew he was a lawyer. Maybe he should tell her about the ranch and wells. That was a memory David enjoyed. He and the twins had been on their horses. It had been a little over six months after they had buried their father. What a sight that had been. They hadn't been close. For all his talk about needing his help, Gramps hadn't let them near the drilling. but even from a distance they had been able to see that black gold spewing forth. The three of them had just sat there on their horses, reveling in the sight

The oil had meant an end to scrimping and saving, but a portion of the land was black and would take time to heal. Thank God, Gramps hadn't let any of them put on airs because of the money. Other than better clothing, and education, the only really extravagance Gramps had allowed was the second-hand Studebaker for graduation.

No, he wouldn't tell her yet. It was too nice knowing she had married him, not the Diamond MiK. The family had lived well since then, but nothing spectacular. Mom had gotten involved with a lot of charity work. She had spruced up the house a bit and updated the plumbing and kitchen and added the wash room. Gramps had insisted on adding a bathroom onto Mamaw Deedee's cabin. After he had started working at Jefferson, Colby, and Smith he had made a few good investments on his own, but even so his main extravagances had been the car and some custom made suits. Maybe three years in the army and this girl beside him deserved a little more than that. Could be it was time for the McKaids to live a little. A married man had to think of the future.

* * * * *

When they reached Hollywood, they checked into the Hollywood Roosevelt Hotel. Cindy had told him flat out that the one on Wilshire was too expensive. He hadn't enlightened her. Hollywood might be her hometown, but evidently she didn't know that the hotel was favored by some of the stars. From the outside it didn't look that grand. She was right on one count though. It was closer to her home. When they reached their room, he told the bellboy to wait.

"Cindy honey, fish that ivory thing out of your suitcase while I get my dress uniform." He handed both, along with a bill, to the boy. "They need a good pressing. Think you can have them back in an hour?"

"Yes, sir." The boy pocketed the money and left.

"I take it, you want me to wear that home."

"With your boots and new hat. You look sexy as hell in that get-up. Think your family might like to go to the *Brown Derby* for dinner?"

" I don't think my brothers are ready for anything that fancy. There's a place on Sunset called *The Haufbrau Gardens*." *Did she really want to look sexy facing her father*?

"A favorite of yours?"

"I was there once. Sophie told me about it. Her father takes her mother there on special occasions. They have a gypsy violinist roaming around. I can't quite see my eight-year-old brothers at the Brown Derby. If Mom has ration stamps left, we could pick up a roast, and I could cook. It would be a lot cheaper."

"You're probably right about the boys. Maybe the Derby wouldn't be suitable for them." He picked up the telephone book. "I'll call for reservations. Six o'clock sound all right for them?"

"Fine. Leticia ought to be home by then. Why didn't you tell me you are a lawyer?"

"You didn't ask."

"You said you had a couple of cows."

"Honey, any real Texan worth his salt owns cows. At thirty I better have a way to support us."

"Does any real Texan always have a thirty-eight under the front seat of his car?"

"If he's not wearing it." He grinned. "Only he's usually driving a pick-up with his rifle in a gun rack behind his head."

Neatly pressed, the uniform and dress were returned in half an hour. After she dressed, Cindy looked at herself in the full-length mirror. David did get a charge out of the way she looked, but how would her family react? She looked expensive. He wanted them to see her as his wife, not their daughter. The white Lady Stetson with its leather tie under her chin matched the color of her hand tooled boots. What would her father say? He would have to tell the man a few things.

* * * * *

Lucy was nervous. She'd had a lot of arguments with her father, but in spite of having been so angry with him, she loved her whole family. She wanted them to accept David as one of them. He was her choice, but he was going to come as a shock, and Dad was going to have something to say about not being married in the church.

When David pulled into the driveway the boys were in the yard, involved in a rousing shootout. When they saw the convertible, all three cap guns dropped to the ground. Jimmy ran for the house, shouting at the top of his lungs. "Mom, Dad, Lucy's home, and she's got a soldier with her, and he's got a convertible."

She was sure the whole block heard him. The neighbor next door, who was spending his Saturday afternoon mowing his grass, stopped to watch them. Jack stood in front of the car, hands on his hips, just looking at her, and Jason hopped up on the running board and looked **int**o the back seat.

"Will you take me for a ride, Sergeant?"

"Later." David turned to her. "The triplets?"

"This one's Jason. The loud mouth is Jimmy, and the cheerful one in front of us is Jack."

"How do you tell them apart."

"Practice. Jason, get down off there so David can get out."

Her brother simply edged toward the back seat.

"Grab that suitcase," David told the boy as he stepped out and around the car to open the door for Lucy. He gave her a quick kiss. "You ready?"

"You kiss her again, mister, you're in trouble." Jack stood in front of the car, hands on his hips in his best tough guy imitation.

"I'm bigger than you are," David tossed back.

"Yeah, but there's three of us," Jack growled. He looked at her. "Wow, look at those boots. You look just like *Dale Evans*."

"She's prettier," David told him.

"Lucy's been in Las Vegas," Jason screeched. He had looked into the shopping bag resting on the backseat floor. and pulled out the three caps. He clamped one on his head and tossed one to Jack. "There's three, so they're for us."

"Brothers," she muttered. "Now the whole neighborhood knows where we've been." Then to top it off, across the street Sophie was coming out of her front door. "Jack, pick up those guns. You know you're not supposed to leave toys in the grass." She reached for David's hand and took a deep breath. "Let's go in and get it over with."

Chapter 13

Lucy held fast to David's hand as they entered the house. Her parents were waiting in the living room. Her mother was untying her apron. Her grim faced father looked at David, then at her.

"We've got rules in this house, Lucinda. I told the police that my daughter would never willingly go with a strange man. It looks like I was wrong. I never thought I had to spell it out that as long as you are under my roof you are not staying overnight with any man. You have been a trial at times, but I did think we raised you with a sense of some kind of moral decency. You can't be staying away for three days and just waltz in like nothing is wrong. You. . ."

"Dad . . ."

"Let me finish. You tell your friend to take his convertible and get the hell out of this house right now." His words held more sadness than anger. "To think a daughter of mine would disgrace us with a thing like this. We need to speak alone."

'"David isn't going anywhere." Her words were unnaturally soft. She was hoping to avoid a yelling match. "Anything you have to say, you can say right now. If he goes, I go. He's my husband. I am Mrs. David McKaid."

For a long moment her father just looked at her. He shook his head at the protective way David had his arm around her. "By a justice of the peace, I suppose. I know you've always been a trial, but I did think, in spite of all your foolish questions, you were a good Catholic girl."

"By a minister," she snapped, forgetting her determination to speak softly, "and I'm sure God listens to him as much as he does a dried up old priest who thinks a woman is only good barefoot and pregnant." She could feel David's arm tense ever so slightly. "If we're all such good Catholics why don't you and Mom and all the rest have sixteen kids. Just once can't you be happy for me?"

"Lucy."

"You didn't tell me you were Catholic," David said.

"It's like the lawyer thing. You didn't ask. Not a very good one." She was glad he had his arm around her. She needed it. "Be happy for me, Dad."

She held out her left hand. Her father glanced at the rings.

"Very pretty pieces of glass."

"I beg your pardon, Mr. Rollins," David said. "I wouldn't insult your daughter with glass. The jeweler described the engagement ring as a perfect, blue white, emerald cut. I have the proper documentation for both rings so they can be insured when we get to Texas."

"Then heaven help my daughter. How many years will it take before they are paid for. Lucy, do you realize what you've put us through? Your mother's been half out of her mind with worry."

"I had other things on my mind."

"That is obvious."

"Easy there," David murmured. "Of course they were worried." He looked at both her parents. "We were just swept off our feet. We didn't give much thought to what you must have been going through. I couldn't resist buying her things. I'm proud to call your daughter my wife."

"Looks like you served your country well enough," Mark conceded as he inspected David. "I don't know why she kept you such a secret. I hope you know what you've got yourself into. She's a handful."

"Car really does have a Texas license plate," Jason yelled.

"Mind your manners, young man," her mother told him. "What will the sergeant think of you."

"It's David, ma'am, and I'm used to younger brothers. I had two."

"Had?"

"Guadalcanal and D-Day, sir. It devastated my mother."

For the moment that statement was enough to quiet her father. Perhaps he was glad the boys were only eight.

"Well," he finally said, "you look to be the best she's ever brought home. The house isn't big, but the divan makes into a bed."

"That's kind of you, sir, but we're at the Hollywood Roosevelt. We'll be leaving for Texas Monday. We'd like to take you out dinner tonight. I favored the Brown Derby, but Cindy thinks the Haufbrau Gardens is more family oriented."

She was sure it was, but she also knew it would be cheaper.

"Her name is Lucy. Lucinda Jane Rollins. You have a job before the war?"

"Her name is Lucinda McKaid, but I like calling her Cindy. I'm a lawyer, but with my brothers gone I'll have to help with the livestock."

"In this house it's Lucy. Didn't ever figure you'd end up on a farm." He was looking at her as he said it. "You've been a big help to your mother, but you sure don't do anything outside."

"In Texas we call it a ranch." David words were quiet and respectful. He smiled as he looked down at her. "Honey, why don't you and your mother take that suitcase your brother's holding and gather your things together while I get acquainted with your father."

She and her mother went to the bedroom. Lucy placed the empty suitcase on the bed, opened a drawer, and started transferring her clothes. Her mother sat on the bed beside the suitcase.

"He's not a bit intimidated by your father. Why didn't you tell us you were seeing someone?"

"I wasn't." She was taking her time, folding the clothes neatly. "David's a lawyer. I think it would take more than Dad to intimidate him. I met him Wednesday night."

"Lucy." Her mother reached over to touch her hand. "This is no way to forget Jerry. We can have it annulled."

"Jerry's history. David's the best thing that ever happened to me."

"Lucy, listen to me. He looks quite a bit older than you."

"He's thirty."

"Another older man. You've never dated anyone your own age. Not that you don't look pretty, but, you didn't have that dress and those boots when you left the house." Her mother touched the suitcase. "CM? Where did you pick that up?"

"Cindy McKaid, Mom. It's what he calls me. We have our marriage license out in the car." She held out her left hand. "Aren't they gorgeous? As far as being older - Mom, the younger they are, the stupider they are. They can't think of anything but getting a girl into bed."

"And David didn't?

"This was different. I wanted it, too. I knew he was the one for me."

"You need time to know more about him." Her mother glanced at the diamonds. "If they are real, it's a poor basis for marriage. We can have it annulled." She was repeating herself. "Father O'Toole can tell us how."

"No, we can't. Get real, Mom. We've spent the last few days and nights together. I believe that's called consummating the marriage. An annulment is out of the question, and Father O'Toole doesn't have anything to say about it. I'm twenty. I can make my own decisions. You know I've been questioning him ever since I was a little girl. I'm sick and tired of hearing how women are meant to be obedient little nobodies. I can't help but wonder who dreamed up that bit about Eve being made from Adam's rib. Maybe if they let priests marry they'd have some idea of what the real world is all about."

She started to tuck in her little thirty-five millimeter camera, but changed her mind. She would take some pictures before they left. Instead she turned to the small closet she shared with her sisters and started taking out what belonged to her.

"It has nothing to do with Jerry. I mean it. When David makes love to me nothing else matters."

"Well, that's not a bad thing." Her mother stood and hugged her. Lucy never remembered her doing that before. "I hope it will be enough. I'm going to miss you. Texas is a long ways away. It's going to be a different kind of life." She took a few steps, closed the door, and once again sat on the bed. "We've never talked about marriage, have we?"

"A little late for the birds and bees."

"You've known about that for a long time, but there's more to marriage than the bed."

"I didn't sleep with anyone." She hesitated with the faded, blue jumpsuits she had worn at work, then folded them and added them to the rest of her meager wardrobe. Everything fit into the one suitcase. "Does that surprise you?"

"To be honest, I'm not sure. Just don't argue about everything. Keep him happy enough that he won't want to stray. Talk to each other, and don't keep secrets. Do you know when your father and I talk about things?"

"To use your own words, I honestly never thought you talk to each other."

"At night. In bed." Her mother looked embarrassed and hesitant. "At night, Lucy. As the children come, it's the one time you can be alone. In bed, in the dark, after. . ."

"After sex?" she supplied.

"Yes. Without either one, you won't have a good marriage. They are equally important."

"Thank you." She meant it. She leaned forward and kissed her mother's cheek. "It sounds like good advice."

"What do you know about him?"

"His family has cows. He went to Texas U whatever that is. He cares about his mother. I just found out this morning he's a lawyer, and I can't stop him from buying me things. You should have seen him this morning when the California Patrol stopped us. There he was with a gun pointing at him, and he asked for identification, and when they told me to get out of the car, he told me to sit until he was sure I was safe. Doesn't that sound like I hit the jackpot?"

"It sounds like maybe God was looking after you. Don't lose your faith even if you did decide to marry outside the church." Once again her mother hesitated. "The rings and your clothes are expensive. I can see that, but you said his family has a few cows. If he's spending his mustering out pay on you, they might not have a lot of money. When your father and I were married. . . Lucy, we went from the church to a chicken dinner Mama had waiting in the oven. You were young when we left Chicago. I don't know how much you remember."

"We lived with Grandma and Grandpa Smith, didn't we?"

"They converted the second floor into an apartment, but, yes, essentially we lived with them. When we were married we went straight from the church back to the house I'd lived in all my life. We ate dinner in the kitchen, and only when evening came did we have a chance to go upstairs to my bedroom. It was right over the old dining room that my father had turned into their bedroom. It wasn't the way I had pictured living after getting married. I don't think you would be happy living like that."

Not an ideal way to start a marriage. Could she have been so free and easy with David under similar circumstances? She didn't think so.

"We had been married almost ten years." Her mother gave her an odd look. "Lucy, your father must never know this, but I just couldn't take it any longer. I hated every minute we stayed in that house. We had no privacy. Papa thought he had the right to walk upstairs anytime he wanted. I wrote to my brother, asking if he could somehow get Mark a job out here, but your father couldn't make up his mind about Brad's offer. I knew you were the one thing that could push him over the edge. You have always been his favorite. He had been unhappy about Father insisting that you go to St. Mary's. He wanted you to go to public school. I broke three of Mama's precious Sunday plates before Papa lost his temper, accused you of doing it and spanked you. You came to me, crying, telling me you hadn't touched them. I told you to sit on the steps and tell your father all about it."

Her mother smiled at the memory. "You did, and he stormed into the house, and to this day I have never seen him as angry as he was then. No one was going to spank his little princess, but I think it was the fact that Papa pulled down your panties and spanked you on your bare bottom that really set him off. I knew Papa would do that. It was the way he always punished us. I could hear your father screaming at your grandfather. He even threatened to kill him if he ever did it again. We went to the ice cream parlor to talk. It was the only place we felt alone. Our own apartment, and we didn't feel comfortable talking in it. That's when he decided we would move out here. He told me we were going to leave in two weeks. If we could have managed it, I think we would have left that very night."

Lucy started to say something, but her mother kept talking.

"It wasn't easy living with them," her mother continued. "When we told them Lily was on her way - Lucy, I couldn't stand it any longer. My father actually came upstairs the next day and told me if I didn't start saying no to Mark, I would end up with a dozen children. He said he didn't. . ." She took her daughter's hand, her voice shaky. "What he actually said, was that he didn't want to hear our bed squeaking more than once a week, if then. Can you imagine a father telling his daughter something like that? He had no right." It was almost as though she was speaking to herself. "He had no right. I've forgiven him for a lot, but I'll never forgive him for that."

"I think you just gave me the best advice I could have." She squeezed her mother's hand and smiled.

"I do have one other secret. I don't always vote the way your father tells me to. It's a little thing, but it makes me feel like a person."

Lucy looked at her mother's expression and felt that for the first time it was possible that she understood her.

"Lucy, you're the girl I wish I had been. I was so glad. After ten years I was finally going to have my own home. If I wanted pot roast on Sunday instead of fried chicken, I could cook it."

"I'm glad you told me." The pot roast versus chicken might sound like a small thing, but obviously to her mother it was not. "I can't really explain it. Sophie and I went downtown. It was like a big party. Everyone was kissing and shouting. I saw David, and he looked absolutely lost. Then he smiled and started my way. When he kissed me, I knew life wouldn't be worth living unless we were together. I'll learn to hoe potatoes or whatever they grow in Texas. I'll learn to milk a cow if I have to. I'll do anything I have to, as long as I know we'll be in the same bed when night comes."

"You will manage. You always do. Leticia's got a date tonight."

"Not with Eddie, I hope."

"I'm afraid so. I wish she was more like you. I worry about her. You know I never thought much of Jerry, but I always felt you could take care of yourself. Eddie? I just don't think he respects women the way he should. I have a bad feeling about him. Tish is not as strong as you are."

"She can bring him along. It will give her a chance to see him at a family dinner."

"Even the boys don't like him."

"I'll see if I can't talk to her again. I've never understood how he has so much time off. Most servicemen don't have that much time away from base. Eddie must have a lot of friends though. He usually shows up in a borrowed car."

Chapter 14

Out in the living room of the small house David looked at the triplets. "If you boys want to go outside and play, after I talk to your father, I'll take you for a ride, and we can pick up some ice cream."

"You know how to handle boys," her father remarked after the trio left the room.

"I wanted a chance to talk to you alone, sir. I'm sorry we caused you to worry. We were just so caught up in the moment, we didn't think of anyone else."

"How long have you been dating Lucy?"

"How long isn't important." No way was he going to tell this man how he had met his daughter. "I knew I was going to marry her the moment I saw her, but there's a few things I haven't told her. I am telling you so you won't worry about her future."

"Secrets? Lucy has a history of picking the wrong man."

"She told about him." David smiled at the memory. "She flushed his ring down the toilet as soon as we got to Las Vegas. The thing is, I mentioned that we have a cow or two, and she jumped to the conclusion that I'm a farmer."

"That ring on her finger looks a bit expensive for an army sergeant. You talk like an educated man. What are you?"

"I am a lawyer, but the family business isn't a farm. I didn't realize just how good it would feel to know that she was marrying me and not the Diamond MiK. I've enjoyed the way she tells me I'm spending too much money, but I intend to tell her the truth before we get home."

"And this Diamond MiK is the family business?"

"A ranch near Austin. Not the biggest, but big enough. There's enough water on it to make it profitable unless a big drought comes along. We've got a few wells on it."

"I guess water's pretty important in that part of the country."

"It is, but oil pays better. Your daughter's rings are paid for. I wrote a check for them."

That got his new father-in-law's attention. Oh, yes, he could still see it. The excitement and the knowledge that he and his twin brothers could go to any school they wanted. It was fine when the others had come in, but that first one was a golden memory. Gramps had taken Mom into Austin for new clothes. He had known exactly what he had been doing when he picked out those rings.

"I'll tell Cindy soon. She deserves a chance to relax and enjoy the trip home. Right now I think she may be envisioning a future picking cotton and pinching pennies."

"That says something about how she feels about you." The man shook his head. "Lucy's never dated boys her own age. She's good in the kitchen, and she started helping with the younger ones as soon as they were born, but she won't have anything to do with yard work. How old are you?"

"Thirty."

"You're a lawyer, and you have money. How come you're only a sergeant?"

"I can put on the lonesome cowboy act when I need to. I tried to tell one of the twins why, but he didn't listen. Tim went to OCS and became one of those ninety day wonders. Dress up your uniform with anything above a sergeant's stripes and you're just making yourself a good target. I preferred trying to stay alive. I just wanted to tell you, so you wouldn't worry about Cindy. I'll take good care of her." David turned. He didn't want to get into the religious thing. "If it's alright with you, I'll take the boys for that ice cream now."

* * * * *

Lucy was closing the suitcase as Jack bounced through the door.

"We got chocolate and strawberry ice cream out here," he announced. "David took us after it in the convertible. He really is from Texas, and he says you're the prettiest girl he ever met. I'm supposed to put your suitcase in the trunk." He paused to take a breath. "He got shot in the hip and leg and he has the purple heart. He says if we visit, he'll teach us to ride a horse. He's swell, not like that loser Letitia's dating. You better keep him."

"Slow down," she told him. "He is swell, isn't he?" She was pleased with her brother's enthusiasm. "I plan on keeping him." She snapped the suitcase closed. "Mom, would you take my coat out? Jack, do you think you can get my easel and art supplies out from under the bed?"

After her mother left the room Lucy closed the door. She nodded to her brother as he held her box and easel.

"Why don't you boys like Eddie?"

"He's a creep, and he tries to get rid of us when we stay close to Lily."

"Lily?" That surprised her. "He comes to see Tish."

"Not after school. He's been here a lot of times in the afternoon. Lily's afraid of him. If you or Mom aren't here she wants us to stay in the same room with her. We can be real pests when we want to be. He sure gets mad at us, but we're sure not going to let him hurt Lily."

Lucy wondered if she had been missing something. Her brother's words disturbed her. She was glad David had made a conquest of at least one member of her family. She let Jack take the suitcase from the bed. She picked up the box with her sketches and art supplies. Taking that and her easel, she followed her brother out of the room. David and her father were sitting in the living room. She leaned the easel against the wall and sat next to her new husband, where he could put his arm around her.

"You really are an artist, honey?"

"I play around with charcoal when I have time."

"She's good," her father told him. "She did those pictures on the wall over there."

David rose and walked over to look at the two framed pictures of her parents. They were done in charcoal, but color was there in a threaded needle, scissors, and a bolt of cloth in her mother's background . Her father was surrounded by open ledgers, pens, and pencils. They weren't signed. He turned to look at her.

"That, my girl, is more than playing around with charcoal."

"It's just something I enjoy."

She's good," her father told him. "You got a prize when you latched on to Lucy."

That statement startled her, as did the way her father had calmed down and seemed to accept David.

"She's talented, and she's a good cook. She knows how to iron a shirt so it's done right, and she's had plenty of experience changing diapers." He looked at her. "Don't blush, Lucy. You've spent a couple of days and nights together so it's a possibility. You didn't need to make us worry about you though. Your mother's been going around here like a chicken with its head chopped off."

"You've done your share of that," her mother told him. "You better call the police and tell them she came home."

"I think they already know it," David told them. "We were stopped on the highway. Scared Cindy half to death by pointing guns at us. Guess they figured I'd assaulted her and was ready to finish her off."

Lucy saw Sophie on the porch swing and motioned for her to come in. "Thanks for the stolen car and kidnapping story. What prompted that flight of fancy?"

"I didn't know what to think. The last time I saw you - well when you weren't home in the morning - I know your opinion of tall, dark, and handsome, and he must be six feet if he's an inch." She grabbed Cindy's hand. "Where have you been?"

"Las Vegas." Wriggling loose, Lucy displayed her rings.

"Ooh." Sophie looked over to David. "What bank did you rob?"

"Never figured that to be a good idea," was his reply.

Lucy didn't know how, but evidently David had managed to win her father's approval. Either that, or her father was making the best of a bad situation.

She took her mother and Sophie out to the car and showed them the western outfit David had bought for her; gave her mother the silver broach, took the bolo tie in for her father; and gave the boys the belts and holsters.

They told them all about the colonel and his wife and the Las Vegas hotel, and showed them the pictures that had been taken during the ceremony. Her mother sent the boys to clean up and put on their Sunday clothes. When Leticia and Lily came home everyone hugged and kissed and told it all over again. Both girls liked the earrings. Lucy had been sure they would.

Reservations had been made for six, but Tish's sailor wasn't picking her up until six-thirty, so David called and changed the time to seven and told them there would be one more than originally planned.

At one point in the afternoon, the two men took off. When they came back they had camellia corsages. Her mother and the girls' were white. Lucy's was a deep rose color. She didn't say anything, but she thought a lot. David was going to have to learn to be a little careful about his spending habits. Just by itself dinner was going to cost a fortune. At least she had talked him out of the Brown Derby.

Chapter 15

Lucy helped the boys with their neckties. When it was time to leave the three didn't have to ask to ride in the convertible. David just said, "Hop in boys." He opened the door for her. "Hang onto your hat, honey. We'll leave the top down."

Her parents and Lily took the family car, and Tish rode with her sailor in the old Chevy he had arrived in. Lucy noted that he did not open the car door for her sister. "Get your little behind in," was what he said.

"He could have asked Mom and Dad to ride with them," she told David. "It would have saved Dad's gas coupons."

"Lily wouldn't ride with him," Jason said. "She hates him."

"Sure wish you weren't going all the way to Texas," Jack told them.

Lucy smiled, thinking that the convertible had something to do with that remark.

In the restaurant the waiter asked if the boys would be wanting the children's plate.

"Goodness, no," her mother told him after she had looked at the menu. "They will eat it all and ask to finish mine. David, since this is a special occasion, why don't we all just order the sauerbraten? That is, if you like beef."

"I certainly do, ma'am. I'm looking forward to getting back to eating our own home grown meat. We always pamper a couple of young steers by feeding them corn. Gramps is probably getting ready to butcher one about now." He looked at the waiter. "Sauerbraten all around, and if I could see the wine menu?"

Lucy smiled. There it was again, the mixture of a down-home country boy and suave man about town. If nothing else, she had fallen in love with a very interesting man.

"No girly drink for me," Eddie announced. "Me and the little girl here'll have a beer, and that there soubr'nt don't sound very American to me. Since the army's paying I'll have a T-bone and make sure it's done good. Don't like eating an animal before it's been killed."

Lucy glanced at her sister, then at her father. She was quick to look away from his frown of disapproval . Was Eddie trying to be as ill-mannered as possible, or just didn't he know any better? How stupid could Trish be to be dating such a loud mouthed idiot? The waiter was the only one who managed to keep a smile. "Your ID, miss."

"Oh, I'll have ice tea." Her eighteen-year-old sister looked uncomfortable as she spoke. "I don't drink."

"Lily, what would you like?" David words were quiet. "I didn't mean to exclude you two girls."

"Tea's fine for me."

"Lucy just ran off to Las Vegas and married David," Jimmy told the waiter. "He's a whole lot nicer than some boyfriends."

"Don't talk so much," her mother told him.

"That's all right, ma'am." The waiter just smiled. "Boys will be boys." On his way to the kitchen he paused by the gypsy violinist who was soon at the table serenading them. That made the place perfect as far as Lucy was concerned. It was one of the reasons she had suggested the restaurant. David seemed to be getting along surprisingly well with her father.

"Cindy tells me you're a bookkeeper," he was saying. "Have you been with CBS long?

"Fifteen years. I was with a radio station in Chicago before we came out here."

"Is it a good place to work?"

"Lucy," Tish asked, "where's the ladies room? "

"I'll show you." Wondering if her sister wanted to talk to her, she picked up her purse as she rose.

* * * * *

"I didn't have a chance to talk to you alone at home," her sister said as she emerged from the stall and started washing her hands. "It looks like we both made the same mistake at the same time. How far along are you?"

You're not. . ." Lipstick in hand, she turned from the mirror. "Oh, Tish, don't tell me you're pregnant."

"We're going to get married. Eddie's father is a minister and he wants him to marry us."

"That's not why I married David." She just looked at her sister, not wanting to believe what she was hearing. "Don't do it. Not Eddie. You deserve someone better."

"Isn't that what Mom and Dad told you about Jerry? It didn't stop you, did it?"

"I didn't sleep with Jerry. "

"Sure. you didn't," her sister sneered. "Remember how we used to worry about undressing. Ridiculous, wasn't it?" Letitia giggled as she reached for a paper towel. "Eddie loves watching me. You know how it is. Men have needs. It's important for their health." She looked away, her voice faltering. "He said if I really loved him - after all it's what we women are supposed to. . ." Her words trailed off.

"You didn't fall for that line?" Lucy asked. "Tish, how could you? He has the manners of a pig, and he drinks too much. Jack says Lily's afraid of him."

"It isn't a line, and Lily's jealous. He told me how she came on to him. We're getting married."

"Don't do it."

"I love him, and he loves me. We can't wait much longer. I'm three months along. I'll start showing soon, so we have to get married right away."

"No you don't." She felt like shaking her sister. "I think the church has a home for unwed mothers-to-be. Mom and Dad can talk to Father Reilly. I don't envy you telling them. It's going to take their minds off me. That's for sure."

"Eddie's from Georgia. We'll get married there. He and his father both want it that way. His father's a minister."

"If he's from Georgia, he sure lost his southern accent. Don't do it. He's about the rudest person I've ever seen."

"You're not the only one who can snag a husband."

"I did not. . ."

"Sure you didn't." Trish discarded the paper towel. "You just climb out a window on Wednesday night and come home Saturday in a convertible and wearing expensive new clothes. Well, I'm just as tired of it all as you are. Yeah, don't get a good paying wartime job, Dad says. Just keep on being cooped up in an office while your family's living in a dinky little house and helping pay the bills. Maybe he'll still have a job, but he'll never move to a house big enough for all of us. Well, Lily's lucky. She's finally going to have a room all to herself. I took my money out of the bank Friday, and we're leaving tomorrow."

"Well, I hope you have enough sense to keep it in your own purse." She was angry that her sister could be so stupid. When had she changed so? From the sound of it, Eddie's ways were rubbing off on her. Had she been feeling so sorry for herself that she hadn't noticed what was happening to her sister?

"A man takes care of his woman, and Eddie's all man. He said a hundred and thirty two dollars isn't much, but with what he's got we'll get to Georgia."

The way she said it told Lucy her sister had already turned over her meager savings.

"His folks have a resort on a lake, and his father's a minister. You could be a little happy for me."

"I wish I could be." On an impulse, Lucy opened her purse and took out the bills David had given her, holding them between her fingers for a moment. "I'll give these to you if you promise to keep them hidden in the back of your wallet and not tell Eddie you have them."

"That doesn't seem right," Lily pouted. "It would make it seem like I don't trust him."

"I'm your sister. Trust me on this. Promise me, Letitia. If you ever need me, call me. Keep them hidden or they go back in my purse. It's a hundred dollars."

"I don't like it, but I promise." Her eyes were focused on the money.

"Good." She folded the bills and tucked them between the pictures in her sister's wallet. "Tomorrow we'll talk about how to tell Mom and Dad."

Tish turned and walked out of the ladies room. Lucy followed, not knowing what else she could say. She certainly hadn't expected that conversation. She only hoped David wouldn't mind that she had given her the money. Monday she would close out her own small bank account. When the two reached the table salads had been served, and a waiter was offering David a sample of the wine.

"It will do," he told the man who then started pouring. She was surprised when her father had no comment as her glass was filled.

"You have a husband to care for you now," he told her. "You answer to him, not me. David, are you taking Route 66?".

"Part of the road needs work, but it's still the best way to go," David said. "We're going to take our time going home. At Winslow we'll make a detour to the Grand Canyon. I want Cindy to see it. They tell me it is really worth the trip. I want to see it myself. If it's open, I hear they have a half decent hotel there."

"I imagine it's changed a good deal since we drove it in 1930."

"Cindy didn't mention that."

"She was not quite six. When we were going over some of those mountains she had her head covered up. I've always figured after that she decided nothing else could scare her. She hasn't been afraid of anything since. There were some sad sights along that road back then."

"I have four new tires and a good spare. One of the mechanics at the fort scrounged them for me. I wrecked two coming across.

Those army convoys tore things up in quite a few spots." David looked her way. "Do you have a camera, Cindy?"

"A cheap one, but it takes good pictures."

"We'll stock up on film."

"Why do you call her Cindy?" Jack asked. "Her name's Lucy."

David reached for her hand. "Just my name for her. She looks more like a Cindy than a Lucy."

"That's nuts."

"No it isn't," Jason said. "She looks like Cinderella in that dress."

"Maybe she is at that," David told him. He looked at her father. "Mr. Rollins, if one of the girls will baby sit tomorrow night, we would like to take you and Mrs. Rollins to the Brown Derby."

"David, I thought we settled that. You can't keep spending money like this."

"Just the four of us, Cindy girl. The old man would have my hide if he found out I didn't go when I had the chance."

"I think Lily could stay with the boys. I guess you know about taking extra water and gas across the desert. I imagine there are more motor courts than when we made the trip."

That trip from Grandma and Grandpa Smith's was only a dim memory. Mostly Lucy remembered her parents singing *California Here We Come,* Tish asking when they were going to get to Uncle Brad's, and the smell of Lily's diapers. For a good part of the trip baby Lily had been in a basket between her and Tish.

"Have you read Steinbeck's *Grapes of Wrath?*" he mother asked.

"Mom had us all read it." He was suddenly serious. "She told us to say a prayer of thanks that we didn't have to live it."

"Sounds like she's a good woman," her mother said. "Did your father agree?"

"She is, Ma'am. We lost Pop when I was thirteen."

"Oh, I am sorry."

"One of those things." He hesitated. "He and a bull got in an argument and the bull had a few too many pounds on him. My grandfather kept us all in line though. Sometimes I've thought he was stricter than my father ever would have been."

It was all quiet for a moment.

"This meat's as good as Lucy makes," Jimmy piped up, breaking the silence. "Do we get dessert, too?"

"Ask your mother," David told him.

When Eddie and Tish decided to leave early, Lucy thought of the first time she had seen her sister with the sailor. There was just something about him she didn't like, especially after what Jack had said. From the breath he usually had, he probably drank too much.. She had noticed that though Eddie had offered the chair next to him, Lily had taken a seat between Jason and Jack. "David, do you happen to have one of those business cards of yours?"

"Jefferson, Colby, and Smith would fire me if I didn't."

"Could we give one to Lily and Tish? I'd like my sisters to know where we'll be."

Willingly he not only gave cards to both girls but to her father and the boys as well.

"We'll be at the house in the morning," she told Tish as she and the sailor left. "We will have a chance to talk some more then."

Chapter 16

Lucy was well aware that the lace gown David had picked out was not going to stay on long, but she enjoyed knowing that he was watching as she slipped into it. She had never even thought of owning, much less wearing, anything like it.

"You were right," he told her. "It was the perfect place to take the family. The boys got a kick out of that violinist."

"They're firmly convinced he really is a gypsy."

"He made quite a sight in that costume and he plays quite well. We'll have to have the boys visit us. I promised to teach them to ride."

"I really don't think Dad can afford trips across the country."

"We'll take care of that." He reached for her hand, pulling her down to his lap. "Just the family though. No boyfriends."

"Does that mean you have the same opinion of Eddie as I do?"

"Your sister could do a lot better. I have seen his type too often. Have they been going together long?"

"A little over four months. I've heard people saying things about someone being born in a barn, but I think a pig sty would be more like it for him, and to say Tish wanted a beer right in front of my parents - that was uncalled for. He likes showing those tattoos to the boys. I don't know why sailors think it's so cool to get the ugly things."

"They figure it makes them men. I hope your sister's not serious about him."

"She told me she's three months pregnant." She frowned. "She said they're going to get married at his home in Georgia. It seems his father is a minister. She told me that three or four times. She also said they have lakeside resort there. The more I think of that the odder it sounds. What's a minister doing running a resort? Jack said Lily wanted the three of them to stay close when he was around. He thinks she's afraid of him. Evidently he's been around when Mom and I weren't."

"I don't like the sound of that. Is that why you gave her my card?" He put his arms around her. "You take care of them, don't you?"

"I always have." All at once she realized that she was going to miss them. She could still remember the day her father had come home with the news about the boys. It had been almost two whole days after Dad had taken Mom to the hospital.

She had been looking forward to her twelfth birthday when her mother had told her and her sisters she was going to have a baby. She promptly did what she always did. She went to the library to find books about pregnancy and babies.

She had decided early on that she could find the answer to anything in the library. With increasing frequency, she was finding out that what she learned on her own didn't always agree with what Father O'Toole preached. It was hard to forget how the librarian had looked at the books she was checking out and had peered over her glasses at her, the woman's gray hair almost slipping out its sturdy bun. Miss Emily Grote went to St. Bartholomew's and was Mom's friend.

"Lucy Rollins, you haven't gone and gotten yourself in trouble, have you?"

"Mom's going to have a baby, and I want to know what she's supposed to do or not do. I heard Aunt Jane say thirty-nine is too old to be having babies."

"Well, I'll just say it is a bit unusual." She stamped the cards. "Maybe when you finish these you might want to read something on baby care. I imagine Gracie will need help."

Miss Grote hadn't had any idea how true her words had been. She was wearing an apron over her school dress when her father had walked through the back door. She had just finished making scrambled egg sandwiches for the lunch bags. Little Lily had been putting them into the brown paper bags, and Tish had been washing up the breakfast dishes. She had been worried. She had read about women dying when they gave birth. Mom had been so tired for the last few months.

"Aunt Jane brought supper over last night. Did Mom have the baby yet?"

"Is it a boy or a girl?" Tish asked.

"The doctor had to do what they call a Caesarian, but she's resting easy."

"What's a ca-caesarian?" Lilly stumbled over the word.

"It's an operation to take the baby out." She had been surprised at how disheveled her father had looked. It was unusual to see him with his tie hanging loose and in a wrinkled shirt with the top buttons undone. *"Do we have another sister?"*

"I'm going to need your help today, Lucy, but first do you suppose I could have one of those sandwiches?" He was running his hand through his hair. His glance rested on the lunch bags Lil had so carefully wrapped.

"I have time to fix you some fried eggs."

"The sandwich will do."

"Dad," Tish screeched, "is it a boy or a girl?"

"Boys." He reached for one of the bags.

"Twins? Do they look alike?"

"Triplets. Far as we can tell, you look at one you're seeing all three." He unwrapped the sandwich and opened the ice box for the milk bottle. Lucy put a clean glass on the table. "We named them James, Jackson, and Jason. The nurses tied ribbons around their ankles so we can tell which is which. Letitia, I want you and Lil to go on to school. Lucy, you'll have to miss school today. We need to go back down to that used furniture store. One crib isn't going to be

enough. Uncle Brad has a friend with a truck. He's going to borrow it and meet us there."

She could still remember the feeling that had gone through her with that statement. Dad and Uncle Brad had added the third bedroom just the year before, and it had been hers. She had enjoyed the brief time she had with her own room. Lily had inherited the spot in the double bed beside Tish. Her parents had gotten Lil's old crib from the attic and set it up in their own bedroom. Not voicing her thoughts, she had just gotten into the car and tried to enjoy sitting in the front seat with her father, but hovering deep inside her had been the image of three cribs that would have to fit somewhere in the small house. Triplets. No wonder Mom had gotten so big. It wasn't until they were in the shabby store in downtown L.A. that she had finally commented.

"Dad, those two extra cribs aren't going to fit in you and Mom's room."

"Princess, you're just going to have to move back in with Tish and Lily."

"Dad." It wasn't fair. "I'm too old for that. We can't sleep three in a bed like some old hillbilly family. I'm a young woman now." She blushed, not wanting to mention her periods had started a few months earlier.

"It will only be for now, Lucy. Things will improve. I'll be getting a raise, and we can find a bigger house."

"I have two daybeds cheap," the store owner chimed in. "Maybe there is room for one of them. They don't take up as much room as a bed." Eagerly he led them to the other side of the store. At one time one of the two daybeds may have been a handsome thing with carved walnut arms and back, but it was marred by scratches and gouges. The shop owner had managed to polish the brass of the second specimen.

"Seven dollars for this one. Ten for the brass. It's a nice piece for such a pretty girl."

"I don't know, Lucy. It's just that we weren't expecting three babies. Your mama won't be able to nurse them, so that means buying formula and three times the diapers." Mark looked at his brother-in-law. "We were just starting to get ahead of things, and

now this. I know babies are a blessing, but it's more blessing than we needed right now."

"Maybe nine for the brass one," the man told them.

She hadn't said a thing, afraid she would start crying if she did. She would have rather slept on the floor than three in a bed.

"I'll buy it for her," Uncle Brad suddenly said. "It should fit under the window in that room."

"I'll buy it for you, Princess." Her father sighed. "I'll have the single bed to sell. Can we make a deal?" he asked the man.

The thing wrong with the memory was that things hadn't gotten any better. The promised bigger house had never materialized. Her hated daybed was still by the window. Maybe that was what had driven Letitia into Eddie's arms. She did smile at the memory of what she had done the day the triplets came home.

"What are you thinking about?" David's voice brought her back to the present. "You looked as though you were miles away."

"Just thinking about the day the boys were born. I missed the final arithmetic test that day, but the teacher let me make it up. I was afraid they would lose the ribbons the nurses had tied on, so I put nail polish on their toenails. Dad had a fit, but we kept doing it until they started to school, and Jason got hold of my polish remover."

"Were your parents expecting triplets?"

"Later mom told me the doctor had said maybe twins, but they only had one crib ready. Dad and Uncle Brad had just finished adding my bedroom on the year before. I had to move back in with Tish and Lil." She touched his hand. "I hope you don't mind. I put the hundred dollars you gave me between the pictures in Tish's wallet. She let Eddie take what she had. I'll close out my own account before we leave. I'm going to try to talk to her again tomorrow."

"Let's hope she keeps it. Maybe your mother should talk to her."

"There isn't going to be any way to avoid telling both of them . Us getting married is one thing, but Tish getting pregnant without being married is going to be a whole lot worse."

"That's understandable."

"I argue with Dad. Tish has always been so quiet it's hard to tell how she feels It bothered her more than it did me that we didn't have much of an allowance in school. The boys were very well behaved, weren't they?" She didn't want to talk about her sister. "It was their first experience with eating out."

"They were perfect little gentlemen weren't they? Are they always so well behaved?"

"If there's a chance to get in trouble, they'll find it."

"That's what I figured. That's why I promised them five dollars apiece for behaving themselves."

"You didn't?"

"It worked."

" David, they only get fifty cents a week for an allowance."

"I know. They told me. I like your family. Reminds me of home when we were younger." He was pushing up the red lace. "Would I be out of line if I asked about that tall, dark, handsome thing?"

"I must have forgotten about it when I saw you. I always thought too tall would hurt my neck looking up. Too good looking usually thinks he's God's gift to women." She looked at him and smiled. "I was wrong. Watching you when you were half a block away, I was hoping you'd see me. I guess there really is an exception to every rule. You are perfect." She lifted her hips a bit, making it easier for his efforts with the gown. "I never believed in love at first sight, but the minute you touched me it was almost like an electric shock. I told my mother that when you make love to me nothing else matters. I don't know how it happened, but I love you. I don't know what good I'll be on a farm, but I'll try."

"You'll be just what I need, but I'm beginning to see we're going to have a real problem with you nagging me about my spending habits."

"Nagging?" she asked. "Is that what I've been doing?"

"Close to it, but I've enjoyed hearing you worry about money." His hand left the lace to caress her face. "Think maybe it's time I tell you how it really is. It's told me a lot about you, and to be honest, it's mighty nice knowing you married me, not the Diamond MiK."

"The Diamond what?"

"Our ranch. It's actually supposed to be the Diamond MK, but Timothy started pronouncing it MiK when he was learning to talk, and we all picked it up."

"A ranch like in the movies?" Her skepticism showed.

"Hollywood pretties it up a bit. We don't have a lot of range wars or Indians with tomahawks. When I told your father I won't know about the stock until we round them up this fall, I meant it."

"Does that make you a cowboy or a lawyer?" *Just how much was she supposed to find out in one day? First he was a lawyer. Now a rancher?*

"That's debatable. I'm not sure how things are going to play out. Timothy was the one who was starting to take charge. Now we'll have to wait and see. Taylor was going to be a vet. He would have made a fine one. He was good around the animals. I told your father so he wouldn't be worried about you. He managed to give me some fatherly advice."

"When did he have a chance to do that?"

"When we went for the corsages. He said you're bossy, but you'll probably settle down with a home of your own. I promised him you would have that. I'm supposed to be honest with you, not keep secrets, and he doesn't think you'd take it very well if I took up with any other women."

"He's right about that." She didn't add that it would about break her heart in two. "Mom said no secrets and keep you happy. I took that to mean in bed. She also said to talk to each other."

"About the secret thing. The firm wants me back. Just let me enjoy doing things for you. My bank account is a little more than adequate. Jefferson, Colby, and Smith aren't stingy when it comes to charging hours, and I've made a few profitable investments." He gave her one of his gentle kisses. "Did you really tell your mother that?"

"Uh-huh. Funny, I pictured you in a western, but I cast you as the villain, not the owner. Is your ranch big?"

"Big enough. While we're talking, maybe there's another item we should clear up. We've had a pretty intense few days. Kissing you? Girl, I've never had anyone hit me the way you did. I just plain had to have you as soon as possible, and I had the feeling maybe you felt the same."

"I did."

This afternoon when you said you weren't a very good Catholic, did you mean that?"

"I always mean what I say." She drew back a little to look up at him. "We didn't go to Catholic schools. In catechism class I got mad at the priest when he said women couldn't be priests. I shocked my parents when I refused to believe that God chooses the Pope. I told them that the Cardinals do, and that they are just a bunch of old men. I told Father O'Toole that I should be allowed to read what I wanted without having the church tell me what they didn't want me to read. Since I left high school I don't remember the last time I went to confession, although Mom and Dad don't know that."

"Are you an atheist?"

"No." She shook her head. "I just believe that God is for everyone. I've read a lot of books. God is bigger than any one church or any one name. All religions seems to believe in the same basic ten commandments. Father O'Toole didn't seem too happy when he saw I had a book about the early days of the church. I've never been able to decide if those men that put the bible together hated women or were afraid of us. They sure made us insignificant."

"Mamaw Deedee's going to love you," he whispered. "We go to a little Methodist church in the country and a bigger one when we're in Austin. Will you go with us?"

"Wither though goest, I will go. Thy people shall be my people."

"The book of Ruth."

"I do know the bible. Its stories show how people should live. It's about right and wrong." She hesitated. "Mom did tell me she has one secret she's never told Dad."

"That blows that bit of advice."

"She's wise not to tell him." Cindy smiled at the memory. "She doesn't always vote for whoever Dad tells her to vote for. Are you going to tell me who to vote for?"

That brought a smile to his face. “Honey, you climb through windows. Heaven help the man who tells you what to do.”

“With you being a college graduate and a lawyer,” she asked, “shouldn’t you have been an officer? I thought men like that were sent to OCS and came out second lieutenants”

“Your father asked me the same thing. I didn’t want to be an officer. I just put on a good old boy act to convince them I was just another cowboy. They didn’t buy it, but I rejected the idea. The last thing I wanted was to go to Officers Candidate School.”

“When are you going to wear that sport jacket you have in your duffle bag?”

“As long as we’re traveling the uniform is an asset. I’ll get into civvies when we get home. Now quit talking, Mrs. McKaid, and kiss me.”

She quit worrying about what she was going to do about Tish. It could wait until tomorrow.

Chapter 17

Sunday morning Lucy gently refused to wear another of her new dresses. She was actually starting to think of herself as Cindy, but thought her parents would be more comfortable seeing her in something familiar. "Mom doesn't have anything really special to wear tonight," she explained to David.

"Love you in anything you have on," had been his reply, "and all those buttons down the back might make it more fun undressing you when we get back. That extra little skirt around your waist is sort of sexy."

"It's called a peplum." Surveying herself in the mirror, she had never considered the green two piece dress sexy, but then David seemed to think that about anything she wore. She put the red hat on her head and was pulling on the red gloves when it suddenly occurred to her that this was the way she had been dressed the night she had met Jerry. Sophie had laughed at the idea of the red and green combination in September.

Both Dorsey brothers were getting together after years of almost hating each other. She and Sophie and Tish had decided that nothing would keep them away from that. Getting to the pier wasn't like walking down to Sunset Boulevard to the Palladium. They had to take the red car out to the beach, and they had to watch the time so they wouldn't miss the last car of the night to get home. Sophie and Leticia had both worn sweaters, but she had figured that the ballroom on the pier would be stuffed to the gills with people.

She had been right about the crowd. After being used to the Palladium, it was surprising to realize the ball room just looked like an old barn with Jimmy Dorsey's band at one end and Tommy at the other. Since she just adored Tommy and his trombone they stood close to his end, watching the band play, when a sailor asked her to dance.

When Jimmy band started playing another sailor tapped her on the shoulder.

"Where do I buy the tickets?" he asked.

She didn't need his accent to know he was from New York. A lot of those boys from New York and New Jersey asked the same question at the Palladium.

"We don't have Dime a Dance *places here. We just come to listen and dance."*

After one dance with a fourth sailor she managed to steer him over in front of the bandstand and introduce him to Leticia, where she suggested he have the next dance with her. As she turned back to watch the band play, she had bumped into a well worn jacket. It's owner smelled of peppermint.

"That was nice of you."

His sun bleached hair had been as rumpled as his clothes, tan trousers, plaid jacket, and a plaid shirt that had probably never known a tie. Evidently he hadn't bothered to shave for the evening because there was more than just a hint of five o'clock shadow. His smile was nice though, as if truly appreciating her, not looking her over like a hawk ready to dive on its prey.

"She's my sister and a little shy."

"Dance?" he held out his hand. "It's not often the prettiest girl in sight almost falls into my arms."

Tommy's band was playing Paper Doll. *They edged into the dancing crowd.*

"My name's Jerry." He was a couple inches taller than her and her high heels, but not so tall as to be uncomfortable.

"I'm Lucy."

"Hello, Lucy. I was wondering how I could get you away from the navy. Four of them in a row. One dance apiece."

"I was looking for one safe for my sister."

"What's your criteria?"

"First one claimed to be shipping out tomorrow morning."

"That's bad?"

"Make me happy, baby. Be patriotic, and send a fellow off with a beautiful memory."

They danced together very nicely.

"So what wrong with that?"

"You're kidding, I hope."

"Yeah, I guess I am. How about the second?"

"Why does a sailor have thirteen buttons on his uniform?"

"I suppose you know the answer."

"Every girl in L.A. knows that one. To give a girl thirteen chances to say no."

"I'll have to remember not to use that if I'm ever in the navy. How did number three fail?"

"Beer breath."

"You're particular."

"About my sister? You better believe it."

The number ended and they stood there waiting for the next one. He was holding her hand.

"If I'm number five for another sister I pass. I like you."

"Lily's at home. She's too young. Sophie lives across the street. She can take care of herself."

As the band started playing Besame Mucho, *they started dancing again. He had been a pretty good dancer, and he had started crooning the words real soft like. His voice wasn't half bad. They had found themselves close to a wall and somehow had stopped dancing. Lucy leaned against the wall because there wasn't any place to sit. He lifted her left hand.*

"Has every man in L.A. lost his mind?" he asked.

"What is that supposed to mean?"

"The prettiest girl here and no ring on your finger."

"Maybe I just haven't met the right man yet."

"Life Saver?" He pulled a roll from his pocket. So that's why he smelled of peppermint. "You smoke?"

"I tried it when I was seventeen and didn't like it." She slipped the Life Saver into her mouth.

"Good, I hate kissing a girl who tastes like tobacco."

"What makes you think you're going to kiss me?"

"Maybe not tonight, but I will." He took her arm. He was looking at his watch.

"I'd better find my sister and friend," she told him

"Not yet. We can't talk here. Did you get your hand stamped when you came in?" She nodded. "There's a bar across the way. We could get to know each other over there. They're only serving soft drinks here."

He had been easing her toward the exit, and that had made her nervous. He had surprised her though, stopping by the door, nodding to the man sitting at the table.

"This is Lucy. We're going to duck out for half an hour. She's got a sister and girl friend here." He looked at her. "Their names again?"

"Leticia and Sophie." That had made her feel better. If he had had anything nasty in mind, he wouldn't have done that. Outside she had looked at him. "Are you with one of the bands?"

"Moonlighting with security."

After the heat in the ballroom the night air was chilly. She was wishing she'd worn her suit. There was barely enough moonlight to keep them from stumbling as they hurried across the boardwalk and around to a darkened door. The place was as bare as the ballroom. Plain old wood, with a few tables, and three booths, one of which they had headed for. There were only a couple of people in the place.

"Everyone must be over with the bands. What do you drink?"

"Rum and Coke."

He had gone over to the bar and came back with the drinks and a bowl of pretzels. He sat down next to her, and put his arm around her.

"You're cold, girl."

"I'll warm up."

"Glad to hear that."

She had picked up a pretzel, realizing how he might interpret that remark. "I should have had a jacket," she added.

"Evenings on the beach can get cold. You have a job?"

"I run a spot welding machine."

"A little thing like you welding? That doesn't seem right."

"A big machine with levers and buttons. It's not hard work. We're supposed to pick things up ourselves, but usually some of the men do it for us if it's heavy. It's a small place. We're working ten hours a day, six days a weeks."

"You ought to be making good money."

"I give my father a good deal of it and buy a few things for Mom. My three brothers eat a lot." She had munched on a pretzel and washed it down with a few sips of her drink.

"That's quite a houseful. Three brothers and a sister."

"Two sisters. Lily is only fourteen. She's mad because Dad said she was too young to come tonight. How about you? Do you have any brothers and sisters?"

"An only child. Mom must have figured one of me was enough."

She had munched on a few more pretzels and downed a few more sips of rum and coke. Jerry had been doing the same, his arm still around her.

"What do you do?"

"A little of this, and a little of that. I answer a few casting calls when I get the chance."

They were facing the door, so she had seen the man come in, look around, and head for their booth. He had placed his newspaper on the table.

"Pretty girl, Jerry."

"Yeah, she is." He hadn't introduced her. "I'll see you later."

"Downtown next time."

The man had walked over to the bar and ordered a beer. Jerry had picked up the newspaper, and after a few minutes slipped an envelope into his inside pocket.

"Still cold?"

"Some. I should have had better sense than to leave my sweater at home."

"Let me take you and the other two home. My car's nothing to brag about, but it runs." He had taken off his jacket and put it around her shoulders. While doing it he had managed to kiss her cheek. "That's for starters. We can do it better later

"Better save your gas," she told him. "We live in Hollywood."

"Almost on my way." He had leaned over and kissed her cheek again. "I could get in the habit of doing this."

When they got back to the ballroom the band was playing They're Either Too Young or Too Old. *He took his jacket back, and when they started* I'll Be Seeing You, *they danced. He crooned the words a good deal of the time. Evidently he was one of the Hollywood Hopefuls*

A few dances later they collected Leticia and Sophie, and with the two of them in the back seat of an old Ford they had headed for Hollywood.

Jerry had stopped the car in front of the house. Sophie slipped out and headed across the street to her place. Leticia hesitated.

"I'll be in a few minutes" she had told her, and Leticia said, "Sure, you will," and gone inside. As soon as he saw the door close Jerry put his arms around her and it wasn't anything like the brief kiss in the bar had been. When he lifted his head his fingers played around her ears.

"This isn't a good idea, girl. Not for me, and it sure isn't for you, but I want to see you again."

"Are you married?" She was not going to get involved with a married man, even if she did find him attractive.

"No. but I used you tonight and I don't think you're that kind of a girl."

"What was in the envelope?" She had been wondering all along. It didn't exactly seem to be anything honest.

"He owed me some money. What are you? Twenty-two, twenty-three?"

"Nineteen."

He looked over to the small house. "Must be pretty crowded."

"We manage"

"What would you say if I told you I've got a flat not too far away?" He was still playing around with her ear.

"I'd say I'd better go in. I usually cook Sunday dinner so Mom can go to church with the boys. That means I have to get up for early Mass."

"Damn it, girl, we really aren't good for each other." But he had kissed her again and walked her to the door, where there was another long kiss. "Can't seem to stop doing that. I'll pick you up at six-thirty."

She turned from the mirror. He hadn't been worth it. It had been almost eight when he had shown up. All the broken dates, the tears and heartaches. The moment David had kissed her she had known that what she had felt for Jerry was nothing like the way David made her feel.

"I love you, David Stanley McKaid," she whispered as she took his hand. "I'm so glad I went down to Hill Street."

"You're going to miss your family. You're almost a second mother to them."

"The difference is, I might miss them, but I couldn't bear to be away from you."

"We'd better go. You want to talk to your sister."

Chapter 18

Cindy was alarmed when her youngest sister hopped off the porch swing and rushed to the car almost before David turned off the key.

"We've got a problem, Lucinda."

It wasn't the words which alarmed her, as much as the tone and the haste. Lil using her full name let her know it must be a real problem. A look that serious wasn't a time for nicknames. She reached out to her sister. "It can't be that bad."

"It's worse. Letitia's gone. After I went in our room last night all her things were gone." The words were tumbling out as fast as she could say them. "After you left last night, I went in and every last thing she owns was gone. I mean. after the way Dad carried on when you didn't come home - I didn't know what to do. I was afraid to say anything. I wanted to ask you what to do, but I didn't want to use the telephone. Mom and Dad might have heard me. This morning I just told Mom Tish had a headache and needed to sleep in, and that I would stay home from church to take care of her. It will be about half an hour before there're back. I don't know what to do. How am I going to tell them? Dad's going to hit the ceiling."

"Slow down," David told her. "Let's go in the house and talk this over. Last night she told your big sister there were complications."

"Yeah, she's stupid and in real trouble."

The three of them went into the house.

"How old is she?" David asked.

"Eighteen." Lucy said. "No one is going believe she was kidnapped. Dad will call the police again."

"It won't do any good. I'm not up on California law, but I'm pretty sure at eighteen she can do as she pleases."

"She's dumber than I thought she was. She's going to have a baby." Lily's tone let them know what she thought of that.

"She told you?" Lucy asked. That was a surprise.

"No," Tish frowned at her, "but I'm not stupid. For awhile she was throwing up every morning, and she's always had bad cramps every month. She usually asks me for some of my Kotex. I don't know what she spends her money on. She's always broke. She's not going to be able to keep it a secret much longer. What she sees in that bum I'll never know."

"Jack told me you're afraid of him. Has he ever touched you?"

"He tried, but I took care of that." Her youngest sister's words had an almost triumphant ring to them. "The jerk's really mad at me. I just don't want him to have a chance to get even with me."

"What happened?"

"I was picking up after the boys one day. They had left some cars and trucks in the middle of the living room floor. They were out shopping with Mom. Eddie just walked in and put his arm around me. I told him not to, and he just said something about it being time I learned how to treat a man." She looked at Lucy. "You know how you told me to jab a man with my knee. Well it really works. He yelled and grabbed himself and started swearing at me. He was using words even the boys in school don't use." She saw David flinch. "Actually he was down on the floor swearing at me and calling me all sorts of nasty names, so I kicked him as well."

"I didn't know what to do. I was afraid to stay in the house with him, but I didn't want him near me, so I went out on the porch and sat on the swing, but I picked up the baseball bat first. I think it was a good thing Mom drove in when she did. The boys brought in the groceries. When we went inside Eddie was sitting on the divan. After awhile he mumbled something about coming back when Letitia got home and left. He's come around a couple of times, but the boys stay around when that happens."

Lucy just stared at her sister. Lil had always been the closest thing the family had to a tomboy, but she had never imagined her capable of anything like that. David was just shaking his head.

"You Rollins girls beat anything I've ever encountered. Hat pins and baseball bats. Heaven help the man who tries anything with either of you. Unfortunately, I have a feeling Letitia isn't as astute."

'From what she said last night," she remarked, "she fell for that *men have needs* line."

"Any idea of how to tell your parents?"

"I hate to spoil the day for Mom," Lil said. "She is really excited about going to the Brown Derby, and she doesn't get to go out very often."

"I imagine she is." Lucy thought a moment. "Mom and Dad don't ever go anywhere except to Aunt Jane's and Uncle Brad's. Let's not tell them right away. You've already lied to them. Once more won't hurt. We can tell them Eddie came by and they went out for lunch and a movie. You can offer to watch the boys, and we won't say anything until we get home."

"Better still," David offered, "we'll tell them at the restaurant after we finish dinner and a drink or two. That way we can talk calmly and quietly, and the boys won't have to hear it all."

She liked that idea because she couldn't imagine her father making a scene in public. She just wanted her last day at home to be as pleasant as possible.

Lucy put on an apron and opened the ice box.

"Since we're going out tonight we don't need much for lunch, but the boys and you have to eat."

"Why don't we just have sandwiches?" Lily asked. The boys will like that."

She took an egg carton from the ice box. "David, will you take Lil down to the store and pick up a dozen eggs, and some potato chips? I'll boil these and we'll have egg salad sandwiches."

"You really do know how to cook?" He seemed amused.

"I started cooking when I was eleven."

Lucy was alone when her parents and the boys came from church. They weren't too pleased to discover that the daughter who had had a headache wicked enough to keep her away from church had managed to recover enough to go out with her boyfriend. However, they accepted the story, and the family spent a good part of the day with a monopoly board on the dining room table.

At the Brown Derby, Lucy was quite aware that even though they had reservations, a crisp new bill had exchanged hands. The McKaids and Rollins were seated at a very prominent table. The food was fine, the service excellent, and the conversation centered around talk of Texas weather, her father's job, and tales of childhood. Lucy was surprised at how interested David was in the details of her father's work. It was during desert and coffee that David became serious.

"I realize our marriage came as quite a shock to both of you. It wasn't something we planned. It just happened, but we're confident that we did the right thing. Unfortunately all surprises aren't always pleasant. Cindy has something she wants to tell you. We would appreciate it is you listened quietly."

"I should have known," her father said. "You're in the family way." His hand went to the glass in front of him.

"No," she reached across the table. "Don't pick up that glass yet. I wouldn't want to see you spill it. I'm not the one you have to worry about. Lil didn't know quite how to tell you, so she concocted that story of a headache." She kept her voice calm and steady, keeping her eyes on her father. "Last night there was a reason Tish and Eddie left the restaurant before we did. They went home to collect all her things. I imagine they are well on their way to Georgia by now. He wants his father to marry them. It seems he is a minister."

"A fine example you set." He kept his voice low, but she could see the anger he felt.

"I had nothing to do with it, Dad. When we went to the ladies room last night she told me she's going to make you a grandfather in six months."

"No, not with that no good bum. I'll make her come back. She can give the little bastard up for adoption."

"We raised you girls right," her mother said. "Where did we go wrong?"

"You didn't go wrong. You've been good parents. It just happens."

"She's eighteen," David said. "She can get married if she wants."

"Your father was right." Lucy watched as her father turned to her mother. "Hollywood is a God forsaken place. We should never have come here."

"Nonsense, Mark. Papa was a stubborn old fool. Our Letitia will come home someday, and we will welcome her and her child. Now finish your desert, dear. David is paying for it, and we don't waste food."

Lucy's eyes widened. Her mother was as amazing as when she had told her about Grandma Smith's dishes. She had never thought that her mother had a mind of her own.

"Why Georgia?" her father asked.

"She said his father is a minister and he wanted him to marry them."

"I have never believed that sailor is a southerner."

"Aren't ministers like priests?" her mother asked. "They go where their superiors send them."

"That's right, Mother Robbins. It's entirely possible that's why he doesn't have the accent." David looked at her mother. "I hope you don't mind me calling you Mother Robbins."

"Of course not. It sounds just fine."

Lucy had a feeling that her husband was just trying to speak of the best possibilities. Then, again, ministers sons did have a reputation of rebellion.

Chapter 19

Earlier that morning ,for the first time Lucy, had looked in the cracked mirror on the wall of little cabin, and realized that she was looking at Cindy, not Lucy. Cindy McKaid was heading toward Texas and a new life with a stranger who was her husband. Dad had always called her his little princess. Now, for the first time in her life she felt like one. What would living on a ranch be like? Maybe the new home wouldn't be much, but it would be hers and David's and that was enough to make it worth looking forward to.

They were sitting in the little roadside café across from the shabby cabins in Victorville. Maybe the toast had been soggy, but the eggs had been perfect. The coffee wasn't anything to brag about, but it had cooled off enough to drink. The suitcases were back in the convertible. David was in his fatigues. She wore a skirt and blouse and a wide brimmed hat. It was still about an hour before the sun would show itself.

"Can I run a suggestion past you?" he asked. "If you don't like the idea, tell me."

"What about?"

"Every Labor Day we put on a barbeque. We have for years."

"Will your whole family be there? Aunts, uncles, and cousins?"

"Neighbors, friends, the people that work around the place." The words rolled out casually. "It's two weeks until Labor Day. If we arrived then it would be a good chance to introduce you to everyone."

She didn't answer immediately. Instead she picked up the coffee mug. The brown liquid seemed to fascinate her. She spoke without looking up.

"David, have you told them you're out of the army?"

"Gramps might be guessing, but I didn't say so. T.J. knows I should be."

" When you talked to him, did you tell him about me? Am I going to be a surprise?"

"A very welcome surprise. Mom's been nagging me for years about getting married."

"To Betty Lou?"

"No way. They would disown me. Betty Lou is the only one who thinks we are engaged."

"Has it ever occurred to you that there might be something wrong with her?"

"The thing wrong with her is that she was born a Simpson. They've been interbreeding for generations. About the barbeque? I'd be proud to stand up and tell them all that I've got the prettiest wife around, but if you think it would be too much at one time, I'll understand."

"We did surprise Mom and Dad." Maybe he would understand, but it didn't take a genius to realize that this was what he wanted to do. "It sounds fine to me. We'll have two weeks all to ourselves. Who is T.J.?"

"Thomas Lee Jefferson is the senior partner in my law firm. He. . ." David took her hand. "I hope you won't think badly of me. He and the senator thought Mom had suffered enough by losing both my brothers. They didn't want to see me sent to the Pacific. They pulled in a few favors and that's how I got discharged early. They were still shipping soldiers over to the Pacific. No one knew the war was about over."

For a moment, Cindy couldn't say anything. David had walked up to her on Hill Street and taken her breath away with a kiss, one soldier of all the men celebrating that night. One by one, his revelations were overwhelming her. Now there was mention of a senator. When would the surprises stop? Reaching across the little table she put her right hand over his as he held her left.

"No family should lose all its sons. Roosevelt said that. But, David, I'm just a twenty year old from a big family. I didn't go to college. We're a meat loaf and left over family. How am I going to fit into your life? You're talking ranches, senior partners, and now senators?"

"Cindy girl, you're going to fit in just fine. Don't you worry about that. He's just a State Senator. Finish your coffee so we can get started."

"There's no hurry," she told him. "We have two weeks to get there."

"We do want to get across that desert before the heat of the afternoon. If you're through with that coffee, we'll pay the check and get started."

The old man at the counter rang up the money on the ancient cash register. "You got extra water and gas with you?"

"I've been across before."

"Leastwise you got a decent car. Some of the heaps I seen comin' through before the war - coulda called it dead man's road back then. I just like to ask anyway."

"Never hurts to ask. I thank you for your concern."

* * * * *

David watched his bride as her eyes swept across the shapes and colors of the Grand Canyon. She was utterly captivated. He couldn't imagine any girl he had known to be so natural. He blessed the impulse that had led him to Hill Street that night.

"It's gorgeous. I didn't know rocks could be so colorful. And that little, bitty stream down there is so far away."

"That little, bitty stream is a raging torrent of a river." He was looking at her face, not at the age-old rock formations. The awe and wonder in it made her even more beautiful. What a prize he had found in this girl. What would she think when they arrived at the ranch?

He watched as she raised the cheap, little camera again and again. He would have to get her a better one. A twinge of doubt ran through him. He had thought he was resigned to running the ranch. That was to be Timothy's job, but Tim wasn't coming home. He was under tons of water somewhere near those islands in the Pacific. Taylor stayed somewhere in France, buried with all the others who had lost their lives on D-Day. Twins, who had always been together, torn so far apart by a war.

Gramps couldn't live forever. All he could honorably do was exchange the uniform for a pair of Levis and a rope, but what he could have accomplished with this woman at his side. Young as she was, she would hold her own in Austin. Until this moment he hadn't realized how much it hurt to give up a dream. He really should tell her about the oil wells, but that could wait. For now he just wanted to enjoy her.

"Can you imagine what it would look like when the sun rises or sets?" she asked.

Her words bought him back to reality. "Suppose we find out."

"Would you mind if I get out my pastels? I can work from the snapshots, but I'd love to do one here."

"You can do anything you like. Don't you know that? I'll get your easel." They started walking to the car. "I'll have to get a set of keys made for you. I'll walk over and see about a room for the night. I'm not even sure they have the hotel open for business."

While she worked at her easel, he leaned against the low wall, watching her. Every so often she glanced his way.

"Do you want a *Dr. Pepper*?" He started to move.

"Don't move. I like you just where you are."

When she closed her box of colors, he walked over to see what she had done.

"My God," he blurted out, "you didn't tell me." She had captured the great stones, but they were only a background for a fine charcoal portrait of him. "Where did you study?"

"I've always been able to capture people. I took art all through high school. I've never had too much time to indulge myself."

"Indulge yourself? It's what you should be doing. When I saw the portraits of your parents on the wall I noticed you didn't sign them. You should. A background of books and pens for your father, and clouds for your mother. What a unique idea. Sign them, girl. You'll be famous someday."

"After the way Mom took the news about Tish I think I should have added a bar a of steel for her." She picked up a dark charcoal and sketched in a name, C M.

He liked that and smiled. His mother and grandmother were going to love her. That thought made him realize that they really should pick up gifts to take back to them. Perhaps Navaho rugs would be nice, but he didn't want ones from the tourist traps along the highway. He wanted authentic, not cheap imitations made for the tourist trade. Shopping should be good in Albuquerque, and they did have some good hotels there. He would call ahead for reservations. Cindy's mother might appreciate one as well. It would make a good Christmas gift.

* * * * *

They saw the Painted Desert. They studied Indian ruins. They made love in dingy cabins, and hotels. She made quick sketches of them all. She also took her turn at driving along straight roads and mountainous ones. The empty suitcases filled with souvenirs, clothing, and maps.

When they reached Albuquerque, Cindy said nothing about a cabin being cheaper. She'd been hot for days. Thoughts of a long bath, a good meal, and perhaps the most comfortable mattress of the trip shut out all financial considerations. The hotel had pictures of movie stars who had stayed there. The suite turned out to be all she had hoped for. She and David didn't have to lug their suitcases to the room themselves. After five and a half days of being in the car it was next to heaven.

"We'll just relax today," David told her. "tomorrow we'll see what the town has to offer."

"Sounds wonderful."

They relaxed in the hotel, and the following morning enjoyed walking around the Old Town part of the city. There were small shops, but there were also curbside stalls. They stopped often to look, but soon they back-tracked their way to an outdoor stall where an Indian girl was showing someone a rug. Off to one side sat a man who looked so old Cindy wondered how long he had been alive. David touched one of the rugs.

"Good day to you, Grandfather. Your daughter weaves beautiful rugs."

"Manners of the old ones," the Indian replied. "Who taught you our ways?"

"My great-grandmother. She is called Deedee, but that is not her Cheyenne name. My grandfather sometimes called her Speaks Softly. She and my grandfather thought I should know something of her heritage."

"Did your grandfather have a name?"

"Patrick Ryan, but Mamaw Deedee says her people gave him the name Talks a Lot."

Cindy watched the old men nod. In spite of the way David had addressed him, she felt sure he was not his grandfather.

"I didn't know him, but I've heard it said he was a good story teller. They said her father demanded fifteen horses when he took her away. He was a young man, but she was younger. Those days are long past."

"He is no longer with us, but grandmother is still well, although it's been a few years since she has delivered any babies." David took her hand. "This is my wife, Cindy. I am David McKaid. We're on our way home to Texas, and want rugs for my mother and grandmother. Perhaps onc to give her mother as well. Will you take a check for them? We are staying here today and tomorrow."

The old Indian nodded, and David turned to her. "You pick the three out."

"They're all beautiful."

They were, the colors were vibrant, the designs so perfectly symmetrical. She selected three and heard David ask, "Do you have a large one? My mother put oriental rugs down, but I've always envisioned one made by your people."

"One granddaughter is weaving one now, but it will be a month or two before she finishes it."

"Would you ship it?" Again the nod. "Cindy, why don't you go over to that pottery shop and pick out a couple of nice pieces for us?"

She had an idea that David didn't want her to know how much he was paying for the rugs, but she didn't voice her suspicion. California had a lot of small houses built in the Spanish style. David had mentioned a house of their own. Something like that would be nice, maybe something they could add on a room or two in the future. She had seen some pottery and baskets that she liked. A short time later when she looked up, David was on his way to join her and the old Indian was nowhere to be seen.

"He isn't really your grandfather, is he?" she asked.

"It's a term of respect for the aged. I didn't want him to put on the ignorant, *me heap big Indian* act. He's probably on the way to the bank to have them call and verify the check. I told him to ship them all at one time when ours is ready. Find anything you like?" Sight unseen, he had bought the larger rug.

They stayed on Route 66 until they at last, in Texas, they turned off and headed for Dallas where they stayed in an upscale hotel.

It was Sunday. The following day they would be home in time for the Labor Day barbeque. She would be meeting his family and a few friends.

Chapter 20

At David's request Cindy was once again wearing the white crepe. It did look good with the white boots, but she was understandably a little nervous. She did want his mother and grandfather to like her.

"Isn't it a little formal for an outdoor barbeque?" she asked. David was wearing his dress uniform. The heavy jacket was on the bed next to the white Stetson from Las Vegas. The sun outside the Dallas hotel was a lot hotter than the California sun she was used to. She didn't envy him in that heavy uniform.

"You look just the way I think you should. Close your eyes."

She did. She felt his hands fasten a clasp at the back of her neck.

"Now open them, Mrs. McKaid."

Her hand went to the silver and turquoise. "You bought it. It's the one in Las Vegas that matches my earrings."

"You're going to knock them dead." He kissed her. "I love you, girl. I want the whole world to know it. Now let's be on our way. By the time we get there everyone should have a full belly and a chance to mellow out."

Cindy watched the fences roll by, saw an occasional watering hole, some cows, and once in awhile an oil well. After all the oil wells clustered together in the Baldwin Hill, she wasn't too impressed by the solitary wells. They didn't seem too important. The posted speed limit hadn't seemed to matter much. They had passed one sheriff's car. The driver had just beeped his horn and waved. Miles later she had her first glimpse of the M and K inside a diamond as David turned the car and stopped in front of a metal gate topped by a wrought iron arc. It was the same emblem that was on David's boots and ID bracelet. While he was out of the car opening the gate she looked around.

To the left and maybe a hundred yards or so back was a very old looking three story house and what looked like a used car lot. A large area around the house was fenced in. A wide porch spanned the front and one side of it. Other buildings were scattered about behind the house. A good distance to the right was a clump of green trees. There was nothing else other than a few cows. It didn't seem to be an inspiring sight. She wondered. Did David's grandfather sell cars to make ends meet?

With the ease of a man who had spent a lifetime doing it, David got back in the car, drove through, and once again got out to close the gate.

"The trees over there," he told her as he buttoned his jacket. "That's where I want our house. There's some fine limbs for a swing for the children. Close enough to the road to watch them while they wait for the school bus we're going to have one of these days."

"Sounds like you have it all planned. What is it going go look like."

"Think maybe we should have your input on that. At least four bedrooms, and a studio for your art work. We'll make it the biggest showplace around." He closed the car door.

"Can we have two bathrooms?" It was the first thing to pop into her mind. What a lovely thought. David was planning their future home.

"Spoken like a girl from a big family." He laughed. "We can have as many bathrooms as you want, maybe one just for us off our bedroom. Roll up your window. It's dusty along here."

Inside a second fence opening she saw a few good cars, and a host of beat-up ones and dusty pick-ups. The pick-ups outnumbered the cars. The Buick rumbled over a series of pipes buried in the ground.

"Cattle guard," he explained.

"Who does the guarding?"

"With their hooves the stock can't cross. Keeps them out without a gate."

The grass was green in spots, brown in others. Children were playing in the yard. A few men were busy with a game of horse shoes. On the porch some people were in chairs, others perched on the railings. All looked up to see who the late comers were.

* * * * *

When the McKaids put on a barbeque Betty Lou Simpson always made sure she was there with her father and brother. She sat on the front porch railing, her rough hands holding a beer. Miss Margarita and old Buck always knew how to put on a feed. She usually got to take home some of the leftovers. She was getting tired of stew herself, but Pa still hadn't bought that stove she wanted. She was thinking that once she and Davy got hitched things would be better. Pa and E2 wouldn't be able to boss her around anymore.

Allas had to be on her guard around Pa. He'd believed what she'd told him after the old man had that heart attack. She might have been only twelve, but she had known how to take care of people who didn't treat her right. It was real easy if you knew how, and she had kept Pa from bothering her the way the old man had.

She'd forgotten to iron the only clean gingham shirt she could find, and her fingernails weren't quite clean. She'd been too busy in her attic room with Davy's things - his old lunch box, the broken belt buckle, the dried up old snake skin he'd thrown at her, the flower girl basket from the day he'd proposed, and the little pillow for the ring. Holding that pillow, Davy had looked so grown-up in his shirt, tie, and first pair of good long pants.

Pa and Elmer never went up in the attic. Just in case though, she had all her things wrapped in the old blanket she'd snitched from the MK stables. She often took them out, remembering each event, reminding herself that she was just as powerful as Davy's old

Deedee and knew how to take care of people who were in the way. Most every night she said her little prayer.

The old lady was staying in her cabin this night, and she was glad. She didn't cotton to the old Indian. Could look right though you, she could. Be glad when the old woman died. She'd lived past her days. That was for sure.

Like he'd promised, E2'd been hanging around the ranch, hoping to get hired for the round-up, and he'd heard that Davy had gotten out of the army early. They'd been expecting him home before this. Miss Margarita was getting anxious. Old T.J. had probably managed the whole thing. Well, old T.J. just had another think comin' if he thought Davy was goin' back to Austin. With the twins both getting kilt, Davy was going to have to stay on the ranch cause Buck was no spring chicken.

That suited her fine, because she didn't like being around Davy's fancy lawyer friends. Them and their high faluten ways. Course, once they were married, Davy would buy her some dresses, and she'd be able to boss Elena around just like Miss Margarita did. It wouldn't be right to keep calling her that though. Couldn't decide if she should call her Ma, or Mom. Nobody'd look down on her once she married Davy.

Davy would probably add Pa's forty acres to the Diamond MiK. Then they could all live in this big house with its indoor plumbin'. She sure was glad Davy was comin' home. She was twenty-eight and high time they got hitched. She'd waited long enough. She wanted a baby, and she was going to be a good mother. Wouldn't run off like her own ma'm had.

She looked down at her dusty boots. Maybe she should go round back where the food was, but if Davy came home she wanted to be the first one he'd see. All the little children were playing a game of tag here, and the old folks in the chairs were talking to each other. She sort of wished she'd put on her dress, but that didn't seem right for a barbeque. Anyways she was more comfortable in her old shirt and levis. Miss Margarita was wearing one of her colorful long skirts. She always looked so nice.

Davy hadn't had time to buy the ring when he was home on leave, so one day when Pa had taken her to town with him she'd bought one. Only cost a dollar, and she'd had the ribbon at home. Wore it around her neck, reminding her that Davy was all hers.

When she saw the convertible come through the gate she turned so fast she dropped the beer bottle, and it splashed onto the porch and her boots. She flew off the porch. It had to be him. Davy was the only one in the county with a convertible. She saw him get out, and before he had the door closed she had her arms around him.

"Davy, you're home." It was then she saw the girl in her spankin' new white cowboy hat and fancy dress, and when she rounded the car that bitch had on the prettiest white, embroidered boots Betty Lou had ever seen. "Who's she?" she sneered.

That's when the girl stopped in front of her.

* * * * *

When Cindy saw the redhead wrap her arms around David, she was overwhelmed by a jealousy she hadn't known herself capable of having. No one was going to cling to her husband like that. Very calmly she stepped out of the car and over to the two.

"He doesn't have a sister," she murmured, "and you're not old enough to be his mother, so kindly get your hands off my husband."

"He's my feeancé, so don't tell me what to do. I've got a ring." The girl's high pitched voice echoed around the yard.

"If you have a ring," David told her, his voice gentle. but almost weary. "you bought it yourself."

"You didn't have time, so I had to pick it out myself. You did propose to me. Where'd she come from?. Who is she?"

"Cindy is my wife." He was trying to back away. "Betty Lou, will you please let go of me."

"Liar! Liar! You can't be married to her. We're promised. You proposed."

"We were children, Betty Lou," David told her. "Your grandfather was going to shoot my horse. Remember?"

Cindy watched the girl drop her arms and stare at him. Her face twisted into an ugly threatening thing. "I hate you, David McKaid. How long do you think Miss Fancy Pants will last around here?" Her face vicious with hatred, the redhead turned to stare at her. "You damned bitch. You'll be sorry you ever met him." She spun around, ran to a battered pick-up parked next to a white Cadillac, revved it up, and shot out the gate.

Even the children had stopped their game to stare.

"By golly, Davy, looks like you got yourself a spunky one." The gravelly voice came from behind Cindy. "Took you long enough to get here."

Chapter 21

Cindy hadn't noticed him, a gray haired old man in a blue work shirt and levis. There wasn't any doubt about it. She had to be looking at David's grandfather. His face aged by a lifetime outdoors, she could picture David looking just like him someday which was odd because they didn't look anything alike. He just came up to David's shoulder, but he had that same look of knowing who he was, and that he wasn't anyone to tangle with. What a wonderful candidate for her charcoals.

"Cindy's special," David said. "No sense in rushing a honeymoon. I really didn't intend to humiliate Betty Lou in front of everyone."

"Bout the only way you could do it. I know'd you didn't give her that ring. Know how you feel about her, and you sure wouldn't give a girl a dinky, little thing like that." He took her arm. "Most everybody's out back. Had a hunch you two might show up today. There's still plenty of food left. Let's go introduce this little girl proper like."

"T.J. here?"

"He brought the senator and his wife."

He led the way around to the back of the house, where the size of the crowd just about took her breath away. There was no way she had been prepared for all the people she saw. She was looking at rows of picnic tables with half empty bowls of food, benches, lawn chairs, and men, women, and children of all ages. Off to one side music was coming from a violin, a bass, a banjo, and a guitar. To her dismay, off a ways she saw what looked like four old fashioned out houses. A short way back sat quaint little log cabin . All that was missing was a couple of horses tethered to the back porch. The people from the front porch had followed them around the house. The children were finding their parents, no doubt eager to tell them of the confrontation with Betty Lou.

Several men started to say something, but David put his fingers to his lips as he walked up behind a slim woman wearing a colorful Mexican skirt and a white blouse. He slipped his arms around her.

"How's Mamacita tonight?"

"Davy." The one quiet word resonated with happiness. She turned. "You're finally home."

It was only too obvious where her husband got his black hair and well tanned look. His mother must have been quite a beauty when she was younger. Cindy was suddenly glad she had taken Spanish in school and hoped she remembered what she had learned. Maybe the red-headed Irishman David had told her about was in her background, but she looked more like the Mexican grandfather he had mentioned. The woman looked so happy to see her son, but it took only a moment for her new mother-in-law to switch her attention to her.

"And here's your lovely young lady."

"She's family, Mom. Meet your daughter-in-law, Cindy. Isn't she the prettiest thing you ever saw?"

"Of course she is." With no hesitation the woman hugged Cindy and kissed her on the cheek. "Shame on you for not telling me so we could have a proper reception." She might look Mexican, but her English was perfect.

"See why you needed those greenbacks," his grandfather commented. "Here I figured you must have forgotten how to play poker."

His grandfather walked over to the musicians, and when they started playing the *Wedding March* the hubbub of voices quieted. From somewhere a harmonica joined in. David cleared a spot on a table, jumped up on it, and extended his hand to her. With his grandfather's help, she found herself almost lifted up to stand beside him.

"Home for good, folks." David's voice rang out loud and clear. "Gonna to hang up this uniform and hide it in the closet. While I was in California I discovered something. Hollywood might be full of movie stars and producers, but just plain people out number them. I took one look at this little girl and by golly, I knew we were meant for each other. Changed her name to Mrs. David McKaid. So, y'all meet my wife, Cindy. She's smart, she's beautiful, and would you believe, she's been on my back about spending too much money."

That brought laughter to most.

"Now all we have to do is show her that the Diamond MiK and Texas are the best places in the whole US of A." The place erupted in cheers, whoops, and calls for him to kiss the bride, which he gladly did.

She was relieved when his grandfather held out his hand to help her off the table. David jumped down to join her. He quickly discarded the hot uniform jacket and tie. A coke bottle was shoved into his hands. Most of rest of the afternoon and evening became a confused blur to her. The men were slapping David on the back and making all sorts of remarks. She was hugged and kissed by men and women alike.

"What'll you have, little girl?" his grandfather asked.

"Cindy prefers rum and coke," David told him. "She's pretty particular about it. Insists on mixing it herself. There's a bottle of *Barcardi* in the car. I knew we wouldn't have any." He tossed his keys to the old man. "Have someone take our luggage in." It was a request, but there was also the confidence of a man used to giving orders.

"If you see Elena," his mother said, "tell her that David's room needs airing out."

"Steve here?" David asked his grandfather.

"He's here someplace. You were right about him. He knows his cattle, and he's easy to like. He's got a way with men as well as cattle."

There was potato salad, hamburgers, slices of tender beef in a barbeque sauce, and red-hot chili. In a large pit there was the remains of what must have once been a cow. She assured the doubters that she made her chili just as hot, but after she tasted it she didn't let on that it wasn't true. It stung all the way down. There was enough beer to float a battleship, along with some of the hard stuff.

At one point David introduced her to the senior partner of his law firm. She thought T.J. Jefferson looked the part. A little shorter than David, he had the husky build and white hair of an elder statesman. Of course he wore jeans, boots, and a cowboy hat just like everyone else. The lone exception was the state senator who was with him. Senator Whitney Clayton was on the lean side, with a voice surprisingly strong for such a short little man. His gray suit and Stetson were almost the same color as his hair. He put his arm around her as he shook her hand. *Did everyone in Texas hug everyone else?*

"Trust our Davy to find a little gal who will look good for the photographers. I'll talk to the missus about having the two of you over for supper one of these nights soon. She's around here somewhere."

"Give us a chance to get settled in," David told him.

"Housing situation's terrible," T.J. said. "You can use the firm's apartment until you find something."

"About that. . ."

"Let's not bore this little girl with business. How about we go up on the porch and talk a bit, after I get Cindy something to drink."

"Please, don't bother," she told him. "I would really rather have glass of that ice tea."

* * * * *

David and T.J. both perched on the railing of the back porch. David had his back to the house. He was keeping his eyes on his young wife. No surprise that his grandfather was watching her as well. His mother was at her side. He had been sure that the three would connect. She made a pretty picture in that dress and the boots. He wondered how long it would be until they could slip away to his room.

"Relax, boy. She's in good hands. Margarita and Buck are both overjoyed you got yourself a wife. UCLA her school?"

"Cindy's the oldest of six," David told him. "Two sisters almost in stair steps. She has three brothers. Her father's a bookkeeper. She's been working ever since she graduated from Hollywood High. She ran a welding machine until Germany surrendered. Gave half her salary to her father, but I'm pretty sure she helped out more than that."

"Religion?"

"Catholic, but according to her not a good one."

"Church wedding?" He frowned.

"Las Vegas."

"Good enough. She know about our plans?"

David shook his head. "Not yet."

"She is a looker. What is she? Twenty-three? Twenty-four? Any garbage that could come up later?"

"She's twenty." David was a little uncomfortable. "About that. Since I'm the only one left, it looks like I'm going to have to stick around and run the place."

T.J. took his time taking a cigar out of his pocket, offering one to David He took it, but slipped it into his own breast pocket.. T.J. bit off the end of his before lighting it.

"Buck's been afraid you'd feel that way. Talk to him before you make any decisions. He doesn't want you wasting your education. The senator was going to wait a few years, but he changed his mind. He hasn't admitted it, but I have an idea it's a health issue. He's going to announce his plans for retirement before the next election. He'll give you time to get on the ticket. You'll be a shoe-in. A veteran with all those medals, and when you and that little girl of yours get into a good Baptist church, no one will be able to touch you."

"You know we're Methodist." David told him, "and you know how I feel about changing. No way would Cindy be happy with a fire and brimstone preacher." He grinned a bit. "I hear she was arguing with her priest when she was a child."

"Looks like you did your homework. Who picked out the diamond? You or her?"

"You're off base." Once again David shook his head. "Cindy didn't know anything about the Diamond MiK until a few days after the wedding. I still haven't told her about the oil. She has been on my back all the time about spending too much. Kept telling me to get cheaper hotels. Had a devil of a time getting her to let me take her and her folks to the *Brown Derby."* David eased himself off the railing.

"You think real hard, boy," T.J. drawled. "It's your future and it's what you've always wanted. We need new blood in Austin." He held out his hand to keep David from walking away. "I hear Betty Lou didn't take it too well. I offered to take the Elmers home. She raced out with the pick-up. Think she'll cause any trouble?"

"She's always trouble. I don't want her anywhere near Cindy. I'll make sure everyone knows she's not to step foot on Diamond MiK land." He was looking out at his bride and his mother. "I'll talk to the old man, but right now all I want is a home, a family, and a little stability in my life."

"Go on, and get back to your wife. You haven't taken your eyes off her all the time we've been talking. When you were here on leave you should have told folks you were seeing someone. Might have made it easier."

"I wasn't." David smiled. He knew it was best to be honest with the man. "Confidentially T.J., I saw her on street on VJ Day, and knew she was the one as soon as I touched her. We were in Las Vegas the next day. The friend she was with was worried when she didn't show up at home. They had a APB out on me as a kidnapper. Got stopped by the California Patrol on our way back to see her folks."

T.J. let loose with a deep belly laugh. He stood and slapped David on the back.

"Buck always said when you fell, you'd fall hard. You take a couple of weeks to think it over. Man in your condition can't think straight for awhile." Before the two parted, the man had one more comment. “You take a good look at the way you introduced her to us. You could have told her to go casual like everyone else.”

“Cindy looks good in anything she wears.”

“Yeah, boy, I bet she does, but she didn’t get that outfit at Goodwill. Beats anything her sister has.”

A question nagged in the back of his mind about that remark, but T.J. had already walked off the porch. Besides, his focus was on Cindy.

* * * * *

Along about nine, Cindy noticed the ones with small children starting to leave, but soon others started drifting away as well. David’s mother, whose name she had discovered was Margarita, took her by the hand and beckoned to David. “Your luggage is in your room. I had Elena air it out. You should have told us about Cindy, and it would have been thoughtful if you had told her a little about us. I had to assure her the out houses were only dug for today. We do have indoor plumbing.”

“Thought it was only fair since we didn’t tell her folks until after we tied the knot. Just took the plumbing thing for granted. Is Mamaw Deedee all right? There was a light in her cabin, but I haven’t seen her around. I want Cindy to meet her.”

“Tomorrow will be soon enough. She’s tending a little girl who was hurt bad.”

“Brought her into the cabin?” His surprise showed.

“She’s someone special.” She took both their hands. “I’m happy for both of you, and, David, I had a talk with T.J. You listen to him, you hear me. You found us a gem when you brought Steve home.”

“Speaking of Steve, I never did see him around.”

“Pretty Girl’s due to foal. He’s probably been with her.”

“Tonight? Someone should have told me. Both arriving the same day, seems only right that the foal ought to belong to Cindy.” He took her arm. “We’ll be back, Mom. I want Cindy to see this.”

“She’s not dressed for the stables.”

“We won’t worry about that.” He almost said it over his shoulder as he hustled Cindy around to the car.

Chapter 22

"She's a beauty," he told her as her drove a short few hundred yards to another fenced in area. She barely had time to notice the few horses milling about the corral as he hurried her into a rough building which looked as though it had seen better days.

Inside it was neat and clean, filled with saddles, brushes, buckets, and covered tubs. Two sets of four semi-enclosed stalls were opposite each other. Cindy didn't have time to wonder what all the various equipment was for, or to take in the pungent mixture of odors. She almost had the now familiar feeling of being on some kind of a movie set. She wouldn't have been surprised to have Roy Rogers or Gene Autry show up. The sight of a beautiful Palomino in the stall heightened the feeling. She recalled the Rose Parade and wondered if Leo Carrillo and his silver saddle were somewhere close

A man in ragged pants and a dirty undershirt looked up from the stall his arms were leaning on. Almost as tall as David, he had a well-worn straw hat covering an unruly thatch of blond hair. Several days of whiskers, and a full-blown mustache that almost hid his face. A long blue tattoo of a snake ran down one arm. He grinned and clapped the tattooed arm on David's shoulder.

"Good to see you back, Sarge. You're just in time."

"How is she?"

"See for yourself. She doesn't need any help. Who's the pretty lady?"

"My wife. Name's Cindy. Tell you about it later."

Cindy gripped David's hand as two little legs and a nose emerged from the back of the mare. She held her breath at her first sight of a living, breathing animal coming into the world, and she clenched David's hand even harder as it dropped to the straw beneath. The mare turned to nudge her baby as it struggled to stand on its own wobbly legs. She took a good look at the animal. Her coat was smooth and almost as bright as a newly minted penny, the tail and mane the creamy color of an eggshell. She was busy licking her baby dry.

"I'm sure glad we have towels to do that."

Both David and Steve laughed.

"You won't even have to eat the afterbirth."

"*What a revolting thought.* That was amazing. I'm glad we got here in time. She's beautiful. I think Palominos are the prettiest horses of all."

"You know about horses?" David showed his surprise.

"Anyone who's watched the Rose Parade knows what a Palomino looks like. We've watched Leo Carrillo prance around on that horse of his every year. They make a big deal out of his Palomino and silver saddle. The year the boys were born someone gave Dad tickets to the game. He took me. Mom wasn't feeling well enough to go."

"You have twin brothers, too?" Steve asked.

"Triplets."

They watched as the mare cleaned up her baby; watched the little one struggling to get all four feet spread out on the straw filled ground. Cindy laughed.

"He's adorable."

"He or she, it's yours."

Steve was smiling. "Your grandfather said she'd breed true. That one's going to be a carbon copy of its mother."

"She always does if Tiger's the sire. If she could have I think Mom would have kept everyone one she 's had." David eased the door of the stall open "

"Careful, Sarge. She might be a bit skittish."

"Not with me. She might be Mom's horse, but she knows me." He took the carrot Steve handed him and ran his hand along the mare's side. "Good girl," he murmured softly. "You'll have that little one up and running at your side in no time at all." It was almost as though he was talking to a lover.

Pretty Girl promptly nickered a greeting and daintily plucked the carrot from his hand. David took the opportunity to run his hand along the little one's underside. A smile lit up his face.

"What are you going to name her, Cindy? She's all yours."

"Isn't a horse's name supposed to be important?"

"It can be anything you want. She'll be a high stepping show-off just like her mama."

"If her mama's Pretty Girl can she be Lady?"

"Lucy's Lady. I like that. It puts her right there in your family." For a moment he was busy helping the newcomer find her mother's teat. With that accomplished he stroked Pretty Girl's neck. "Step inside, Cindy. Let your Lady know who you are."

With only a slight hesitation, Cindy obeyed. A baby was a baby, and no matter what else they were, they were there to be loved. She stretched out a hand to stoke the newborn.

When they were out of the stall, David took her in his arms and kissed her. "Congratulations, Mrs. McKaid." His smile was wonderful to see. "Welcome to the Diamond MiK. You're a real Texas wife with your own horse. I knew you'd fit right in. Let's go tell Mom and Gramps about your wedding present."

"That's the damnedest thing I ever saw." Steve remarked. "Any girl I've ever know would have been worried about her dress and those fancy boots."

"Cindy's not any girl. She's something special. Cindy, this is Steve White. We were in the same outfit. He's from Wyoming and wanted a warmer climate, so I hired him to be our new foreman. He's a good guy even if he does have that snake on his arm."

She held out her hand. “Glad to know you, Steve.” She wrinkled her nose. “David, from the way you smell, I must smell like a horse.”

“Nothing wrong with that.”

Back at the house, they joined his mother and grandfather.

“She dropped as easy as always. She belongs to Cindy. She named her Lady. We’ll put it down as Lucy’s Lady. It fits right in there with her family.” His mother nodded. “Her name is Lucinda Jane Robbins McKaid,” he explained. “Her family calls her Lucy. I like Cindy better. Her sister’s are Lily and Letitia. He brothers are Jimmy, Jack, and Jason.”

“Triplets?” His mother caught her breath on the word.

“Just the boys,” Cindy told her. “Leticia’s eighteen, and Lily is almost fifteen. Dad calls us his Little Ladies. David and I have already agreed that we’d prefer one at a time.”

He laughed at her, and shook his head at those around them. “No, Mom, you are not going to be a grandmother yet. Give us time. Right now I think it’s time to call it a day. It’s been a long one, and I’m sure Cindy’s tired. I know I am. We’ve had it for tonight. We’ve been on the road for two weeks. We’ll talk some more in the morning.”

* * * * *

Cindy was tired, but it was her mind more than her body. No way had she expected such a crowd. So many people, a state senator, the horse - the stable? It was a lot to take in, especially Betty Lou. She had never had an enemy before, but she knew she had one now. It was going to be hard to forget the look on the woman’s face.

She wasn’t, however, too tired to appreciate the room David led her into. It held a washing machine, laundry tubs, hooks, shelves, a chair, and work boots. Several boot jacks lay on the floor.

“No muddy boots past this point,” David told her. He put his foot into the curve of one of the boot jacks laying on the floor, easing his foot out of the leather. As he followed with the second boot, Cindy started to do the same. The screen door opened, and a young Mexican boy rushed in.

"No, no, Senora McKaid, not the white ones."

"He's right. Sit down, honey and let him help you with them. Manuel, we'll have to get some white polish for those."

"I have some." The boy shrugged. "Your grandfather said he picked it up by mistake when he was in town the other day."

"The old man must be slipping. Manuel is Elena's grandson. It's his responsibility to keep the boots and this room clean. He hopes to be a doctor someday."

"Thank you," she told the boy as he pulled off the boots.

"I will find some white leather to line a boot jack." He was running a loving hand along the embroidery on the boot. "Buenos..."

"English, boy," David said. "English if you want to be an educated man."

In their stocking feet, she and David walked into the kitchen bigger that Cindy had ever imagined. The long oak table and chairs were worn and from another era, but the big gas stove sitting next to an old fashioned wood stove was modern as could be. The room even held two white refrigerators, something her mother was longing for. Most surprising of all was the enormous fireplace on the outside wall. It was a meld of the very old, and the very new.

The same could be said of the adjoining room. Stretching all the way across the front of the house, the living room still managed to have a warm, lived in look. It, too, had an overly large fireplace. At one end there was a radio beside an upright victrola which had been converted to a record player. Overstuffed chairs and a divan were grouped around them.

The opposite end of the room held an old oak library table and two tall china cabinets. A Tiffany lamp with its multicolored glass was off to one end of the table. Three framed pictures were on the opposite end. Since one was of David, she came to the conclusion that the two look-alikes were his twin brothers. A small, framed snapshot was there as well. All three, each holding the reins of a horse, had that self important look that only young boys could manage.

One lace curtain was drawn aside, prominently displaying the stars in the window, a blue one for David and two gold ones for the twins. Brown and yellow draperies flanked each window. Two Oriental looking rugs graced the polished wood floor. She recalled David mentioning them in Albuquerque and wondered if maybe they were the real thing. David told her there was an office as well, but that he would wait until tomorrow to show her that.

Her high school days of working in the furniture store let her realize that the house wasn't furnished with secondhand cast-offs. It had a lived in look that made one forget that it had probably cost quite a sum to furnish it.

"The house looks pretty old." They were walking up the stairway.

"It predates the Civil War. The bathroom is at the end of the hall. We'll have to do with a single bed for tonight. Don't be disappointed in my room. I haven't bothered doing anything with it since my high school days." He opened the last door on the right. He was looking at her as he held the door open. She looked into the room and laughed.

"I think you just ruined the image of school boys. Are you sure this is your room?"

David just stared what she was looking at. The shiny brass bed, with a pristine quilt sporting a large multicolored star, was the one from his mother's room. Lace curtains were at the window, and the blue rug on the floor looked new. David's duffle bag was leaning against a tall chest of drawers. Her suitcases had been placed next to a matching ladies vanity with a three way mirror. An old fashioned Tiffany lamp lit the room. A fan atop the chest of drawers did its best to cool the room.

"Strange taste for a high school boy," she remarked.

David looked as though someone had punched him in the stomach.

"It just occurred to me," he said, "that Mom and Gramps were almost expecting us today. Something T.J. said — how did he know you have a sister?" He closed the door and turned the big old fashioned key. "I don't know what is going on, but it's late, and it's been hours since I held you in my arms." He walked over to close and lock the open window and pull down the shade. He shoved the straight chair under the door knob. "I don't know how they knew we were married, but if anyone is planning a shivaree tonight, I will deal with them tomorrow."

Cindy was touching the quilt.

"It's handmade. What a beautiful design."

"The Star of Texas. Mom made three of them years ago for the time we married." He took her in his arms. "Welcome home, Mrs. McKaid. It was thoughtful of them, but I am certainly going to get some answers tomorrow."

* * * * *

In the shack that lay smack dab in the center of the forty acres next to the Diamond MK, Betty Lou Simpson waited for both the Elmers to come home. When they arrived she lit into her father and brother.

"He cain't do it," she raged. "We was promised. We'll sue him for that there breach of promise I read about. We can sue him for it all, and he'll have to marry me to git it back."

"Betty Lou," he father said, "You're not agonna do that. There's not a lawyer in Texas that's going up against that bunch."

"I told you and told you," E2 insisted. "Only reason he said that was cause Papap threatened to shoot old Sally. Everybody in the church heard that. Besides we were all three just children."

"He proposed to me," she yelled. "I said yes."

"Go to bed, girl."

"Don't tell me what to do, old man. I'm not even yours to boss. Papaw told me I was probably his'n. Said my ma liked him better." In her rage she swept the cup of coffee she has been drinking off the table. E2 moved the kerosene lantern out of her reach.

"Maybe," the old man said. "and maybe not. I knew we were sharin' her. She weren't nothing but a whore I picked up in Austin. Don't know why God had to burden me with you. Go to bed."

"I'll kill her. I'll kill both of you."

"You're not killing anybody," her brother said. "Go to bed like Pa said and forget about him David McKaid's married and he didn't marry the likes of you. There's nothing you can do about it. He even gave her the filly Pretty Girl had tonight."

"I'll make him sorry he done that." She went up to her attic room, but she didn't sleep. She held on to Davy's belt buckle and said her prayer.

Davy McKaid is handsome and dark.
Davy McKaid always tells the truth.
Davy asked me and I said yes.
Someday soon, Mrs. David McKaid I will be.

But this time she added some lines

The bitch can't have him
And Davy can't give her Pretty Girl's foal cause Davy's mine.

Chapter 23

As they walked down the stairs together, Cindy couldn't help thinking what a rugged looking husband she had. She was used to seeing him in uniform or naked, but true to his word, he had put his uniform in the closet. Dressed in a pair of Levis and a checkered shirt, he was the very picture of a cowboy. Because he had said they would be going to see her wedding gift, she had chosen to wear one of the faded blue jumpsuits she had worn to work. Each time she put it on, she recalled her father's first reaction to it. His little ladies were supposed to wear dresses not pants.

David's mother and grandfather were already sitting at one end of the big table. The older Mexican woman at the stove was what one would call pleasingly plump, her hair a mixture of black and gray. "Coffee's ready," she called out.

As she had noticed the night before, the kitchen looked easy to work in. She took the offered seat beside his grandfather. The cook slid cups of coffee, and bowls of fresh sliced peaches before her and David.

"Thanks, Elena. Cindy likes just one egg, over easy and one piece of toast."

"So, Davy, after all those skinny, dark-haired idiots you ran around with," the woman told him as she was inspecting the jump suit, "you went with the magazine ads. You brought us a little blonde Rosie the Riveter."

"It was a welding machine," she told the woman.

"Good. Always, I knew he wouldn't settle for a useless socialite. Our little Manuel?" She smiled. "I think he fell in love with you and your pretty boots last night."

"I thought I'd show Cindy around before it gets too hot," David told them, "but first we'll see how Pretty Girl and Lady are doing. This afternoon I'd like to look at the books and get an idea of how we're doing."

"When are you going into Austin?" his mother asked.

"Things have changed, Mom. Tim isn't exactly here to take charge."

"You didn't become a lawyer to spend your days cutting the balls off those danged doggies." His grandfather stared at him over his coffee cup. "I reckon I can still handle things around here."

"We can discuss it after I go over the books. First I have a call to make." He rose and walked over to the old fashioned phone hanging on the wall. Cindy had seen the old fashioned telephone without a dial in the movies, but she was surprised to see one still in use. David picked up the ear piece and listened for a moment. "Ladies, this is David. Glad you think she's pretty, but could I have the line for just a few minutes." He grinned and waited for a moment. "Morning, Jess. Get Elmer Simpson for me. Either one, but not Betty Lou."

It was several minutes before he spoke again. "Sorry I didn't get a chance to talk to you last night. I've asked you enough times to try to talk some sense into that sister of yours." He listened. "She not half as angry as I am. You tell her and you tell old Elmer Number 1 that if she ever again steps foot on our land she'll be a trespasser and treated as one."

He glanced over to the table. His mother was frowning.

"I mean it, E2. You can tell them something else as well. If my wife stubs her toe, I'll blame Betty Lou. If she falls off a horse, I'll blame her. If Cindy gets hold of a bad batch of green beans, I'll send for the sheriff after I've strangled her ." Another pause. "It's not your fault you've got a crazy sister. I'll tell Steve you're on the payroll. The three of you have to eat. Just tell both of them what I said because I am serious. Betty Lou steps one foot on the place, she risks getting shot."

* * * * *

"Stew for breakfast," Elmer Number 1 roared. "What in the hell's gotten into you, girl?"

"Don't see no new stove in here. do you, old man. Told you all you're gettin' is stew. Don't even see the leftovers you brought home."

"Didn't see me with any, did you?"

"We got a delivery to make?" the older man asked his son as he hung up the telephone.

"That was David . He said he'll tell that new foreman to hire me." He looked at his sister. "Had a message for you, Betty Lou."

"Bout time he paid some attention to me. Bet he already knows that girl and her fancy ways don't fit in."

"Don't get your hopes up. Said if you're found on the Diamond Mik, you'll be a trespassing, and they just might shoot you. Where'd you go this morning. Heard the truck come in about three-thirty."

"You must have been dreaming." she snapped I didn't go nowheres and don't you start tellin' anybody I did."

* * * * *

When David hung up the telephone and took his place at the breakfast table, his mother was looking at him.

"Isn't that a bit drastic, even for Betty Lou? Who was on the line?"

"Milly Gaiter. I didn't recognize the other one."

"Everyone in the county will know what you said."

"I'm counting on it. Four people picked up to listen in. I know we couldn't do anything about it before, but now that the war is over we have to get a dial-up system around here. One with private lines. I can't do business over this antiquated party line. I'll talk to the sheriff later today. First I want to talk to Steve about the foreman's house."

"He's not using it," his grandfather told him.

"Living in the bunk house with the men? That's not a good idea."

"Got himself one of those little trailers. Not much more than a bed and a stove. Says a man alone doesn't need all that much room. A couple of the men have asked about it, but he told them they would have to talk to you."

"I'm glad it's empty." David sat down and picked up his coffee mug. "Cindy and I will use it until we get our house built."

"There is enough room here," his mother said.

"Nonnegotiable. I promised Cindy's mother and father that she would have her own house and bathroom." Both his mother and his grandfather looked surprised. "One she doesn't have to share with three brothers and two sisters. We need our own place."

"Did T.J. take care of that little matter we discussed when you were home last time?" his grandfather asked.

"Turns out Elmer Number 1 took out a mortgage three years before the war. The paper work is at the firm. He's not always on time with the payments."

"You going to foreclose?"

"Not unless I have to."

"Either Elmer know you bought the note?"

"No."

"Better locate that still first."

"I've known that for years. Tim and Taylor found it when they were fifteen. I can have it busted up anytime I want. I'll have to before long. The damned thing is on our side of the line."

"On our land?" his grandfather thundered.

"Evidently the first Elmer had a modicum of sense. No one's going to look for his damn still on the Diamond MiK. I'm not going to tell you where it is, but unless they keep some filled jars stored away some other place, they will be out of business by the end of the week."

"Don't swear," his mother said. "You've changed."

"War and Betty Lou does that to a man. I don't know which is worse." He took a couple of apples from the bowl and put one in front of Cindy. "We'll go see how your Lady is doing as soon as we finish eating. Want her to get to know you before we turn them out to pasture."

"I've never been near a horse before last night," she told him.

"Didn't think you had. We're going to have to teach you to ride."

She wasn't sure she wanted to get that familiar with horses.

Elena placed both their plates on the table just as the door to the wash room opened. Steve stood there, his hat in his hand, a gun in the worn holster on his leg.

"Shooting rattlers?" David asked.

"Sorry to interrupt your breakfast, Sarge, but we've got a problem at the stables."

Chapter 24

Both David and his grandfather were on their feet instantly. "What's wrong?"

"There's no easy way to say it." He look apologetically at the women. "Pretty Girl's down, and the little filly's in big trouble."

"I will call Doc Kelso." His mother moved toward the telephone.

"Maybe he can do something for Pretty Girl, ma'am, but he can't help the little one." The foreman looked disgusted. "We'll have to put her down. She's got two shattered legs."

"How in the hell can an hours old filly break two legs?" David was reaching for his boots.

"I'd say it's more how did someone get in there to break them. They're not just broken, they're shattered. Nothing with four legs does this kind of damage. Looks like someone was in there with something pretty heavy."

"Is Pretty Girl hurt?" Margarita asked.

"No marks on her, but she's down, Miss Margarita, and not looking good."

"Margarita, call the sheriff," his grandfather ordered. "You and the girl stay here. You don't need to see this."

"Betty Lou," David was muttering. "The damn bitch has gone crazy and there's probably no way in hell we're going to be able to prove it."

"Maybe, maybe not. From what I could see, whoever did it sliced off an ear as well. Maybe as a souvenir? I can't think of any other reason for a thing like that."

The three men went out, leaving Cindy at a loss for words. His mother and Elena just looked at each other.

David must be wrong." his mother finally said. "Even Betty Lou wouldn't do anything like that."

"She's an evil one," Elena insisted. "Even Father Torres makes the sign of the cross if she crosses his path."

"That's superstition. I know the rumors, but it's just that she has this fixation on David."

"You didn't see her reaction when we arrived last night." Cindy couldn't help making the remark. "If looks really could kill, I'd be dead right now. I didn't know anyone could hate like that."

"Don't you ever be alone with her." The words came from a gray haired Indian woman walking through the door. Her faded blouse was plain, her flowered skirt long, and her eyes dark as David's. Two long braids fell down her back. Her face was lined with the signs of age, but she stood erect as a youngster as she glided silently into the room. "I delivered that girl, and I've never told anyone what I did that night."

Her eyes caught Cindy's and she realized that she was looking at David's Cheyenne great-grandmother.

"Girl, I prayed to every spirit I know. I prayed for forgiveness that night, not because I strangled that baby, but because I hadn't done it. When I touched that little thing, it was all I could do to clean her up because I could feel the evil bottled up in her." She crossed the room, letting her hand rest of Cindy's shoulder. "Welcome to the family, dear. You may call me Deedee. I am glad to meet my David's wife, and sorry to have bad news greet you so soon."

"David, has told me about you. He thinks you're pretty special."

"Do you know what Betty Lou's mother said to me when I handed her that child?" She was talking to the three of them. "Even after twenty-eight years, I have never forgotten her words. She looked at me and said, 'I'll feed her, but as soon as she's weaned, I'm outa here. I ain't bein' no brood mare for either of the Elmers." She swore she had been better off in the cat house in Austin where her husband had found her than in that hell hole of the Simpsons. David's right, but he's also right when he says you will never prove it. She's a sly one, trickier than her coyote cousins."

The not so distant sound of a gun going off caused the women to close their eyes for a moment. It was Deedee who moved to the telephone to call the sheriff.

"Elena," David's mother said, "would you please fix another egg for Cindy? I'm sure that one is cold by now."

"Don't waste it," she said automatically. "It won't be the first time I've eaten one cold."

"It won't be wasted, dear. The dogs will have it. Elena, when you have it ready, why don't you pour yourself a cup of coffee and sit down." She moved the plate with the cold egg and toast aside. "The men are trying to protect us against the world again, so we might as well have ourselves some girl talk. Is your little guest doing better this morning, Mama Deedee?"

"She still has pain, but she's better. The bleeding has stopped, so she's healing. It's her mind hurting her most. She's been up a bit, but she still isn't saying anything new."

"That's one good thing this war has done. They are getting the injured up sooner. They are even sending new mothers home in two days instead of ten." David's mother touched Cindy's left hand. "Your rings are lovely, dear."

"He spent too much on them." Sitting in the kitchen she felt awkward having the big diamond reflecting the morning sunlight. "I keep telling him I don't expect him to be spending all his money on me, but he won't listen." She noted the surprised look the three women exchanged. "When we all went out to dinner, one of the boys said I looked like Cinderella. Sometimes that's how David makes me feel."

"David hasn't told you. . ."

"Oh, I know he's a lawyer, but he says he's probably going to stay here on the ranch."

"You mustn't let him do that." His mother looked concerned. "He has worked too hard on his career. Did you have a big wedding?"

"We went to Las Vegas." She smiled at the memory. "David asked a colonel and his wife to be witnesses. He didn't even know him, but he walked right up to him and asked."

"That sounds like our Davy." Elena put the fresh plate in front of her. "Eat, before it gets cold."

"Elena is like one of the family," David's mother explained. "She's been with us forever."

"The girl might need me." David's grandmother nodded to her granddaughter. "After you talk to them, have them come to see us." She touched Cindy on the shoulder. "Make sure our David follows his heart. Don't let him settle or anything less. He will need your encouragement." She left just as the foreman entered the laundry room. He stopped at the doorway to the kitchen.

"Sarge says his wife has a camera and can he use it. Wants to take some pictures before the sheriff gets here."

Cindy rose immediately and went upstairs to get it.

* * * * *

Cindy watched David and his grandfather take off their boots. Elena was on her feet immediately, filling two mugs with fresh, hot coffee. David walked over and sat down.

"Sorry about leaving you alone your first morning here, but it was nasty business." He sounded weary. "Putting down an animal is hard enough, but when it's a favorite it's bad." He was looking at his mother.

"Is Pretty Girl all right?" she asked.

"Some of the men are taking care of her and the filly. It looks like her heart just gave out."

"Doc Kelso was so sure she was strong enough for the breeding." Tears threatened her eyes. "She was about eighteen years old. She was our first Palomino. Your father gave her to me for my birthday."

"Traded two steers for her," his grandfather added.

"You were twenty-five," David said. "I remember. Doc Kelso asked if he could take some blood samples to look at. Said he had been so sure she didn't have any heart problems." He sat at the table, fingering the mug, but not drinking. "Showing Cindy around will have to wait for another day. I'm going to see if I can get hold of an army Jeep. It would be just the thing for getting around the place."

"We do have some gentle horses she can use."

"Cindy doesn't know one end of a horse from the other."

"David."

"Sorry, honey. I just meant you're a city girl and can't ride. We'll take care of that, but for now tires will have to do. A Jeep would come in handy. They can go any place." He looked from her to his mother and then to his grandfather. "Now is as good a time as any to clear up a few things. I should have caught it earlier in the evening, but it wasn't until we got to my room that it came together. Just how did you know I was bringing home the prettiest girl in California?"

"You want to tell them, Margarita, or shall I?" The old man was busy stirring the four spoonful of sugar into his coffee, absent mindedly adding a fifth. "It was your idea to fix up that room."

"It wasn't easy to get it together in eight days. Actually it was T.J. who gave me the idea."

"Just tell them what happened."

Chapter 25

"T.J. had a telephone call from a policeman in Oklahoma City." His mother was looking at her rather than David. "The man was at a cheap little motor court waiting for an ambulance. Evidently the place didn't have - well, T.J. said it had quite a reputation. Not the kind of place decent people go to. No one had called them, but this policeman and his partner were checking out a car that had been stolen the day before. They heard a lot of screaming and carrying on. T.J. said he thought, that given the nature of the place, they might not have investigated if a sailor hadn't rushed out and made for the very car that they were looking at. One went after him, while the other went into the room to see what he could find." She paused.

"He told T.J. a girl on the bed was just about unconscious," his grandfather put in. "When the policeman tried to get her name all she said was 'Call Lucy and David.' After that it was just mumbling. She had been badly beaten and seemed in pretty bad shape. The way T.J. told it, no one knew she was losing her baby until the ambulance arrived."

"Holy Mother of God," Cindy breathed. "You're talking about Tish."

"The girl's purse had been emptied out. She had no wallet, no money, no identification of any kind. The only thing they did find was David's card and a lipstick laying on the floor."

His grandfather took a sip of coffee and grimaced. "Elena, empty out this slop and fill it up again. It's sweet enough to kill." He handed the cook his mug. "When the policeman called T.J.," taking up the story, "he figured she was a client David had taken on. Said he knew David well enough to disbelieve he'd be mixed up in a thing like that. He told the policemen to take her to a good hospital and that he would pay for whatever expenses there would be. Asked Senator Clayton to go with him to investigate. Said he didn't want anyone else involved until they knew who she was, but he figured it would be a good idea to have a reliable witness. They flew up in James' Piper Cub. He said when the girl finally came to after she came out of the operating room all she would say was that Lucy said to call. She kept repeating it. 'Lucy said to call her and David.' Not knowing what else to do, they brought her here."

"Into the Austin airport?" David asked.

"Nope. Landed here in the pasture," his grandfather told him. "T.J. said he wanted to keep it quiet until he knew what it was all about. We made sure no one was around while Steve and I took her to Deedee. He's kept in touch with the police back there. Found out that the sailor had been AWOL for quite awhile. Said the Shore Patrol took him. With a string of stolen cars they can link to him to and a charge of desertion, the navy will take care of him, and the little girl will never have to be involved. You know what a girl has to go through in a case like that. The police said the sailor was pretty well liquored up. T.J. figured that's the way you would want it."

"Is she all right?" Cindy wanted to know.

"Mama Deedee been taking good care of her," his mother put in. "According to her, she just keeps saying the same thing over and over. She says her Lucy married David and would be here, and that Lucy was right."

"We figured that meant David would show up married to some kind of saint." The old man said the last part with a grin that reminded her of David. "You call her Cindy, but Lucy sort of makes sense if your name's Lucinda."

"We all told her Eddie was no good, but she wouldn't listen." Cindy turned David. "Your grandmother came in while you were gone. She said to see her after we talked. Oh, David." She reached for his hand. "I've brought you nothing but trouble."

"You aren't responsible for what happened in the stable, and where would your sister be right now if you hadn't given her my card. The police would have figured she made her living on her back, and I've met some of those ladies around the courthouse. I don't imagine the Oklahoma police treat them with any more respect than our Austin ones do. T.J. must have made sure she got good care."

He sure did," his grandfather said. "Insisted that they take her to the best hospital in Oklahoma City."

* * * * *

David hugged his grandmother when she opened the screen door of her little cabin. It was truly a quaint thing, small and built of logs. As always the porch was spotless. Her two wooden rocking chairs flanked a table made of a huge spool that had originally held cable.

"Cindy tells me you two have already met."

"The sister with two names."

"Her family calls her Lucy." For just a moment he grinned at his grandmother. "Trouble is, Mamaw Deedee, Lucy sounded like a lace petticoat waving in the breeze. Just didn't seem right for a girl whose kisses set a man on fire."

"Told you, boy. Told you you'd come home with a bride. Cut it pretty close, didn't you?" Her smile was brief. "Did you do it properly out there in the barn?" she asked.

"Just like you taught me. I whispered in her ear, told her she'd soon be running on all four legs in a sea of green grass, and that her dam was waiting with all the milk she could drink."

"Was Pretty Girl hurt?"

"I really don't know. She was gone before we got out there. Doc Kelso was pretty sure it was her heart, but he wasn't absolutely sure.

"That horse was strong as an ox," his grandmother stated. "The girl tends her flower garden faithfully, but she's got some nasty things growing there." As always she refused to call Betty Lou by name. "She thinks I haven't seen it, but I have. Tell Doc to look for digitalis. She's very proud of the way her Foxglove blooms." She took Lucy's left hand in both of hers. "Come in Lucinda. What a lovely name. I told David that he would come home with the perfect mate. Told him he would know you right away."

His grandmother's cabin was always comforting. A stone fireplace was at one end of the living room, but it was smaller, cozier, and years newer than those in the main house. David could remember when it had been added, one of the two things Mamaw Deedee had wanted after the wells started producing. The other had been the bathroom added on the back side of the bedroom..

Glass bottles of various colors were at the windows, letting prisms of light float through the air. The walls were covered with animal skins and tapestries. Herbs and grasses hung in bundles, drying in the air.

Cindy's sister lay on the old, brown couch. Dragons swirled around the red kimono she wore. It was one his brother had sent from Hawaii. He caught a glimpse of a cast on Letitia's left arm.

"I should have listened to you," the girl whispered as she saw Cindy. "He's a monster."

"It's all right, Tish." Cindy knelt beside her sister and began stroking her hair. "We all make mistakes. What happened?"

"Don't ask. I'm so ashamed. I'll never be all right again. Thanks to him, I can never have another chance to be a mother. They had to take out my insides."

"Talk to me, Tish. Tell me what happened. You can talk to me." Her voice was soft as she comforted her sister. "We've always talked, Tish. You listened when I hurt, when no one else cared. You have to talk or you'll never get over it. It will keep festering inside you and never let you be healed. You know how you were always after me because I sat and talked instead of dancing. Those sailors and marines needed to talk to someone. It helps. Really it does."

He followed his grandmother's nod and sat beside her on the stone hearth where they would be out of the way.

"No." Letitia was shaking her head in protest.

"You're hurting inside, just like those boys were. Some because knew they had killed, and some of them felt guilty about being alive because it was a friend's blood they saw instead of their own." Cindy's voice as low. "What they did and saw hurt their very souls. They needed to talk to someone and they knew they would never see me again. Maybe that's what the confessional is all about. Talking the bad out into the open instead of letting it grow inside?"

It was a new insight into the girl he had married. There was a reason she seemed older than her years. He could picture her holding a young soldier's hand, easing the pain of war. If he had felt the horror of what they had been through, what must it be for the young men who had just started their way into manhood? How could Cindy, at twenty, realize that they would never talk to mothers, wives, or sisters about what they had done. It wasn't only her brothers and sisters she protected. Her own passions ran deep.

"He didn't love me, Lucy. He wasn't going to marry me. I know that now. I don't even know who he really is, but I know he's evil. I should have listened to you."

"Did you take the bus that night?"

"He had a car. It didn't take me long to realize he didn't borrow those cars. He stole them."

David watched the two girls together. Leticia was holding Cindy's hand. They looked so much alike. In his mind he was picturing how the scene must have looked to the policeman as he had entered that sleazy room. .

"After the third car," Tish was saying, "he started bragging about how he could hot wire anything on wheels. He said he wouldn't get caught because he'd been dodging the shore patrol for months. Then he told me - Lucy," he said "I couldn't tell anyone because if I did I would go to jail too."

"What happened in Oklahoma City?"

"It was just getting dark when we checked into the cabin. We hadn't even brought in our things, not that I had much. I had everything I owned in a couple of paper sacks, but someone must have stolen them out of the car because the first morning when we had stopped to eat breakfast and got back to the car they were gone. Eddy said it was my fault for having them in the back seat instead of the trunk, but I know I had put them in the trunk. All I had left was what I was wearing and my purse. I was tired, and when I said I was hungry, he said he would get something and bring it back. It was always that way. I spent all my time in the car or a room. He said it was for my own protection. I waited for what seemed like hours. When he did come back. . ."

She was looking at the ceiling, at the walls, at anywhere but her sister's face.

"Go on."

"He was drunk, Lucy, and it wasn't the first time. He had bottle of beer in his hands but no food. I told him again how hungry I was. He was angry and said he'd lost his money in a crap game. I really was hungry. We hadn't eaten all day, and I was so hungry I thought I was going to be sick. When I looked at the map. I couldn't even figure out what we were doing in Oklahoma. It wasn't the shortest way to Georgia."

She was trying to sit up. Cindy helped her and sat next to her, cradling her sister in her arms.

"He - he - he told me I was going to have to earn our dinner, that. . .oh, Lucy, he said he had a Marine lined up who was looking for a nice little blonde, and that he'd taught me well how to please a man. Lucy, I panicked. He was acting crazy, telling me about a man in Detroit who was going to pay him for teaching me to be a good little - little I can't say it, Lucy. I'm not one of those girls. I could never do that."

"Of course, you're not that kind of girl," she crooned.

Her sister was crying; his wife was trying not to.

"I know I promised, but I was so afraid and so hungry. I told him to leave me alone, that I was going home. 'We're broke, little darling,' he told me, and that was when I blurted out that you had given me money. I - I should have listened to you. It was like he was a different person, hitting me, swearing at me, calling me names because I'd held back the money. I tried to get away. When I said something about the baby, he shoved me so hard I fell backwards onto the bed, and said he'd take care of that. He took that beer bottle, and - oh, dear God, Lucy, it hurt. I thought I was going to die."

He watched his bride's face and knew she was having a hard time concealing her true feelings. As long as he lived, he would never again stand in a courtroom to defend a man accused of rape.

"You're safe now," Cindy told her.

"When Mom and Dad find out. . ."

"We'll have to make sure they never find out."

His grandmother rose, motioning toward the door. Out on the porch she took a deep, cleansing breath. "She finally talked. You be good to that wife of yours. She's a very special person. That sister of hers needs something to love right now. Do you remember Freddy Gomez's big dog?"

"That big German Shepherd who's part wolf?"

"Manuel has been telling me about the pups she has. Find out if there's a nice little female left. They should be weaned by now."

Half an hour later he walked back into the cabin, depositing a little brown and black ball of fur onto his sister-in-law's lap. "Take good care of her, honey," he told her. "She's going to be a big one. You take care of her, and she'll take care of you." The tears had disappeared. She almost smiled as the puppy licked her face. "You'll have to think of a good name for her."

"She's precious." Tish stroked the puppy. "That's what I'll call her. She can be Precious."

"Good name for a dog that's going to grow into almost eighty pounds." He smiled. What a name for a puppy who was definitely not going to grow into a lap dog.

* * * * *

As David walked Cindy back to the main house she was quiet. "Looks like your instincts were right about Eddie."

"I know I didn't like him, but I never thought of anything like that. How could any man do something like that?"

"Some men - there's just no polite way to describe them. There's a lot of nastiness that goes on. Going back home and having your father say, 'I told you so' might not be the best thing for her."

"We can't let them know what really happened. It would devastate them, and it would make it harder for her to forget it all.. She's always been the quiet one. I usually had to decide what we did when we were young. When we went to the Palladium I usually found someone for her to dance with."

" She will probably never forget it, but she will have to learn to live with it. She won't be ready to go anywhere for awhile. If she likes, she can stay here. "

"That's generous of you."

"Mom would probably welcome her. There's four bedrooms on the second floor, and Elena's room and storage space on the third."

"He tried to kill her over the money. How could he get that angry?"

"I don't think it was all anger," he told her. "He was just teaching her what happens when a lady of the evening tries to defy her pimp. Mamaw Deedee told me she's got some nasty bruises, but he made sure he didn't touch her face. When you gave her that card, it looks like you saved her life."

One more favor he owed T.J. and the senator. One more thing to make it harder to stay on the ranch.

Chapter 26

Cindy didn't how, but she decided that she was not going to let her sister suffer the humiliation she would endure if their parents found out the truth of what had happened.

The evening meal was quiet. David had told his grandfather that he didn't think any of the other horses were in danger, but that Steve would be sleeping in the stable

"Tomorrow I am going to arrange for some security around the place," he said.

Cindy felt a trifle uncomfortable during both the noon meal and supper. Steve had joined them at noontime. Elena had served tender t-bone steaks, fried potatoes, greens, corn, and topped off by a berry cobbler. Cindy had enjoyed all the eating out and not having to make beds, but she wasn't sure how she felt about having someone serve her at home. Would she ever feel comfortable in a house where an amiable Mexican woman and her daughter did all the cooking and housework.

She had been gently refused when she had offered to help clear the table and wash the dishes. The whole day had been troubling, starting with the way David had talked on the telephone about Betty Lou. Remembering the woman's words the day before she felt responsible for David's mother losing her favorite horse.

She didn't even want to think about how the little one had suffered. And Tish? What kind of a God let something like that happen?

If she had felt almost overwhelmed yesterday, this evening she felt almost lost. Every time David had mentioned taking over the ranch, someone seemed to object. Deedee had told her to be sure he followed his heart. Wasn't the ranch the most important thing to him?

After the evening meal she stood by the old library table, looking at the pictures of the three McKaid brothers. The pictures must have been taken when the boys were young. David looked to be in his early teens. The twins were younger. They looked every bit as alike as her brothers did. The black and white didn't show what color hair they had but David had mentioned them being redheads. David was evidently the only one who had inherited his grandmother's dusky look and jet black hair.

"Ready to turn in?" David asked as he came through the door.

"It's been quite a day."

"Not the way I had planned on having our first day home. Things aren't usually this complicated." As he put his arms around her she felt safe and, to her surprise, at home. "I wanted the day to be so perfect. I had things I wanted to show you."

"Do you really think Betty Lou did it?"

"Unfortunately, she's the only possible suspect. I'm taking you into Austin tomorrow."

"I'd rather stay here. It's your home, and Tish may need me."

"If we can get it all done, it will be just for the day. Your sister couldn't be in better hands. Mamaw Deedee is taking good care of her. I have to talk to T.J. about how we're going to handle her being here. We don't want any scandal to follow her around. Mom and Gramps said there's some talk in town that the girl Deedee's is taking care of is local and thinking about learning the old ways. T.J. might have planted that idea."

"You said he's the senior partner. Does that make him your boss?"

"One of them."

"Why would he fly his plane out to help Tish just because she had your card?"

"He's also my god-father, and I've always thought he's been in love with Mom." He started massaging the back of her neck, a habit she had learned to love. "We'll have a busy day tomorrow. I want to see about security. We can't take any chances of something worse happening. We'll want to start looking for a car for you. That might take some time. They aren't going to be able to switch from wartime production to cars over night I want put out word about finding Palominos for you and Mom. We've always ridden them in the parades. We need to find an architect for our house. I want to get that started as soon as possible. We'll drop in at the firm and talk to T.J."

"David, building a house going to. . ."

"Don't say it." The warning was firm. His fingers were on her lips. "Don't say one more word about what something is going to cost. I had planned on taking you out to see the wells today, but I'll just have to tell you. We can't go into Austin without you knowing the truth."

"What truth?"

"Cindy, until I was fourteen, things were pretty bleak around here. Then our first gusher came in. Honey, you don't ever have to say it again. We're - I think the mundane term is filthy rich. Those oil wells changed our lives."

Oil wells? She stared at him, too shocked to speak. He had oil wells, and she had been telling him not to spend so much on her? She had argued against so much. She just didn't know what to say.

"We're going to build a house that will be the envy of everyone who drives past it. Gramps and Mom have been saving for future generations. That's us. It's time the McKaids started living a little."

"What must you have thought of me?"

"Just that I've been proud of you. I have an idea that you're the kind of woman who will help me do some good in this world. I'll always know you married me, not the Diamond MiK."

Maybe she should have realized it earlier. Certainly the jeweler on Hollywood Boulevard hadn't hesitated to take his check for the rings. The reality of it, though, didn't make her want to go out and start spending money. She already had more than she had ever dreamed of having.

"Do me a favor tomorrow," he said. "When I introduce you to the firm, I want them to see the real you. Wear that suit your mother made and the hat you had on when we met. When I saw you standing in the street as though you didn't belong there, I knew you were the one Mamaw Deedee promised me."

"I don't think I was alive until you kissed me," she told him.. " I love you so much."

"You'll never know how much it means to me that you married me without knowing anything about the ranch or wells."

They were lost in another kiss until David suddenly pulled away and took her hand.

"It isn't much, but the foreman's house is going to give us some privacy. Nite, Mom," he said as he turned to go up the stairs.

She followed his glance to the doorway of the family office where his mother stood watching them, and she felt a rosy glow spread across her face.

"It's all right, honey," he whispered. "We're married, and she's smiling. She's probably thinking grandchildren."

It was a possibility. They hadn't been doing anything prevent it. She might not know what they were, but she knew there were ways to do so. Father Reilly had spent many sermons talking against them.

Chapter 27

"It isn't a very big town, is it?

Cindy made the comment as David stopped the car in front of the Kaidville Bank. They were a few miles west of the ranch house. Her first surprise was that the town had the family name. Her second was the size of Kaidville. The small brick bank building was flanked on one side by a slightly larger general store and on the other by an even larger feed store. A small Methodist church had been at the beginning of the block. Opposite it had been house holding a doctor's office. At the end of the block she saw a Catholic Church. Evidently the Catholics outnumbered the Methodists. The cemetery behind looked to be the older and larger of the two.

"Almost a six hundred people," David told her. The school house, funeral parlor, American Legion Post, and Masonic temple are in the next block. We've got a city hall, a jail, and a stop sign. The school house is next to the Baptist church."

Once again David ignored the speed limit as he drove into Austin. She hadn't known what to expect, but the Colby building was large, modern, and had revolving doors to walk though. She had a new checkbook in her purse; the one that Calvin Jesup, the president of the little bank in Kaidville had handed her; one that had a ridiculous amount of money on the first line.

Inside the marbled walls of the Colby Building, David took her hand and headed toward the bank of elevators. As requested, she was dressed in her beige suit and red hat. David had on the sport jacket that had been in his duffle bag sport jacket, slacks, and a pair of white boots embroidered in black with the MK brand, and of course, a white Stetson on his head. All the men seemed to favor the western style hats either in felt or straw.

After yesterday's events, it was a relief to be alone and away from the ranch. With all they had done during the previous two weeks, she wasn't too edgy about meeting his former co-workers. After all, she had met T.J. and a state senator Monday at the barbeque. What was hard to get used to was the fact that David really had all that money.

It had been one surprise after another ever since the California State Patrol had stopped them that day when they were on their way back to Hollywood. Now she thought maybe the only question was whether David would practice law, or stay on the ranch. His mother, grandfather, and grandmother had all seem to indicate that he shouldn't choose the ranch. She didn't know why they were concerned. David loved the place. Whatever it was, she thought that decision should be left to him. He should do what he really wanted to do.

His hand felt just as comforting as it had when she had thought he was a simple farmer. An ancient black man sat just inside one of the elevators, patiently waiting on his little stool. Uniformed girls manned the others.

"Glad to see you're still here, Sam." David nodded to the man.

"Yes, sir, Mr. McKaid." The man was all smiles. "Done heard you got yourself a pretty little wife. Mr. Jefferson's makin' sure everybody knows. You want the seventh or the eighth floor?"

"Eighth. Main offices. Architectural Design still here?"

"Still on the fourth."

"Sam's been here since the building opened," David told her as the door closed and the elevator rose.

When they stepped out of the elevator on the eighth floor once again she was feeling that she was on a movie set. A very pretty secretary sat at a white desk inside a door that had proclaimed that it was T.J. Jefferson's office. Her black dress was subdued, but it showed off a well endowed figure. David smiled at her.

"Still here I see. How is that little one doing?"

"Not so little. He started high school last week."

"Cindy, this is Zelda. She's been T.J.'s secretary for quite a few years."

"A lot of broken hearts around here today, Mr. McKaid. Go on in. T.J.'s expecting you."

Inside T.J. stepped around from the biggest desk she had ever seen, shaking David's hand, hugging her, and making sure she was comfortable in one of the big leather chairs, all in one smooth motion. He seemed to be one of those men who seems to want you to feel comfortable, all the while you are remembering that he is a very important person. He perched one hip on the edge of his desk.

"I hear you had some trouble out at the ranch."

"Damn party line." David scowled at him. "Man can't take a piss without the whole county knowing it."

"Careful, David, there's a lady present."

"Cindy's got three brothers."

"Yes, and if I heard them talking like that I'd tan their eight-year-old hides."

"Sorry, honey. I'll have to remember I'm not in the army any longer."

The look he gave her was one of surprise. She loved David, but she wasn't about to let him talk like that. She did have her standards. Little Jack had found that out when he was four and whipped out his little ding-dong in the back yard.

"You really think Betty Lou could do a thing like that?" T.J. asked.

"I know she could. She's mean enough and even if she does look to be all skin and bones, I've seen her sling fifty pounds of feed over her shoulder easy as a man. She's kicked more than one dog. If you want the honest truth, I've always wondered about Elsie Mae's saddle coming loose, and why she was out there alone at night. At the funeral Betty Lou asked me if I wasn't sorry I had let her sit next to me at to the church social."

"That's a pretty serious accusation. You were just what? Fourteen?"

As she listened to his words, a chill ran through Cindy . She wouldn't soon forget the way Betty Lou had looked at her or the words she had spoken..

"Thirteen," David said. "A month before the bull got Pop. Elsie Mae wasn't afraid of much, but she wouldn't have gone off riding by herself at night. That's why I warned E2. I figured word would get around. I've got some calls to make while we're here. No sense in letting the whole county know what we're doing. Some of those women must spend most of their time waiting for someone to make a call. They pick up and listen in quick enough. We're going to get a decent telephone system if I have to fund it myself."

"You have a point," T.J. said. "A man can't conduct business over a party line. It has been mentioned, but we couldn't do anything about it until the war was over. It will take some time."

"We have to do something about a lot of things." David leaned forward. "This state can grow, but not unless we make air conditioning common. We've got the potential, but not if every small town has nothing but party lines, and what man is going to want to move his family down here when he finds out his children will be going to a one room school house?" Her husband was more animated than usual. His words had passion behind them.

"You seem to have done pretty well coming from a one room school."

"A bit of tutoring on the side after the wells started producing is what got the three of us into decent schools. You know that. Keep the cowboy image. People love that, but we've got to move us into this post war world ready to compete. Dallas and Houston are going to grow. Austin needs to do the same."

"Men like you are just what we need." T.J. picked up a cigar from the ashtray on his desk, pointing it at David more than smoking it. "We need you here in Austin. You got yourself a good foreman. Knows his cattle; gets along with the men even if he isn't a Texan. Buck's no spring chicken, but he's still going strong. Find yourself another bookkeeper. With his gift of gab, Raymond would make a dandy PR man to handle your campaign. You're young, but people respect the McKaids. It's a well known name."

Campaign? That word startled her even more than the oil wells had. Was there more than a law office under consideration?

"I'm needed at the ranch," David once again stated.

"You hear Buck telling you that? You bring any clothes with you?"

"We're just in for the day."

"Colby's having a thing tonight."

"Cindy doesn't have any gowns yet, and my tux doesn't fit any better than anything else I owned before the war. I intend to see Levi while we're here."

"It's not formal, but it's a pretty important occasion. You better wear a suit, not a sport jacket. The press will be there."

David's glance rested on her, then went back to T.J.

'Just what is this occasion?"

She wondered as well. Just what was it that T.J. was wanting from her husband?

"Introducing the new partner here at Jefferson, Colby, and Smith. We made the decision last week, but as far as the press goes, it's been pending since the week before you received that draft notice."

David didn't say a word. T.J. eased himself off the desk and took her arm.

"Come on, honey. Let's show your hubby his new office."

He walked them down the hall. David frowned when he saw the gold lettering spelling out his name on the door. Another brunette in a black dress sat at a desk.

"Good morning, Mr. McKaid."

"Good morning, Jinny."

"Jinny's going to act as your secretary for now," T.J. said. "She did do some work for you before. You can keep her or get someone else if you want."

The inner office was on a corner with two large windows, books filling half of the shelves that made up one wall. The desk was smaller than the one in T.J.'s office, but still larger than normal

An intercom, a telephone, and a gold pen and pencil set sat on it in lonesome splendor. Two chairs, identical to the leather ones in T.J.s office, were there. David's law degree, a picture of his mother and grandfather, and a blow-up of the Diamond MiK brand were on the fourth wall.

She watched David as he touched the desk, looked at his diploma, and turned to stare out the window at the Austin street below.

"I wasn't prepared for this. Why now?"

"You would have been here before this if it hadn't been for Hitler and his war."

"I had two brothers then."

The way he said it hurt her inside, but in that moment a realization hit her. He had first mentioned it the night they had met. He had said it to her father. Each time it had been the same. He had never said he wanted to run the ranch. Yes, he loved it, but all along, it had been that his grandfather needed him; that his brothers weren't alive to be there. It was a duty, not a desire. She knew what that was like. How often had she wanted to sketch, not iron the clothes for Mom or run the vacuum cleaner? She walked over to stand beside him, touching his hand.

"David," she almost whispered the words, "what is it that you were planning before the war?"

"The Diamond MiK needs me, honey."

"That's not what everyone told me yesterday. Is this what they were telling me you should do?"

"Honey," T.J. said, "your hubby has talked of nothing but politics ever since he was fifteen. He's going to be representing the district in Austin first, but one of these days he'll be in Washington. We need men like him, men that care about this country and the people in it."

"I can't let Gramps down," he said.

"From the way they all three talked yesterday, I think that's what you'll be doing if you turn this down," she told him. "Your grandmother told me to be sure you followed your heart. We can still build our house. You can commute to work. It didn't take us that long to get here."

"It won't be easy." He took her in his arms and looked into her eyes. "I worked here, but the Diamond Mik has always been home."

"Nothing in my life has been easy. Even President Roosevelt had his Shangri-La to go to when he needed to get away."

"I haven't touched a law book in three years."

"Don't worry about it," T.J. told him. "You haven't forgotten what you know."

"Doesn't the announcement usually come before the name on the door?"

"Maybe, we were thinking of the old story about the farmer who hung a carrot on a stick ."

"And hung it in front of his mule," David finished. "Fancy carrot you're ramming down my throat." He paused. "Give me a few weeks. I want to make sure I have the right people at the ranch. Cousin Ray and I go a long way back. I'm not sure I'll be comfortable with someone outside the family taking over the books. We want to get started on a house. There's a lot that has to be done. We've been married less than a month."

"Take a couple of months if you need it. James will wait with his announcement. Spring might be better anyway." She watched as he handed David two key rings. "Use the company apartment when you're in town until you find something for yourself. Housing is a big problem.. What are you going to do about that little problem you had yesterday."

"It's not a little problem. You know how Mom felt about Pretty Girl, and I gave the filly to Cindy as a wedding present. The first thing I've given her, and it's taken away. I'm not going to forgive that. It's not just the sentiment though. It's going to take a bundle to replace them. I've made up mind. I won't foreclose yet, but after tomorrow the only income the Simpsons will have is what E2 makes at the round-up."

"No one's found that still yet," the man warned.

"They've been looking in all the wrong places. The twins found it years ago. I'm taking Steve and some dynamite there tomorrow."

"Don't get caught trespassing."

"That's the hell of it." David slipped the keys into his pocket. "Excuse the language, Cindy. It's in what's almost a cave and it's on our land. Steve blew up a few bridges. He can take care of it without any trouble. We'll make sure no one's inside, destroy what's there, and cause a rockslide to erase all trace of it all."

"Make sure you do a good job." The attorney showed his concern. "If word ever got out that there was a still on the Diamond MiK it would be bad. Eight o'clock at Colby's place."

"Mom and Buck know?"

"They're both set to come in for it."

She watched as David went to the desk. "I remember Jinny getting engaged. Does she have any children?" All of a sudden he was all business.

"Boy about two. Last I heard her mother takes care of him. Her husband's plane didn't make it back to England."

"Too many of them didn't." She watched as he flipped a switch on the intercom.

"Jinny."

"Yes, Mr. McKaid."

"Get my mother on the line and tell her to bring my wife's brown dress and anything else she might need. Tell her I will need my cuff links and bolo tie. She will know the ones I want. She can take it all to the company apartment. Tell her we will all be staying overnight. Then get hold of Levi Goldman. Tell him I'll be in and in need of a suit for tonight. After that get a couple of nice potted plants; something impressive for my office and a small one for your desk. You can come in every day or two, water them, and forward any mail to the ranch. Until I tell you differently those are your only duties. Play with your son, maybe take him to a park. If I do send the rest of my law books in, shelve them for me."

"Yes, sir, Mr. McKaid. Welcome back."

Chapter 28

David had started buying his clothes from Levi Goldman while still at Texas U. The shop was still in the same location. The clerks were new, but the white haired owner hurried to meet them.

"David, how good it is to see you home."

"It's good to see you, Levi. You're looking spry as ever."

"And what a lovely young lady you have with you."

"My wife." He turned to her. "Cindy, honey, this is Levi Goldman. He's the best tailor in Austin. Levi, I'd like you to meet my wife"

"I'm glad to meet you, Mr. Goldman." She offered her hand.

"It's about time there should be a Mrs. McKaid. All you soldiers bringing back such pretty wives." The tailor looked at her and then nodded to David. "And all of you back with shoulders a bit wider. What can we do for you today?"

"Just like my secretary told you. I need a suit for tonight. It will have to be off the rack. I need to be wearing it by eight o'clock."

"Senator Colby's reception." The man once again nodded. "I heard the rumors. A corner office no less. I will have to start calling you Mr. McKaid."

"Levi, you've called me David since I bought my first suit. You just keep on calling me that."

"Congratulations. Navy blue as usual?"

For a moment he couldn't reply. Levi Goldman's question evoked a memory. He was seeing Mom standing there with the rifle in hand and Mamaw Deedee beating on the triangle. "Maybe something different," Levi repeated.

No." He shook his head. "We'll keep it navy blue. I'll need a shirt, cuff links of course."

He didn't like the memory. It made him think of the following day. Tim had walked into the Houston Army recruiting station, having no idea that his twin was with two friends talking to the Marine recruiter. There was an up-side though. He had found the girl he needed. Him in his lawyer mode and her in that brown dress with the little pearls around the neckline and cuff, they were going to make quite a striking couple. God, but she had looked good when she had tried it on. It clung to her in all the right places.

David took the suit Levi selected from the rack and stepped into the small cubicle. Before he had a chance to put on the double breasted coat, Levi stepped inside.

"David," the man kept his voice low, "it might be that it's none of my business, but I've known you since you were a boy. Is your cousin Ray still keeping your books?"

"Gramps wouldn't let anyone else do it."

"I only heard this second hand mind you, but it was from a good source. Ray has been playing with some big players here and in Dallas. They aren't the biggest games in town, but big enough for my source to wonder. Everyone knows that Ray is only a bookkeeper at the diamond MK. Buck's the one who owns it all."

"Uncle Raymond never wanted anything that got his hands dirty. Ray's the same. Maybe I better look into it." He gave a grateful nod to the tailor. "Thanks for telling me."

"Like I said, it might be none of my business, but I've always liked you boys. It broke my heart to hear about your brothers." He stepped back out.

David buttoned the coat, stepped out, and smiled at his wife as the tailor marked it for alterations, but he thought about what he had heard. It would bear looking into. He commented that he would come in later to talk about what else he would be needing. Levi told him the suit would be ready in two hours.

"Have it sent to the company apartment. We have a lot to do yet."

"I'll do that. Wear it in good health."

The next hour was spent having lunch, then it was back to the Colby Building, this time on the fourth floor where he introduced Cindy to an old friend.

"Robert and I were roommates from our first year at Texas U. We were pretty wild until we decided we better settle down and study. From the looks of the office, Architectural Designs is doing well." He turned to his friend. "We need a house, Robert. I want to put it by that clump of trees. You always said it would be a dandy place for one."

"I believe I've always said that a house there would be making a statement."

"More than a statement, Robert. Make it your masterpiece. It's time some McKaid money was spent. We want at least six bedrooms."

"Sounds like a good start. Brick, of course." The architect was smiling. "Anything else?"

"Plenty of bathrooms."

"Closets," Cindy put in. "Big closets and a lot of them, and shouldn't it look like Texas?"

"We'll want to be in it by Thanksgiving." That's what he said, but he actually had little hope it would happen.

"That won't be easy. I can have some preliminary plans to look at by the end of the week. Anything else you can think of?"

"A studio for Cindy."

"What kind?"

"She's an artist. One of these days she's going to make the McKaid name famous."

"That means the light has to be considered."

"One more thing," This was important. Cindy was not used to the heat she would find during the Texas summers. "I want central heat for winter nights, and air conditioning for summer heat."

"Not a bad idea, and you can afford it."

"Who's good with security? Someone was in the stables early yesterday morning."

"I read about that in this morning's paper. The Palomino's heart gave out, and the filly had broken legs"

"Mamaw Deedee doesn't think the heart attack came on by itself. The filly was Cindy's wedding present."

"Colby's son is the best. He's on the second floor."

"Do you know where I can pick up a few sticks of dynamite? Someone who can keep his mouth shut about it."

"My Uncle Bo. You might think about him for your contractor. He's still the best around, and if anyone can get you in by Thanksgiving it will be him. I can bring it out tomorrow morning. I'll bring a well digger with me as well. We'll want to look around. With all those trees, there's bound to be water underneath."

"Fine. I'll have my foreman ready. He did some demolition work in the Army. If you hear of any Palominos geldings for sale, let me know. I'm in the market for two."

* * * * *

"Last stop," he told Cindy as the elevator took them down to the second floor. "After we take care of some security issues we'll go to the apartment."

Just as he had expected, Colby Security had a more discreet look. The lettering on the door was smaller, the office plainer, but the chairs just as comfortable. Luke Colby did not look like the policeman he had once been. David was hoping to make the apartment before Mom and Gramps arrived. They might be able to give the bed a test run.

"I read about the trouble you had out at the ranch yesterday," Luke said.

"I won't lay blame on any one person because I don't have proof, but I need a few good men watching the place. You wouldn't happen to have a woman who could act as secretary for my wife."

"David, I don't need. . ."

"Yes, you do, honey." He took her hand, but kept his focus on the ex cop. "I want someone with my wife, someone who can ride, handle a gun, and take care of a woman who is, let's say, is a redhead who can heave around a feed sack and threw out a pretty nasty threat when she saw Cindy."

"Do you have anything you can take to the sheriff?"

"Unfortunately, no. Any number of people heard her tell Cindy she'd be sorry she ever met me. That would be nothing in court. You had to be there and see it happen. I have never worried about her before, but coupled with the fact that she bought herself a ring and has been wearing around her neck and the way she turned on me Monday, I don't mind telling you I'm worried enough to be here."

"The newspaper just gave the bare facts. How bad was it?"

"I had to put the little filly out of her misery. Her legs weren't broken. They were crushed. Pretty Girl was already gone. Doc Kelso was pretty sure it was a heart attack, but he took some blood samples. Mamaw Deedee thinks he should check for digitalis. No one stays in the stable at night, but that changed as of last night. I want someone around the house as well."

"We can do that."

"When we were young things seemed to happen to anyone who got in her way."

"I take it we're talking about the Simpson girl?"

"Who else?"

"We have a couple of older women working for us, but someone younger might be less obvious." He turned to Cindy. "The newspaper said you're from Hollywood. One of my nieces finally wore me down. She's young, but good. You can call her as your secretary. Are you a good enough actress to pretend you don't know anything about horses?"

"I wouldn't have to pretend," she told him. "Until the other night the closest I've ever been to a horse was watching the Rose Parade. I don't really need a secretary."

"No one knows that. She's good at a lot of things. She also taught my grandchildren to ride. I will arrange to have her meet you." Luke turned back to David. "I'll send a couple of men out tonight, and I'll be out there tomorrow to assess the situation. I presume you'll be at Dad's tonight."

"We've been invited."

"Congratulations."

"They made it pretty hard to turn done."

Chapter 29

"Expensive looking," Cindy remarked as she looked around, "but it looks like an oversize hotel suite." For one brief moment she thought of how her life had changed. Less than three weeks ago she hadn't stepped foot into a hotel room, much less a suite. She had learned to enjoy traveling, to appreciate a good hotel.

The two bedroom apartment was bigger than the house off Vine Street. It had a Spanish look to it, the furniture heavy, one bedroom with a double bed, the other held twin beds. The pictures on the wall were of cowboys, horses, and even one featuring an oil well against a stark blue sky. One end of the beige and brown living room held a desk, a telephone, and a bookcase filled with an assortment of books. Stationary on the desk had a heading which read **Jefferson, Colby, and Smith**. The dining room could easily seat ten, and the kitchen could serve snacks and drinks, but no real food was in sight. Meals would have to be eaten out. The bathroom was all white with remarkably thick towels and terrycloth robes.

"That's the idea," David told her. "Keep your mind on business, all the time remembering that you are the guest of the best law firm in Texas." A doorbell sounded. "There goes our few private moments."

"Everything all right, Mr. McKaid?" the doorman following David's mother and grandfather asked, placing two suitcases on the floor.

"Just fine. We'll take it from here"

David's mother kissed her on the cheek as she placed Cindy's cosmetic case on the coffee table.

"I couldn't find your jewel box, dear, but I did bring this."

"I'll take that bed divan." his grandfather called out over his shoulder as he took a suitcase and a cosmetic case into one bedroom. "If we want to get anything to eat tonight we'd better start thinking about where to go."

"I already made reservations," David told him.

"I don't have a jewel box," Cindy said, "but the necklace David bought me is in that case."

"Turquoise won't do with that dress. You can wear my pearls. They will go well with it."

Two and a half hours later Cindy picked up her husband's bolo tie. The silver diamond shape, rimmed with gold and showing the gold M and K, matched the cuff links he was putting in his shirt as well as being the design on his boots. That wasn't all it matched. The heavy silver chain on her arm might have his name and serial number engraved on the underside, but the gold diamond and initials on top had the same design as the wrought iron gate at the ranch.

"It doesn't stand for McKaid. It's the same as your ID bracelet. It's the Diamond MiK brand, isn't it?"

"Wondered how long it would take you to make the connection." He once again had that engaging grin. "I had to give it to you. When a man finds something that belongs to him, he just plain has to put his brand on it."

"You were branding me?" That thought irritated her.

"Don't be mad, honey." He left one cuff link dangling half in and half out of its buttonhole, as he took her in his arms. "It does stand for McKaid as well, but I couldn't let you get away. Halfway through that first kiss I was afraid I was going to bust right out of my britches, and don't tell me you didn't feel the same."

"I did, but don't you ever forget it works two ways. If I belong to you, you belong to me. Maybe I'll have to learn to shoot one of those gun after all. I might have to use it if I ever found you with someone else."

"Wouldn't have it any other way. Shall I show you why that will never happen?"

"We'll be late as it is."

"I intend to be late. Let them wonder if we really intend to show up."

He held out his arm for her to finish with the cuff link. Odd how that small gesture made her really feel like a wife. This certainly wasn't the way she had thought married life would be. Almost three weeks and she still hadn't cooked a meal for her husband, and now, during dinner at the restaurant, he and his mother had been coaching her about reporters and photographers.

"I guess we can't keep Mom and Gramps waiting. Just keep in mind what we talked about. They might be lawyers and their wives, but they are no better or no worse anyone else you've ever known. They will all be curious about you. That's only natural. At school one of my professors told us to always picture the opposition naked, but I don't want you looking at any man like that. Just picture the reporters as wearing flannel pajamas. That ought to work as well. Be nice to them though. We will always need to be on the good side of the press. We need them as much as they need us."

"Maybe a bunny costume with floppy ears and a big cotton ball for a tail?" she asked.

"Perfect." He picked up his suit coat. "If you can climb out windows, you can face the people you meet tonight."

"You look like an attorney," she told him, at the same time remembering that at the ranch he had looked like a cowboy. "I've never been to anything like this before." It was the same thing she had said during dinner. "Do I look all right?"

"You will be the loveliest lady there. Mom was right. The pearls are perfect. I had hoped we could ease into things a little slower, but it isn't happening. Just you remember that T.J. was impressed with you, and you did meet the senator and his wife Monday. You will do fine."

She fingered the double strand that glowed against the brown fabric. Her mother-in-law's pearls were undoubtedly the real thing. She did want to make David proud of her, but could she do it?

"Don't be nervous, honey." His lips brushed her cheek. "Just remember you have one thing no one else has."

"What's that."

"All my love. I love everything about you. You're my other half."

She smiled. That helped. It was the first time he had said it.

* * * * *

As David turned the Buick into a circular driveway Cindy was hoping she didn't look as nervous as she felt. The many cars lining the drive did little to reassure her. There weren't as many as had been at the barbeque, but none had a rattletrap look, and there were no dusty pick-ups. The stone house was by no means a mansion, but it was certainly larger than any private home she had ever been in.

David stopped the car in front of the door, ignoring the fact the he was beside another car and was blocking the driveway. He left his keys in the ignition. Once inside, both he and his grandfather handed the black butler their hats. David hadn't mentioned him. When she saw David's mother tucking her gloves into her purse, she did the same.

"Good evening, Mr. McKaid, Mr. Buck. Your ladies look lovely tonight. Mr. Colby told us there was a new Mrs. McKaid. Might I say that we are all glad to see you safely home and with such a lovely bride."

"Thank you, Josiah. The driveway is filled. I left the keys in the car. Think you could have one of the boys park it for me?"

"That won't be a problem, sir." Though his words sounded prim and proper, a smile went with them. "I believe they have been awaiting your arrival."

T.J. walked over to greet them as they entered a crowded room. At least he was one familiar face. She thought she recognized others, but she wasn't sure. There had been so many people at the barbeque. After that morning visit to the offices, she did feel that T.J. approved of her. Several colored girls in attractive black and white costumes were wandering around with trays of champagne glasses and tasty tidbits.

"I was beginning to wonder if you had changed your mind," T.J. boomed out.

"Just had a few things to do this afternoon, and you know how it is with women getting dressed."

"Worth every minute of waiting," T.J. said as he managed to tuck David's mother's arm under his. "Two of the prettiest ladies in Texas."

Heads turned as he led them over to a grand piano where a man was playing a quiet tune. He stopped the music as T.J. nodded and raised his voice.

"Ladies and gentlemen." Conversation stopped. "If you don't have a glass in your hand, I suggest you get one."

He waited until the girls with trays circulated.

"We have looked forward to the return of one our brightest young attorneys. He served his country well. We are delighted to have him back with us where he belongs. Join me in a toast to Jefferson, Colby, and Smith's newest partner and his bride, Mr. and Mrs. David Stanley McKaid."

The glasses were raised, but without any murmurs of surprise. Even the reporters and photographer had heard the rumors. Once again she shook hands with so many people that she didn't even try to remember names. She was so glad David was staying at her side.

"Can I get a couple good shots of you and your bride?" a photographer asked David.

The flashbulbs went off, and somehow she and David were seated in a corner talking to a couple of reporters. T.J. stood close by.

"Didn't I hear you were from Hollywood? What pictures have you been in?"

"The closest I ever came to the movies was watching them. I'm just your average, every day girl. I ran a welding machine until shortly after the Germans surrendered."

"Your father? Is he in the business?"

My father is a bookkeeper. There's nothing glamorous about my life. We've lived in the same house since I was six. We live in Hollywood because that's where his job is. I have two sisters and three brothers, and I am sure that when everything settles down, I will miss them."

"Where did you meet David?"

She turned. They had gone over possible questions at dinner. David had said to let him field that one. "Would you like to answer that, darling?"

"Certainly." David smiled. "We met at a rather important occasion in downtown Los Angeles. I almost didn't attend, but as soon as we met, I was glad I decided to go. If you don't mind now, I see someone I want my wife to meet."

"What a wonderful answer," she whispered as he whisked her away. "I'll have to remember it." That was the first time she learned that her husband could answer a question truthfully by skirting the whole truth.

T.J. followed them across the room. "Walk over to Margarita and Buck. Leave your wife with your mother, and you and Buck join me in Colby's den."

* * * * *

David nodded to T.J., the senator, and the other man. Levi's words sprang to his mind, but he smiled at his cousin even as he wondered why Ray was present. Ray knew ranching, and could throw a rope almost as well as anyone, but the bookkeeper could usually be found indoors. How could he afford high stakes games? His side if the family didn't have that kind of money.

"You didn't say what the important event in L.A. was," Ray commented.

"Just a party some of us were invited to attend. Hollywood went all out to make all servicemen feel welcome."

"Something she said Monday," T.J. said, "made me think that she didn't expect such a crowd or know much about the ranch."

"You don't know how good it felt to know that it was me that interested her and not the money. I didn't tell her about the ranch until a few days after the wedding. I only told her about the oil last night." He was pleased that both T.J. and his grandfather liked his wife. "She's the oldest of six, and from what I saw she's had a hand in raising her brothers. I know she helped out financially."

"I was listening to her talk to the reporters," T.J. said. "She's evidently going to miss her family."

"It's only natural that she will." He thought having Tish close by might help, but he certainly wasn't going to mention that in front of Ray. He turned to the senator. "I understand you intend to retire."

"I figure it's about time I paid I little more attention to family. Gladys and I are going to be great-grandparents in three months. Time to hand over the reins to you young ones. Might take her on some trips when things get back to normal. She'd like that."

"Whit and I think Ray here would be a good man to run your campaign." T.J. said. "David, you'd better start looking for another bookkeeper.

"Now wait a minute," Ray bellowed. "I don't recall telling you I was ready to change jobs. I've been part of this outfit for fifteen years." His gaze went from man to man. "That's right, aint it Buck? You been happy with me. Right?"

"We all have, Ray," David told him, all the while thinking that he had better get his hands on the books as soon as possible. His cousin was protesting too loudly. Thank God he had visited Levi Goldman. "I would rather keep the books in the family," he told T.J. "We have time to think about it."

"April," the senator said. "That's when I'll make the announcement."

"Shall we rejoin the ladies?" T.J. asked.

"You go on," David told him. ""I want to call my foreman and find out how things are out in the stable and corral."

When he was alone, he called and talked, not to Steve but to Elena. "Go into the office," he told her. "In the bottom left hand drawer of the desk you'll find ledgers, the books Ray takes care of on Tuesdays and Thursdays. Take them up to your room until I come home tomorrow. If Ray comes around, you know nothing about them. You'll find the key to the drawer in the cigar humidor. Lock the drawer after you get the books, keep the key for me."

His hand was slow as he hung up. He did know of another bookkeeper in the family. Having three active boys around might be good for his mother. She tried not to show it, but losing both the twins had hit her hard, and now she had lost Pretty Girl. Life been throwing her too many curves."

David pictured the boys as he had first seen them, their cap guns in hand during a mock shoot out, the way they had strapped on the holsters he and Cindy had bought in Las Vegas. Never a replacement for his brothers, but perhaps a distraction, and he had promised them he would teach them to ride. It was worth thinking about. He might have someone investigate, find out how good he was and how much he made. He had mentioned that they had moved from Chicago when Cindy was about six. She had mentioned an aunt and uncle, but no other relatives.

Her mother seemed like a meek little housewife, but at the Brown Derby she had surprised him. She might be one of those quiet women who ruled the roost without their husbands ever realizing it. The very fact that the thought came to him had him wondering if Cindy was going to be like her mother. She had certainly had her say in T.J.;s office that afternoon. They were going to be quite a pair. He was going to keep her safe, and he was going to build her a house she would love.

* * * * *

"I was there with a girl friend." Cindy and her mother-in-law were talking to Senator Colby's wife and several other women. "Until I saw his stripes, I thought David was an officer. He just had that look. I think I fell in love with him the moment we met."

"He should have let Whitney get him a commission," Mrs. Colby said. "Did you and David have a big wedding?"

"We eloped to Las Vegas." She hesitated just a bit. "My sisters and I decided quite some time ago that would be best. The boys are triplets, and we would rather have Dad use the money for their education." The smile on her mother-in-law's face told her that she had said the right thing in the right way. That had been her suggestion at dinner. She had been sure the question would come up. "I can't think of a better way to have a wedding. It was so romantic. If you're ever in Las Vegas you should stay at the Hotel El Rancho Vegas. It's perfect. The colonel and his wife who stood up with us were very nice. He had been stationed in Texas once." It was true, but if David was an important part of the law firm, she wasn't going to let the wives patronize her. She could be a name dropper when it would help.

A younger woman, who was probably a few years older than she was, joined the little group, kissing Mrs. Colby on the cheek.

"Hello, Auntie. You're looking wonderful."

"You look happy. Have you got a new boy friend?"

"Not a chance. All the good ones are taken. I'm happy because I finally quit my job. When I went to work for Uncle Luke I didn't know he would keep me in the secretarial pool forever." She greeted David's mother. "Of course I will have to find another job quickly. I do have rent to pay." She held out her hand. "You must be David's wife. I'm Eleanor Colby. Uncle Luke said he met you this afternoon."

"I'm Cindy." Was this the girl who was supposed to meet her?

"I hope you know you've dashed a lot of hopes around here. There has been more than one girl waiting for David to come home. I think it will be ever so nice having someone new around. If you like, we can practice barrel racing together. Do you have your own horse?"

"I'm afraid not." She wasn't even sure what barrel racing was. It sounded improbable. "Yesterday morning David told his mother I don't know one end of a horse from another. I do know that much, but I'm not sure I've even thought about riding one."

"Oh, you must. You can't be on a spread like the Diamond MiK without riding. I know David will be busy, but he will find time to teach you."

"If you have time, could you come out and tell me a little about it?" Luke Colby hadn't wasted any time. This girl was definitely the one he talked about. She reached out to touch her arm. It wasn't an instinctive gesture, but if she was going to fit in, as

David had said, she was going to have to learn to touch and hug. It seemed that all these Texans did so. "You could start by telling me what barrel racing is."

"Oh, dear, we are going to have to teach you a lot."

"It might be a good idea," David's mother said, "if we stayed over until tomorrow and buy you some proper clothing for riding. You don't want to use those pretty white boots for everyday wear."

David walked over in time to hear that remark.

"I want to be back at the ranch before noon, but you could spend a few hours shopping before going home. Hello, Eleanor. Mom, make sure she gets gloves. She doesn't want to ruin her hands." He reached down for her hand "We'll find a couple of geldings for you and Mom, but with your talent, your art comes first."

"You didn't tell us your were an artist," Mrs. Colby said.

"After we have it framed, we will show you the portrait she did of me at the Grand Canyon." He smiled at all the ladies. "She has a remarkable talent." He looked at his mother. "You and Gramps stay as long as you like. I gave Gramps the spare key. Cindy and I have been on the go ever since eight-thirty this morning. I think it's time for us to leave."

"How long have you been married?" Eleanor asked.

"Three weeks tomorrow."

"Well you two love birds just toddle off. You've been here long enough, but David, if Cindy needs an assistant,. I'm in the market for a job. We can't have a Mrs. McKaid who doesn't even know about barrel racing."

"Come out to the ranch, and we'll discuss it," David told her. "First you'll have to assure Cindy that you're not an old girlfriend. I've been informed that I'll be shot if I get too close to one of those."

"Now that's what I calll a good Texas wife. I'm going to like you, Cindy."

Chapter 30

David was up and dressed before the sun made an appearance. Cindy stirred, half awake.

"Go back to sleep." he told her. "I want to catch Steve before he gets started on the day's work."

By eight-thirty o'clock he and Steve were inspecting part of the fence. A short distant away a river meandered its slow passage though the pasture and past an outcropping of rock.

"You're right." Steve told him. "At first glance it's fine, but it would be quick work to open it up wide enough to get a truck through."

"Next week, get someone out here stringing up more wire. I want five strands of barbed wire along this section between us and the Simpsons. Too low to crawl under and too high to jump"

"I can have someone out here tomorrow."

"We don't need a gate between us and the Simpsons, but next week will do. We're going to raise some dust today, and I don't want anyone asking why."

"What goes with that family anyway. They can't be as bad as they say."

"Whatever you've heard, take it as gospel. The term white trash was invented for them. E2 is the only one who has a lick of sense. Probably the only one who doesn't think that because a woman lives on the place she's fair game."

"E2 his real name?"

"If you're a Simpson man, your name is Elmer. The number just says how far down the ladder you are. When the old man dies, you move up. The only thing they do know is how to make damn fine moonshine. No one's ever gone blind drinking it, but after today the men in these parts will have to look elsewhere. We're here to dry up the supply."

"Do you lose many head off those little cliffs over there?"

"Not that we've noticed. There's easy access to the river here. That might be why this spot was chosen. More than likely it was just plain spite. From what I've been told our two families have never gotten along. We've been trying to buy their forty acres for as long as anyone can remember. Now I have the means, but somehow, as much as I hate Betty Lou, I can't see myself doing it." He had one foot in the stirrup, preparing to mount Tiger. "I'll show you why we're here."

Steve mounted his horse, and the two rode the short way to the bushes and trees growing up against the small cliff. The bushes were old enough and green enough to make a man think their roots must run deep. A heavy rain always brought the creek water close. When he dismounted and let the reins fall from Tiger's head, Steve followed suit.

"I haven't been in here in years, but I'm sure it's still here."

It was just as he remembered. He led the way through the narrow opening behind the bushes and around several man size rocks. Five feet in from a deep overhang he stopped. It hadn't changed much. Empty mason jars were still stacked along one side along with empty jugs. A couple of crates were probably used for stools. The big vat and copper tubing were the same as he had seen years before. There were a couple more propane tanks than there had been back then. A black nothingness at the back seemed to indicate that it might be the entrance to a cave. He would have to bring a couple of strong flashlights to make sure no one was back there.

Steve whistled. “Looks like you’ve got yourself something illegal going on here.”

“It’s not ours. My brothers found it when they were young. I found them out back of one of the out buildings drunk as a couple of skunks. I gave them their choice of telling me where they found the stuff or me telling Mom. It’s probably been here for generations. The Simpsons have been the chief suppliers for as long as anyone can remember. I know for a fact that the revenuers have gone over their forty acres more than once. Everyone knows they make it, but no one has located this. The older I get, the more it worries me. Think you can demolish it?”

“Those propane tanks should go up pretty good, but few sticks of dynamite would help.”

“Can you do it without a detonator? I don’t want to advertise what we’re hauling out here. I want it destroyed, inaccessible and not talked about.”

Steve took his time looking around, inspecting it all.

“With those propane tank here, I will want to be far enough away. Give me enough cord or rope and some gasoline and I’ll rearrange the landscape.”

“It will be here by noon. My architect is coming out to look over the location for our house. He will have it with him. We’ll see if we can’t do it before my grandfather and the women get back from Austin.”

“You building your own house? Your mother’s been pretty busy getting your room redone. I heard her telling your grandfather how much it meant to have you at home again.”

“I know she’s disappointed.” He had hated seeing that look of on his mother’s face, but he knew Cindy needed her own home. “I made a promise to Cindy’s father. He asked me to give his daughter a home of her own. Evidently they lived with her in-laws for years, and it was not an arrangement he and her mother enjoyed. We’ll be living in the foreman’s house until ours is built.”

“Not exactly the lap of luxury.”

“Cindy didn’t marry me for my money. She didn’t know I had any.” He led the way back to the horses.

* * * * *

Cindy relaxed in the back seat. David's mother had slipped off her shoes. She did the same. His grandfather was driving the old Chevy. She couldn't quite believe how much money she had spent. She still wasn't completely comfortable about that. What would David say when he found out that she had bought for Tish as well? That had been at his mother's insistence

"Mama Deedee tells me she doesn't have a thing," she had said. "Buck told me she was wearing a hospital gown when they landed in the pasture. Buck and Steve had a mattress in the back of the pick-up to take her to Deedee's cabin. They had her wrapped in a light hospital blanket. Evidently her sailor had trashed all her things because no one found them."

As a result Cindy had three dresses, a skirt and blouse, and under clothes for her sister. They had been the same size for years, so she was sure they would fit. For herself she had picked out three gingham blouses and three pair of blue jeans. She also had a light brown Lady Stetson, a straw hat, and a pair of riding boots that Margarita had insisted upon. His mother had also suggested buying two boxes of expensive thank you notes, saying that there would be wedding presents coming.

It was early evening before they arrived home. Robert had left word that a well digger would be out the next day. Elena was busy in the kitchen. Before all the packages were inside, David and Steve rode in. David dismounted and kissed her.

"Did you have a good day, honey?

"I spent a lot of money. I bought some things for Tish. I hope you don't mind."

"I'm sure she needs them."

"Looks like you've been working?" his grandfather commented.

"It would take some heavy equipment to clean up the mess we left behind. I'll join you for supper as soon as I get Tiger taken care of and get washed up. Elena has supper ready."

Cindy had planned on going to the little cabin to see Tish, but just as soon as David had washed up, Elena had super on the table. After they had eaten they walked into that big living room, and for a moment she thought maybe she had been dreaming and forgotten to wake up. There on the library table was a magnificent silver tea set from T.J. and beside it was a cut glass punch bowl with a silver ladle and two dozen darling little cups. The card with those was signed by Senator Colby and his wife. She was going to need those thank you notes. Maybe it wasn't all a fairytale, but she was finding out how Cinderella must have felt.

Chapter 31

While David was out riding and in the stables Cindy wrote her first two thank you cards. She still had some one cent stamps in her purse. She had only sent her family one postcard apiece, and one to Sophie. Probably she should have sent more. She put three on each envelope and looked at her mother-in-law. "Where do I mail these?" she asked.

"I will have some mail myself. Just leave them on the little table by the door." Margarita glanced down at Cindy's feet. "If you and David plan to go out with Robert and the well digger and watch the water witch, low heels or boots might be more comfortable. High heels tend to dig into the dirt. You do look a lot better in the blue jeans and blouse. That jump suit Monday looked pretty well worn."

"I wore them for over two years at the aircraft factory. We had to wear pants and either tie back our hair or wear snoods. I'll get my boots. I don't have any low heels. I've read about witching for water, but does anyone really believe in it." In this day and age it did sound rather odd.

"If it's Barney who is going to drill, he won't do it unless it's been witched. Do you mind if I go out with you and David to watch?

David can show us where you're going to put your little honeymoon house."

"I'd love to have you come." She slipped off her shoes and placed them on the staircase, thinking she would pick them up next time she went upstairs. She didn't correct Margarita, wondering what David's mother would think when she saw their house being built. What they had talked about the previous day was definitely not a little house. "I'm going to take Tish the things we bought her. I won't be long".

She still felt as though she was in a different world as she sat in the wash room, putting the boot hooks through the leather loops and pulling on the brown boots she had bought the day before. She couldn't help thinking that the ranch house wasn't what went with so much money. The furniture and all were a lot newer than what was in her parents' house, but it had a homey, lived in look, nothing like the big houses in Beverly Hills where the rich movie stars lived. And the grandmother living in the little log cabin in back? She didn't think that was because they were ashamed of her. David obviously adored her.

As she mounted the steps to the little porch with its old rocking chairs, she felt that perhaps the little cabin was his grandmother's choice. When she stepped inside, it was as though she was stepping into an older world, one that would really appreciate the Navaho rug when it arrived. Her sister, still wrapped in that lovely red kimono, sat on the old sofa, caressing the puppy David had brought her on Tuesday.

"Mamaw Deedee just figured maybe she needed something to love," David had told her later. Evidently it had been a good move. Tish looked slightly better, maybe a little calmer.

"You have clothes for your sister," Deedee said. "Good. It's about time she has something of her own to wear." She lifted the puppy from Tish's lap. "Time Precious should go out and piddle. You and Tish can talk."

"Who is T.J.?" Tish asked as Deedee closed the screen door behind herself and walked off the porch with the puppy.

"He's David's godfather and the senior partner in his law firm. He and Senator Whitney Clayton brought you in from Oklahoma City."

"Senator?" her sister exclaimed. "Where on earth are we anyway?"

"It's called the Diamond MiK. Austin is about an hour away."

"Texas?"

"Of course."

"Does David work here?" she asked. "I thought he was a lawyer. Deedee said this T.J. person told her I'm not to go outside."

"David told me he and T.J. are trying to figure out a way for it to look like you are just arriving from Hollywood. After you are well," she added. "They don't want anyone to know what happened to you. They want to hush up any scandal before it can start. He said something like that would follow you around the rest of your life."

"How could I have been so stupid? It's all a little hazy. I know the nurse gave me a shot of something for pain before we left the hospital and it really knocked me out, but it was starting to wear off. I'm pretty sure I was in an airplane. That much I remember." She ran her hand through her hair. "Imagine? My first ride in one and I can't even remember it. It seems were there two men who carried me over here in the back of a truck." Tish didn't seem to know what to do with her hands.

"David's grandfather and Steve, brought you in from the pasture where the plane landed. Steve is the ranch foreman. David met him when they were in the army. All the rest of the people who work here were away on errands of one kind or another. They didn't want anyone to know about you until they found out who you were and why you had David's card."

"I hope you understand all that because I sure don't." She held up one of the blouses. "Lucy, these are pretty, but how I can I pay you? I don't have anything anymore. Eddie took the money you gave me. You tried to tell me, but I didn't listen. I sure wish I had. When Eddie found out I had a hundred dollars I hadn't told him about, he just exploded. Can't we have him arrested for what he did to me?"

"It wouldn't be a good idea." Cindy took her sister's hand. "Don't even think about it. It's over. He was AWOL, and he was stealing cars and who knows what else. T.J. told us the Shore Patrol took him."

"How can I not worry?" Her sister was doing her best not to cry. "I don't think I can ever forget what he did to me. How can I? After what he did, I'll never have another baby. I guess I'm just lucky to be alive, but I'm a burden to you and David. It must have cost a lot to have those men come out to get me. Now all these clothes and a nurse. . ."

"Didn't she tell you?" Cindy was shocked. "Deedee is David's great-grandmother."

"Grandmother? But she's. . ." Tish hesitated.

"She's Cheyenne and a medicine woman." Cindy nodded her head and smiled. The words came slowly. She didn't want her sister to think less of David because of his family. "It must be quite a story. David told me that Deedee's husband was an Irish mountain man, a hunter, a trapper, and a scout. Actually, he said he rode with Kit Carson. Can you just imagine that? It's all so unbelievable. When I met David— Tish, he told me he had a couple of cows. I thought he was a farmer."

"Just where did you meet him? You didn't tell me you were going out to see someone."

"I wasn't. I just met David that night when I crawled out the window." She was glad Tish didn't seem to realize she hadn't answered her question about prosecuting Eddie. She would let David explain why it wouldn't be a good idea. "Sophie and I went downtown to Hill Street. It was like New Years Eve, only better." Her eyes lit up at the memory. It was a night she would remember forever. "Right there in the middle of the street he kissed me, and, oh, Tish, it was like magic. I couldn't get Jerry's ring off my finger fast enough. I managed to slide it off with my gloves, but David still noticed it. We spent a couple of hours in Tony's bar. No one was drinking much. David doesn't like to drink. Last night at Senator Colby's house he made one glass of champagne last all evening."

"I bet he made sure you drank though."

"You know Sophie and I have our two drink rule. David didn't even finish his. I should have seen the signs. He didn't sound like a hick farmer but after he kissed me, I was so crazy about him, I didn't care what he was. We took Sophie home and went to that big hotel in Wilshire Blvd. I was afraid he was spending all his mustering out pay. He said we'd go to Las Vegas that night but that the car didn't have enough gas to get us there, and, of course, gas stations aren't open that late. We had to wait for morning when they opened."

"So what exactly is that husband of yours? A cowboy on a ranch or a lawyer? That convertible he owns is pretty fancy for a cowboy."

"David doesn't work here. He owns it. At least his family does." Cindy's voice mellowed. "Tish, last night we were actually at a State Senator's house. Senator Colby is one of the partner's in the law firm. They made David a partner and had a party to announce it. It's a big stone house with a butler, a grand piano and a couple of cute black maids walking around serving drinks and hors d'oeurvres." She took a deep breath and looked at her sister. "The newspapers interviewed us and took pictures. They were talking about David maybe going into politics. Not only is this his ranch, there are oil wells on it."

"Ooh." It was a long, drawn out ooh, accompanied by shocked look. "Guess I don't need to worry about paying you."

"Not this time. That first night, David said I didn't look like a Lucy. He called me Cindy. Who would have thought that I'd turn out to be like Cinderella?" She leaned forward to kiss her sister on the cheek. "I have to go now, but I'll be back. There's a well digger coming out. I can't believe it, but they have someone come out and try to find where to drill by walking around with a stick. I want to see that. David's having a house built just for us. Wish me luck. To tell truth, Tish, this whole thing scares the heck out of me. What if I mess things up for David? I'd never forgive myself."

Chapter 32

David lifted the saddle off Tiger, quite aware of the man leaning against the wall.

"Thought we were friends, Davy."

"I hope we still are."

"Pa and me, we went out to start cooking. All we found was a mess of rocks. Pa's pretty mad. Didn't know friends blow up each other's property." His words held the flat monotone of a man dredged in hopelessness. "You being a lawyer, ain't there some kind of a law against that?"

Without looking at E2, David put the saddle in place and started brushing down Tiger.

"Not if someone's granddaddy put his illegal still on someone else's property. That was downright sneaky of him. What I do on my own property is my business, not yours. You've been the trespassers."

"A hundred or so yards in. How'd you find it anyway? Wasn't much room to get in between those rocks. You come home from the war having a stranger take over, and almost the first thing you do is blow it up. What if Pa had been inside?"

"We checked that out. Didn't want to have anyone hurt." He went on brushing down his horse. "Steve's no stranger. We were in the same outfit. He's a good man. I've known that still was there for years."

"How'd you find it?"

"The twins found that damn thing when they were fifteen. I found them both behind the pump house, stinking drunk. If Mom or Gramps had found them, there would have been hell to pay. It was tell me where it was or tell them. I didn't give them much of a choice." David looked up. "I never knew what to do about it until one day I was watching Steve set some charges to blow up a bridge. It came to me then. There was a man right there who was not only a good friend, he was a cowboy who was sick of rounding up newborns in the Wyoming snow and who knew how to blow things up safely."

He shook his head. "I'd just gotten word about Tim and was feeling pretty low, thinking about him and Taylor. Offered Steve the job that night."

"Life's been hard enough, Davy." E2 didn't move. "All Pa knows how to do is make his moonshine, and Betty Lou might be smart about some things, but she sure ain't smart enough to hold down a job. Aunt Adelaide was the only woman who ever stuck around, and she fell down the steps and killed herself after she married your uncle. With my own ma dying when I was born, I never knew her, and Pa sure likes to remind Betty Lou that hers run off cause she couldn't stand changing her skinny butt."

"That still has worried me all these years, thinking of what would happen if the Feds found it. The trouble was, I knew it was probably the only thing keeping you all alive. I always figured I didn't have to worry about the sheriff. He was never too keen about looking for it, but I know for sure the Feds have searched your property more than once. It would have been a disaster for us if they had ever found it on McKaid land." David went to the other side of his horse. "On our land, not yours." His voice hardened. "That wasn't right."

"I try, Davy, but it's hard. No one wants to hire me because my name's Simpson. Decided years ago I'll never marry. No girl would want to have me anyway, and I'm damned sure I don't want to bring any more idiots into this world. Time we stopped this lunacy of Elmer 1, 2, and 3. Been a laughing stock all my life because of it."

"I'll pay you double wages during round-up, and after that I'll put a good word in for you at the feed store. Mamaw Deedee says it's going to be a hard winter. Did you tell that sister of yours about the foal the other night?"

"Might have mentioned it. She was still up and angry when Pa and I got home. Everyone who was still here heard about you giving it to your wife as a wedding present. I kept telling her you weren't ever gonna to marry a Simpson."

David finished currying Tiger and turned him loose.

"Putting a gun to that little foal sickened me. She had promise, and Mom thought the world of Pretty Girl, mainly because she was the last thing Pop had a chance to give her." He turned away. "Make sure the gates are all fastened. I'll tell Elena to fix a basket for you to take home."

"Can't figure you out, Davy. First you blow up our income, then you feed us."

"It's like I always told you, E2. You may be a Simpson, but you haven't got a mean bone in your body. Anyone else would have left a long time ago."

"They're kin. Someone's got to make sure they don't starve."

"You just tell your kin to remember what I said about your sister. She threatened Cindy Monday night. Betty Lou's a skinny thing, but she's strong. While we're at it, you'd better destroy those Foxglove flowers she's so proud of. Mamaw Deedee thinks she might raise them for more than their looks. They're deadly, you know."

"Hell, you think I don't have better sense than to cross my sister? I wouldn't be surprised if everything in that garden wasn't poison. I've stepped careful around her ever since I come to be Elmer Number2 stead of 3. Tell the truth, Davy, I've always figured she's the first Simpson woman strong enough to not be getting it from every man on the place. Don't think Pa's ever touched the girl. Not so sure about the old man. She hated him as far back as that wedding. Tell the truth, I always sort of figured she thought if you married her, she'd be free of the place. That bun in Aunt Adelaide's belly might not have been your uncle's."

"Anyone sees her on the Diamond MiK, she's a trespasser. Wish I could prove it. Anyone else would have at least killed the filly outright instead of crushing its legs and letting it suffer. I'm the one who had to put a bullet in her. Don't forget that because I won't. Pop traded two steers for Pretty Girl just so Mom got the Palomino she wanted, and that was when things were damned tough around here."

"I'll do my best. I always told her you'd never marry her. By the way, congratulations. Saw the piece in the paper about you being a partner in your law firm. Your wife's a real beauty."

* * * * *

As Cindy reached the back porch of the main house a pick-up with a horse trailer pulled into the yard. Eleanor Colby hopped out. She was dressed in jeans, boots, and hat, and was holding a limp bread sack filled with a few cookies. A crumpled piece of paper was tied to the piece of string holding it closed.

"Hi, Cindy. I figured I might as well bring my horse. David probably has room for him."

"Hello, Eleanor. As soon as they get here, we're going to go find out where our well will be."

"Go get a hat, girl. Don't be out in this sun without one. Right now, I want to know if anyone around here has an old dog they need to get rid of. Elena or Buck ought to know."

"That's an odd thing to want."

"It's the quickest way to find out about these cookies." She waved the bread sack in the air. "It was tied to the gate."

"A gift?" she asked.

"Looks like it. It's your name scrawled on the paper. It should have been brought up to the house. It looks like I got here just in time." She started toward the back porch. "The first thing I have to tell you is, don't eat anything unless you know where it came from. Lab tests take time. It might sound cruel, but we want to know if you're in danger. If the dog starts to suffer a bullet will take care if it quickly."

Cindy stopped dead in her tracks. "That's a terrible thing to do."

"Would you rather be the guinea pig? Like I said, lab tests take time. David's paying me to protect you, not the livestock."

The words did little to quell Cindy's anger at the idea, but the hat probably was a good idea. She didn't want a sunburned face. She went into the house, jammed a hat on her head, and was frowning when she and Margarita walked out the back door. The ranch pick-up was parked near Eleanor's horse trailer. David, Buck, and Steve were all talking to Eleanor.. She was still holding the bread sack

"We'll put her in a stall for now," David was saying.

Cindy went to him. "I don't need a nursemaid, David. Eleanor can take her horse home. We never had a dog at home but if we had, we sure wouldn't have ended its days by trying to poison it." The words came softly but were firm..

"I'm sorry if I offended you." Eleanor broke the awkward silence which suddenly descended on the little group. "I didn't like the idea, but I thought it would be best if we knew as soon as possible if there is someone after you."

* * * * *

David put his arm around his wife. Maybe she was in a new environment, but she was still the girl who had looked up at him saying, "I'm old enough to do as I please." Still the oldest child, taking care of the younger ones even when the younger one was a non-existent dog.

"I told Eleanor that it was completely unnecessary. Poison is a woman's weapon. A man will use a gun, choke or beat his victim, or cut a brake line, but will practically never use poison. The cookies will go to a lab, not to find out, but to verify our suspicions. Betty Lou's the only one who would try anything this stupid. I under estimated her capacity for hating." He touched her cheek. "Let Eleanor stay for my peace of mind, if for no other reason."

"It's her choice," Eleanor said. "I really am sorry if I offended you. Last night, I somehow got the impression that David and his family, and even T.J., were all trying to protect a fragile, little city girl. I see I was wrong. That's not you anymore than it's true that I'm the bubble headed dilettante people think I am. David has been telling me about Betty Lou Simpson and how she reacted when she found out about your marriage. If you have a half-crazed woman after you, there should be someone who can concentrate on you without the pressure of doing his or her own thing."

The sound of engines distracted them. The two cars coming up the gravel drive were followed by a flat-bed carrying drilling equipment and pipe. Luke Colby and Robert both joined the group. Both men wore jeans, boots, and the ever present western hat.

"Getting settled in?" Luke asked his niece. "Problems?"

"Someone left these tied to the gate." Eleanor handed the cookies to her uncle. "A hand written note says they are for the new bride. It seems to us that something like that should be analyzed."

Cindy looked up at her husband. "Didn't I hear you say something about putting Eleanor's horse in a stall?"

"We'll have someone see to it."

"Not you," David said as Steve started forward. "We don't need trucks coming in this way once the builders start. We will need our own gate, so we might as well put it in now. I'll show you where. Shall we get started?"

"Bet this little gal's never ridden a tailgate." Buck's eye twinkled as he moved to the back of the pick-up and opened it up.

"First time for everything." David swung her up and took his place beside her. "Hang on to the hinge. honey. Drive it a little slow, Gramps."

Chapter 33

Cindy, along with everyone else, watched as the old man inspected a tree, selected the end of a branch, and stripped the leaves until he had a Y about a foot long. Slowly he started walking the area, the top ends of the Y curving into his hands; the single end horizontal to the ground.

"Not everyone can do it," David explained. "I can't. Neither can Gramps or Mom. Both Tim and Taylor could. To her surprise the stick suddenly turned downward. The man crisscrossed the area several times, each time the branch dipped down at the same spot. "Might have to go deep," he remarked as the stick kept bobbing up and down slightly.

"Didn't figure on a shallow one." The well digger walked over and gave a few taps to a stake to mark the spot.

"That will work out fine," Robert said. "We can put the house in front of the well and run the septic lines out to the field. Start drilling. Just remember we want water, not oil," he joked.

Soon Robert had blue prints spread out along the hood of his car.

"This is something I designed a few years back, thinking of it for myself someday. I think we can adapt it to what you want." He pointed to the center. "Living area here, a long one just like you have in the house now. Kitchen and dining behind, two bedrooms on either side with a bathroom in each wing. Above the living area we put your wife's studio. We'll be far enough away from the trees to have good light. We could put in a skylight if you like."

"Is this another room?" Cindy indicated a spot in front of what he had called the living area."

"A semi enclosed patio, maybe just a low brick wall. We can make the walls strong enough for adding a second story over the bedrooms. It will cost more, but save in the long run."

"Got a pencil?" David asked. When Robert handed him one, he reached over and sketched out rooms on the right." Put five rooms here, a master bedroom all across the end. A private bath, closets big enough to walk into. Comfortable chairs and maybe a little ladies desk could go by this window.

"A retreat for the lady of the house?" Robert asked.

"Right. Make this section three rooms long. First one on the right can be my office. Make the bathrooms big enough to move around in. I've got a couple of buddies who came home in wheelchairs."

"No problem. Wider doors for closets and bathrooms. You might want to use two of those rooms for a nursery and playroom someday."

"Spanish style," David commented. "Give it an old Mexico look— maybe stucco with a red tile roof. I saw a few in Southern California that looked pretty nice. When we went through Arizona and New Mexico we did some shopping. We have some Navaho rugs and pottery coming."

"Whitish brick would look about the same."

"Could we have big glass windows looking out on the patio?" she asked.

"It's your house. Mrs. McKaid. You can have whatever you want. David, what about the left wing? To keep it symmetrical we could make part of it a garage. The entrance to that should be in the rear close to the kitchen."

David nodded his approval. "Fine."

His grandfather was standing in front of the car looking at the plans.

"Seems to me I heard someone complaining when I wanted to build back in forty-one. Something about the old home place meaning a lot to us McKaids. Don't recall your checking account being big enough for a palace like this. You needing something fancy now just because you're a partner in that law firm of yours?"

"Jefferson, Colby, and Smith has nothing to do with the house Cindy and I are building." David met his grandfather's eyes. "Have you forgotten what you gave me when I became a fully fledged lawyer, what you intended for the twins when they got their degrees? "

"Much your ranch as mine," he agreed. "I know that. You and your mother's names are on all the papers same as mine."

"You've always said you were saving it for the future. Well, the future is here. Our children will be the future. When people drive past, I want them to be saying, That's where the McKaids live.' I'm mighty grateful for all you've done for us. You didn't let us become narrow minded, stuck-up, little rich kids. You made sure we didn't grow up thinking we were better than anyone else just because we had money. Don't forget I was fifteen when that well came in. Except for fixing up the inside, having decent clothes to wear, and our pick of a university, we basically lived the same way we always had. I'm going to try to raise my children the same way. They'll do their share of chores around the place, but this house is going to be good enough for anyone, even the President of the United States.

"Aiming high, boy."

"Not me. Not yet." He shook his head. "Not yet. In the past few years I've seen enough to know that a country that keeps its colored soldiers in kitchens isn't ready to have a president with Indian and Mexican blood in him, but I'm going make sure my sons will live in a better world— one that calls all men equal. I've met men with PHDs who served as mess attendants just because the color of their skin offended men in high places, and along with it, I served under white men who let men die because they themselves were ignorant and arrogant bastards. If that doesn't change, someday this country of ours will be in real trouble right here at home."

Cindy smiled to herself, knowing that her husband had just made his first brief campaign speech. Maybe she had lived in Hollywood most of her life, but she was a California girl who knew what kind discrimination was rampant. After all, neither she nor David had mentioned his blood lines to her parents. She would have to ease into that when she wrote home.

"Think we ought to have a swimming pool, honey?" he asked her.

"I think that would be nice."

"Put it in the plans," he told Robert. "We don't have to put it in until next spring. Make that a three car garage in back. About time the McKaids start living it up a bit."

"Think the boy's head swelled up with all that shooting over there, Margarita?"

"I don't think so, Buck," his mother said. "I think it will be a big improvement over the foreman's house."

"Think of it as helping our people around here. A lot of workmen are going to be drawing a paycheck for awhile. We will be employing others when it's a done deal."

So the children she would have were the future. Cindy liked the sound of that. How had all this happened. Maybe her mother had been right after all. Maybe there really was a God who was looking after he.

* * * * *

On Friday afternoon Eleanor drove off in her pick-up and horse trailer. When she returned, Cindy and David admired the black horse she led out.

"That little pony's a beauty all right, but we have more than enough in the pasture," David said

"All of which are working horses. I used this one for my brother's two girls. He's used to having someone new on his back." She offered the lead rope to Cindy. His name is Seth. Stay on his left side just about where I am standing. We are going to stand here and talk for a few minutes, and then you are going to walk him over to the stable. When we get there stroke his neck and tell him what a good boy he is and give him this apple"

"That's not the way I learned to ride a horse," David told her.

"And that's probably because your father sat you on one almost as soon as you could walk. He probably carried you on one before that."

Though she had always enjoyed the cowboy movies, riding a horse had never been on Cindy's *things to do* list. She took the rope into her hands the way Eleanor showed her. Not once there on Hill Street had she considered it. Not even in Las Vegas as she said, "I do," had she considered the fact that if she married David, she would have to start sitting on top of an animal big enough to crush her. She did her best to smile as she and Eleanor started walking toward the gate. David had called it a pony, but it looked like a horse to her. David waited until they were through the gate before getting into the pick-up to drive the horse trailer to where their own was kept.

Later that night, in the privacy of their bedroom, she asked David if he would talk to her sister.

"Tish can't seem to understand why Eddie wasn't arrested for what he did to her. Maybe you can explain it better than I can."

"Doesn't she understand what it would be like on the witness stand?"

"Would it really be that bad?"

"It would be brutal." He had his arms around her. "I wanted us to be by ourselves in the foreman's house, but I didn't figure on anything like what's been going on. It hasn't been the kind of welcome I wanted. With Betty Lou on a rampage, I'll feel better if we stay here. I don't want you to be alone."

"Everything is happening so fast. We haven't even been here a week, and look at all the things that we've done. Do we really need a house that big?"

"Need? Probably not, but it's what I've thought about for years. At first I didn't want Gramps to build, but after a few years I realized that I felt that way because I wanted to be the one to build it. Mom and Mamaw Deedee always told me I would find the right girl someday, and sometimes when it got really cold over there in Europe, when we were half frozen with the snow and half asleep with weariness, the only thing that kept my feet going was picturing myself sitting in front of a roaring fire with a wife tucked under my arm and children playing on the floor. Sometimes that was all that kept me going. I think even the boys from the north learned to hate snow."

"Your mother asked me if we were going to go to church with them Sunday, " she said after a small lull. A chill ran through her as she pictured a line of men so tired they slept while walking. What must it be like in snow and cold? She only had vague remembrances about sitting on a sled being pulled by her father.

"What did you tell her?"

"I told her we would."

Chapter 34

Cindy took the hand the preacher offered her. David had introduced him as Reverend Cooper.

"Welcome to our congregation, Mrs. McKaid. I fear we'll seem small to someone from Hollywood."

"Hollywood is just another town. My family isn't rich." Had she said the wrong thing? After all the McKaids were wealthy beyond her comprehension. She held on to David's hand as they stepped into the little church and walked down to the front pew. It was her first glimpse of the inside of a Protestant church. There were no stained glass windows, no fancy altar, and no kneeling pads. *Did they kneel on the floor?* There was an altar rail, but behind it was a simple table holding a large bible There was a cross on the back wall, a chair on the right, and four chairs on the left, maybe they were for the choir, because there was a piano just the right of their pew.

She discovered that there was no choir; the congregation sang the hymns; they didn't kneel; and her hands felt empty without her missal. It was different from anything she had experienced, but then everything in Texas was. It was like a whole new world. She was aware that protestants didn't have a confessional, but not that communion was broken pieces of soda crackers with grape juice and no fasting.

The piano player was adequate, but no virtuoso. Reverend Pearson greeted all, remarked how wonderful it was to have David and his bride home at last, and preached a sermon on forgiveness and how the world needed to heal.

After the service was over, she and David stood with the preacher and shook hands with all forty-one of the parishioners and David's mother even invited the preacher and his family to join them for dinner the following Sunday.

Back at the ranch, as they changed into blue jeans and shirts, David asked her how she had liked the church.

"It's very plain, but everyone is very friendly." *Where was the beauty and pageantry she had always felt in church? The service had seemed so drab and humdrum. I'll get used to it,* she thought. *All brides have to adjust to a new life. The trouble is, I have two lives to adjust to— this ranch and Austin.*

"Eleanor wants you to walk Seth after dinner. He'll need to be brushed down a bit."

* * * * *

The well came in with pure, sweet water. David ordered a bricked-up pump house built to enclose it with white bricks, of course. The new gate was cut wide enough to allow large trucks to turn in, and soon a copy of the brand was above it, this one accompanied by the words The Diamond MK. David started writing check after check.

Because the report on the cookies came back with word that they were indeed laced with rat poison, Cindy and David didn't go to the foreman's little house. They spent their days and nights in the brass bed Margarita had so lovingly prepared. Eleanor took over one of the remaining bedrooms on the second floor.. The large bedroom on the third floor became the repository for the wedding presents which kept coming. Though Eleanor helped Cindy keep a record of who sent what, and was usually able to add details about the senders, Cindy insisted on writing all the thank you notes herself.

Within a week Robert had the house plans completed and approved. David hired Colby Construction, and Bo Colby was on site supervising the pouring of the concrete slab.

Think you can get it done by Thanksgiving?" David asked him.

"I'll be honest with you, son. We'll be lucky if it's completed by Christmas. You've got yourself one hell of a house here, and it isn't easy to get some of what we need. I think I know what we can do for you though. Looks like the north wing has the master bedroom. Right?"

David nodded.

"We'll get the two by fours and maybe the roof on the south wing, and other than that leave it untouched for now. You don't need those rooms right away. Let the garage wait as well. We'll rough in your wife's studio and the rooms up there, and finish off the master bedroom, kitchen, and great room so you can furnish them. Do that and we'll have you in by Thanksgiving."

"Get the front patio in as well. Cindy will want to show that to her folks."

"They going to be coming in for the holidays?"

"I haven't told anyone yet, so don't mention it."

"I was looking at the plans last night. Something struck me. You sure you don't want a bathroom up there by those rooms opposite the studio? If they're for the help, it might be a good idea. Robert said your wife's an artist. She might want somewhere to wash up."

"I don't know what they are for yet, but you have a point. Put it all in."

"You and your wife will be wanting to pick out some of the fixtures before long. I'll give you the plumbing house address. One other thing. You know anybody with a beat up old black Ford pick-up?"

"Could belong to the Simpsons. Why?"

"It's been driving by real slow like several times a day."

"If a red-head is driving it, she's been warned to stay away. She threatened my wife. Thanks for telling me."

David went from the site to find Steve.

"Four strands of barbed wire in Texas law means no trespassing, but I'm ordering signs. When they come have someone ready to post them along the fence line."

"How many?"

"I'll let you know as soon as I figure out how much fence we have along the front and the Simpson's side."

Just as he turned to enter the house his mother stepped out.

"Mom, do you know any good decorators?" he asked.

"A couple. Since you're going for a Southwestern look, Maurice would be my choice."

"Isn't he. . ."

"A New Yorker? Yes, but he's in love with the look you want. He's a bit flakey and will darling Cindy to death, but he won't try to steal her away. He's good at what he does. Speaking of which, you were right when you said Cindy's talented. She's collecting quite a portfolio of what she calls sketches. They look like more than that to me."

"I don't think she realizes how talented she really is. Once we get the house out of the way, I want to invite a couple of gallery owners in. I'm thinking of giving her a decent camera for Christmas. Right now I just want to get her on that pony Eleanor's got her taking care of."

"She won't admit it, but I think she's scared to death of it."

"Her father said she hasn't been afraid of anything since she as six."

* * * * *

"You're actually riding a horse?" Tish asked.

"Well, not yet." Cindy took her place on the sofa as Deedee took the puppy outside for a walk. "I'm feeding him and grooming him, and learning about saddles and such. I sat on him this morning, but we didn't actually ride. You're looking better, but you still shouldn't go out walking."

"I could walk Precious myself."

"Deedee doesn't mind doing it." She decided to be honest with her. "Tish, no one here knows you're my sister. They think a local girl has come to learn from Deedee."

"Well, I'm learning a lot but I'm sure not local. What's the big deal about it?"

"It's like I told you before, David and T.J. don't want people talking about you, or having a scandal circulating about either of us. It's important for you and for us not to have anyone know what really happened. People talk."

"I want Eddie to be arrested for what he did to me. I want him to know he can't get away with it."

"You need to get your strength back.. For my sake," she pleaded. "just stay inside for now."

"Strange, isn't it, how our lives have changed? I haven't asked you. Are Mom and Dad mad at me?"

"I haven't told them you're here. Mom is worried about you. Dad was pretty upset, but I think he'll get over it. I guess we both disappointed him. I'm not sure if he thinks I'm really married since we didn't have a church ceremony." *Her father would be all right with her sister now that she wasn't going to present him with a grandchild. Poor Tish. Never to be a mother.* "I have to go now. Eat a little more. You've lost weight."

She left to go to the stables with Eleanor. She intended to feed Seth a couple of carrots. She had grown to like the little beast. Putting the heavy saddle on him was left to others, but she learned the importance of checking to make sure it was cinched properly. It was drilled into her that she did not want to find herself on a loose saddle.

"When we were children one of the local girls died because her saddle came loose," David told her. "She should have known better than to ride out without telling anyone. I will worry less if you just ride with either me or Eleanor for now."

"Don't worry about that. I don't think I'll ever really feel comfortable being out of sight of the house."

Chapter 35

David looked around the table. Everyone was seated just as he wanted. Cindy was on his right with his mother next to her. Gramps sat at his left and Cousin Ray was seated on the other side of him. As the one who had called the family conference, he sat at the head of the table. Though he was aware that Ray was eyeing the ledgers, he ignored him and casually rested his right hand atop the books. He would have to thank Levi Goldman for his tip. Ray did indeed have a problem.

"If this is a family conference," Ray said, "what's your ditsy, little blonde doing here?"

"My wife," David informed him, "is a closer member of this family than you are. You may apologize now, and if I ever again hear you refer to her with anything but the respect she deserves, you will be sorry."

"No insult intended, Mrs. McKaid."

It was a lie, but David let it ride. "Gramps, when was the last time you had the book audited?"

"Audited? Davy, we've never had call to do that. If you can't trust kin, who can you trust?"

"Who indeed?" He looked at his mother. "Mom can you tell me what Xavier Freeman does around the place?"

"I have never heard of the man," she answered quickly. "With a name like that, I certainly would have remembered him. I am sure he doesn't work for us."

"He draws a weekly paycheck. Ray," he shifted his gaze, "can you tell me why Xavier doesn't have a social security number?"

"Shucks, Davy," his grandfather said, "is that why you called this here meeting? I coulda told you that. Some years back Ray was a little short, so I told him to invent a name and write himself a check. It was a onetime thing. You're wrong about weekly checks."

"Buck's been doing a fine job of keeping this outfit running, boy." Ray made a move to rise. "If that's all you called me in for, I'm leaving. Just because you're some hot shot lawyer now, you don't need to be thinking you can come in here and start taking over."

"Sit, and don't call me boy." The sit was a firm order. When Ray pushed back his chair, he added, "Sit, or we will all sit here together until Sheriff Brady joins us. I haven't intended to call him in on this, but if I have to, I will."

Ray sat.

"How many years ago was that, Gramps?"

"Don't rightly remember. Maybe two, three years before the war."

"I have only the books for the last three years." He lifted some papers from the top ledger and handed them around. "I had Jinny type these up. It's a list of the checks our Xavier cashed during the last three years. The first of those years our Xavier was earning a hundred dollars a week. A princely sum compared to what anyone else on the place made. It seems he was a pretty valuable employee. Hard to believe, but his salary doubled to two hundred a week last year. So far this year, you will notice, he has earned about twelve thousand dollars." He looked at his cousin. "It doesn't take a lawyer to recognize an embezzlement scheme, Ray. Since you are a McKaid, I don't think we need to cause a scandal. I will give you three month severance pay, meaning, of course, your regular salary. Xavier has already been dropped from the payroll."

His grandfather looked stunned.

"You can't fire me, boy," Ray barked. "Buck runs this outfit."

"You call me boy once more, I might change my mind about the sheriff."

"Maybe I run it, and maybe I don't," Buck said, "but David and Margarita have as much say as I do." All at once he looked a little older. "Looks like I was wrong. Should have caught this years ago. He probably doesn't deserve it, David, but think we could make that a year? At forty-six he's going to have a tough time finding anything. All the jobs will be going to the boys coming home."

"Six months. Is that all right with you, Mother?'

She nodded.

"Cindy?"

"It sounds unbelievably generous."

"Be in my office in Austin tomorrow at three. I'll have the severance papers drawn up by then."

"I'm not signing anything."

"No signature, no checks. It's that simple. It's more than you deserve, but we don't need a scandal around the McKaid name. We'll make that in weekly checks," he added. "Give you the whole thing at once, you'd take it to Dallas and blow it all. I'd stay away from those poker games if I was you. You may leave now." It was a definite dismissal.

It was quiet until they heard his pick-up take off.

"He'll be there," his mother said.

"Poker games, huh. I always trusted Ray. How'd you find out anyway?"

"A little bird whispered in my ear."

"It was chicken feed compared to what he could have taken. Who's going to do the books now?"

"It's not how much. It's the fact he took it, and it was escalating. There are other discrepancies that I didn't mention. The cost of feed and fertilizer for instance. I'm pretty sure he's taken a lot more than just what I mentioned. I have had one of the men who does investigating work for the firm look into someone. If you agree, we will offer him more than he's making now, plus moving expenses." He didn't want his grandfather to feel that he was pushing him aside. "He's being underpaid for what he does and for the length of time he's been with his present employer."

"If you can't trust kin, how do you think you can trust this fellow?"

"I would trust this man with my life. I was impressed when I talked to him at dinner one night. He and his wife will be coming in to discuss it few days before Thanksgiving." He reached over for his wife's hand. "I think it's pretty safe to say I can trust him. After all, I am married to his oldest daughter."

"Dad?" Cindy asked, real surprise in her eyes.

He smiled and nodded.

"Will the boys and Lil be coming, too?"

"They all have to find out if the climate suits them. I believe the train tickets are being delivered to him today. Travel is still tight. I could only get Pullman seats. So far he doesn't know who is making the offer. Don't mention it when you write or call them."

* * * * *

Daily, David and Cindy checked the work on their house. After the workmen left for the day the two of them wandered through the place. They would be happy if the promise that the kitchen, living room, and the master bedroom would be livable by Thanksgiving became a reality . Both were eager to be out of the main house. He had sent the rest of his law books to Austin and planned to start working in October.

In the middle of September he and Cindy walked in from her riding lesson. Both were dressed in blue jeans, boots, and gingham shirts.

"Shall we talk to Tish now?" David asked.

"She must be feeling pretty good. She's getting cranky about staying inside all the time. She just can't accept the fact that it's better not to have Eddie arrested."

"I've thought of a way I can make her face that fact." They walked back to the little cabin. "You looked more sure of yourself today," he said. smiling down at her.

"I'm beginning to enjoy it. Eleanor's a good teacher. Wait until the boys know I'm riding a horse every day. Before I mail it, I want you to read the letter I wrote. There's so much I want to tell them, and I think part of it will be better written than told on the phone."

"About Mom and Mamaw?"

"Just the ranch, your mother and grandfather for now. At the end I said I would tell them about your grandmother later because the letter was getting pretty long."

"I got wind of a couple of young palomino geldings for sale. The timing is perfect. We'll have Steve look them over. It will be a good reason for him to be away from the ranch."

"I still don't see why your brother's horses won't do."

"You heard what Mom said. She can't bear to see anyone else riding them. Gramps and I talked it over, and we're both glad she feels that way. They would be too much for you to handle, and Mom isn't as young as she used to be. Gramps suggestion of a Dude Ranch makes good sense. They would get good care at one of those. I'm putting out some feelers. This paperwork is getting me down. Don't mention that part of our plans to your sister." He hugged his grandmother as she opened the screen door. "I hear your girl is getting cranky."

"Just getting itchy feet."

"I feel like I'm in jail," Tish told him.

"Sit down and be comfortable. You, too, Cindy. Your sister has ice tea ready. That girl sure is taken with that Frigidaire. She says your mother would like the ice cubes for sure."

"Maybe now that the war is over Dad will buy her one." She sat down, taking the glass Tish held out. "You're looking good, Tish."

"I feel good, but I also feel like I'm in prison."

"We think maybe it's time you're paroled." David took a sip of his tea. "First you'll have to tell us what you have decided. Is it staying here, or are you going back to California? Are you going home like a puppy dog with its tail dragging?"

Tish leaned forward to pick up Precious, who seemed to have doubled in size in the three weeks since David had brought her in.

"I don't know if they would even let me in the house after the way I sneaked away, but I do know what they've always said about dogs. The boys would love Precious, but Mom wouldn't want her." She was stroking the puppy, looking down at it rather than at Cindy and David. "I think what I would really like is to be a nurse. Maybe I could learn to be a midwife as well and help Deedee, but I don't see how I could afford it. Deedee says some nursing schools want you to have some college first."

A look passed between David and his grandmother. "Think she'd make a good one?" Deedee nodded. "Tish, I'm going to show you once and for all why you don't want Eddie arrested." He turned a straight chair around, placing it next to the table. "Come over and sit here."

Tish moved to the chair. David took the puppy from her. "You're on the witness stand. Witnesses don't get to hold puppies. Sit up straight," he commanded. "The jury is watching you— twelve men and women listening to every word you have to say. There's a court stenographer taking it all down. The courtroom is a public place. It's filled with people who want to hear the whole sordid story. If it's juicy enough, the reporters will be racing each other for telephones when it's over for the day." He paused a moment. "Your folks will be sitting in the front row. Jimmy, Jack, and Jason won't be with them, but their classmates will be hearing their parents talk about you. Those brothers of yours will hear all the details. You can count on that."

"David. . ."

"The only thing you're allowed to do," he snapped, "is answer questions, and answer them truthfully. You're under oath to do that. Perjury will send you to jail. The prosecutor has finished. His questions were hard, but he treated you with kid gloves because he wants to win his case. Maybe he's wants that for you and maybe it's only for his own career, but he wants it."

He placed his tea on the table.

"Now it's my turn. I'm the defense attorney." He turned to look at her. "Miss Robins, how long have you known Mr. Lawson?

"I met him in April."

"Who introduced you?"

"No one."

"You mean you just let him pick you up off the street?"

"Well, you see, I worked at Woolworth's. Eddie bought a bottle of perfume and then handed it to me, saying— he said I reminded him of a gardenia and should wear it. It sounds silly now, but it was so. . . "

"Just answer the question please. In other words, you just let a strange sailor pick you up."

"Well, he was in the navy, and we were supposed to be nice to our boys in blue."

"Nice?" he raised his right hand to lips curled into a sardonic smile. "I guess that's one word for it, but I doubt if all girls were as nice as you were to him."

"I didn't know he was a deserter."

"Tish," David said, "The DA has probably objected to my last remark and the judge has had it stricken from the record, but the jury has heard it. You are only allowed to answer the questions you are asked, and whatever Eddie was or wasn't, or the fact that he is a deserter has no bearing on the case. It won't be allowed to be mentioned. That remark would be stricken from the record as well." He returned to his lawyer mode. "Did you start having sex with him the first time you went out with him?"

"That's none of your business."

At that point the judge will order you to answer the question. The next questions will probably be when did you decide to get pregnant so he would have to marry you. Why you sneaked out of the house to run away with him. There's only your word about a marriage proposal. He didn't even give you a ring to wear. Can you sit on the stand and tell in graphic details what he did to you in that motel room?"

"That isn't fair." She was almost crying.

"No, it isn't. David." Cindy couldn't believe what she was hearing.

"No," David agreed, "but to defend his client he has to go after Tish. He'll probably come up with a witness who heard Eddie soliciting for her services. It isn't right, but it's the way these cases usually go. T.J. has found out that Eddie was AWOL long enough that he was classified as a deserter. He was stationed up at the Great Lakes when he walked away. It's a wonder he eluded the

Shore Patrol for as long as he did. No branch of the military takes kindly to deserters, especially during a war. Technically, he could be shot. but I doubt if that will happen. Add that to the fact that there's a string of car robberies and who knows what else. Let it go, Tish. He isn't going to be a free man for a long, long time. You'll only hurt yourself and your family. There is no way you want to tell a whole room full of people what you told your sister, and tell it in more graphic details."

"I guess Deedee's right." Tish sighed. "She's been telling me that hating him will only make me old and bitter before my time. I guess Precious and I want to stay here if I'm welcome."

"You're more than welcome." David picked up the puppy and put her back on Tish's lap. "What are you feeding that creature. She's sure not the runt of the litter." He sat down. "Other than the three of us, we've managed it so no one but Gramps and Steve has seen you. Mom hasn't even come in. Steve knows you were robbed and beaten, but that's all he knows. Mom and Steve know nothing of the baby, and we're keeping it that way." His mother did know, but he thought Tish would be more comfortable not knowing that.

"It's as I told you," Deedee said. "You have a second chance to live your life. Your life wasn't saved by accident. The man is being punished. Put it behind you or it will eat you alive."

"Listen to her," David said gently.

"I can't spend my whole life just sitting in here."

"You're not going to. In a few days I'm sending Steve to Tennessee to look at some horses. While he's at it, he's going to drive you up to Oklahoma City. We've found an old suitcase for you. He'll buy you a ticket on the Greyhound bus and see that you get on it before he leaves you."

"While you're in Oklahoma City," Cindy said, "buy yourself a dress and a coat. Maybe Steve can locate a Goodwill store for you to shop in. You'll only have the hundred dollars I gave you, so be careful how you spend it. You'll want to eat on the way down. You've got the clothes I bought for you. Your story to Mom and Dad and Lil will be that you had a miscarriage and decided all of us were right in our opinion of Eddie. You sneaked out while he was asleep and took the bus to here. No one else, not even the boys, is to know about the baby. I'm sure Mom and Dad haven't told them about that. You call us before the bus leaves and ask if we can meet you in Austin. It's party line, so don't say anything else. The way some people listen in to the conversations, it's impossible to keep a secret."

"I don't have the money."

"Yes, you do." She handed her sister the package she had put together. "There's everything you need in it, a wallet, lipstick, a compact, and some handkerchiefs. You'll have to get a new social security card later. You've always liked my straw-hat with the flowers. You can have that."

"It's not that we don't want to buy you new things," David said, "but it has to look as though your story is real. My mother has suggested that if you decide to stay here, we will take care of whatever schooling you want. She hasn't met you, but she and Mamaw Deedee have talked about you. You haven't been out looking us over, so you won't have to pretend to be seeing it all for the first time."

"This all seems pretty complicated."

"It's simple. We just tell Mom and Dad you got as far as Oklahoma City, had a miscarriage, and decided you didn't have to get married after all." Cindy kissed her sister on the cheek, and scratched Precious under her chin. "It will save a lot of embarrassing questions. Welcome to Texas. It's going to be sort of nice to have you around. I hope you are learning something about training a dog. I saw her mother the other day. She's part German Shepherd and part wolf, and really big."

"Will they let her on the bus."

"Leave her here," Deedee told her. "I will give her to you as a welcoming gift."

"Steve will be here for you at ten-thirty Friday night. Wear your sweater. It might get chilly in Oklahoma."

"You'll be fine," Cindy told her sister, but once outside the little cabin she was shaking her head.

"It does sound complicated, David."

"T.J. came up with it. He had the idea when he heard about the palominos in Tennessee. It will all depend on her. Let's hope she can keep it a secret. You know you sister best."

"I had no idea she was sleeping with Eddie, so I guess she can. They say middle children can be difficult and that's what she was before the boys came along. I think she resented me at times. I tried so hard to keep Dad from calling me his little princess."

"Would you like to go unto Austin tomorrow? Jinny called to tell me that her folks have that apartment over their garage cleaned up."

"A place of our own? I'd love it. Would Eleanor have to come with us?"

"She can stay with her parents. She can be with you during the day. I need to start going into the office once in a while. Want to read me that letter now?"

Chapter 36

Once up in their bedroom, Cindy picked up the letter she had written, offering it to him.

"You read it to me."

She seated herself in the comfortable chair David had added to the room. He stretched out on the bed.

"More comfortable over here," he said.

"Let me read this first."

"We'll probably hear it sooner if you stay there," he admitted.

Dear Mom, Dad, and all,

It's been an amazing six weeks . David hasn't gone back to work yet, but he says he better drop in at the office before long. They have been very understanding about him staying here at the ranch. We might go in to Austin soon to look at an apartment. I imagine the housing crunch is as bad back in California as it is here. David's secretary found this little three room apartment. She said it isn't much, but they are holding it until we look at it. It's over her parents' garage. An elderly aunt was living in it until she fell coming down the steps. Once David starts working we will be in Austin a lot, so we have to have a place to stay.

Austin is a very nice town. Not as big as L.A. of course, but it's the capital of Texas. It has some nice shops, and you can go to Dallas if you can't find what you want here. I haven't been there yet, but Maurice says we will have to go there soon. I think I mentioned in my last letter that Maurice is helping me pick out things for the house. He has some really good ideas. He also thinks I have a good sense of color. When I showed him some of my sketches he said he would like to bring a friend who is a painter around to see them. I still don't know his last name. He says names aren't important.

By the way, if he's the reason you said in your last letter that I should remember that I'm a married woman, you don't have to worry. He doesn't feel the same way about women that you do.

I am beginning to see why people are so fond of their horses. Yesterday, Eleanor and I rode around the ranch for about an hour. They keep telling me Seth is a pony, but I guess I can't tell the difference between a horse and a pony. They both look the same to me. I think I did tell you that David has two Palominos. There are quite a few horses in the pasture. The men take their pick of them during the round-up. Most of them have their own saddles but the horses belong to the ranch. Eleanor and I went out one day to watch them brand. I was going to do some sketches but we didn't stay long. I know it has to be done. But those poor little calves were bawling their little heads off. You would too if you had a hot iron jammed against you and a knife cutting off your private parts. David said I'll get used to it, but I'm not so sure.

I think if I ever ride alone I should take a compass with me. The place is so big I might get lost and never find my way home. Margarita says I'll learn. She is David's mother. She and his grandfather want me to call them by their first names. I feel a little awkward doing it, but they said they have never had a girl around the place. Buck is really nice. He calls me David's little gal. He's not as tall as David, but he looks real nice on Sundays when he dresses up in a suit for church. I can picture David looking something like him when he gets old. I don't know why that is because they don't look anything alike.

David favors his mother and grandmother. You will like Margarita if you ever get a chance to meet her. She must have been a really beautiful girl because she is still real pretty. She's happy to have David home, but she's sad, too. She misses David's brothers. She won't let anyone ride their Palominos. They are going to sell them to a Dude Ranch. Her hair is black just like David's. Her father was from one of the oldest families in Texas. She says they can trace their family almost all the way back to the Conquistadors who came from Spain and conquered the Incas. They had a big ranch at one time, but somehow they lost it after Steven Austin and other Americanos came here. Guess I will have to start reading up on my Texas history.

She has a really long name. I think that must be a family thing. It's Margarita Maria Namid Gomez McKaid. She told me Namid is an Indian name that means Laughs a Lot. It was her mother's name. Gomez, of course, is her father's last name. David's father was killed by a bull when he was thirteen, but she still puts flowers on his grave every Sunday before church. It isn't a big church, but the cemetery is big. Not as big as the Catholic one, though.

Our house is coming along fairly well. They have the bedroom walls up. Not the bricks yet. The windows are in the bedrooms and bathrooms. Imagine having more than one bathroom. They are waiting for the big windows in the living room and dining room. Did you know that when they build a house they bring in the bathtubs while there are only two by fours up? The red tiles for the roof were delivered yesterday.

I think this letter is getting a little long. I'll tell you more about David's great-grandmother in my next letter. Boys, you be real good and help Mom. David says he'll teach you to ride if you ever come in here. He might even let you try some target practice. I've gotten pretty good. I can usually hit what I aim at, but that's only with the little 38 David bought for me. I haven't tried a rifle yet.

There's not much to see around here, just a lot of land and fences, but I'm getting used to it. I miss you all. Lil, are you used to sleeping alone yet?

Write me sometime.
Love to you all,
Lucy(Cindy)
P.S. One more thing. I'm pretty sure you're going to be grandparents come next May. (Come next May. There I'm already talking like a

Texan.) I'm lucky though. I haven't been sick in the morning. Maybe it's Elena's cooking.

She looked over at her husband and smiled at the way he was grinning.

"Get yourself over here, Mrs. McKaid. Wondered when you were going to say something."

"How did you know?"

"Hell, honey, cows and horses come in season, but any fool knows his wife is supposed to bleed every month and you sure haven't. We must have done it right nearly first time we tried. What do you want? A girl or boy?"

"I'll take what we can get. I just hope it's only one."

"We better ask Mamaw Deedee if all this riding's good for you." He put his arms around, grinned, and kissed her. "If it's a girl we'll call her Victoria. A boy can be Victor."

"That's," she started to say awful, but caught herself. "You know I sort of like Victoria. It would probably get shortened to Vicky or Vic though."

* * * * *

It had been close, but as Cindy sat on the large green sofa with David's arm around her, she was happy. No, she was ecstatic. Just yesterday the sofa and its matching chairs had been delivered. She had been baking cookies in her own oven when the patio furniture arrived. The dining room wasn't finished, but there were folding tables and chairs waiting to be placed at the other end of the huge living room. The empty flooring gleamed at that end. The half they were sitting in held the Navaho rug which had arrived ten days earlier. David had ordered a second one for the empty end.

The pot roasts in the kitchen were starting to smell good. There were two just to make sure there was enough for thirteen people. Margarita and Buck would be joining them later. She liked the slight tang of the vinegar she had added after browning the meat. The ranch beef might not need it for tenderizing, but she liked the taste it gave to the meat and gravy. She wanted the meal to be perfect. Sometime within the hour Steve and the limousine David had hired would be arriving with her family.

She smoothed out the fabric of the dark green velvet of her dress, then touched her finger to the white collar. In a matching chair, Tish was biting her lower lip and fidgeting with her fingers. Her dress was identical except for being blue. Both still wore their blonde hair in a page boy style. Precious lay tethered at her feet. With six new people arriving, David had suggested that Tish keep the puppy on her new leash.

Eleanor relaxed in the chair closest to the fireplace. Logs were laid, but though it was the middle of November it wasn't yet cool enough for lighting a fire. David thought it would probably be by evening. The Navaho rug looked quite at home in the room. Later in the day David and his grandfather would be putting the tables and chairs up at the empty end of the room.. It was the only way to accommodate everyone around the same table. She didn't want it done until her family had taken their first tour of the house. Fresh flowers filled the pottery on the heavy end tables. After a few days of moving in they all felt entitled to relax, but it wasn't easy to do so.

"We could almost pass for twins again," Tish commented.

"You've lost weight." She didn't want to say anything about the wary, half haunted look Tish still had. Her sister had changed so much, but how could she not after what she had been though. "You need to eat more."

"You sound just like Mom and Deedee."

"Weight loss or not," Eleanor commented, "there's no doubt that you two are sisters,"

Cindy was pleased with the room, pleased with the all the rooms Bo Colby and his crew had finished off— her wonderful kitchen with its mud room, David's den, their bedroom with its private bath, and this magnificent room.

What a feeling it had been the last two nights, knowing that except for Eleanor on a cot in David's unfurnished den, they were alone in their own home. Remembering her talk with her mother, she wondered how her parents had managed to stay married living up above Grandma and Grandpa Smith for ten whole years. As she said her prayers each night, she thanked God for meeting David and for the fact that the brass bed in his room hadn't squeaked. How had her life turned out so perfect?

A small apartment in Austin, and this huge new house, even though most of it wasn't finished. What would Mom and Dad think of it? That brass bed was a beautiful piece of furniture, and they had brought the lovely Star of Texas quilt over here, but left the bed itself behind. It just didn't fit with the look they wanted. Maurice had been wonderful, guiding her to just the right heavy furniture to carry out the Spanish look.

"It is a bit large," David agreed. "That far wall should be covered with book shelves. I'll to tell Bo to add them."

"Maybe I should take Precious out," Tish remarked.

"Let's all go out on the patio and wait," Cindy said. "They ought to be here soon. It might be nice to have the ice tea and glasses waiting out there."

Very much the lady of the house, she headed for her kitchen with all its latest appliances and gadgets. With her own selections and all the wedding presents, she had everything a housewife could possibly want. She had talked David out of hiring a cook, but had agreed to have one of Elena's daughters-in-law help with the cleaning. Probably as her pregnancy progressed she would be glad of that. She remembered how sick and how tired her mother had been with the boys. Of course, Mom had been almost forty.

Eleanor joined her in the kitchen, with an offer to help carry the tray of glasses. Cindy liked the tray and the heavy, old fashioned tumblers and matching pitcher. Just one of the many wedding presents— one that was very appropriate for the McKaid Hacienda, which was what they had begun calling their new home. When some had found out about the look they wanted, they had raided their attics for long unwanted and unused, and almost antique items.

Tish was sitting on the low brick wall when they came out the door, and Eleanor elected to join her. Cindy hoped it wouldn't leave marks on her sister's dress. They had actually driven up to Dallas to shop for them, and they had been expensive. She didn't say anything though. Tish was nervous enough as it was.

"Good idea." David was seated at the wrought iron table with the glass top.

"Help yourself," she said. "I'll get some of the cookies I baked yesterday." They were her brothers' favorite. What would they think of this house and the ranch? Would Dad want to work for David and Buck? They had deliberately kept Tish unaware of that possibility. Before returning to the patio she turned the meat in the two dutch ovens. After what everyone said about mothers-in-law, she felt so lucky. Margarita had said she and David should have a chance to greet her folks without them.

"I want everything to be perfect," she once again told herself.

Ten minutes later Steve drove up in the limousine.

"It's Lucy and Tish," one of the triplets yelled as the three of them spilled out of the limo. Cindy had her arms around all three of her brothers even before her parents and Lily were out of the long vehicle.

"This is a surprise." Mark walked up and shook David's hand. "Until we came through that gate with that big sign overhead I had no idea it was you. Why all the secrecy?"

"I didn't know how you might feel about working for your son-in-law. Welcome to Texas." He hugged her mother and Lily, then backed away slightly as a white van drove up. "Excuse me. We weren't expecting anyone else."

Chapter 37

David started toward the van as it rolled to a stop behind the limousine. It was the electric company's van, but the driver had a cap pulled down, covering his face. There was no need for it to be here. Something was off. The driver was turning toward the open window and raising his right arm. David's hand just automatically reached for the little .22 in his pocket. It wasn't much of a gun, but he hadn't wanted to alarm her folks by having his .38 strapped on, a precaution he'd been taking ever since the Simpson's old Ford had increased its daily meandering up and down the road.

A shot rang out, and Tish screamed as she fell from the low wall. He turned just in time to see Cindy grab one of the heavy, old-fashioned glasses and throw it straight through open window of the van. Tea sloshed out as it went straight through to the head of the shooter, bounced off and spraying glass splinters as it hit the ground.

Chaos erupted. The figure in the van was yelling. The boys and Gracie added their shocked screams. Lily just stood where she was, staring at the van. Tish was crying, holding a bloody hand to her shoulder. Precious added to the confusion by running toward the strangers with loud puppy barks and her leash dragging behind her. Cindy's father simply had a stunned look on his face.

"You shot my sister," Cindy yelled.

"Stand back, everyone," David ordered. He aimed, not for the driver who had her hands to her face, red hair now streaming out from the fallen cap, but at both tires. The van settled into a lop-sided look as the air whistled out.

"Die, you bitch," Betty Lou yelled "Davy's mine. All mine. You can't have him."

Eleanor flew off her perch on the bricks, raced to the van with a gun in her hand, pulled open the door, and yanked the girl to the ground.

"Ow, that hurts. I'm hurt."

"Don't expect sympathy from me." Eleanor jerked her to her feet. "You're lucky I don't shoot you here and now." She pulled the woman's right arm behind her back, then looked at Cindy. "You throw a mean glass of tea, girl."

"That's what happens when you play ball a lot with three little boys."

"Go inside and look in my purse. There's a pair of handcuffs in it."

The boy were all talking at once. Gracie's purse was on the ground. She was helping Tish to a chair and trying to stop the blood with a handkerchief. Cindy was hovering at her side, but left to get the handcuffs.

"Hadn't you better get a doctor?" Mark asked.

"My grandmother will take care of her. If she needs a doctor we'll get her there." He looked over to where several pick-ups were speeding their way across the field. "I think everyone heard the shots." He slipped the .22 back into his pocket.

"Hold still," Eleanor ordered. "God, girl, you smell like you haven't had a bath in weeks."

Cindy handed her the cuffs. Betty Lou was twisting and stamping her feet as Eleanor fastened them behind her back.

"How'd you get two of 'em, Davy?" she wailed. "Two of 'em. We was promised. You proposed. We was gonna get hitched."

Eleanor dodged as Betty Lou tried to butt her with her head.

"I was nine years old and your grandfather threatened to shoot Sally."

"We have to get married. It's the only way I'll get ever away. I didn't know you had two of 'em. They can't have you. You can't have two wives. They can't have you. You're mine. We're promised."

Both pick-ups came to abrupt stops, with family and men rushing to their rescue. Deedee and his mother went directly to Tish's side.

"You all right?" Buck asked to no one in particular.

"She's crazy," Cindy said. "Somebody needs to put her away."

"Don't worry," Eleanor told her. "She'll be getting put away all right. This will do it."

Eleanor forced Betty Lou onto a chair.

"That hurts."

"You think that bullet in Tish's shoulder doesn't?"

"Scissors or a knife," Deedee demanded, "and some towels."

"Easy there, girl." David handed his grandmother his pocket knife and moved behind the chair, putting a light hand on his sister-in law's cheek. "Your mother is holding your hand. I'm going to hold you so you don't move so Mamaw Deedee can see how bad your shoulder is. I don't think it's done any real damage. Betty Lou never could hit what she aimed at. Try to count to a hundred for me." He looked over to his mother. "Call the sheriff. Steve, you stay here. The rest of you men can go on back to the bunk house. Betty Lou evidently meant to kill my wife, but shot her sister instead. Since you weren't here, you don't need to be here when the sheriff arrives."

Cindy handed Deedee a couple of tea towels she had taken from the kitchen.

"Eighteen, twenty, twenty-one, twenty. . ." Deep breaths came between the counts as Deedee sliced through velvet and slip and brassiere straps.

"Steve, you know where Doc's house is?"

"Yes. ma'am. I had one of the boys over there during the summer."

"Then let's get this girl into that fancy car over there. The cartridge's lodged against the bone. It's going hurt getting it out, and he can dull the pain while he does it. I can't. Tish, can you hold these towels against your shoulder while we get you in the car?"

"I- I'll try." Blood was seeping down her already bloody dress. "I- I've hurt worse than this."

"I know, girl, but that doesn't make this hurt any less."

"I'll go with you," Gracie said. "I'm her mother."

"I will, too," Cindy said.

"You better stay here to talk to the sheriff." David moved to her side.

"I'm Deedee," his grandmother told Gracie. "Tish, try to breathe deeply once you get in. Then I will hold pressure on it until we get to Doc's house." She glanced away. "Davy, you tell the sheriff where to find us."

As soon as the three were on their way to the doctor's, Cindy started to clean up. Eleanor stopped her. "Don't touch anything yet. Sheriff Brady will need to see it."

"Wow," Jason exclaimed. "This is some hotel they're building here in the middle of nowhere."

"A real live shootout just like in the movies," Jack added.

"Lucy saved the day," Jimmy chimed in. "Lucy always knows what to do."

"It's not a hotel," David told them. "This is our home, but it's not quite finished yet." Even in the heat of what had happened, he smiled at the fact that the triplets were obviously proud of their sister. Maybe they were too young and had watched too many westerns to realize that things could have turned out much differently. "It needs a lot of work yet." He looked at her father. "We're usually a little more civilized that this. Mom," he took her hand, "I'd like you to meet Cindy's father, Mark Rollins, and these three are Jimmy , Jack, and Jason."

He hesitated a bit, not quite knowing what to call his father-in-law. Mother Rollins was alright, but Father Rollins sounded like a priest.. Fortunately he and Cindy were on the same wave length. She came to his rescue

"Dad, this is David's mother, Margarita and his grandfather Buck."

"She's a bitch. She a damn stinking. . ." Betty Lou began shouting again.

"Betty Lou Simpson," Margarita interrupted, "you don't talk like that. These little boys don't need to hear that kind of language."

"Yes,um, Miss Margarita." She clamped her mouth shut.

"Betty Lou's our neighbor," David explained. "She has been causing trouble ever since we arrived home. I think our marriage pushed her over the edge. I would like to say she will be prosecuted for attempted murder, but, regretfully, I imagine she will be judged incompetent to stand trial and be sent to the State Hospital for the Criminally Insane. Eleanor has been here as Cindy's secretary, but she's with a security firm I hired."

"No," Betty Lou screamed. "I won't go nowheres. Davy, you can't be married to her. We're promised."

"Excuse me a moment," Cindy said. "I'd better check on the meat. Lily will you see that the boys get some cookies." She looked at Betty Lou. "I don't add rat poison to my cookies, or I'd offer you one."

David followed her to the kitchen. "Are you all right?" She took the lid off one dutch oven and started turning the meat. "Cindy," he repeated gently, "are you all right?"

"How can I be? My sister's been shot." The words came slowly. "I wanted everything to be perfect. I've brought you trouble again."

"You've brought me nothing but happiness." He took the fork from her hand, placed it in the spoon holder on the range, and turned her around. "It's over, honey. Neither one of us will ever have to worry about Betty Lou again. It's not about you or anything you did. I've always thought she was capable of murder. She should have been put away before this, but there's never been any proof." His arms went around her. "Don't ever blame yourself, my darling. Tish will be all right."

"She didn't need this, too."

"She'll be fine. Didn't you hear her tell Mamaw that she's hurt worse than this. Tish will be just fine. You just start having good thoughts. You don't want to have our little Victoria hearing bad things, do you?"

"You really think she can hear me think?"

"She's part of you, and will be until next May. Now let's go back out and wait for Sheriff Brady. He going to want to hear from all of us." He kissed the top of her head. "What a wonderful person you are. What made you think of throwing that glass at her?"

"I can't believe I did that. I guess I wasn't thinking. I was mad. I don't like hating someone, but I just hate hearing that woman's name "

"She's going to have quite a bruise on her face and probably one beautiful black eye. You just relax . We don't want little Victoria to be upset, do we?"

"You think she knows how I feel?"

"Mamaw Deedee says she does."

"I guess I'll believe her. From what she's told Tish, she's seen a lot of babies being born. Tish says she's ninety-seven. She can't be that old, can she?"

"It sounds about right. Now let's go out there and make your family feel welcome."

Chapter 38

David smiled as his young bride replaced the lid. She really did know how to cook. The odors coming from the two dutch ovens proved that. They walked hand in hand out to the patio where they found Steve and the sheriff were talking to his grandfather.

"Steve flagged me down as I was heading this way," the sheriff said. "Moss at the electric company called and said his van was missing, and that the Simpson's truck was parked in its place. I thought I better see how things were out here." He looked at Betty Lou sitting with her hands cuffed behind her back. "Looks like you had trouble all right. He says to read Steve said. He says it was your wife's sister who was shot."

"Sitting there pretty as you please just a trying to trick me into shooting the wrong one," Betty Lou mumbled.

"Every time she opens her mouth she incriminates herself," David said.

"Who all saw it.?"

"Everyone here except Mom and Gramps. Cindy's family just came in from California."

"Steve filled me in." The sheriff nodded. "Look, David, why don't I just take her in and lock her up, and we'll take care of all this tomorrow." He walked over and looked at the van. "What happened to the tires?

"David shot them dead," Jack called out.

"Well, sonny, looks like they're dead all right."

"Tell Moss I'll have someone replace them."

"Looks like he's past due for new ones anyway. Why don't you just have someone patch 'em up and let the old skinflint buy his own." He looked over to Eleanor. "Your handcuffs?" She nodded. "Want to ride along and tell me all about it?"

"If you don't mind, Brady, I've been looking forward to Cindy's pot roast. Seems David married himself a good cook. Can I come in tomorrow?"

"Sure."

"Brady," David said, "I believe this gives you cause enough to get a warrant to search the Simpson place. You might find that foal's ear."

"No," Betty Lou screamed, "You cain't do that. I got my rights. I was just protecting my own man. We're promised. He couldn't marry her. Leave my things alone. The attic's mine. They're not really married. They cain't be. Davy's mine, all mine. Mine, mine, mine. Everyone knows it. Stay outa my house."

"I hear you, girl," the sheriff said. "Now let's get in my car nice and peaceable like."

He helped the sheriff bundle her into the back seat. She kept raving that no one could touch her things.

"Pretty much tells us there's something worth looking at," the sheriff said before sliding behind the wheel.

David nodded.

"Why don't you all go inside?" Margarita said. "I'm going over and see what Elena has to scrub away those blood stains."

Don't bother," David said. "Blood's not going to come out of those stones. I'll have Bo replace that section."

* * * * *

The room didn't seem quite as large with her father, three growing boys, Lily, Margarita, and Buck in it. Cindy noticed the way her father was looking at the empty half of the room.

"It will probably be a year before we finish this room."

"We're waiting for a rug," David explained. "The Navaho woman who wove this one is doing another for us. It's a slow process."

"Will it be the same as this one?" Lily asked.

"Probably not. We don' know what it will look like. The Navaho women don't try to duplicate their designs."

Jimmy looked around, obviously uncomfortable. He had always had the weakest bladder of the three. It was one of the differences between the boys that she was aware of. A slight smile curled around her face. Jimmy had been the one who had initiated the distance contest a few years before. She has scolded them good, telling them if they didn't keep their little ding-dongs in their pants where they belonged, she would tell Mon and Dad about it.

"Would you like to see the rest of the house?" *If our baby is a boy, will he do the same thing?* Her smile turned into a sigh. Knowing boys, he probably would. "There isn't too much to see yet," she added, "but would you like to see it? There's a bathroom off the kitchen and one in our bedroom."

"We have really pushed the builder," David told her father. "I told the him to get these rooms first. It will probably be February or March before it's all finished. You boys can help me set us up some tables and chairs later on. I borrowed then from the lodge hall, but your sister wouldn't let me set them up until you arrived."

"Elks or Moose?" Mark asked.

That was one item she hadn't mentioned in her letters home. He and Uncle Brad belonged to the Knights of Columbus. They had always made it clear what they thought of the Masons. Both David and his grandfather belonged, and David had started going to their monthly meetings.

"Masons," she said as she stood. "Let's start with the kitchen."

Cindy absolutely adored her new kitchen, all the counter space, the tiled floor, the little breakfast nook to one side, and enough cupboards to fill with whatever she accumulated. Why would she ever want to hire a cook to work in it?

"Are you all right with cooking?" her father asked. "Your mother. . ."

"I know. Mom couldn't stand the smell of food. I wasn't even sure I was pregnant until Deedee told me not all women get morning sickness. She even said I don't have to take naps if I'm not tired."

"You take care of my girl," he told David. "Mothers to be are delicate."

"Nonsense, Mr. Rollins." David's mother was frowning. "We don't have time to be delicate."

"Mom's health has always been a worry." Cindy didn't want to upset her father. "Lily, I hope you're helping her."

"I am, but I'm not as good at housework as you were. I'm babysitting for Mrs. Lathum after school. I take care of Roger and Mary until she gets home from work. She doesn't know if her husband will ever come home. They know he parachuted out of his plane, but they don't know if he was taken prisoner or killed."

"We miss you and Letitia," her father said.

"Maybe you won't have to miss us."

"It's a lot to think about, Lucy."

"No talk of business today," David told him. "Today is just about family."

Cindy led them to the door that led to the wash room. The wash room separating the kitchen from the dirt outside was almost a carbon copy of the one at the main house. The washing machine was newer and the built in tubs were still unused, but there was a chair for sitting and hooks for hanging. The towels hanging in the little bathroom with the shower were the khaki ones from David's duffle bag.

"When you've been working outside you need a place to wash up," she explained.

"Sometimes you just gotta go." Jimmy scooted in, slamming the door shut.

"We're going to put you up with Mom and Gramps," David said. "The only bedroom finished here is ours. As soon as Steve gets back I'll have him take your things over."

When Jimmy emerged from the bathroom, Cindy took them down to the hall to their bedroom. As soon as Lily stepped inside she gasped. "Oh, Lucy, it's the most beautiful room I've ever seen."

"It is something," her father agreed.

"I like it." Cindy smiled. "Maurice showed me what wonderful things you can find at antique shops and auction houses. I could never have done this by myself."

The decorator had insisted on the thick, dark green wall-to-wall carpeting. The heavy four poster bed with its brocade canopy made the Star of Texas quilt even more impressive. The two over-stuffed chairs by a little drop leaf table were the exact shade of the carpeting. The little antique ladies desk by the window actually held a long feathered quill. A straight chair with a needlepoint seat waited in front of it. Three of her sketches of the ranch were grouped together on one wall. Both the dresser and chest were of the same vintage as the bed. Lamps with frosted glass globes sat on the night stands. There was a ceiling light was above the desk. The textured wallpaper with its pale yellow background and green leaves added a hint of sunshine.

"Looks like you're taking real good care of my girl," Mark said.

"Trying to, sir."

"I had no idea," Cindy murmured, "that when David said I looked more like a Cindy, he meant Cinderella."

"The thought never occurred to me, honey." He turned to the boys. "Want to help me set up a couple of those folding tables now?"

"Sure. What's upstairs?" Jason asked.

"A big empty space right now," David told him. "One of these days it will be a studio for your sister work to in."

* * * * *

By the time Steve ushered Tish and the two older women in, the tables were covered with tablecloths, dishes and silverware. David noted the care with which the big blond man in worn jeans seated the still shaky girl. Tish's left arm was in a sling. Maybe he was wrong, but Tish seemed to be at ease with his foreman friend.

It might be a sign that she was healing after her ordeal with the sailor. An experience such as hers often left a lasting aversion to men

"You just take it easy, Miss Rollins." Steve turned to him. "Anything else, Sarge. The suitcases are still in the limousine."

"You can take them over to the house later. Why don't you join us for dinner first?"

"I'm not presentable enough." Steve looked down at his jeans."

"Maybe we don't need thirteen at the table. You would be doing us a favor. I want you to meet my in-laws. Later on her father might have some questions about the ranch that you can answer. Did you save the bullet for the sheriff?"

"We did." Deedee told him. "Doc put sulfa powder on it and took a couple of stitches. He wants her to stay with me for a few days so I can watch her to make sure no infection sets in."

"Penicillin would have been better," David commented. "That's what the army pumped through us."

"'I've tried to tell him that a couple of times. He says sulfa works and doesn't have the chance for a reaction like penicillin. He's a stubborn old man who won't keep up with progress."

That statement brought smiles— smiles brought on by the thought of the ninety-seven-year old woman calling the doctor an old man. He was only in his early sixties. On the other hand, she might have a point. Maybe it was time to suggest that he take a younger man into his practice. If what he had in mind came to pass, Kaidville and the surrounding area would soon be growing.

* * * * *

In the intimacy of their bedroom, Cindy turned down the beautiful quilt, folded it neatly, and placed it at the quilt rack standing at the foot of the bed. She was wearing the red negligee David had picked out in Hollywood. He came up behind her, his hands seeking her breasts.

"My favorite sight of my beautiful wife," he whispered.

"I won't be able to wear it much longer. I'll be all stomach and funny looking."

"You'll always be beautiful. Our baby makes you even more so. You glow with a happy, contented look."

"There wasn't much to glow about today." She turned to face him.

"Oh, but there is. We can live a normal life now. Eleanor can go back to Austin tomorrow."

"In a way, I'll miss her. She's taught me so much."

"From now on it will be just the two of us."

"And a slew of construction workers."

"Not at night." He was slipping the lace from her shoulders.

"I like it when you do that," she whispered, pulling him down to offer him her lips.

"My favorite part of the day."

Afterwards as she nestled comfortably in his arm she knew he was smiling.

"You make a very good pot roast, Mrs. McKaid."

"Even if I did have to put it in the oven to keep it warm until they got home. You know, I think Tish must have maneuvered the doctor into saying she should stay with Deedee just so she didn't need to be near to Mom and Dad."

"It's possible. Take your mother and the boys to Deedee's cabin tomorrow. Gramps and I are going to drive your father around the ranch."

Chapter 39

"Our ranch foreman is doing a pretty good job," David said. He and Buck sat in the jeep with Cindy's father. Both Buck and Mark had a beer in their hands. David's held a coke. He had parked under a black walnut tree growing near one of the prettier spots along the river. "Steve can tell you how many bales of Bermuda we put up. He was discharged about six months before I was. I hired him before we got hit. He came here straight from the hospital.. Said he didn't have any ties to keep him in Wyoming. Gramps has been pleased with him."

"An old army buddy," Mark said. "How did you manage to get an army jeep?"

"It helps to know the right people," David admitted.

"Who does the ordering as far as feed goes?"

"Not so much feed as fertilizer and lime," Buck told him. "We just always hope we have enough hay and Milo to feed the herd through the winter months. The calves go off to market soon as they're heavy enough. We do some extra feeding on the ones we butcher. What do you think of the place?"

"It's big all right."

"Actually," David told him, "it isn't all that big. It's the wells that bring in the money. An extra hard winter or a drought can decimate the herd in a hurry."

"How many men have you working for you?"

"It varies with the season. At round-up we hire extra hands. We don't have our own combine. We hire that out on shares. Once the house gets finished we'll be hiring more help for the house. Cindy is refusing to hire a nurse for the baby."

"I'm not surprised. She helped Gracie raise the boys. What about the oil wells?"

"The company sends us the checks. They take care of everything. We do have other investments. If you decide to take the job, Gramps and I will brief you on those."

"Have you been keeping the books yourself or having someone else do them?"

"A cousin was keeping them. There were some questions when I looked them over."

"Embezzlement?" he questioned. "I take it the man is in jail."

"It's really my fault," Buck said. "I figured I could trust a nephew."

"In a way," David explained, "it all might have started years ago by him misinterpreting something that was said. I might not have checked them so thoroughly if someone hadn't told me he had a gambling problem. We didn't want the McKaid name dragged through the mud. There's going to be a vacancy on the school board soon, and I'll probably be appointed to fill it."

"You didn't tell me about that." Buck dropped the empty bottle back into the bucket of melted ice.

"I just found out about it a few days ago. Some of the other districts have been discussing consolidating into one unit and building both a grade school and a high school. We really don't need that forty acres of the Simpsons. Politically speaking. donating it for the sole purpose of building the schools on it would be a good move. That much land's not apt to be turned down. The café might do some extra business on football nights. It could benefit the whole town."

"You finally going to foreclose on them?" his grandfather asked.

"The Diamond MiK foreclosing on the poor? We don't need that. E2 asked me early this morning if we still wanted to buy it. Old Elmer Number One's insisting that if the law sends her away, they should follow. Maybe he's got some crazy notion of helping her escape."

"Well," the old man said, "that's one way to get rid of them. They won't be able to do it though. They might call it a hospital, but it's as tight as any prison we've got."

"I didn't mention that I hold the mortgage." he added. "No need to generate hard feelings. I offered him fifteen dollars an acre."

"Three'd be too much," Buck frowned.

"The two of them have to have something to live on until E2 can find work. I suggested he start calling himself Elmer, Jr." *That was enough on that subject.* He looked at his father-in-law. "You think about it, and talk it over with Mother Rollins. Before you make up your mind, we'll take you into Kaidville and Austin and show you around the town a bit. We could introduce you to Father Torres if you like. Mother Rollins has already met the doctor."

"I'll be honest, David. The way this whole thing was handled I figured maybe there might be something shady about the whole business, but I figured what the hell. Gracie and I have never taken a vacation. It was a train trip for her and the children and a chance to enjoy ourselves on some else's money. The boys had the time of their life sleeping in those upper berths and eating in the diner. I figured I could always say not interested. It's going to take some serious thinking. We've been in California fifteen years now. I have an idea that summer here is going to be a lot hotter than California. I know how Chicago was. We used to sleep out on the front porch sometimes. California was a nice change."

"I'm having air conditioning installed. We could work something out about housing in the contract."

"If I take it, I'll insist on a yearly audit by an outside firm. I know Gracie would like to be here when that grandchild arrives. I guess you're hoping for a boy to take over the place someday."

"That's what everyone thinks." David turned the key to start the jeep. "Girls have an advantage," he muttered. "They don't grow up and go off to fight a war and get themselves shot."

* * * * *

As David and Cindy left the church the first Sunday in December, one of the younger members asked if she could have a moment of their time. Cindy recognized her as the one Margarita had introduced as one of the two school teachers, the one who taught the older children.

"I've gotten myself backed in a corner," the woman told them, "and since it was my idea in the first place Miss Grissom says it's up to me to fix things."

"Why don't you come home and have dinner with us?" Margarita asked.

"It's mostly Mr. David and Miss Cindy I need to talk to."

"We aways have Sunday dinner together," Cindy told the teacher. It hadn't taken her long to discover that Sunday dinner was expected to be cooked by Elena at what Margarita had taken to calling the main house. Since Father Torres had a second church to preside over, Mass was held early. Elena always had dinner ready promptly at twelve, usually a stew or a hearty soup with enough to feed any of the of the hands who felt like joining them. It was a long standing tradition.

"I walked to church."

"We'll see that you get home," David assured her. "I've been wanting to have a talk with you about the school."

Cindy was enjoying the peach cobbler when the teacher looked at her.

"I'm not sure how this whole thing escalated, Mrs. McKaid, but the children voted to have you be Mary in the Christmas play."

"Me?" She put down her spoon and reached for the water glass.

"Miss Grissom says I let it happen, but I didn't expect anything like this. You see, I have this one boy in the eighth grade who wants to be a writer. It's Jose Gonzales. I've been encouraging him because he has written some very good essays. He does seem to be talented, so I suggested that he write a play for the Christmas program. Miss Grissom thought it was a good idea, but. . ."

"But what?" Margarita asked.

"I think I got carried away with the idea. I told him he could be the director and pick out whoever he wanted to play the parts as long as he didn't favor his sisters and brother. The older children got together and said they thought one of the pregnant mothers should be Mary. Four of them are expecting. His mother is one of them. I tried to tell him that with the Baby Jesus in the manger, Mary shouldn't be pregnant, but he insisted she has to be when Joseph knocks on the door." She hesitated and looked around the table. "No one wanted their mother to feel hurt because she wasn't chosen, so Jose finally said Mary should be young and beautiful and everyone knows Mrs. McKaid is expecting, so she could be Mary."

David started laughing. Cindy just looked at her. "Me?"

"Why not?" David suggested. "We should encourage such creativity."

"Maria Lopez volunteered her four month old brother to be the Baby Jesus. She said it was all right with her mother as long as we keep him wrapped in a blanket. I checked that with her mother. They are going to have it in the school yard." Again she hesitated. "Mary— she's supposed to ride up on a donkey. Jose didn't think it was showing favoritism to use his family's mule, since no one has a donkey and they own the only mule around here."

"A mule?"

"I don't suppose those young 'uns have any idea who should be Joseph." Buck was looking at David as he said it.

"As a matter of fact they— well, they have. Jose thinks it would be appropriate if Mr. McKaid— I mean they are all so excited about it. The little ones are going to be angels singing *Silent Night*, and since the shepherds don't have any sheep they are going to put a sign that says sheep on their dogs. I really don't know how I let them all get carried away like this."

"I'm sure they are all very serious about it," Cindy said. "I can picture my brothers dreaming up something like it. If it's all right with you, David, I'd be honored to be their Mary."

Margarita smiled at her. “Tell Miss Grissom it’s fine with us. I’ll even volunteer to furnish the costumes. Just get the sizes of all the angels and shepherds for me.”

“We’ll make the Kaidville School proud.,” David told her.

“By golly,” Buck said, “We ought to get pictures of that.”

Hours later, in their bedroom, David asked if she really wanted to ride a mule.”

“It can’t be any harder than riding a horse, can it?”

“I’ll have someone take pictures, maybe even find someone with a movie camera. We’ll get one of the reporters from the Austin paper to come out and watch it. Mom will probably get some pretty professional looking costumes.”

* * * * *

Monday morning two weeks later, David found a dozen copies of the morning paper on his desk.

“Did your wife enjoy her donkey ride?” his secretary asked.

“As a matter of fact she did. Her three brothers are eight years old. She said it was the sort of thing they would have expected of her.”

“Those little angels are adorable. Where did they find such cute little angel wings?”

T.J. came through the door, newspaper in hand. “Kaidville kids have it right.” he exclaimed, parroting the headline. The entire front page held pictures of the event. “How did you manage this?”

“Actually it was all the children’s idea. The teacher was so embarrassed when she came to talk to us she stuttered. When Cindy said she’d be Mary I couldn’t very well refuse to be Joseph. Mom got into the spirit of things and had the costumes shipped in from New York. I thought it might be nice to have pictures. When I asked Melvin to come, I had no idea they would put us on the front page.”

“A good move. You couldn’t get better publicity. This picture of the little angel crying when she had to take off her wings is a real tear jerker.”

“That’s when Mom decided to let them all keep their costumes.”

"She didn't," Jinny said.

"She did. Mom's a real softie when it comes to little girls. We've always spent Christmas Eve helping her taking baskets around, and she always makes sure there's a doll in it if there's a little girl in the family."

"What's this about you being on the school board."

"Richard McIver died. I'm appointed until the next election."

"What about that mention of a new school and you donating the whole forty acres of the Simpson place?"

"The children need a good education. Consolidation's the only answer."

"You ready to take on a pro bono case? Mexican accused of holding up a gas station. He's got half a dozen people swearing he was at a dance at the time."

Chapter 40

The tree at the main house was very pretty. Cindy had to agree with that. She and David had helped Margarita decorate it. It was seven feet tall and loaded with decorations. The one at their still uncompleted McKaid Hacienda was small and sparsely decorated. New Christmas ornaments were scarce, and snapped up almost as soon as the stores put them out. Margarita had offered her some, but she had declined. She wanted the pleasure of collecting her own, even if it meant not having many this first year.

No one had said anything, but she knew there were still shortages of a lot of things. At times, it bothered her that Bo Colby had been able to furnish the house with all the latest appliances because there was no doubt that without the McKaid money, things would have been a bit more difficult. She had given Margarita the framed sketch of David at the Grand Canyon, and a sketch of Deedee to Buck. She had embroidered a set of pillowcases for Deedee, putting a deer and flowers on each one. For David gift she hadn't used charcoal, only pastels showing the front gate with the old house in the background. The red-gold of a sunset completed the picture. The two Navaho rugs were joint gifts from her and David. She and David gave Tish a pretty new dress.

She unwrapped a warm, red robe from Margarita. "We do have some cool nights," her mother-in-law said. Margarita gave Tish a blue one as well. In January Tish would be taking some courses in Austin at the university, and next fall she would be enrolling in nursing school.

Buck presented her with a necklace, a gold chain with a ruby hanging from it, and matching earrings.

"A good start on your jewelry collection," he said.

"Thank you. They are lovely."

When they had walked in that morning, there had been a rocking chair with a big red bow on one of the wooden arms. "You'll need that to rock that baby," Deedee had told her.

Tish had given her some doilies she had crocheted. They had opened gifts from her family the night before after coming home from delivering Christmas baskets. Cindy had lit candles and they had listened to Christmas carols on the radio. Her best Christmas gift was knowing that her father had accepted David's offer and had contacted a realtor about selling the house in California, and that David had a realtor on the lookout for a rental in Austin.

The boys had each sent David a necktie, ones they had obviously picked out themselves. One had a horse's head on it. A second one had the whole horse, and the third one was bright blue with stars and rhinestones. David had laughed.

"After they arrive and get settled in, we'll dress for dinner once in awhile and I'll wear them then."

David insisted she open his two gifts last. Wondering what they were, she finally unwrapped the two boxes, one long, and one much smaller. The tripod puzzled her until she unwrapped the camera. After turning it over several times she looked at him.

"David, all I know about cameras is that you point them and push a button. I'll never be able to figure out how to operate this one."

"Yes, you will. The owner of the camera shop will teach you. I told him that my wife is smart enough to learn anything. He said that later on you would probably want to start developing your own film, so I told Bo to put a dark room in your studio."

"No chemicals until after the baby gets here," Deedee warned them.

For a moment she was silent. "Thank you for your faith in me," she finally said. Would she ever get used to this life she had fallen into? Suddenly her hands went to her stomach.

"What's wrong, honey?"

"Nothing." She smiled at the wonder of it. "I just felt the baby move."

* * * * *

Cindy looked around the room. The flames in the huge fireplace gave it all an old-timey look. The bottles in the little table beside the old library table proved that Margarita knew her guests well. There was a favorite brand of scotch for T.J. and the senator alongside Buck's Canadian Club. If she had wanted it, a bottle of Bacardi was there, but seeing that David had only a coke, she left the rum untouched. They would, however, join the others in the champagne toast at midnight. Actually the only evidence that it was New Years Eve were those champagne glasses waiting between the Tiffany lamp and her art work. Margarita had placed the framed sketches of David and Deedee beside her sons childhood pictures.

She looked over the small group, fairly certain that she was remembering who was who. T.J. and Senator Clayton and his wife were there, of course. It was the first time she had met B.J. Smith, the third part of Jefferson, Colby, and Smith. Though he seemed almost as ancient as Deedee, his handshake had been firm. Deedee had firmly declined to attend, and Tish had preferred to celebrate the night with her. Buck looked good in his gray suit. At her side, her husband was his good looking self in his double breasted navy suit and subdued tie. Margarita looked stunning in her little black dress and pearls.

In her pale green dress and new ruby necklace and earrings, Cindy just hoped she would look as good when her child was thirty. She would soon going have to shop for maternity clothes. A mere fraction of an inch stood between her and split seams. This week the soft flutterings of her baby were making her pregnancy more real. A baby of her own. The boys had been so tiny when Mom had come home with them. Maybe her baby was lucky she had experience with newborns. Deedee had been so pleased when she had told her that she planned on breast feeding her child. Several articles she had read said bottles were better, but she didn't think so.

In a corner, she saw Margarita and T.J. laughing together. Briefly, she wondered why the two had never married. David was right. The man did care for her.

The pudgy little man in the black suit was connected to the University, and the tall woman in gray was his wife. The man talking to Buck was the editor of the Austin newspaper. His wife was the cute little blonde in red, the only one who was drinking too much..

"Penny for your thoughts?" David asked.

"Just making sure I remember everyone's name. "Gerald Everly?" She nodded toward the man who was examining one of the sketches. "He brought the girl who is talking to Senator Clayton's wife. You said he has a gallery in Dallas, but I don't think Maurice took me there."

"It's an art gallery, not furniture." The man replaced the sketch and picked up the other one. "Let's join him." David took her arm and walked her over to the library table. The man turned, the sketch still in his hand..

"C.M.?" he asked. "Dare I hope it stands for Cindy McKaid?" His voice was smooth and deep. He was looking at her, not David.

"It does," she admitted.

"Make it Cindy M. A remarkable likeness. I've met Deedee. The window with the sun shining through her colored bottles, her long pipe? What made you include them?"

"They are part of who she is."

"And is the Grand Canyon part of who David is?"

"At the moment it was. He wanted me to see it. We were there on our honeymoon."

"David McKaid," he turned to her husband, "a small blonde artist is the last person in the world I ever expected to see you marry." He looked back at her. "Would you care to show me your portfolio one of these days."

At that she was the one smiling. "I have a few sketches. I would hardly call them a portfolio."

"Then you would be wrong. Who did you study with?"

"Only my high school art teacher, Miss Emily Wilson."

"A high school teacher?" He looked startled. "She must be a remarkable woman. Please, Mrs. McKaid," he pleaded, "don't let anyone else represent you. I want you all to myself."

"I told you she was talented," David told him. "A studio for her was an essential part of our house plans."

"Have you anything in oils?"

"I was lucky to be able to afford pastels and sketching pads."

"I doubt if that is any longer a problem."

"Deedee says no chemicals for now."

"My grandmother," David added, "wouldn't even let her go into our own house for the first week after the kitchen was painted."

"The new acrylic paints don't have the odor, but neither do they have the versatility of oil." He turned to return the framed pastel to its spot next to the one of David. "I would like to see the others you have. Shall we say next week? I will be in Austin again on Thursday to see about the small gallery I am opening there."

At midnight they welcomed 1946 with a glass of champagne and a kiss.

"Has it been a good year for you?" David whispered.

"A very good year. Sometimes I still can't believe all this is real."

"We'll go into Austin Wednesday. You can shop for some clothes while I'm at the office. I'll be surprised if Gerald doesn't show some of your work at his grand opening. We'll stop at the camera shop as well so you can start learning to use your new one." Cindy reached for his hand and placed it on her belly. The baby was moving. He smiled at her. "That's real, Mrs. McKaid."

"'I'm glad Deedee and the doctor both think there's only one. Mom couldn't sleep with the three of them kicking her.

Chapter 41

"You've been here a week, Mr. Rollins." It was the first week in February. David looked across the desk at his father-in-law. "You wanted that much time to go over the books. What is your opinion of the Diamond MiK?"

"The first thing I have to say is that you should stop calling me Mr. Rollins. I'm your employee. It's entirely inappropriate for me to call you David while you add a Mr. to my name. Call me Mark. It seems to work between Lucy and your people."

"If it makes you comfortable."

"As to business, you're a wealthy family, David. Your books are more of a mess than I expected. I don't know who the cousin was that you had doing them, but whoever it was has been playing fast and loose with them. You should have had him arrested."

"I know, but politically, it wouldn't have been a good move, and just for the record I did do a thorough background check before I offered you the job. I didn't make the offer just because you're Cindy's father. As soon as I checked those books, we— just say we made arrangements. The severance package was more than he deserved, but I didn't want a scandal attached to our name."

"May I make a suggestion or two?"

"I'll be glad to listen." David picked up the pencil laying in front of him.

"You have obviously made some very good investments that are in your name only. Your mother supports a number of charities. Who holds the title to the land?"

"It's held jointly. Gramps added my mother's name shortly after my father was killed. He didn't want her moving off somewhere. He added my name after I received my law degree and planned to do the same with my brothers. Some of the acreage belongs to my grandmother, and I acquired the forty acres of the Simpsons, but donated that for the new school."

"A good tax move. I don't have a degree. I only went to business school to learn bookkeeping, but I did take a few night school courses over the years. First, I think it would be to your advantage to incorporate. You're a lawyer. I would have thought you should know that."

"Not my field. I'm a criminal lawyer." He dropped all pretense of taking notes.

"Then hire a good man. I'm sure you know someone. The second thing is, I think you ought to have an office in Austin. Anyone you do business with isn't going to be impressed with an office in the home and an antiquated phone service."

"You are right, of course, on both points. We've only been home five months. I don't want my grandfather to feel that I'm pushing him aside. He's done very well by the ranch. A few of us are working on the phone thing. Meanwhile, bear with me and use this as your office. I'll see about incorporating. I might even put a few assets in Cindy's name so I know she and the baby will always have no worries."

"It should be done before you incorporate. Not to change the subject, but what is this show in Houston that the boys are so excited about. Lucy took them shopping and outfitted them with boots and hats."

Knowing how excited the boys were, David smiled. "So I've heard. It's the Houston Livestock and Rodeo Show. Happens every year. Steve's been grooming our prize bull to show. A couple of the local children have rabbits they are taking. Mother and Buck and

I will be riding in the parade. Cindy's not quite ready for that yet She'll have to wait until next year. I'm sure you'll enjoy it. I know the boys will. This room can accommodate another desk. Order one."

"I'll need another file cabinet."

"Order whatever you need. Have them bill the ranch. Your California CPA certification won't be any good here. Take care of that." Never again would the McKaids be blindsided. "Cindy and I will be spending the next few days in Austin. I have a trial coming up."

* * * * *

It was March. David had the three men sitting around the small work table in his den. It had been raining. He knew they all appreciated the fact that he had insisted on black topping the driveway in from the road. Since they had all known him most of his life they were comfortable with his cup of coffee while they each had a fine brandy. Cal had been the last to arrive.

"Long time no see," Robert told Cal.

"This meeting isn't about the house." David knew both Robert and Bo were surprised to see the banker/mayor of Kaidville. I have an idea all of you might be interested in." He leaned forward slightly. "There's one basic problem all over the country now."

"Shortages," Robert said. "People have money and not a lot to spend it on. The automobile people have lists of people waiting for a new car."

"That too." David nodded. "I had Cindy on one for a little sports car, but she wants a station wagon."

Robert grinned. "Whose fault is that?"

"Housing," David said, ignoring his friends reference to the coming addition to the family. "GIs coming home with wives and no place to live except with their folks. If you don't mind, I'd like to have Cindy tell you about something she and her family did a year or so ago." He went to the door and called her in. "Tell them about the day you all inspected the houses in the Baldwin Hills." He gave her his chair while he perched on the edge of his desk.

"I imagine you all know that I didn't come from a family with the kind of money David has," she began. "My parents bought the house we lived in when we moved to California back in 1930. It was in a nice location, but with six children we really could have used something bigger. We girls saw an ad in the paper and talked to Mom. She persuaded Dad to look at some new houses they were building in the Baldwin Hills. They called it a housing development. Mom and we three girls really fell in love with the houses the minute we walked in. If I remember correctly all the houses would be pretty much the same, but some were two bedrooms and some three. They all had what they called a bath and a half, just no tub in the one bathroom."

She looked almost wistful as she spoke. "Mom tried really hard to talk Dad into buying one, but they were asking five thousand dollars for them That was more than twice what he had paid for our little house back in 1930, and he had that paid off free and clear. He said he just couldn't see going into debt, especially," she did smile a little, "since he had two daughters old enough to get married, one of whom threatened to get her own apartment every time he said something she didn't like. Those houses weren't luxurious, but they were nice and really were affordable for the working man. As far as I know they sold out in less than two weeks. At least they stopped advertising them."

"Thanks, honey." He offered her his hand. "You can go back to your book now." He had already told her that Bo and Cal probably wouldn't be comfortable talking business if she stayed. He closed the door behind her.

"I guess I don't have to tell you which daughter he was talking about. There's no reason we can't do the same thing here. The Diamond MiK runs on both sides of the highway. Kaidville isn't that far from Austin, and as you know, we surround it. Call it Golden Acres or some such thing, and advertise it as country living and an ideal place for bringing up your children."

"You're talking big bucks," Robert said.

"We have the perfect set-up. We have an architect, a construction company, and a banker, and I've got the land. Maybe make it quarter acre plots. The Diamond Mik will keep the land around it planted in Milo and Bermuda for hay. That will keep the cattle away from the houses. I hear old man Slocum hit an artesian well. With couple more of those maybe we could even have our own little water company."

"The school's not big enough for the children that would be moving in," Bo said.

"We're planning on consolidating and building some decent schools. Our children deserve modern schools."

"Wouldn't that require school buses?"

"We're factoring in that cost. We will be donating the Simpson's acreage for the schools."

Can't day I blame you for foreclosing on them," the banker remarked, "not after they way she tried to kill your wife."

"How would that look? I bought the land and managed it so they didn't know I held the mortgage. Old Elmer Number 1 wanted to move as soon as they shipped Betty Lou out. As soon as the sheriff says I can, we're burning the house."

"Did she really have your old lunch bucket and a buckle you lost?" Robert wanted to know.

"That, plus the foal's ear. a bloody baseball bat, and a hair ribbon she claims Elsie Mae Ritter gave her. Elsie Mae fell from her horse when we were twelve. She evidently went for a midnight ride and her saddle fell off when something spooked her horse. I remember how her mother cried because they wouldn't open the casket for a last goodbye. Elsie Mae and I had sat together at the church social. I have always remembered how Betty Lou told her she'd be sorry. Ray's father swears she must have pushed Adele down the stairs and used the baseball bat on her. She was only a child, but she's always had a temper. Uncle Raymond never quite got over losing that baby."

"A real little Lizzie Borden," Cal commented.

"The donation is contingent upon having the schools built on the land." David wondered why he had shared that memory. "It's a good location. I think the whole thing will go through without a hitch."

"You forgot to say we have our own lawyer," Cal said.

"I'm a criminal lawyer. We'll need a corporate man, and preferably not one connected to Jefferson, Colby, and Smith. Someone is going to do it. Why not us? I can talk Buck and Mom into investing in it. Between all of us we can swing it, and of course, we'll do all our business with your little bank." What he didn't say was that the three of them would be fifty percent of the company. Transfer some money to Cindy's account and it could be fifty-one percent for the McKaids.

"What acreage were thinking of using?" Bo asked.

"Next to the Methodist church. That would mean that people would be driving through Kaidville if they are coming from Austin. The gas station would be between them and Austin. It would improve his business. Draw up two basic floor plans, maybe sit some of them sideways on the lot. Perhaps we could find someone with a nursery to locate close by. They're going to want to plant things."

"You would want to incorporate," Bo said. "You can't just donate the land, but you can sell it at favorable price with an option to buy more in the future."

"Of course." *But not at the same price*, he thought.

"You have a name for this thing?"

"I'm open for suggestions."

"Lone Star Housing," Robert said. "We can call the area Lone Star Acres."

By the time the evening ended Lone Star Housing was on its way to becoming a reality.

Chapter 42

Can I get you anything?" At last his wife was finally sitting. Cindy had been on her feet most of the day. Almost to her due date, she should be resting. He put the newspaper aside and looked at the wind and rain pounding at the window. The bag she had packed was in the car. Tomorrow she would go unto Austin with him, and they would stay at the apartment until the baby was born. When the time came, he didn't want to be driving the miles between the ranch and the hospital.

"It was a dark and stormy night." David laughed as he said it. "I had an English professor who always said that was one way a story should never start."

"Well it is dark and with all the rain I think that qualifies as stormy. I hope your mother and Buck don't try to come home in this."

"Mom has the key to the apartment. She said if the storm came up they would stay over. If she wasn't on the board they wouldn't have gone. This spring concert is one of their major fundraisers for the hospital." He stood. "I'll go check on Mamaw Deedee. I won't be long."

"I'll go with you."

"You'll get drenched."

"Not if I stay in the car while you go in."

"Come on then, but stay dry. You should be taking it easy, and all you've done the last two days is run around cleaning a house that doesn't need cleaning. Maria told me how you have been doing most of what she's paid to do. You want to relax. The baby's due in a couple of days." He really did appreciate what she was trying to do. She knew that once in awhile the thunder still had him flinching as though the big guns were booming.

Even if the weather hadn't had the pasture soggy, he wouldn't have taken the shortcut through the field, going instead out to the highway and down to the main gate. Cindy was too close to her time for a rough ride.

"Just checking to make sure you're all right," he told his grandmother after he entered the cabin. "That storm is pretty rough."

"I'm just fine, David," she told him. "You should be home with your wife."

"She's in the car. She insisted on driving over with me. I've been trying to tell her it's time to go bed, but she insists she's not tired. She should be. Maria said she's been cleaning the whole house and baking as though we were expecting company."

"She's nesting." He questioned her with a look. "Getting ready for that baby. Maybe I'd better go over to the house and stay with you."

"It isn't due until the end of the week. You know we're planning to go into Austin until it comes so we'll be close . . ." He broke off as the door was pushed open by a thoroughly drenched Cindy. She was panting as though she had been running.

"My water broke," she gasped. "I think I'm having the baby."

"It's not time." He shook his head even as watched her hands go to her back and her face contorted with a moan of pain.

Deedee quickly moved to close the door and draw her farther into the room. "David, go in my bedroom and strip the bed. There's an oil cloth in the bottom drawer along with clean sheets."

"It's too early."

"Do it, Davy. Babies have their own time tables. I haven't delivered a baby in ten years, but I haven't forgotten how. You will have to be my assistant."

"I can't." *Deliver his own baby? Was Deedee losing her mind?* "I don't know anything about babies."

"Nonsense. You've been helping pull calves and foals since you were fourteen. Now get that sheet pulled nice and tight," she ordered, "and after that boil me a sharp knife for ten minutes. and get me some clean towels from the closet. Cindy, let's get you out of these wet clothes. I've got an old flannel robe you can put on. It's not fancy, but it's warm and dry. Has the pain let up?"

"No."

The look on Cindy's face was enough to send him into the bedroom to obey Mamaw Deedee's instructions. His heart racing, he yanked off the pillow, the spread, and the sheets, letting them fly into a corner as he opened the bottom drawer of the old dresser. He'd had plenty of practice making his own bed as a boy, but Deedee wanted this one tight enough for any army inspection. How in the hell was he going to be able to watch his beautiful wife go through the agony of childbirth? The oil cloth and fresh sheet. It wasn't supposed to happen this way. He was supposed to be pacing the waiting room floor as Cindy was in the delivery room surrounded by doctors and nurses, and here he was preparing a birthing bed.

He left the room to put the water and knife on the kitchen range, then getting the towels. He obeyed instructions, held his wife's hand as the pains came faster than the doctor had predicted, and listened to murmurings from Deedee about how the old ways were. How women of the tribe gave birth squatting with two women on either side, but white women had to lie on a bed. He tried to close his ears to the screams his wife couldn't hold back as the child left her body.

A scant two hours later he looked down at the tiny form in his arms, a makeshift diaper around his tiny bottom, a fluffy yellow towel his blanket, his first born son who was going to grow into a boy riding horses, learning to read, and maybe someday have his name on a ballot. Gently he placed him in his wife's arms.

"Our son, Cindy. You've given me a son. He's beautiful. What shall we call him?"

She cradled the child in her arms. "Victoria would have been fine," she told him, "but honestly, David, Victor or Vic sounds like an Italian gangster."

"We can't have that, can we? Our son will be an important man. How about Shawn Ryan McKaid? Does that sound important enough? It was my other grandfather's name."

"Maybe important enough to be a Chief Justice of the Supreme Court." She pulled her eyes away from their son and looked at him. "Remember what you told me the night we met?"

"I remember I told you I was going to marry you."

"You said I had nice hips and came from good breeding stock."

"That was a pretty stupid thing to say to a girl I was trying to impress."

"That's what I thought at the time. Was Shawn Ryan the one who rode with Kit Carson?"

"He was," Deedee stated. "He was a fearless man. He lived with my tribe for almost six years. Don't expect to have them all this easy, girl. David, you did fine. He's a fine, healthy child."

She sat down in the old rocker she kept in the room and leaned back. She looked exhausted. "I remember how it was in the old days. You would have been declared unclean until you purified yourself. Men of the tribe weren't allowed to be around women in their blood times. It made them unclean." She closed her eyes. "My father asked for fifteen horses for me. Shawn gave him twelve horses and two fine Navaho blankets. He was an important man, my father. I learned my healing arts from him. I've never told anyone, but my father sent us away."

When she opened her eyes there was deep down sadness in them.

"When the buffalo started disappearing, he knew the white man was going to win. He never understood why they wanted to annihilate us, but he said one of us should survive to tell the world we weren't uncivilized savages. He told me go with my husband, to his people, to learn their ways, but to never forget ours. I obeyed, but how I missed the freedom of the plains. I had to learn to eat and dress like a white woman. I've tried to teach you some of our ways. I have even tried to write some of it down. My husband was a good man. He lived with my people for about six years." She spread out her hands. "I must be getting old. I already mentioned that. The gods have been good to me. I've lived to deliver my great-great-grandson. Teach him well, David. When it's light, bury the afterbirth, and when your parents come home, present your son and tell them his name. It's the Cheyenne way. You chose well when you finally found your mate. Cherish her. Teach your son."

"Thank you for telling us that," Cindy told her.

"They call me Deedee, but my Cheyenne name is Woman Who Heals. When I was a child it was She Who Laughs. I will call you Earth Mother. Stay the night. I am very tired. I will rest these old bones on the sofa."

In the ensuing silence, the baby nuzzled around until he found a nipple and learned to take nourishment from it.

"Already he knows how to get what he wants." David pulled up the rocking chair his grandmother had vacated and spent the rest of the night making sure his son did not fall from Cindy's sleeping arms. Even with her hair a tangled mess, he marveled at how beautiful she looked.

Once the rain stopped, a wolf pack howled in the distance. A chill ran down David's spine, and he reached out to touch his son to make sure he was breathing, and kissed his wife's forehead, grateful to find no trace of fever on it. Out in his dog house, Precious joined his wild cousins in their mournful sounding song, and for a few moments the other dogs on the ranch came to life in nature's mournful symphony. Then it was quiet until the distant coyotes started their song.

He sat back in the chair. Maybe he should check on his grandmother, but he was tired. Delivering his own child was definitely not the same as tending a cow or a mare. Thank the Lord up above it had been an easy delivery. Next time he was going to send her to the hospital early even if it meant a two week stay. For a brief time his eyes closed in an exhausted sleep.

When the sun rose and was well on its way through its daily orbit, he went out of the room to talk to his grandmother. He came back to lift young Shawn from Cindy's arms. Tears unashamedly made their way down his cheeks.

"She's gone, Cindy," he said. "Mamaw Deedee slipped away from us during the night. What is it the preachers say? The Lord giveth and the Lord taketh away. Lord, how I am going to miss her."

Chapter 43

"Mom, Cal and Reverend Cooper want to talk to you and Gramps." David whispered the words in his mother's ear as she stood by the casket.

"She looks so peaceful. I had forgotten she had the dress."

"I'm glad you chose it. It's the way she would have wanted to be dressed."

More than one person had commented that any museum in the country would have paid a small fortune for the elk skin dress with all its fancy beadwork. He took his mother's elbow.

"I think she was just waiting for Shawn to be born. They need you in the office." This time her black dress fit her. For some reason that thought floated though his mind as he led her through the crowd to where the Cal and the funeral director waited with both the minister and Father Torres.

"There have been so many people here," the funeral director said, "that I have had to put out a second guest book. We are worried about tomorrow. The chapel will not be big enough to hold everyone."

"Your grandmother was respected in these parts," the minister told her. "She delivered several generations of them and doctored, goodness knows, how many more. Father Torres and I have a solution."

"If it's alright with you," David told her, "our good mayor here," he nodded to Cal, his friend, banker, business partner, and for the last fifteen years, mayor of Kaidville, "has proposed blocking the highway in front of the church for an outdoor service. The weather is good. All the chairs from here and both churches can be set outside. If we need more, there's always the VFW and the Lodge hall."

"Do whatever you feel is necessary," his mother told him. "It's overwhelming to see how many people care. I'm glad we persuaded Cindy not to come, but she's insisting on being here with the baby tomorrow. Do you think you can have something a little more comfortable than a folding chair for her?"

"I will insist upon it," David assured her.

"There's one other thing we would like to discus." Father Torres was looking at him. "David, I'm sure you know that Texas law allows private cemeteries on a person's own land."

"True, but why should we be thinking of that."

"David, Miss Margarita, surely you know that Deedee's Indian dress is priceless."

"Surely," his mother said, "no one would dig up a grave just for an Indian dress."

"There are no limits to what some men will do for money," Father Torres said. "A priest knows that. What some ask absolution for can sometimes chill our souls. I'm not saying it would happen, but that elk skin dress is probably the only one of its kind that is left. Temptation would be great."

"There's no way we could have the cemetery guarded," the Reverend Pearson added..

"Deedee wasn't one of my flock," Father Torres said, "but she was a fine woman. Everyone loved her. No one would think it odd if you wanted to fence in a garden in her honor."

"Let me get this straight," his grandfather asked. "You're asking us to bury an empty casket tomorrow. Wouldn't some of the pall bearers notice it was too light?"

"She didn't weigh much more than a couple of bags of feed." That was the funeral director.

"It's Mom's decision." He looked at his mother. Tears were in her eyes.

"She would like to be on the ranch. Her people didn't have cemeteries and fancy coffins. Just the thought that someone would dig her up for that beautiful dress is more than I can bear. At home we will know that she is safe. Plant some native wildflowers and put up some bird houses." She touched his arm. "Put her near your house, David. It will outlast the homestead."

* * * * *

At one o'clock the following afternoon not only was Cindy seated in a comfortable arm chair, Margarita, David and Buck were as well. They were to one side of the open casket placed in front of the church steps. A microphone was beside a lectern, and some of the flowers had already started to wilt in the May sun. David nodded to Mark. He and Gracie were to whisk Cindy and the baby away as soon as the service was over. Neither David nor his mother wanted her and the baby exposed to the crowd any longer than necessary. Young Shawn was safely swaddled in a proper diaper and a soft blanket to shield his tender skin and eyes.

After the volunteer choir had sung, and all had said their words, David rose, took the baby, whose diaper Cindy and been quietly unpinning, and stepped up on the church steps.

"Deedee Ryan," he told the crowd of mourners, "left this world happy and contented because the last thing she did was to deliver her great-great-grandson. Her last words were of the old Cheyenne ways. She asked us to remember them. I honor her memory. She was called Deedee, but she told us her name was Woman Who Heals." He lifted the naked baby for all to see. "I have a son. His name is Shawn Ryan McKaid. In my heart I shall call him He Who Is In A Hurry. It is the Cheyenne way."

Unashamedly he let his tears fall on his son's soft skin as he mourned his ninety-seven year old grandmother and went to his wife's side.

* * * * *

"You did it again." David didn't need to see the newspaper spread out on T.J.s desk. In the past twenty-four hours he had seen it all too often. There on the front page, he was holding the naked baby aloft for all to see. The headline said "Naming Ceremony." The write-up below began, "Several hundred people crowded the streets of Kaidville to lay to rest a beloved Cheyenne midwife and medicine woman. At her funeral her great-grandson and local lawyer, David McKaid, honored her last wish that he present his newborn son to the world in an ancient way, a baby he had helped her deliver just days before."

Inside pages recounted her life and had pictures of Cindy and her parents as they had walked away, of Letitia in tears, and of the crowd in the street. It also mentioned his mother and her charities.

"I didn't do it for the publicity. They've made a circus out of it."

"No, David," T.J. said. " they have presented her life it a very good way."

"How did they get the photographers down there so fast?"

"The paper sent someone was down to cover the funeral. When he saw the chairs being carried out, he made a hurried telephone call. It's not every day a major highway gets blocked off. I understand a movie crew hit the blockade while they were returning from a shoot down on the gulf. They are probably going to use the footage as a human interest story."

"In every movie theater in America, I suppose. Don't I have a say in that?"

"You made it a public event when you moved it to the middle of main highway."

"What choice did we have? The crowd was three times the size of the chapel?"

T.J. folded the paper and tucked in under his arm. "Whitney is going to announce his retirement tomorrow and express the hope that you will take his place on the ticket."

"Isn't thirty a bit young?" David asked. "It seems to me there's something about being thirty-five."

"Only for the presidency," T. J. told him. "Will Ray be your campaign manager? With his gift for gab, he'll be good at it. I presume that's why you have your father-in-law doing the books."

"You presumed wrong." David reached for the pipe he had started smoking. "Ray is to have nothing to do with anything. I was hoping I wouldn't have to tell you. We've kept it under wraps. He has a gambling problem, and the Diamond Mik was supporting it. It was getting out of hand. Mark told me he wanted us to have the books audited every year. It's something Gramps never thought of doing."

* * * * *

A week later while an engraved granite stone was being placed in the cemetery behind the church, a bronze plaque was being fastened to the newly fenced in area that could be seen from both the road and the new house. It simply read, "In memory of Deedee, a woman of the land." A gardener was busy creating a haven of rest. A young Live Oak tree was planted, wild blackberries would cover the fence, and in the spring daffodils and blue bonnets would bloom. Baby rabbits and birds would find a home where an old Cheyenne woman rested in peace.

Epilogue

Cindy was thrilled with the crowd. everything pointed to the fact that Shawn was sure to be the next Vice President. They were sitting next to their oldest son at the head table, his wife on his other side. Margarita was on the other side of the emcee along with her husband, T.J. At one table in front of them, sat her mother and the rest of the family, Jimmy, Jack, and Jason with their wives, Trish and Steve, their own daughters and their husbands. It was too bad her other son couldn't be here as well. Ted was in the Gulf seeing to a problem on one of the oil platforms. She wished her father and Buck had lived to see this day.

From the looks of the crowd, every democrat in Texas who had enough money for the exorbitantly priced ticket was enjoying a good Texas steak. All were dressed in their best. She was wearing a stunning new gown. Who could have ever believed that Lucinda Rollins would be wearing a designer gown that showed off the diamond necklace that had been David's fifty year anniversary gift?

What a life it had been. Their house was the grandest thing she could have imagined. Her pastels were in Gerald Everly's little gallery, and she was getting some wonderful photographs with her new cameras. Both sold well. After the children had grown up she had started having more time to devote to her career.

Lone Star Housing's first houses had sold out fast. Now it was bigger than any of them had imagined back in the forties. She and David had been at the last two inaugural balls. The Diamond MiK had hosted a barbeque for the president himself. David had held his senate seat for three terms, D.C. that is, not Austin.

A secret service man was speaking in a low voice to David, something about a man who insisted that he needed to talk to David immediately.

"It's something about his sister, sir. She's run off from a hospital."

She could feel the way David stiffened.

"I won't be long." David leaned over to kiss her as he said it. It all happened so fast. A gray haired waitress turned, raised her am, and a shot rang out. David slumped against her, but not before she saw a figure in worn jeans streak out from somewhere, grabbing the waitress. Screams rang out from everywhere. A table overturned as a second shot exploded. Three doctors rushed away from their tables to be at Cindy's side, lifting her bleeding husband from her.

"It's his shoulder," one of them told her. "He'll live."

Cindy looked across to where E2 stood over his bleeding sister. "I saw it all," she said, speaking clearly and loud enough to be heard. "The gun went off accidentally while they were struggling." She wanted to be certain that all should know what she had seen.

"Betty Lou never could shoot straight," David whispered. All Cindy could think of was that if he hadn't leaned over to kiss her, he would have been proven wrong.

Cindy's Comments

My name is, as they say in the newspapers, Lucinda Jane McKaid, nee Rollins. I have just finished reading this story, and I do marvel at the wonderful life I have had. I am blessed with a wonderful husband, three daughters, and two sons, and seven grandchildren. My husband still had his seat in the Senate in Washington, but his heart had always been at the Diamond Mik. Shawn did win the election, but he became president by default. My photographs and pastels still sell well. No, I did not ever want to work in oils.

My family adjusted quite well to living in Texas. Tish finished her courses. I don't think she has ever gotten over the fact that RNs no longer dress in white and wear the little caps of their schools. She and Steve married and took over Deedee's little cabin. They never had any children, of course, but they raised a lot of German Sheppard pups. She lost Steve a few years back.

If you met them, you would think my three brothers were born Texans. When the visit us, they ride, drink bear, and talk man talk. Jimmy is a lawyer; Jack hosts the evening news for an Ohio television station; and Jack, believe it or not, has seven best selling mysteries under his belt. Lily has three daughters, and not one of them has a name starting with L.

I was raised as a good Catholic girl and became a good Methodist wife. I have tried to live right, to be honest, kind, and truthful. Only once in my life have I told a really grievous lie.

After that banquet we all heard how old Elmer Number 1 somehow got a job at the State Hospital for the Criminally Insane. No one was quite clear on just how Betty Lou escaped. Certainly at her age. no one could have expected it. We do know old Elmer Number 1 had always declared, "I had to do somethin'. She might be my daughter and she might be jist be my sister, but she sure as blankety-blank doesn't belong in a hospital like that. It jest ain't right. The McKaids took our land and put her there with all those crazy ones." If the old man had still been alive, he certainly would have put himself behind bars with that statement..

That night at the banquet, E2 had trouble getting in. He wanted to warn David, but it took the sound of that gun to distract the secret service man detaining him. E2 had aways been quick on his feet. He knew what he was doing, as he sprinted over to that demented sister of his. It's been a good many years since then, but I can still see it in my mind. As far as I was concerned, there was only one thing I could say when they started questioning me.

I looked at the doctors. I looked at the policeman. I looked at the secret service men. If it has been necessary, I would even have sat in a courtroom and looked a District Attorney in the eye and told him it was an accident. It was the only thing I could say. She had to be stopped.

What I never told anyone, was that I saw E2 wrestle that gun away from Betty Lou and jam it straight into her throat before he pulled the trigger. If David hadn't leaned over to kiss me, she would have hit her target all right. No one ever called him E2 after that night. He's just plain Simpson. He's never been a bad sort. He has worked around the ranch for years. David had him help teach our grandchildren to ride. It's like David said. He's the only Simpson who ever had a lick of sense.

THE END